ENEMY OF TALIONIS

TALIONIS SERIES
BOOK THREE

C.J. MILACCI

JOURNEY PERSPECTIVE PUBLISHING WITH FAYETTE PRESS

Enemy of Talionis

Copyright © 2024 by C.J. Milacci

Published by Journey Perspective Publishing

Philadelphia, PA, USA

ISBN: 978-1-958230-12-1 (printed softcover)

ISBN: 978-1-958230-13-8 (printed hardback)

ISBN: 978-1-958230-11-4 (ebook)

Cover design by Emilie Haney

Editing by Becca Wierwille

Proofreading by Chris Pearce

Typesetting by C.J. Milacci

Find out more at www.cjmilacci.com

It is not the critic who counts; not the man who points out how the strong man stumbles, or where the doer of deeds could have done them better. The credit belongs to the man who is actually in the arena, whose face is marred by dust and sweat and blood; who strives valiantly; who errs, who comes short again and again, because there is no effort without error and shortcoming; but who does actually strive to do the deeds; who knows great enthusiasms, the great devotions; who spends himself in a worthy cause; who at the best knows in the end the triumph of high achievement, and who at the worst, if he fails, at least fails while daring greatly, so that his place shall never be with those cold and timid souls who neither know victory nor defeat.

— THEODORE ROOSEVELT

To my dad, the man in the arena.

Dad, thank you for teaching me how to stand courageously and fight for those who can't fight for themselves, for being a man who will run into the battle, even when no one else will, and for showing me what a true hero looks like. I love you!

Eryndale

CHAPTER

ONE

We've faced more enemies in the past twenty-four hours than I wish was possible.

And we're still being brought into Eryndale by a dozen scouts like we're dangerous. Criminals.

How can we be *here* right now? After everything we've been through, it feels ... impossible.

I shift, and the bindings on my wrist cut into my skin. My body pulses like one giant bruise, the scrapes on my arms and legs stinging as a gentle breeze blows by.

We are perched on a high outcropping overlooking the refuge city, at the beginning of a long bridge. Yet, now that the scouts took off the hood covering my head, all I can do is focus on my friends, not the scenery before me.

Nika, Matthias, Shane, Bryson, and Ari are bound as well, each one of them sporting their own set of injuries. Dried blood cakes our faces and exposed skin. Our clothes are torn and dirty.

This is the most unkempt I've ever seen Nika. Her curls hang limp, and her normally rich dark complexion is almost waxy with pain and exhaustion.

Bryson lets out a low moan, his head bowed. Two of our captors—scouts I guess—are practically carrying him.

Ari stands as close to her brother as possible, straining against her restraints as she leans toward him.

The siblings normally look alike with matching blond hair and creamy skin. But Bryson's skin is a sickly pale-green color, and pain drips sweat off his brow. His strong runner's build is nowhere to be found. Right now, Ari could easily beat him in a race, despite her sheer lack of athleticism.

Blood stains his pant leg from where J's arrow found it's mark. Even though the scouts bandaged him up, he lost a lot of blood. Especially since he had to walk so much on the wounded limb. Now that we're here, hopefully he'll receive some treatment.

Although the six of us are here, together, I can't help but think about Nalani. Hopefully she's recovering from nearly drowning. Catori and Davey will take care of her I'm sure, but it's strange to not have her here with us after escaping Talionis together.

I drag my gaze away to take in the scenery before me.

My jaw drops, hanging like a door with a loose hinge.

Mountains guard the valley on every side, and the sun shines overhead, as though bathing the refuge city in its approval. Groves of trees crane up to the sky, and a brook meanders through the valley. Buildings seem to grow out of the trees at varying heights. Snatches of colorful fabric blow in the breeze, billowing out of open windows.

"Bria." Nika's voice next to me draws my attention before someone gives me a light shove in the back.

Max, the leader of the group of scouts who captured us, is walking away from the outcropping and toward the bridge leading into Eryndale. We're clearly expected to follow.

Small black braids bounce against his head as he walks, and thankfully, he moderates his pace. None of us are in good enough shape to move at more than a slow crawl. Something about the man is comforting, despite the fact that he brought us here bound like criminals.

Enya, the scout who led me through the forest while I was blindfolded, is nearby, and so is Chul-Min Lee and a few other scouts whose names I don't know. Zoe is with another scout at the back of the group. From the conversation I overheard between her and Max last night, I don't think she's thrilled with the way we're being treated. Which makes me like her.

With each step closer to Eryndale, the more the city demands to be noticed.

Flowers and gardens shout out their triumphant display of color, from wild flowers growing on the valley floor, to window boxes, to well-maintained gardens placed in what appear to be strategic places throughout the city. Suspended from the trees are rope ladders and bridges like the one we're on, and walkways hover over the ground, upheld by wooden stilts. Hammocks sway gently in various places, and the sounds of children laughing and playing ring through the air.

The buildings are laid out in a pattern. Bridges connect trees that hold multi-level structures, spinning out in a design of many circles all connected with one another.

And every bit of it feels like a punch in the gut. This is *Eryndale*.

And it's bigger than I ever imagined.

The place I've wanted to come to for longer than I can remember. The place I thought I could start over, become a scout, make a difference in the region. Discover my purpose. But as I stare at it, the strange feeling of being in a new environment draws me into its grasp.

Why do I feel like I felt when I woke in Talionis?

Nothing is familiar. It's not home.

As connected as every one of those buildings are to one another, I'm not connected here. I roll my shoulders, trying to detach the feeling, but it clings to me, leaving a sour taste in my mouth. This wasn't how Eryndale was supposed to feel.

Hope was supposed to overcome me here, along with the belief that Ark could be defeated.

So why do I feel lonelier now than I did with that sack over my head an hour ago? Why is the tiny bit of hope leaking out of me?

I clench my fists, and the motion causes the bindings to bite into my wrists. Proof that these scouts think we're a danger to the refuge city.

We've fought for days to get here, to find safety. We've lived more nightmares than I dreamed possible. But I'm not sure if any of it even matters.

Storm's precious face comes to mind.

Standing in the transport.

Held by Laban.

Screaming my name.

They found her. Somehow, they found her. And now Laban and Demetrius Ark have two of the people who mean the most to me.

Storm. And Cai, the mentor who taught me so much. My uncle.

As though he can sense my thoughts, Matthias appears next to me. His blue eyes gaze into mine for a moment as we continue down the bridge. They seem more vibrant than ever as they shine against his deeply tanned skin. His disheveled hair sticks out in crazy angles, debris dusting the dark locks. I suddenly wish my hands were no longer bound so I could take his hand in mine.

The thought warms my cheeks, and I turn away before I reveal the depths of my emotions. He and I care about each other. We know that. But at the moment, I'm so vulnerable and tired that I think I might do or say something stupid.

Max leads us over different bridges before we come to the first rim of the city. The sight of massive buildings upheld by trees, and sweet smelling wildflowers, and murmurs of people going about their business engulf me more with every step. My friends and I gawk wide-eyed at everything we pass, and I allow the magnificence of the city to distract me.

It's reminiscent of seeing Talionis for the first time, but so different. Talionis was cold, hard, unyielding. Eryndale flows with the valley, grows with the trees, and seems to laugh with every child.

I want to feel comfortable here. I want to be *excited* to be here. And I want to belong.

But how can I fully belong anywhere when I feel so shredded by everything that's happened?

The two outermost rims that we come to first have stations

with scouts on alert. I peer inside the open door of a structure. It holds simple cots, rifles, a crossbow, and several knives, a control or radio panel of some sort, and a small kitchen and living area.

Max speaks briefly with a scout, then we continue on our way. Balconies surround each building, and as we pass, scouts come out and watch us with eyes that refuse to reveal their thoughts. They hide their emotions toward us the way I did toward those I knew I could never trust in Talionis.

Which does nothing to make me feel more comfortable.

After the first two rims of scouts and their stations, the next few seem to be houses. My mouth waters at the smell of a fragrant tomato sauce being prepared. Matthias's stomach growls as we pass someone's residence who is pulling freshly baked bread from the oven. Nika and I share a grin, which is the most at ease I've felt since seeing the city.

Enya waves at different people as we pass, calling out greetings—sometimes to people on the same level as us, sometimes down at a lower level, or up to someone on the level right above us, which seems to be the highest level.

"I've never seen anything like this," Nika says as we both pause to look to the ground.

"Keep walking." Enya gives me a light nudge. "You'll have plenty of time to see it later."

We obey her command and continue forward.

Up and down each tree there are different platforms and houses through every rim we pass, some having as many as five levels. People lounge in nets hanging from thick branches, their chatter slowing as we pass so they can stare at us.

I almost want to be annoyed by their stares, but I can't blame them. We must be a sight. Six teens, bound and beaten up. Bryson looking like he's ready to pass out, unable to take a step without the support of the scouts on either side of him. Shane's face carved into an angry expression.

Then Matthias smiles his most engaging smile, and lifts his bound hands in a wave. "How's it going?"

Two of the people staring avert their gaze, but one girl, who looks to be around our age, smiles and waves back.

I press my lips together and attempt to tamp down the flare of jealousy.

The closer we draw to the center of the city, the more elaborate and larger the structures become. It's like the town center found in different villages I've traveled to with my mom, with stores and businesses. Only this center is raised up in the air with layers throughout the trees.

A sign on a door we pass catches my attention: *Center-Post for Sphere 11*. I hesitate, squinting to see through a window into the lit space inside. Enya presses her hands against my back, propelling me forward, but my curiosity pulls at me.

"What's a Center Post?" I ask Enya.

She sweeps her dark hair over her shoulder and gives me a sideways glance. "You're nosy."

"Mm-hmm," Nika says from my other side.

I roll my eyes but say nothing as we come to a halt. No time for more questions.

We have stopped in front of the biggest building in Eryndale —at least the biggest I've seen. My guess is this is the one in the center of all the others. Several trees hold it up. It stretches into the canopy of leaves above and reaches down into the lower branches before stopping several feet from the ground. We are easily thirty feet in the air.

Max pauses by the twelve-foot-high double doors and focuses on the two scouts half-carrying Bryson. "Take him down to the infirmary. He needs to be treated. The others can brief the leadership."

The scouts nod and turn to go.

"Wait!" Ari tugs her arm free from Zoe and steps toward her brother. "I'm coming with you." The fierce determination on her face is like nothing I've seen from her before.

Zoe looks at Max, and he inclines his head. Zoe gestures for Enya to go with Ari, and the group makes a slow exit. Shane stares after his girlfriend, but doesn't follow them.

My chest tightens. I don't like our group being split up. Even though we're in Eryndale, I don't feel safe. Catori's warning about a leak within the refuge city rings in my memory. We need to be on guard. Cautious about who we trust.

A deep exhaustion steals over me. Will I ever feel safe again?

There's a low groan, and I glance back to find Max pulling on the thick black handle of the massive doors.

My heart kicks up in my chest, and apprehension tangles with curiosity. I always thought I'd be thrilled in this moment, entering the heart of Eryndale, prepared to train to take my place in the ranks of the scouts.

I never thought I'd be unsure of the welcome I'd receive.

There's a group of people just inside the door, so we don't get far.

"Ah Max, you're back," an older, balding man says, with a clap on his shoulder. He doesn't do more than glance at us. "We've decided to wait to talk with them. Get them cleaned up and settled in scouting station room twenty-one b, and make sure they have something to eat." He nods in our direction before disappearing farther into the building.

The man and two women with him hesitate a moment before following him.

"Wait!" I call after him. "We have a lot we need to share. It's urgent."

They don't look back at us.

Zoe snorts. "Don't bother. If they decided they want to wait, you won't change their minds."

I gape after them, watching until they disappear through a set of doors.

This can't be happening. The leaders were supposed to see us right away, hear us out, and formulate a plan to attack Talionis. There isn't time to delay.

Laban has Cai and Storm. And probably Damara, the woman who took care of Storm, too.

Who knows what's happening to them, even now?

"Hold on." Max strides away from us, face set in determination. He disappears through the same doors the others went through.

A few minutes later, he pokes his head out and waves for us to come.

"Well, I stand corrected," Zoe says. "He must have gone straight to Essie."

"Who's Essie?" Nika asks.

"The woman who founded Eryndale." Zoe leads us forward. "If she calls for a meeting, everyone shows up."

Max leads Nika, Matthias, Shane, and me into a massive circular room with a domed roof. Thick tree branches weave their way through the space, supporting the structure. I stop and gape at the natural beauty of this place. Three rows of seats with desks climb up the walls and circle most of the room, except for the door where we entered. A balcony appears to overlook the entire space, and intricate carvings cover every supporting pillar.

Nika gives a low whistle. "Wow."

"Over here." Max gestures for us to follow him onto a platform in the center of the room.

He quietly dismisses several of the scouts until only he, Zoe, and Chul-Min Lee remain. Men and women file in, taking seats all around us on the ringed platforms with a desk circling the platform in front of them.

The leaders of Eryndale.

After a few moments, the leaders fill the seats, and a thick silence descends on the room.

The balding man we met when we first entered the building sits to the left of us in the front row. A deep scowl mars his face, and he raps his fingers against the desk.

Unease chills the base of my neck. I want to shake off my fears that this will *not* go well. But I can't.

"Well," the man says. "You wanted to speak to us. So start talking."

Nika nudges me in the side.

"We need your help," I blurt.

The man raises his bushy eyebrows, and several other shift, as though impatient.

"Time to elaborate, girl," Nika whispers.

I glare at her. Why *I* became the spokesperson for our group is a question I'll be asking all of them later. I half expect Shane to jump in, but he keeps looking back toward the door, probably wishing he was with Ari.

When I look at Matthias, he gives me a small smile and nods his head. He mouths the words, "You've got this."

"Eh hem." Baldy clears his throat. "Is that all?"

I clench my jaw and force myself not to react out of irritation. "We escaped from Talionis several days ago, and we've risked everything to come here. If you don't help us, many will die."

I launch into a desperate recap of all we've experienced. Being kidnapped and forced into training as soldiers in the hidden city of Talionis. Ark's plans to use teens in a war across the sea in his home country of Sitreea. How we each worked hard to become some of the best recruits, all so we could use our training against the soldiers, sabotage the city, and escape. I share our different skills and how we worked together as a team and lost some friends along the way. But I don't go into details about our losses, and I am careful to leave Cai out of my recounting completely.

Between his fears and Catori's warning about a leak, I don't want to give too much away.

"Since escaping," I continue, focusing on different men and women around the room, "Laban Meritas has been hunting us every step of the way. We have items Ark wants. His battle plans, a key to Sitreea's armory, detailed invasion tactics—even encrypted files. All things he's desperate to get back. And we know too much. Villages have been destroyed in the search for us." My throat thickens as I remember the horrors we witnessed. "Teens and children are being taken to force men and women to aid Talionis as they hunt us down." My jaw trembles, but this time it's from anger. "Ark has sent his most ruthless soldiers after us, and he's hired mercenaries." I shiver at the thought of Laban, and the image of Broche with his mechanical eye.

Although we defeated them—with the help of Callypso—I know that battle isn't over. Laban doesn't give up easily.

Memories of the battle with Laban grip me. It was mere *hours* ago. I can still smell the mud from the battlefield on my clothes, mixed with gunpowder. Still hear the bullets whizzing through the air, the pounding of rain to the earth. Shay's scream for help as Laban dragged her, bleeding and injured, back to the transport.

The girl from my hometown. Someone I've known my whole life. We defeated her, but at what cost? Sure, she's given herself to Talionis, but the horror in her eyes as she faced Laban as a failure . . . I don't know if I'll ever shake the image from my mind.

The thoughts rip through me in a flash, and I press forward in my plea for help. Now is not the time to process all we've been through.

"If you don't do something to stop him, this region will experience far more horrors than you can imagine." The words pass over my lips with a depth and fervor I can't hide.

We desperately need their help.

Storm needs their help.

And, by the looks on many of their faces, they're ready to do something.

I open my mouth, prepared to tell them about Storm, when Baldy stands abruptly.

"How are we supposed to believe this is true?" He gestures at us. "They could easily be spies from the city looking for a way to enter Eryndale and destroy us. And the supposed 'battle plans' merely a diversion to absorb our attention and keep us from focusing on what truly matters."

"What?" I practically screech. "Are you kidding me? Look at us!" I point with my bound hands at my bruised, dirty, blood-caked friends. "We're not spies! They're hunting us, and we need refuge and help. The only reason we're even here is because Callypso and her pirates fought off Laban's unit, before taking us captive herself."

The room erupts in a cacophony of conversations. Did any of them hear my objections?

I clamp my hands, the rope rubbing against my skin as grating to me as this man. How could he think we're from Talionis? Even worse is that two others, a woman and another man, seem to *agree* with him. I glance at Nika. Her expression is shuttered. Matthias's eyes are closed, head bent down. Shane looks ready to either storm from the room or throttle someone.

And at the moment, I can't blame him.

This can't be happening.

"I believe them," Max says, speaking for the first time. His raspy voice rises above the low conversations, bringing them to a halt. "My team has gone through several towns in the east over the past weeks, and we keep hearing the same thing: soldiers from Talionis are entering their villages, kidnapping teens and kids, sometimes injuring townspeople who stand against them, all searching for those they call fugitives from their city." He pauses. "And several towns are completely destroyed."

Baldy pounds the table with a fist. "We know the reports! And we are actively working to contain this issue and bring as many young people to safety as possible." He points a stubby finger at us. "We also know that they're the reason for the terror the villages and towns are experiencing. Having them here is endangering everyone in the city."

"That doesn't mean we shouldn't help them. Eryndale is a *refuge* city," Max argues. "No matter how hard we've tried, we haven't been able to obtain the information we need to get in and stop Talionis. We've just stayed hidden, watched teens get taken, seen towns obliterated. It's time we do something." He grits his teeth, and something behind his words echoes a hurt.

A loss.

It's a sound I know too well, because I hear it in my own voice at times. He has lost someone himself.

"It's time we get them back," Max continues, "and stop this madman. They can help us do that."

It was easy enough to tell Max was the leader in the group that captured us, but here he seems even more intense and passionate, the confidence in what he's saying radiating through the room.

Matthias is watching him, forehead crunched in concentration. I wonder if he senses something familiar about Max like I do.

"We have enough to deal with as it is," a woman who agrees with Baldy says. "The Raiders are moving farther east, and we need to protect villages from them as well. Not to mention this nonsense about Callypso. She's nothing more than a legend."

"Exactly." Baldy nods vigorously. "We know they're spies because they claim they were captured by a myth. How could we trust a word they say?"

I gape at him. He can't be serious. Yet his words about Callypso have others around the room nodding. The memory of Max dismissing Callypso when I told him about her after his team captured us comes back to me. He used the same words as the Eryndale leadership: myth, legend. I should never have mentioned her. All it's doing is ruining our chances of convincing these people to help us.

"Callypso aside, we know Talionis is a threat," a man says. Although he's one of the youngest among the leadership— maybe late thirties—there's a dynamic charisma about him that has others leaning forward to hear what he has to say. His dirty blond hair is well-styled. It's not long but almost . . . swooshy. He probably takes longer to get it to look like that than I take to do my hair for a special occasion. Unless the eccentric Talionis seamstresses, Sampta and Presida, are doing it.

His eyes are intriguing. They're gray . . . or maybe blue? Both colors seem to swirl together. A light scar on his eyebrow gives him a rugged look. It's not scary, like Sergeant Valarius's scar. Instead, somehow, it almost makes him more personable.

He spreads his arms. "Every threat that comes against the people of this region is one we need to guard against."

"Exactly." Max spreads his arms wide. "We cannot claim to be a refuge, to *protect* others, if we're not willing to take a stand against evil. No matter what form it takes or how much it terrifies us. Pretending it's not there doesn't make it go away. It only makes it stronger."

Max's words swell through the room with electrifying passion.

A leader of Eryndale responds, but I shift slightly to see Max better. His dark brown skin is smooth over a broad forehead and full nose. The black braids covering his head are a few inches long, some sticking straight out, others falling down. But when he turns and finds me watching him, his eyes catch mine. They're a deep brown, and again a familiar tug pulls at me. Like I've looked into those eyes before.

My breath catches in my throat, choking me.

Max studies me, and I don't break eye contact.

I know. I know why he's familiar.

Someone else starts talking, and Max looks away to focus on what she's saying. But I hear nothing. My heart beats an unsteady rhythm in my ears, drowning out all other sounds. Those eyes are the same eyes that could look at me and know what I was about to do before I did it. The same eyes that could read a situation and anticipate what was about to happen.

The same eyes I watched drained of life as their owner took my bullet.

Pain and guilt pierce me, sending a burning ache into my chest.

Max is Cade's brother.

That's the person Max lost. The reason for the pain in his voice.

Cade.

My chest constricts, making it difficult to breathe, and a rushing sound fills my ears.

I try to focus on the meeting, but the reality of the loss Max doesn't even know he's experienced won't release me. I lift my bound hands to grab hold of my necklace, feel the smooth seaglass pendant my brother Ezri gave me before he died. I *know* that loss. Know what it feels like to have a brother you love with you one day. And then for him to be ripped from you the next.

Again, I attempt to pull myself back to the meeting, but nothing registers clearly. I think Nika and Matthias answer the questions asked. Nika watches me, and I sense her calm facade for the leaders slipping at my abrupt silence.

None of it matters. At least not right now.

I'm too overwhelmed. Too exhausted to fight with those I thought would be on our side.

Max's passionate call for the leaders of Eryndale to stand up and fight to stop Demetrius Ark, his assurance that we can help them figure out how to do so, his confidence and quiet leadership—all of it echoes Cade. His desperation to do something about Talionis makes sense. He believes his brother is there.

But he's not.

Not anymore.

Like the angry ocean tide sucking me under, guilt begins to drown me. Along with the riptide of grief. I miss Cade. And I wish my rash decisions hadn't cost him his life, even though his actions saved me.

God, You saved my life the day Cade died in my place. But how can I face his brother knowing he'll never be able to see Cade again, all because of me?

CHAPTER

THREE

I don't hear the rest of the meeting. My mind is a swirling ocean of sadness, guilt, and fear. Max is an ally in Eryndale, but will he still be one after I tell him about Cade?

The meeting ends.

Zoe and Chul-Min Lee lead Nika, Matthias, Shane, and me back through the city. Max stays behind with the leaders to continue discussions.

There's more I should have said. Details they need about how we understood the map to get close enough to Eryndale in the first place. How the EUN, Hosea, and Catori helped us. Even details about Callypso to prove she is, indeed, real. Not the myth they want to ignore.

I *think* Matthias and Nika covered some points. But after my realization about Max, I couldn't focus, other than noting that there was less talk about what we experienced and far more arguments about why they shouldn't help.

And fervent accusations about us being spies.

Exhaustion threads its way through my brain as various parts of my body throb in pain. I want to wash up, but even more, I want to collapse onto a bed and sleep. Forget what's happened. Ignore the stress.

Based on the weary slump of my friends' shoulders, the circles rimming their eyes, and the way each of them carries themselves to keep from jostling an injury, I am confident they feel the same as I do.

We wind over the walkways, then Zoe and Chul-Min Lee stop at a small house a few rims out from the center and high in the trees. There are simple cots on the floor and few amenities, but I barely register any of it.

Zoe cuts off our bindings, though the faint red lines on my wrists remain as a reminder.

"We'll take two of you down to the medic so she can check your injuries. And then you can wash up," Zoe says.

"Is that where Ari and Bryson are?" Shane asks.

Zoe nods.

"I'll go first," Shane says.

"Fine." Zoe focuses on the rest of us. "Who else?"

"Matthias will go too," Nika says.

Matthias opens his mouth like he's going to argue, but Nika spears him with a look.

"Okay, guess I'm going too," he mumbles.

I briefly wonder why they don't just bring all of us to the infirmary, but I don't have the energy to ask.

Zoe and Chul-Min Lee usher Shane and Matthias out of the one-room building. There's the distinct sound of a lock sliding into place, and when I look out the window by the door, I see that Nika and I aren't actually alone. Zoe's standing outside. Guarding us.

There are cameras in our quarters as well.

Once again, I'm trapped and being watched.

But the physical entrapment in Eryndale feels like nothing compared to the guilt that's captured my heart. I don't think I'll be able to look Max in the eye again.

When Catori said to watch our backs in Eryndale, did she know they'd treat us like this? Or is there more to worry about?

I sit on a cot and gaze out the window on the side of the hut. The cot shifts as Nika sits next to me, but neither of us speak.

Night has fallen and the room is dark except for the soft moonlight filtering through the windows. Crickets chirp their nighttime song, and pine and the smokey scent of fire mingle in the air. The bright twinkle of electric lights illuminate the city.

Trees wave their branches, swaying to the whim of any breeze blowing by. It doesn't matter if they want to or not. The wind blows, the branches move. That's how it goes. Do the trees ever wish they weren't moved by the slightest desire of something outside of them? Do they wish they could never bend no matter what blew against them?

I hug my knees to my chest. I wish I could stand firm, be unmovable. But my pain, my guilt, my desperation, my fears, they all sway me. Break me. I drop my head on my arms and wince as I bump a bruise on my forehead.

The familiar sound of Nika breathing is almost comforting. I sense the change in it as she prepares to speak, but I don't lift my head.

"I didn't expect them to call us spies, or claim we're liars because we were captured by Callypso," her voice is soft, barely a whisper. "But I think I was most surprised by your silence. What happened, Bria?"

I roll my head to look at her but don't lift it from my arms. "Does your past ever sweep back in and brush away everything you thought you'd worked out? Bring back all the old feelings you thought you'd moved past?" I pause, almost choking on the thick emotions. "Does the work God is doing in your heart ever feel just"—I swallow hard—"temporary? Like it only worked for a little, but the heartache, the pain, the guilt—it's all just lurking in a dark moment, waiting to come back and take over?"

She studies me and doesn't answer right away, but I don't mind. I'm more afraid of her answer than her silence. Afraid she'll confirm my fears: that this God who saved me, who died for me, who will keep me from Hell, isn't actually able to change me. Or really fix my brokenness.

"Yeah, I've felt like that. But like my sister always told me, He's the God of the process. Sometimes He'll work a miracle and change us or heal us right away." She runs a hand through her hair, her face a strange mixture of pain and peace, hurt and hope. "But I have found in my life that most often He takes me through a process to heal me, grow me, to show me Himself." She pauses and looks out the window.

I lift my head up and watch her, less aware of myself. She

keeps her eyes averted, and I study her. Nika is one of the strongest people I know. Yet, in this moment, it's clear that strength cost her something to gain.

"It took me a long time to heal from things in my past. First, I had to face my demons. But when I did, mm, it yanked out all of these terrible emotions." Her jaw clenches, and I wonder what my friend has faced. "It was almost worse at first. I'd figured out how to ignore my pain and scars and let them shape me, but facing them . . . that was a new challenge. And, girl, it *hurt*. But with God's help and the support of my sister, I started to see a miracle. I started to actually forgive, and then to heal."

She traces a cut on the back of her hand. "But it wasn't instantaneous. It was more like watching a plant grow. I didn't see much of anything at first, no matter how hard I looked. The roots were just forming. But then a little green head sprouted and began to grow. Finally, it flowered and produced fruit. I still feel shadows of the pain and stabs of hurt and betrayal at times." She gives me the smallest of smiles. "It's like an old injury that will still ache. But overall, I'm not the same as I was. I've grown and healed." She puts an arm around me and gives me an awkward side hug. "You will too."

Her arm drops away, and I shift so that I'm facing her instead of sitting shoulder to shoulder. She's staring out the window, her expression peaceful and yet contemplative. Nika knows pain, understands it in a deep and personal way.

"What happened to you, Nika?" My question is a whisper, a breeze that would barely stir a small leaf.

Before she can answer, the door swings open. A scout's flashlight is almost blinding since my eyes have adjusted to the darkness. Nika and I both hold up a hand and squint toward the opening.

"Do you people like being in the dark?" Enya flicks on a light.

The entire room brightens, and Matthias, Shane, and Ari enter. They each sport bandages. Matthias has one on his forehead, which flashes my mind back to the moment I thought Laban had killed him. My chest constricts, but Matthias's eyes catch mine and he smiles.

He's alive.

The scent of lavender fills the room. All three of them are clean. I can suddenly feel every speck of dirt caked to my skin, the grime in my hair making my scalp itch.

Nika and I stand at the same time.

Enya nods to us. "I'll bring you two to the medic in five minutes."

I want to argue, but it's no use. We'll get the chance to wash up soon enough.

After Enya closes the door, Nika asks, "How's Bryson?"

Ari tucks her blond hair behind her ear. "He's okay. They said he'll need to rest, but there's no sign of infection." Her face softens in relief, but it's almost immediately replaced by irritation. "I asked when I can get my tech back, and they said the timing is undetermined." Her face pinches and eyes narrow. "How am I supposed to keep track of anything at all if I don't have *resources?*"

I bite down on my lip to keep from laughing. I've never seen Ari this annoyed.

Shane wraps his arm around her and pulls her close. "It's probably protocol."

Ari releases a long breath. "It's rude. They have everything." She lets out a huff. "And they refused to explain their cloaking techniques to keep this city hidden. I *know* they're using them—I can see the signs of the tech. They might as well tell me. I'll figure it out eventually anyway." She crosses her arms over her chest. "I asked if I could just have my screen, and you should have seen them. You'd think I asked to hold them at gunpoint! I mean, who do they think we are?"

The rest of us exchange a look. I guess Shane and Matthias didn't update Ari and Bryson on the meeting with the leadership.

Shane gives her a quick update.

Ari blinks. "If I had my tech, I could show them the proof they need that we're not spies."

"They probably wouldn't believe it." I glance at the door. I scratch my head, and the grittiness in my hair makes me cringe. As much as I want to be with my friends, I *really* want to be clean.

"I wish"—Matthias hesitates and glances up at a camera—"our friend was here. They'd believe him."

Others murmur their agreements. It *would* make things better if Cai were here.

But he's not.

Maybe I can find his son, Azarias, and give him the things Cai sent for him. Perhaps that would help. I keep the thought to myself. No sense getting hopes up for no reason.

Cai's note for his son and the cloth of fabric from the last day they saw each other are tucked into an interior pocket of my jacket that, thankfully, the scouts missed when they searched us. When the time comes, I'll have what I need to prove to Azarias that his dad is still alive.

Hopefully it makes a difference.

The door opens again, and Enya gestures for Nika and me to follow her. We practically leap out of the room.

There's more to sort through than I know what to do with. But I shove it aside as I meander down the well-lit paths to the infirmary.

For the first time in days, I'll finally be able to scrub myself clean.

If only I could just as easily scrub away my fears about what's to come.

FOUR

The next morning, I rise early. Despite our late night and my lack of sleep over the past few days, I still end up wide awake at dawn. Which is just great. I stare at the ceiling as thoughts bombard me. Thoughts about Cade, Max, and Nika. The leadership calling us spies and dismissing everything we stole from Ark as "a trap." Ignoring the threat of Callypso.

I sit up.

All my friends are asleep, except for Nika. She's sitting on her cot, leaning against the wall, watching me. She lifts a hand in silent greeting, and I wave back. With a nod toward the door, she stands.

My forehead wrinkles in confusion. "What?" I whisper.

She puts a finger to her mouth and gestures for me to follow her. I roll off my cot and stand, tiptoeing behind her to the door. The door that is locked, so I'm not entirely sure what Nika plans to do.

She raps on it lightly with two knuckles, and it's opened almost immediately. I follow Nika out the door. The two scouts guarding the entrance look at us.

"We need a bathroom," Nika says, keeping her voice low.

The female scout nods, then shuts and locks the door. She

eyes us for a moment. "You won't give me any trouble, will you?" Her hand rests on the gun at her hip.

"Where exactly are we gonna run?" Nika asks. "I just need to relieve myself. Now, please."

"Are you okay here?" The scout directs her question to her partner.

He leans against the wall of our hut. "Yeah, Lyrics, I'm chill."

Nika and I share a confused look at his word choice, and Lyrics's strange name.

Lyrics rolls her eyes. "Fine. We'll be back in a minute."

She leads us down a short walkway. "Ignore Retro's weird use of words. And my name is Karyss, not Lyrics. The boy likes to give everyone nicknames." She stops at another building. "Bathroom is in there." She nods to the structure. "Don't know why they didn't put you in a building *with* a bathroom," she mumbles, leaning against the railing.

Nika and I enter the facilities without responding. Nika rushes to the small room with a door that houses the toilet and slams it behind her.

"I agree with that scout," she says through the door. "I don't know what fool thought it was a good idea to stuff all five of us in a cramped room without a bathroom."

I smile slightly but don't answer. Now that I'm here, I find I need the bathroom as well. Nika emerges a minute later, and I enter the stall.

Eryndale is impressive. I don't know of many towns with indoor plumbing like this. Let alone in *trees*. I come out, and Nika is drying her hands.

She gives me a wry look. "If we weren't being treated like prisoners, I'd think this place was all right."

I snort out a laugh as I plunge my hands into the water flowing from the sink. "It's not the welcome I thought we'd have when arriving in Eryndale."

"No." Nika's face goes serious. She gives the closed door a quick glance, then focuses on me. "Last night, you never ended up telling me what was actually bothering you or why you got quiet during questioning."

I shift.

"Don't do it," Nika says.

My eyes widen. "Don't do what?"

"Shut down." She stares at her fingers for a moment, picking at one of her nails. Then she looks at me again. "Please, Bria."

I bite my lip, torn between the urge to protect myself by staying silent and the terrifying yet comforting idea of opening up to my friend.

The silence lengthens. Nika sighs and moves toward the door. For once, she won't pressure me to talk.

And I'm disappointed.

"Nika, wait," I say just before she opens the door.

She turns slightly, hand still gripping the handle. "It's okay, Bria. You don't have to tell me."

"It's Max," I say.

Nika drops her hand and faces me fully. "What do you mean? The scout?"

I nod and stare at the floor. "He's, um, well I think that he's . . ." I clear my throat.

"Spit it out, girl."

I bring my gaze up to roll my eyes at her. So much for the *you don't have to tell me*. This is the Nika I know. "I think he's Cade's brother."

Nika blinks, her forehead scrunching.

Before she can respond, Karyss opens the door. "You two done in here?"

Nika appears deep in thought, so I nod.

"Okay, then let's go. I need to get back to my post." She pushes the door open further to allow us out. "And I probably need to supervise more bathroom breaks," she mutters under her breath. "Dumbest secure holding I've ever seen."

If I wasn't so distracted by Nika's lack of response, the scout would amuse me. We follow her in silence back to the hut. When we enter, I'm disappointed to see the others are up or stirring. I want to hear Nika's thoughts, want her to discount what I'm saying, tell me I'm imagining things.

I drop to my cot, ignoring Karyss's question to the others about bathroom needs. Ari jumps at the chance, and Karyss leads her away. Nika sits next to me, her brow smooth.

"I think you're right," she says.

Matthias and Shane are in their own conversation and ignore the two of us.

My stomach drops. That wasn't supposed to be how this went.

"Something about him was familiar," she continues, "but I didn't make the connection until you said it."

"I want to be wrong." My words surprise me, but I don't take them back. "How do I face Cade's *brother?*"

"We'll tell him what happened."

"No." The word is sharp and far louder than I intended.

Matthias and Shane stop talking and stare over at us.

"Nothing to see here." Nika twirls her finger in the air for them to turn back around and leave us be.

The guys watch us for another moment, and Nika gives them a look that apparently scares them enough to turn them away from us. Silence immerses the hut for several moments, then the guys start talking again.

"No," I repeat, this time keeping my voice down. "He's on our side right now. If I tell him, if he knows *I'm* the one responsible for Cade's death, we won't have an ally. We need an ally right now, Nika. You have to admit that."

Nika lays her hand on my forearm. "He needs to know." Her hand tightens slightly. "It's his brother. And if he's anything at all like Cade, knowing what happened will only increase Max's support of us. Trust God here, Bri. We have to do the right thing."

I rub my hand over my face. Her words make sense. They're logical, reasonable. But my mind doesn't want to hear or process any of them. "I don't know."

"I'll tell him then. If it's too hard for you."

My throat constricts. It *is* too hard for me, too painful. I don't want to do it. I want to take Nika's offer and let her handle it. But I know I can't. It needs to be me. Cade died in my place. The least I can do is work up the courage to tell his brother.

"I'll do it," I say. "But I want to do it when I think it's the right time."

Nika watches me for a moment. The door opens, Ari returns, and then Matthias and Shane leave.

As Ari comes to join us, Nika says, "Don't wait too long. The longer you wait to do the right thing, the harder it becomes to do it."

"This is absolutely ridiculous," a woman's raised voice draws my attention. "You open this door right now, Moses DeFort."

"But, Mama, we were ordered to keep them under guard here until the next meet—"

"Of all the ludicrous . . ." The woman's voice trails off.

I stare in bewilderment at Nika and Ari.

"I don't care what they told you. Open the door. *Now.*" The way the woman says the words makes me sit up straighter.

There's no way I would cross her, and I don't even know who she is. The lock clicks, and the door opens.

An older woman with perfectly styled hair, warm golden brown skin, and a fierce expression stands on the other side of the entrance, arms crossed and foot tapping. "This is where they just *stuffed* all these kids?" She enters the room.

All three of us get to our feet, but no one says a word.

Her gaze roves over each of us, and there's almost a softness beneath her bluster. "I'm so sorry, dears." She whirls back to Retro—or Moses?—who's remained at the entrance with wide eyes. "Is this all of them?"

"Why is the door open?" Karyss asks. She comes to an abrupt halt, and Shane and Matthias almost run into her. "Mrs. DeFort, what are you doing here?"

Mrs. DeFort flings her arms into the air. "Two more? There were *five* kids crammed into this room?" She whirls around, taking in the space. "And no bathroom? Whoever made *that* disastrous oversight needs to reconsider their line of work."

Both Karyss and Moses gape at the woman, but no words come out of their mouths.

Mrs. DeFort pinches the bridge of her nose. "I can't believe this." She places a hand on Nika's arm. "This is unacceptable. Eryndale does not treat guests like prisoners. It's not our way." She shakes her head. "Absolutely unbelievable," she says to herself more than anyone else. Then she marches to the door. "Come. All of you. I will not stand for you staying here."

My friends and I stare after the woman.

Karyss and Moses almost trip over themselves trying to get out of Mrs. DeFort's way as she exits.

"But, uh, we can't—" Karyss starts.

"I was not asking your permission, dear." Mrs. DeFort adjusts the cuffs of her jacket. "You'll release all five of them into my care."

She beckons at us to come to her, and we do.

I've come across some of the most evil people to terrorize this region, but somehow being on the wrong side of *this* woman is more scary to me.

Once we've exited the hut, Mrs. DeFort heads down the walkway, further into the heart of Eryndale. I glance back to see Karyss and Moses gaping after us, helpless expressions on their faces.

"I cannot believe they left you poor kids in there overnight." She frowns. "Took me long enough to find you." She pats Ari's arm since she's closest to her. "I'm so sorry this has happened this way. My name is Emmi DeFort, but you can call me Emmi."

I raise my eyebrows. I think I'll be calling her Mrs. DeFort like Karyss did.

"When I heard you all arrived, I wanted to ensure you were treated with kindness." She weaves us through walkways, down stairs, and past clusters of people. "My husband Kassre—you met him, yes?"

After a nod from Matthias, memories of the night we met Kassre DeFort bombard me. It was right after Nate died. A lump thickens my throat, and I swallow it back. Kassre seemed trustworthy enough, even though I still hate the fact that he had to reroute *The Fearless Lady*.

"He radioed me after meeting you when he and Catori connected. Let me just say, I was not happy to hear he left you kids to travel on your own. And I let him know just that. I was unhappy enough that he came out of retirement to handle the mission with Catori, but I understood. But sending kids off into so much danger? He knows better!"

Kassre's comment about his wife laying into him when she heard about him sending us forward on our own makes even more sense now that I've met her.

"I've been awaiting your arrival since he and I spoke. And when I heard what you went through since coming here . . . well, I never!" She shakes her head, mouth pressed into a thin line. "Unacceptable. Completely unacceptable."

She grinds to a halt and whirls to face us. "Oh heavens, I'm sorry. What are your names?"

Matthias is the first to recover and introduce himself, then the rest of us do.

She gives us each a warm smile, then continues forward.

"Will you get in trouble for taking us from where we were assigned?" Matthias asks.

Mrs. DeFort waves a hand through the air. "Oh, I'd like to see them try."

We wind down a spiral staircase until we're at ground level. I think we're somewhere in the eastern part of Eryndale, but I'm not positive. She leads us past a few houses that extend into the trees, and we stop in front of a large and beautiful home. It's a few stories high with balconies on each level. There's a garden overflowing with flowers in the front and a meandering walkway leading to the door.

Mrs. DeFort props her hands on her hips. "Here we are. Home sweet home. Now come on inside, and we'll get you settled in the guest rooms."

Mrs. DeFort gives us a quick tour of the house. A teen girl who looks to be a year or two younger than me steps out of a bedroom on the second floor.

"Oh, Jordyn, dear," Mrs. DeFort says, "meet our guests." She makes quick work of introducing my friends and me to Jordyn. "Jordyn's our youngest." She pats her on the cheek lovingly.

Jordyn smiles, her gray eyes almost shocking against her light brown skin, which is a few shades lighter than her mom's. Her dark hair is a thick swarm of curls that are held back in a long ponytail. I would never have guessed she was Kassre and Emmi's daughter.

"Nice to meet you." Jordyn turns to her mom, eyebrow

quirked. "Moses radioed over and told me what happened. He's afraid Malachi is going to be ticked."

Mrs. DeFort waves a hand through the air. "Nonsense. My boys know they need to mind their elders. Especially their mother."

"I thought the scout guarding us was named Retro," Matthias says.

"Oh, that." Mrs. DeFort scowls. "I give my son a perfectly wonderful name, and he insists all his friends call him *Retro*."

"Mama—" Jordyn starts.

"You're just as bad as he is, Jor Jor. Letting him call you Gator. Really. When Jordyn is such a lovely name."

Jordyn grins. "You didn't even name me Jordyn."

Mrs. DeFort pulls her into a side hug and kisses the top of her head. Their dynamic is unique, and I wonder more about their history.

The two finish the tour, and we learn that the DeForts regularly house visitors, and they have two other sons: Malachi, who's in his late twenties, and Micah, Catori's missing husband.

A thousand questions scream in my mind when Mrs. DeFort shares that bit of information, but the sheen of tears in her eyes keeps me from asking them. It's strange to me that Catori didn't introduce Kassre DeFort as her father-in-law when we met him. But maybe it's too painful for her. She barely mentioned Micah in our time with her aboard *The Fearless Lady*.

Mrs. DeFort shows the guys to one room and then leads the three of us girls to another. The room is spacious and clean with two sets of bunk beds and a desk between them.

"Here you go, dears," she says. "There's a bathroom right down the hall, and this closet has extra blankets if you need them." She opens the closet to show us. "Get settled in. We'll get started on breakfast, so come downstairs when you're ready. And if you need anything, you let me know."

"Thank you for your hospitality," Nika says.

"Oh, that's just how we are," Mrs. DeFort says. She bustles out of the room.

Maybe things in Eryndale will get better after all.

A few hours later, after we enjoy a delicious breakfast of scrambled eggs, bacon, and cinnamon cake baked by Mrs. DeFort, she leads me and my friends back to the same building we were in yesterday. It's time to meet with the leadership again, but after the warm hospitality of the DeFort family and a hot breakfast, I'm feeling more optimistic.

We enter the building. The ceilings are high through this hallway, extending up at least two stories, and elaborate carvings of flowers, wildlife, mountains, rivers, and trees on the walls grab my attention. They're gorgeous. Intricate. There are Bible verses carved among the scenes too.

Mrs. DeFort opens the doors into the hall, and the chattering inside reaches my ears. Nerves flutter in my stomach.

Max is here.

He nods to Mrs. DeFort. "I heard you decided to change up their accommodations, Emmi." He raises his eyebrows. "You know you're making my job harder, right?"

Mrs. DeFort straightens herself to her full height—which is an inch or two shorter than me. Max towers over her, but somehow, she's the one who appears in charge. "These kids will be staying with me, young man. And if you don't let the leadership know, I have no problem marching in there myself." She props her hands on her hips.

Max's lips twitch like he's suppressing a smile. "No, no. It's fine. I'll handle it."

"Good." Mrs. DeFort gives a quick nod. She faces us. "When you come home later, you can tell me all about how things go."

"Emmi," Max says, "you know they're not supposed to talk about—"

She spears him with a sharp look, and Max stops talking.

He knows when an argument won't be won. Just like Cade.

I pull my attention from Max. He can't distract me again today. This meeting is too important.

According to what Mrs. DeFort shared with us at breakfast, we're standing before the Civil Agency of Eryndale, or the C.A.E. It's one of the branches that govern the city. The other branch is the S.O.C., Scout Oversight Committee, but Mrs. DeFort didn't seem to think we'd be going before them. They're more ready to take up the fight against Talionis. The C.A.E. is who we need to win over.

From what Kassre said when he boarded *The Fearless Lady*, most are ready to fight Talionis.

But not all.

I scan the faces of the members of the C.A.E. until I find the balding man who was so vocal against us yesterday. Reginald Finnigan. His eyes collide with mine, and a smug expression covers his face.

I turn away before I give a look I'll regret. I have to keep it together, think clearly, and win everyone over. Even a frustrating man like Reginald Finnigan.

The younger man with swooshy hair who spoke up for us yesterday clears his throat. "Let's get this started, shall we?"

Reginald hefts himself to his feet. "Yes, Gabe. Let's. But first, I'd like to present some concerning evidence."

My shoulders tense. What is he talking about?

He beckons to someone behind us. Two men come forward, arms full. The room waits in silence as they lay the items they're holding on a table several feet in front of me and my friends.

My heart lurches. They're setting out our things.

The map.

The weapons Callypso's pirates didn't know to remove from our packs.

Ark's files of plans.

And Ari's pile of tech.

There's more tech than I even realized. If tension didn't clutter the atmosphere in the room, I'd almost be impressed with all Ari managed to bring with her. But right now, I suspect this won't go well.

"These," Reginald begins once the two men step aside, "are the items confiscated from the group before us. Each item, in my opinion, is an incriminating piece of evidence against them." His nose tilts into the air. "And beyond that, I have it on good authority that one of them is from Talionis."

I force myself to stay still, to wait to say anything until we're asked direct questions, just like Mrs. DeFort recommended. But everything inside me shakes. All the earlier optimism I felt has evaporated.

The DeFort family may be ready to take us in and accept us, but Reginald certainly isn't. And my growing concern is that he'll convince others to side with him.

"What are you talking about, Reginald?" Gabe frowns.

He gestures to the table of items. "They were heading toward us, to Eryndale, armed with all those weapons."

"They've been on the run from Talionis," Max says. "Of course they had weapons!"

Reginald slams his palm onto the desk. "Then explain why they're carrying so much Talionis tech."

Ari shifts, chewing on her lip.

"Not to mention," Reginald continues, "they have a map that was made specifically for Talionis." He crosses his arms over his chest. "And I, along with other trusted members of the C.A.E., have reviewed the so called 'battle plans' they stole, and they're so preposterous to be laughable. Sitreea appears to be the source of all Talionis's resources and technology. There's no way Demetrius Ark could be planning the type of invasion those battle plans indicate under Sitreea's nose. It's all outrageous. As much of a mythical tale as Callypso."

My heartbeat quickens, and I swallow hard. The man's laying everything out like evidence against us. Our pleas and accounts of what we've gone through don't seem to mean anything to him.

I can't contain myself any longer. "Sitreea believes Talionis is an intel-gathering base. Ark hides the teens he's kidnapped every time a Sitreean delegation arrives to inspect the city. They have no idea the scope of his plans!"

Reginald's lip curls. "Absolutely ludicrous. How many lies do you expect us to believe?"He presses his hands on the table in front of him and leans forward, staring at me and my friends. "Every item here proves they're not all they claim to be. They're spies, and we'll be in far more danger if we invite them in than if we treat them as the evidence demands!"

Conversations erupt from the members of the C.A.E., and my friends and I share looks.

"This is not going well," Nika mutters under her breath.

"Enough," Max's voice cuts through the building. "You're judging them without hearing a word from them or giving them a chance to explain."

"They explained plenty last night." Reginald settles back into his chair.

"Let's hear them out," Gabe says. "We've known Talionis posed a threat, and this is the first real opportunity we've had to assess what it is."

"If they tell the truth." Reginald's scowl is so deep, his double chin seems to frown with him.

Gabe focuses on us, ignoring Reginald. "Explain why you have all of this. We need all the information possible to make the best decision we can for the city."

I explain how we needed the map in order to find Eryndale and that we stole it from Ark's safe along with the plans and files and key I told them about last night. Every part of me screams to let them know about Cai—that he was part of this. That he's the reason we even knew to look for the map. Somehow, I think it would help our cause. But I trust Cai too much to go against his instructions.

And my mentor—and uncle—didn't want anyone to know about his involvement until Azarias was told.

Ari passionately shares her reasons for bringing so much tech. She details how it has helped us, from hiding from Talionis soldiers to gathering intel. When she offers to demonstrate how helpful the tech can be, Reginald isn't the only one to shoot her down out of fear of what she might do with access to the equipment.

Before she can argue her points, I jump back in. "Ark's desperate. And he won't stop until he's accomplished his plan. It doesn't matter to him who gets hurt or killed along the way." My eyes skip over to Max, but I don't look at him for long. "We have to stop him, stop Talionis, before it's too late."

Again, conversations break out and the debate continues. Anytime me or one of my friends tries to defend ourselves, we're quickly silenced.

Time drags on until finally Reginald leans back and crosses his arms. "They must remain under guard. They can't be trusted."

Heat flushes my neck. It doesn't matter what we say. The man doesn't want to believe us.

"We were part of the E.U.N.," I say. "Hosea and Catori helped us—they believe us." My eyes search the crowd, desperate to find faces ready to believe what we're saying.

If they don't, what will happen to Storm, to Cai? To my family?

"Then why didn't you enter Eryndale through the E.U.N.?" A woman with glasses who hasn't spoken until now cocks her head. "That's highly irregular."

I clench my jaw. Why does it feel like everything is an argument?

"You couldn't have been with Catori," Reginald interjects before I can respond. "She and her crew were re-routed to help refugees. And Hosea hasn't aided the E.U.N. in years."

"You sit there acting like you know everything," Shane says, his words harsh. "But clearly you don't."

He steps forward, ready for a fight, but before he can say another word, a man who hasn't said anything yet stands.

"We have to stop judging these kids before we have all the facts," he says. "They've come to Eryndale for help. We can't refuse them."

"No, Thaddeus," Reginald says. "They were brought to Eryndale by scouts because they triggered an alarm. Isn't that right, Max?"

Max's hands ball into fists, and he glares at Reginald.

My heart sinks.

"Please answer the question, Max," the woman with glasses says.

"Technically, he's right," Max says. "But we brought them in that way because —"

"That makes things clear enough to me," Reginald interrupts. "I move they remain under guard as spies." He focuses on Max. "Irregardless of what Emmi DeFort may want."

A scout who'd been standing by the doors strides forward. "Are you questioning my mom's loyalty to Eryndale? Everyone here—everyone in the city—knows my family is honorable."

Reginald's face blanches like he knows he crossed a line. "No offense meant, Malachi. But they should not be given further access to Eryndale until we can discern their true motives."

Frustration ripples through me. "We're not spies! We didn't come here to help Talionis infiltrate Eryndale. We need your help to stop them."

"We've been here for a while now." Gabe stands. "Perhaps it would be best to resume this after we've all had time to review what's been shared this morning."

There are nods and murmurs of agreement.

"Fine," Reginald says. "But until we've reached a final decision, they need to remain under watch."

"And they will." Malachi DeFort glares at Reginald. "At my parents' house, with my family."

Reginald opens his mouth as though to argue but seems to think better of it. Instead, he gives a curt nod.

"We'll reconvene this afternoon, then," Gabe says.

Everyone stands, some grouping together to talk, others filing out through different sets of doors. Ari gives a furtive glance at everyone, then slips closer to the table with all the tech.

"What is that girl doing?" Nika mumbles in my ear.

My shoulders tense, but I don't stop Ari. I don't want to draw attention to her. This reminds me too much of the time she had me and Nika help her sneak into a secure wing of the tech building in Talionis during our early days as recruits. Ari can be fearless at times. Reckless, even.

"We should head back to the house," Malachi says.

I startle but try not to look guilty as I nod at him.

Ari is back, a smug smile on her face, which is more than a little concerning. The last thing we need is to do anything that might give Reginald and anyone else reason not to trust us.

WE ARRIVE BACK AT THE DEFORT FAMILY'S HOUSE. MRS. DEFORT meets us at the door and gives her son a warm greeting.

She ushers us all inside. "So, how did it go?"

"Not how we'd hoped," Malachi says, closing the door.

She frowns, then leads us into an open living space with couches. Bryson is there, which fills me with relief. He's healing, and Mrs. DeFort clearly wanted him safe in her home.

After a quick greeting, we share what happened with them. Several times, Mrs. DeFort interrupts to express her outrage, which I find more comforting than I would have expected.

When we finish, she shakes her head. "I'm so sorry. Truly. This isn't how Eryndale should be, but there are those who let fear rule them rather than common sense and decency."

Malachi pats his mom on the back. He's in his late twenties with broad shoulders, close-cut hair, and a well-groomed beard. His skin is a shade darker than his mom's, probably from time in the sun, and his presence is commanding. "We'll get everything worked out." He focuses on me. "You mentioned that you were in the E.U.N. and that Hosea helped you."

Mrs. DeFort's eyes snap to me. "What? He did?"

"Um, yeah?" The words come out like a question. I twist the chain of my necklace around my finger. "It was more of an accident than anything, I guess. We hid in a drainage system near his house, and he found us. But then he helped us and brought us to Catori."

The DeForts share a look that I don't understand.

Then Malachi's gaze sweeps over us. "Hosea rarely helps with the E.U.N. anymore. He had some . . . concerns. And, frankly, they were understandable. But not everyone agreed, and Hosea's stubborn, so he just, well, retired. The fact that he helped you might actually sway some of the C.A.E. to your side."

Before any of us can ask questions, Mrs. DeFort gets to her feet. "Is anyone hungry? It's just about lunchtime."

"I'm always hungry," Matthias says with a grin.

Mrs. DeFort smiles. "I'm sure you are. Our boys are the same way." She winks at Malachi. "Now, why don't you all go freshen up, and I'll get some food together."

With that, she leaves the room. Malachi gives us a somewhat awkward smile and follows her.

Once they've left us alone, Nika sighs. "Why does it always feel like we get just enough information to leave us with a dozen new questions?"

"I didn't think things would be this hard here," I admit. "I thought some of those questions would get answered. Not that we'd have to defend ourselves before the leadership."

"Do you think they'll end up helping us?" Matthias asks.

I shift on the cushioned couch. "I hope so."

Before we arrived, I was confident Eryndale would be the solution. But now, I don't know. And the worst part is we're trapped here while they take their time deciding what to do. Storm and Cai are in Talionis, and I need to get to them. Stopping Ark is important, I know. But if I could at least get Eryndale to agree to help me save Storm and Cai, maybe that would be enough for now.

There's also Derbe. My hometown. Ark has left it standing. For the time being. How much longer will that be the case? Is my family safe there? Or has Ark already taken my brothers, with the help of my aunt?

"At least we have people like the DeForts on our side." Nika nods to the door they left through. "But I'm not sure if it will help if some of us steal things." She gives a pointed look at Ari, who reddens.

"It's not stealing if it was mine to begin with, right?" Her face grows a shade redder as we all look at her.

"What did you take?" Bryson's brow lowers, even as curiosity sparks in his eyes.

She reaches behind her back and tugs a screen out. "This."

"Girl. They're gonna realize that's missing." Nika stands and paces to the window. "Why'd you grab it?"

"There's tech here." Ari holds up a hand. "Just by casually looking around, I can see they're using cameras and sensors as well as ancient types of camouflage techniques to cloak the city from arial view. Not to mention the systems they have in place for communication and training."

"A *casual* look? Really?" Nika says.

Ari ignores her and continues, "I figured if I had some of my gear, I might be able to hack in and find out more information about Eryndale, how it works, and what they know about Talionis."

We stare at her.

"During the meeting, it seemed like they already know something about Talionis." Her eyes dart around the room. "Didn't it?" She gives a nervous chuckle.

"Hacking into their system isn't exactly going to make us look like we're here for their help," I say.

"Good point." Bryson shakes his head at his sister.

Ari's embarrassment fades, and her eyebrows draw down. "They won't know I hacked into their system."

Her confidence would be annoying if it was anyone other than Ari.

Nika presses a hand to her forehead. "You can't assume you're the best and no one can ever figure out that you hacked them."

"Why?"

Nika gives me a bewildered look, and a laugh bursts out of me.

As much as the tech makes me uncomfortable, Ari has insisted over and over again that she "re-coded" everything she brought and there was no way Talionis could track it. And I can't deny the the fact that never once did Laban and his unit find us and haul us back to Talionis because we were using Ari's tech.

I stand and close the door to the room—something I probably should have done sooner. At least it seems like the DeFort family is trustworthy.

"It probably isn't the best move for you to hack into Eryndale," I say. "But if you did, what exactly would you do?"

Ari's face lights up, and she powers on the screen, like I just agreed she should do this.

"First, I'd get a feel for the type of system they're running, and then I would see if I can find any files in their system with intel." She flips her hair over her shoulder and bends closer to the screen. "Like what I did in Talionis."

"But this isn't Talionis," Nika says. "We need Eryndale's help —not to do something that makes them even less likely to trust us."

Ari pauses in her typing and looks up. "But what if I can find something to help convince them *to* trust us?"

Matthias nestles himself deeper into the cushions. "They already don't trust us. Might not hurt to see what we can figure out."

"Great!" Ari starts typing again before anyone else can offer a disagreement.

Shane gives her a peck on the cheek that she doesn't seem to notice. "I'll watch the door." He positions himself at the door, cracking it slightly to see out.

I shake my head, but a smile crosses my face as I sit next to Matthias. This feels so normal that I don't keep Ari from her tech world.

Ari freezes, and the screen drops into her lap.

I tense.

"What's wrong?" Bryson leans closer to his sister.

Ari's eyes are wide. "There's another message from Commander Ark."

Shane closes the door, and spins around.

Bile rises in my throat, but I swallow it down and crowd closer to Ari with my friends.

"Play it," I say. There's no sense delaying. Even though that's exactly what I want to do.

My heart hammers in my ears as Ari raises the screen with shaking fingers.

She presses play.

CHAPTER
SIX

The screen goes black for a second. Then a holographic image of Demetrius Ark bursts from it, sending a chill down my spine.

"Hello, recruits." Ark's slightly accented voice rasps against my ears. "Your prowess in evading capture by my most highly trained soldiers and hired mercenaries is a testament to all you learned in Talionis." His handsome face is calm, collected. And almost pleased.

Like us not being taken by Laban and Broche is a sick test we've passed.

Shane leans in.

"As impressed as I am by your skills," Ark continues, "my patience is growing thin." He links his hands behind his back, and his eyes seem to stare right through me.

My heart beats in my throat. I want to turn off the holograph, stop this evil man—who appears so *normal*—from saying whatever it is he is about to say. But I'm frozen where I am.

"Bria."

My name on his lips sends shockwaves of horror through me.

"You'll be happy to know Storm is now safe in Talionis." He shakes his head. "I can't imagine how terrifying it must have been for the child to be in the Ruins all this time."

No, no, no.

"She is under our watchful care once again." He pauses for an interminable second. "I do hope you return with my items soon. I would hate for her to have an unfortunate . . . accident. Wouldn't you?"

Blood roars in my ears, drowning out the rest of what Ark is saying.

The holograph clicks off.

"We have to go back," I say, desperation feeding every syllable. "She's not safe. He's going to hurt her."

Matthias takes my hand, and I squeeze his so hard my fingers crack. "She's his best bargaining tool, and he knows it."

I try to find a space in my brain to let his logic in, but fear clouds everything. "Eryndale has to do something."

"You're right." Malachi's voice at the door has us all jumping to our feet.

He ambles over and gives a pointed look at the screen in Ari's hand. "But I doubt the leadership will like knowing you took that. You'd all do better to be on your best behavior right now. And bide your time." He looks at each of us. "There are those in Eryndale ready to help you, and that message should be enough to convince those who are on the edge."

"We have people we care about in Talionis," I say. "And they're in danger. Even if Eryndale isn't ready to mount a full attack against Talionis, we have to send a team in to help our friends."

Part of me wants to mention Cai. Maybe Malachi would do something then. But I'm also terrified that my mentor isn't even alive anymore.

Malachi tilts his head, studying me. Then he puts out his hand to Ari. "I'll need to take that."

She hesitates until Nika gives her a light shove. But even as she hands it over, she doesn't let go right away. "I could help. Let me work with your tech team."

Malachi lips tilt into the hint of a smile. "I'll see what I can do." He steps toward the door then pauses. "Mom sent me in to tell you lunch is ready." With that, he leaves.

Once he's out of the room, Shane lets out a growl. "What do

we have to do to get them to help us? Why would we be here if we were spies? It's not logical!"

"We'll convince them." Ari rests her hand on his arm. Shane shrugs her off, and Ari quickly masks her hurt expression.

"This is crazy," Shane says. "What are we supposed to prove? That we're on the run for our lives? That Commander Ark wants us back, dead or alive? That we've risked everything to come here for their help?"

Shane's anger pulses through the room like another person, his voice rising with each question.

"Shane, please calm down," Ari pleads. "You heard Malachi. He's going to—"

"Don't be so naive," Shane interrupts. "If they were going to help us, we wouldn't be in this mess right now."

Ari visibly flinches at his tone and steps back. Bryson's posture stiffens, his hands balling into fists.

"She didn't do anything to you to deserve that tone," Bryson says.

Some of the anger on Shane's face recedes as he looks at Ari. "I'm sorry." He releases a slow breath. "Why are we even here if they're not going to help us?" His voice is quieter now, but there's an undertone of rage that threatens to erupt. "This is pointless. We should have never left Talionis."

The sentence hangs in the air, dripping over us like a suffocating mist.

"Lunch is ready," Mrs. DeFort calls from the other room.

The tension in the room is thick and unyielding.

"Let's go eat," Nika finally says.

I move toward the door and realize I'm still holding Matthias's hand. I give it a light squeeze and let go.

"I need a minute," Shane says.

No one argues with him.

"He's just overwhelmed," Ari says once we exit the room. "He didn't mean it. It's hard for him when he doesn't feel like he belongs somewhere or like he's not wanted."

"Stop, Ari," Bryson says. "Don't do that. Not again. Not with him."

Ari presses her lips together. "But, he's—"

"Gonna have to answer to me if he talks to you like that again," Bryson says, a steel in his words I've never heard before.

No one says anything else, and we make our way to the kitchen and dining area.

Shane's words are darker echoes of my own thoughts in my lowest moments. I may not agree with how he handled himself, but, as much as I want to fault him, I can't. He's as discouraged as the rest of us.

But Bryson's protectiveness toward his sister, the way he's acting now . . . there's something deeper to all of it. And I can't help but wonder what it is.

Max leads us to our third and final meeting before the C.A.E. According to Mrs. DeFort, after this, they'll vote on whether or not to treat us as spies, or accept us as fugitives from Talionis. I'm nervous about the verdict, but the one positive thing is that they haven't been leading us around with bound hands. Which I attribute to Emmi DeFort more than anything.

I feel Nika's eyes on me as we follow Max through the pathways of the city. She was right. The longer I've waited to tell Max about his brother, the harder it's become.

There's always the possibility that they aren't brothers.

But the more time I spend around Max, the less likely that scenario seems to be. And the more likely it becomes one of my friends will put the connection together. I've already seen Matthias and Ari giving Max thoughtful looks. At least I think I have. Maybe I'm imagining it.

"I'll take them to C.A.E., Max." A man in his fifties or so stops us midway to the leadership and breaks me from my thoughts.

I recognize him from our last meeting before the C.A.E. He stood up for us, but I can't remember his name.

"Your little friend is back," the man continues, "and he's talking so fast you could probably get to one of the far west villages in record time with all his energy."

Max laughs. "What, Thaddeus? You can fight off an entire

squad of Raiders but you can't handle Levi's chatter for five minutes?"

Thaddeus shrugs. "I know which battles to fight and the ones I shouldn't waste energy on."

"He's a good kid." Laughter still echoes in Max's voice.

"Then go ahead and have fun with him. I'll take them the rest of the way."

Max taps his chin. "Should I tell Levi you're afraid of him?"

Thaddeus stands taller. "Don't you dare. Or I'll make sure your next mission is less than favorable."

Max only grins at Thaddeus's threat. He takes off to find whoever Levi is. I watch him walk away for a moment. I really need to tell him about Cade. No matter the outcome of this afternoon's meeting.

"Big meeting," Thaddeus says, intruding on my thoughts.

A light breeze stirs the air, and the creaking sound of the bridge we're crossing echoes in the silence that follows his words.

"What do you think will happen?" Nika asks.

He glances over at her. "There are many on your side. All of us scouts believe you. But that could be because we've seen first-hand what the Talionis kidnappings are doing to the villages we're trying to protect. And you've got Gabe on your side. He's a good one to have fighting for you, I guess."

"So, you think we'll be okay?" Ari asks.

Thaddeus shrugs. "Maybe. I don't make predictions when it comes to the politics here though. Want me to figure out scout assignments? Or map out a new village? No problem. I can do that. But that's easy in comparison to navigating the C.A.E." He gives us a sympathetic look. "In fact, my least favorite part of my job is meetings with the C.A.E."

"I thought you were part of the C.A.E," Ari says. "If you're not, why were you in the meeting this morning?"

Thaddeus eyes her and then looks at Nika. "Is she always this inquisitive?"

"Worse," Nika says.

"She should be friends with Levi," Thaddeus mumbles. "I'm one of the lead scouts on the S.O.C."

He stops, and I almost run into him. We're already at the center complex. How did we get here so fast? I'm not sure I'm ready to stand up and fight for them to listen. I'm definitely not ready to hear them say they refuse to believe us.

Especially after seeing the holograph of Ark and hearing his not-so-veiled threats about Storm.

Malachi did bring Ark's message to the leadership ahead of us. Maybe it will help sway some of them to our side.

Thaddeus pauses with his hand on the doorknob. "Reginald Finnigan is looking for reasons not to trust you. He's someone people respect and listen to. You'll need to win him over, or you'll have to find someone who has an equally persuasive voice to fight for you."

"What about Gabe?" Matthias asks. "You said he was on our side. Won't that be enough?"

Thaddeus doesn't respond for a moment, his eyes assessing us. "I hope for your sakes—and for the sake of everyone in the region—that it is. But Gabe's a newer member of the C.A.E. and still earning his place."

His words do nothing to ease the dread knotting within me. He opens the door, and my friends file in one at a time. But I stand in the entrance, unable to take a step forward. This is it. In a short time, I'll know if Eryndale will support us or hinder us.

"You've got to go in, Bria." Thaddeus's voice rumbles next to me. "If you don't, it just makes you look like you're trying to hide something. And we can't let that happen. Talionis needs to be stopped, and this is how we can start fighting."

I turn my gaze to him. A beard covers his face, and there's a raw honesty about him I appreciate. He seems different from some of the others I've met in Eryndale, but I'm not sure why.

"No pressure," I remark. Even though the pressure I feel has mounted with each passing second.

"Good to see you have a sense of humor." His large hand propels me through the doorway. "Now go in there and do what you need to do."

"We aren't spies!" I argue, my neck flushing with a fresh wave of heat. "We didn't come here to find a way for Talionis to stop you. We're here because we need to stop *them*." I clench my hands tighter at my sides.

"We need more than your stories and passionate words." Reginald Finnigan slams his palm onto the desk. "We need proof."

"They'll destroy this region," Matthias says. "I promise you that."

"And we're supposed to believe *you*? A man from Talionis?" Reginald's face pulls into an incredulous sneer. "Not to mention, as I have already stated, your faces are on every screen in every town soldiers from Talionis have terrorized."

Matthias and I look at each other, at a loss. I've already tried to explain why our pictures are everywhere, but Reginald doesn't care. He's so paranoid that Talionis sent us here to trap them, he won't hear any other explanation. Even Ark's hologram didn't sway him. He just claimed it was another ruse to entrench us in Eryndale's favor.

"Tough crowd," Nika mutters under her breath.

My shoulders ache from tension. We've been here for over an hour, and it's only served to increase the accusations against us from Reginald and several others. Even Gabe's support has died down. I guess he wasn't the persuasive voice Thaddeus said we needed. No one has budged Reginald from standing against us. And nothing we've said has helped our case, at least with him.

It didn't matter when we told him the horrors we witnessed or the fear we experienced upon being taken from our homes and forced to be recruits. He didn't even seem moved when I told them about Storm—even *I* could hear the fear in my voice when I said I was worried about what they might do to her.

"Again, I move they remain under guard as spies," Reginald says.

"She's Lily's daughter." Thaddeus gestures to me, and every muscle in my body clenches. "Shouldn't that count for something?"

What does my mom have to do with this?

"Trusting her mother does not mean we trust her!" Reginald argues.

Confusion and longing for my mom weave a tight band around my chest. I'd give just about anything to study cartography with her again. Be held in her arms. But why do *they* trust my mom?

"Talionis represents everything we stand against." Thaddeus stands and presses his hands against the desk in front of him. "We can't continue to sit back and do nothing."

Reginald sits straighter in his chair. "We *are* doing something."

"Come on, Reg," a new voice behind us says.

I turn to see a man about ten to fifteen years older than me enter. He's well-built and dressed like a scout, his skin deeply bronzed from the sun. Confidence pours off him, and several people lean forward as though they're eager to hear what he has to say. He strides to the center of the room, only slightly set apart from me and my friends.

"You can't be serious," the man says. "We stopped really trying to do something about Talionis years ago." He holds up his hand to silence Reginald before he speaks. "Planning, or whatever you want to call it, doesn't count. You know as well as I do that it's time for us to act."

Reginald glares at him, every muscle in his face exercised into a deep scowl, but he doesn't answer.

"We don't have enough information to act yet," says a woman who has been almost as vocally opposed to us as Reginald.

The man turns slowly, observing everyone in the room, then stops when he's facing us. "Max filled me in on what has been going on while I was gone. And I've seen what lengths the soldiers of Talionis are willing to go to get them back." He gestures at us, his gaze catching on each of us. "The time for ignorantly assuming Talionis doesn't matter has passed. Now we need to act. Hard and fast."

Silence settles over the room, allowing the man's words to sink in. Several of the C.A.E. members nod in agreement. The speech seems to sway even those who were so opposed to us a moment ago.

"Well," Reginald says, his voice grating through the quiet, "it's not surprising that as soon as you return from a mission you have an opinion, Azarias. Even if you don't know all the facts."

My heart stops and then begins beating a runaway rhythm in my chest. This is Azarias. This is Cai's son. No wonder he commands attention. He's a lot like his father.

Azarias crosses his arms over his broad chest. "I have an opinion on things that *matter*, Finnigan. This matters."

Reginald rises abruptly, almost toppling his chair. "We stand for peace! That's why Eryndale was founded. Not to go to war!"

Azarias steps toward Reginald. "I know why Eryndale was founded." He spreads out his hands. "Why don't we bring my grandmother in and have her give her opinion on this if you're so deeply concerned we hold fast to what Eryndale was created for?"

"No need to bring me in." A soft voice falls from the balcony above us.

Everyone on the C.A.E. rises to their feet.

"I've witnessed everything." An older woman grasps the railing of the balcony and peers down at us. She must be Essie, the woman who founded Eryndale after the Demise.

Wrinkles line her face and white hair caps her head, but

there's a strength in her demeanor and a beauty to her countenance unlike anyone I've met before. Something about her presence comforts me, while at the same time asking for my respect.

"Please, everyone, sit," Essie says.

I feel like I should obey the gentle command, but there aren't any chairs on the platform where my friends and I are with Azarias, so we remain standing.

"Now, Reggie sweetie." Somehow, I suspect Essie's the only one who could get away with calling Reginald Finnigan *Reggie*. "When you were a young scout, you were one of the most vocal about our need to train scouts to stand up to the Raiders. You recognized that, though we desired peace and even though that was the reason Eryndale was founded, we needed to fight."

Reginald ducks his head. "That was different. It was a defensive move on our part. We had to do it to protect our villages from the Raiders' attacks." He clears his throat, and much of his earlier bravado seems to have wilted. "This would be us initiating the attack. Putting our people in harm's way on purpose."

"If we do nothing," Azarias says, "we're just allowing Talionis to destroy all we've worked for. If we sit back and let them continue to take our kids, the next generation, then we're not who we claim to be." His voice seems to rock the building. Even the outside noises of birds chirping and leaves rustling have dimmed to give way to the passion of his words. "We may not have been formed to be a military. We may not have been created to go to war. And I would never suggest that we go searching for war and battles. But, on my honor, we will fight when we find evil at our doorsteps. We *must* fight, or we will see the next generation taken from us before they have grown enough to experience the peace we claim we stand for."

He marches toward Reginald and doesn't stop until he is directly in front of him. "There is a time for war. There is a time to fight. And that time is *now*."

Reginald's face has paled. "They're stronger than us. More powerful. We will lose."

"If we don't fight, we have already lost."

"I agree," Essie speaks into the quiet that follows Azarias's words. She looks down at me and my friends where we're huddled together. Then she focuses on the members of the C.A.E. "I want your honesty now, my trusted friends. Are you against these young people because you truly believe they are dangerous? Or are you against them because you fear that if you acknowledge the horrors they've witnessed and endured, you will have to face the evil they have somehow survived?"

Her questions thrust like a sword through the room. Every person who has spoken against us drops their gaze. Goosebumps tingle on my arms.

This woman is special.

"But if we fight, we risk the lives and safety of our own children," a woman who has been against us says, her voice small.

"Oh, Margaret," Essie says gently. "The fear of a mother is a very real thing. One I understand well. But we must do for other mothers what we would want them to do for us if we were in their situation."

Margaret's face crumbles, and she drops her head into her hands.

"God has called us to this," Essie says. "Although not all of you share my faith, most of you do. And all of you know I founded this place with the intent to follow God's leading, even when it is difficult." She pauses. "I believe it is time for us to step up and fight. But we will take this decision to a vote before moving forward. Please consider carefully before you cast your decision." Her gaze finds Azarias. "Azarias and Thaddeus, please escort our visitors from the room while we deliberate."

CHAPTER

EIGHT

A thousand thoughts race through my mind as Thaddeus and Azarias lead us from the room.

"How do they know your mom?" Nika whispers next to me.

I shrug but can't find any words to answer her question. My mom isn't from Eryndale. She's from Derbe. All she does for Eryndale is help create maps for the Northeastern region. She's never once talked about traveling all the way here. So why does everyone seem so familiar with her?

And why do they trust her so much?

I cross my arms over my chest and hear the faint rustling of the letter Cai gave me to give to his son. My thoughts ricochet in another direction.

Azarias is Cai's son.

I want—*need*—to tell him about his dad. But the thought chokes me. Is Cai even alive still? Or has Ark decided he only needs one bargaining chip and Storm is enough?

Oh God, let him still be alive. Please.

We step into the warm sunshine. Instead of crossing the bridge to return to the DeForts', Azarias and Thaddeus lead us to the left and onto a wraparound balcony outside of the central hub building.

"We'll wait here," Azarias says. "That way we're close in case they have any further questions, and we'll be nearby to hear the verdict."

He and Thaddeus move away from us and converse quietly.

I watch them, one part of me urging me to follow and tell Azarias about his dad, the other not ready to. Azarias should know about Cai. It's what Cai wanted.

But talking about my uncle means speaking my fears about his safety.

I remove the letter and swatch of fabric from the interior pocket of my jacket, rubbing the fabric between my fingers. I walk a little away from my friends and their conversation, tuck the items into my pants pocket, and lean against the railing.

With an effort, I pull my focus to the view before me of Eryndale. The place I've longed to see since childhood. It's an incredible city. So different from Talionis, but remarkable in its own way. The buildings in the trees, the many and varied walkways and bridges, the hammocks swinging and the nets spread in the branches where kids and adults alike climb or relax.

Sunlight filters through the overhead leaves, and a soft breeze pulls at the ends of my hair. If I had seen all of this at any other time, I imagine I would have felt secure. Excited. Maybe peaceful.

But, thanks to Talionis, I don't only see the beauty of Eryndale. My mind rakes through every potential threat, sees the places where there may be holes in their security, looks for ways to escape. It's like being in a Warfare Strategies Scenario. Or running from Laban and his soldiers through towns and villages.

And I hate it.

I squeeze my eyes shut, wishing I could block out everything I've been through, the ways my mind has been rewired, and just see the good.

The problem is, even if I could shut down the strategic side of my mind, I'd still be on edge, overwhelmed, and with more questions than I ever thought I'd have upon entering Eryndale. And the worst part is that the uneasy feelings, the questions, the uncertainty—all of it reminds me of Talionis.

I grip the railing until my fingers turn white. I wanted to trust these people. I wanted to feel safe. But how can I when they treat me like a spy and a traitor? How can I feel safe when everything is spiraling out of control?

Again.

This isn't how any of this was supposed to go. They were supposed to welcome us in. Hear our story. Help us.

And they weren't supposed to know my mom.

Maybe it shouldn't surprise me. After all, she made the map we used to find Eryndale. At least, I think she did. I probably should have put the pieces together sooner, recognized that my mom is more involved with the refuge city than she let on.

But for a reason I can't identify, it scares me that they know and trust her. It makes me wonder if *I* know her.

I wish Cai was here. That would make everything better. He'd convince them to help us, to fight with us against Talionis. Then they wouldn't look at us like we were traitors or imposters. He could tell Azarias he's alive, and I wouldn't have to. He could help me find answers to my questions about my mom.

But he isn't here. I don't even know if he's alive. I drop my head onto the railing. *God, what do I do?*

"Hey." The railing shifts slightly as Matthias leans against it next to me.

I pull my head up and stare at his handsome face. The urge to fall into his arms and let him hold me sweeps over me, and I turn away.

We may have admitted to one another that our feelings go deeper than friendship. But what does that mean in light of everything before us?

He nudges me with his shoulder. "How are you holding up?"

"How do you think?" I keep my gaze fixed on the pathway below us.

"Me too," he says, his voice soft. We lapse into silence, but it's comfortable. "Do you want to tell Azarias about Cai, or do you want me to?"

I whirl to face him and find him much closer than I realized. "Um, uh, what?"

"You're cute when you're flustered." He winks at me.

I roll my eyes, but my cheeks burn.

"We both know Azarias is Cai's son." His tone is serious now.

"You told me Cai didn't want anyone else to know about his involvement until we told his son. Now that Azarias is here, we can tell him about Cai. Maybe it'll even help our case with the leadership." He places his hand on top of mine. "I'll tell him if you want." He squeezes my hand gently. "You've faced a lot already."

I shift my hand so that I'm holding his, and the flash of joy that dances across Matthias's face at the gesture makes my heart skip a beat. With my other hand, I reach into my pocket again to find the fabric from Cai and the letter he gave me to give Azarias.

I appreciate Matthias's offer, but I need to tell Azarias. It's what Cai wanted.

"No, I'll tell him." My words are shaky and lack confidence. But at least I said them.

Matthias nods and runs his thumb along the back of my hand. As much as I'd rather stay here holding his hand, I can't. I push away from the balcony and take a deep breath. If I don't go tell Azarias now, it'll just get harder.

Something I'm learning the hard way with Max.

Maybe I'll talk to Max after Azarias. Get every conversation I don't want to have over with.

Why is this so hard for me?

I swallow the question and force myself to go to Azarias.

He and Thaddeus stop their conversation as I approach, looking at me expectantly.

"I, uh." I clear my throat and start again, focusing on Azarias. "There's something I need to tell you."

"I believe you, and I agree," he says. "We need to do something about Talionis."

"Yes, but that's not, um, that's not what I needed to say." I blow out a breath, and glance at Thaddeus unsure if I should continue with him here.

"Whatever you want to say to me, you can say to Thaddeus," Azarias says.

He stares at me with eyes so much like Cai's that I blink to break the connection. I remove the letter and worn blue cloth from my pocket and extend them to Azarias. He takes the items from my hands, and a blank expression closes off his face.

"Where did you get this?" His voice is almost harsh.

"Cai, your . . . your father. He gave them to me." I lick my lips. "He wanted me to pass these things along to you. He was a captive in Talionis, too, and he's regretted arguing with you every single day. And he kept the fabric from your shirt that he ripped when you two fought. Actually, he's the main reason we escaped. If it wasn't for him, we wouldn't be here right now." I'm rambling. I clamp my mouth shut as more words clamber to be released. Talking about something I have answers to is surprisingly therapeutic.

Azarias's eyes bore into me, his face hardened into the mask of a soldier. I clench and unclench my hands, pressing my lips together against another onslaught of words. He peers down at the items in his hand and opens the letter. His face slackens in disbelief, and the corner of his mouth twitches.

"I was sure he was dead. But he's alive." His voice is soft, and I wonder if he even realizes Thaddeus and I are still standing here.

There's silence as he rereads the letter.

I should tell him Laban took Cai, but I'm not ready to deliver the bad news.

His head snaps up. "My mom. Where is she? Is she alive too?"

I swallow hard. His mother is Elena. The woman who betrayed me. The woman responsible for my captivity in Talionis. My aunt. I'm not even sure I want to see her alive again. I've tried to forgive her for what she did to me, but sometimes forgiveness seems completely out of my grasp.

"I don't know," I say flatly.

Some of the light dims from Azarias's eyes.

Before I can stop myself, I press forward. "Your mom is my aunt, and not someone we can trust." His eyes narrow in question, but I don't elaborate. "And Talionis captured Cai again, while he was trying to contact the EUN. Right before he was taken, he gave me those. Told me that if anything happened to him, I wasn't to tell anyone else he was alive before I told you." I swallow hard. "I'm sorry he's not with us."

Azarias stares at the letter for a long moment.

He focuses on me, and clamps his hand on my shoulder. "Thank you, Bria."

His hand falls away, and he turns to Thaddeus. "Stay with them for me. I need to go in and tell the C.A.E. what my father said in this letter. It's time we stopped treating them as prisoners and embraced them as our own people."

Azarias strides purposefully toward the door and back into the building we exited.

Thaddeus blows out a low whistle. "Cai's alive. I can hardly believe it." He sounds almost as dazed as Azarias did. A smile lights his face. "If any letter can convince them"—he jabs a thumb at the building—"it's a letter from Cai."

Thaddeus's confidence lifts my spirts. I'm glad Matthias urged me to talk to Azarias right away. Maybe something good will finally happen.

CHAPTER

NINE

"I wonder what's taking so long," Bryson mutters.

We've been waiting outside of the center complex for what feels like hours, but in reality is probably no more than forty-five minutes.

After Azarias went inside, I filled my friends in on what's happening. For the first time in days, a hopeful anticipation stirred among us, but as time has continued to tick by, it's ebbed away. At least for me. Even the breeze from earlier has stopped, leaving the air still and thick.

Everyone is sitting on the balcony, some of us leaning against the railing, others propped against the building. I pick up leaves and small sticks, breaking them into little bits before tossing them back on the ground.

"Maybe," Ari pipes up, "they're working on the plan to stop Talionis, and Azarias forgot we're waiting out here." Her unending positivity always borders between frustrating and almost inspiring.

Today, I'm leaning more toward frustrated.

I throw shreds of leaf to the ground. "More likely, Azarias isn't able to convince them they should trust us. You heard how Reginald Finnigan fought against us. I doubt he'd change his mind easily." I pick up a tiny stick, break it in half, and throw it past where Matthias is sitting. One piece rests on the landing.

The other bounces and falls between the rails and to the ground.

Ari pulls her lip between her teeth, her positive attitude dimming.

Nika raises an eyebrow at me. "Thanks for those cheery words, Bria."

I roll my eyes, but don't respond. I should probably feel a little bad, but I don't. At least not right now.

Thaddeus strolls over and leans his shoulder against the building. "She's probably not wrong." He crosses one leg over the other. "But I know Azarias. Finnigan won't be the one who wins. Just give it a little more time."

The sound of a child's incessant chatter carries to us, breaking into our conversation.

Thaddeus chuckles lightly. "That'll be Levi. I'm telling you, you can hear the kid coming from a mile away." He tries to sound annoyed, but there's a deep affection in his voice he can't hide.

From a ramp to our left, Max walks over with a small blond-haired boy of about six. Max's head is bent toward the boy as he listens to him tell him about how he learned to kayak and that he can do it all by himself. The words tumble out of Levi's mouth so fast I doubt Max could say more than two words even if he wanted to.

Their footsteps reverberate through the balcony as they come closer. Levi's animated hand motions and chatter come to a halt when he sees us sitting on the path in front of him.

"Who are you?" His blue eyes stare at us with open curiosity. "And why are you just sitting here? Don't you have work or something you should be doing?"

"Levi." Thaddeus pushes off from the building. "You have to give them a chance to answer *one* of your questions before you blast them with a dozen more."

"Uncle Thadd! I didn't see you. Guess what!" He steps over Matthias's legs and hurtles toward Thaddeus, apparently no longer interested in who we are and why we're just sitting here. "You left before I could tell you earlier. I learned to kayak all by myself. I don't need *any help*." His arms swoosh through the air animatedly with every word. "So, guess what? We can go kayaking together sometime! And we can have our own boats cause I don't need you to help me." His words gush out of his mouth so fast I can't figure out how he finds time to breathe.

Thaddeus groans, but his eyes twinkle with tenderness. "Oh, great. I can imagine it'll be a fun, peaceful trip. Maybe we can even fish while we're at it. I'm sure *that* would go well." Every word drips with sarcasm, but Levi's face lights up, clearly oblivious.

A low chuckle rumbles from Max.

Levi does a little hop in his excitement. "Yes!" His fist pumps the air. "Great idea, Uncle Thadd. Where's my dad? Let's go find him and ask if we can go now!"

Thaddeus clears his throat. "Uh, well your dad is busy, so I, uh, doubt we can do that today. Plus, um, I have to help, uh . . ." He spears Max with a desperate expression.

"Help with what?" Levi asks.

"Don't look at me." Humor makes Max's words dance. "You got yourself into this one."

"Uncle Thadd, what do you have to help with?" Levi persists.

"Ajax!" Thaddeus says, suddenly. "I have to help a new scout learn how to work with Ajax."

Levi draws in a quick, audible breath. "Can I come?"

Thaddeus's mouth swings open.

"That's what you get for lying to the kid," Max mutters under his breath, shaking his head.

I lean toward Nika. "I thought my brothers could talk my ear off. But they have nothing on this kid."

Nika snorts lightly as she tries to suppress a chuckle.

The sound draws Levi's attention. He spins toward us. "Who are you guys?" He eyes Matthias. "I never seen you here before."

Matthias blinks and looks at me and then Shane. Levi cocks his head to the side, waiting in uncharacteristic silence for an answer.

"We're new here," Matthias says, finding his voice. "My name's Matthias." He reaches a hand toward Levi, and the boy shakes it.

"I'm Levi." He takes a deep breath, his little shoulders rising with the effort, then plunges forward. "Why are you new here?

Where did you come from?" Before Matthias can answer, Levi turns to Ari. "Who are you?"

Ari laughs. "I'm Ari. And that's Bryson. He's my brother. That's Bria, and that's Nika, and that's Shane." She points to each of us in turn.

Levi nods. He focuses on me, his face bunching in concentration. It's as though I can see his brain charging like a transport, preparing to shoot off the ground. I brace myself for a whirlwind conversation, but as he opens his mouth, the door to the building opens, and he spins to see who's coming out.

"Dad!" he exclaims as Azarias comes toward us. Levi runs to him, and Azarias grins broadly and scoops him up.

"Azarias is his *dad?*" Nika's voice swims with surprise, and I feel the same way.

The two look nothing alike. Azarias's skin is several shades darker than Levi's, his hair is black, and his eyes are a deep brown. Levi's hair is so blond it's almost white, and his eyes are a vivid blue.

"Yup," Max answers Nika's question, but something in his one-word answer hints that there is more to that story.

"I see you found Uncle Thadd again," Azarias says as he sets Levi back on the ground.

"Yes!" Levi grins up at his dad.

Thaddeus groans. "All thanks to my *friend* Max."

"Yeah, Uncle Max helped me find him." Levi skips a few feet away and squats to poke at a bug.

"Don't pretend you don't love my kid." Azarias slaps Thaddeus on the shoulder, his eyes sparkling.

"Yeah, yeah. Whatever," Thaddeus says, but he looks over at Levi with a soft smile.

Azarias focuses on us, and we rise to our feet. The light-hearted atmosphere Levi brought with him vanishes as I wait to hear what happened.

I brace myself for Azarias's news, unable to squash the tiny bud of hope poking its head up within me. *Please tell us it went well.*

"So," Azarias begins, his voice grave. The bud of hope wilts inside me, preparing to die completely. "I showed them the letter from my dad." His eyes find mine. "It helped."

Oxygen reenters my lungs in a whoosh. "Okay. So, what now?"

"Now we move slow. Not everyone is completely on your side, but the majority are. They agreed to accept you into Eryndale as refugees and no longer treat you as spies. We're going to work with you to finalize our plan to stop Talionis. After I read my father's letter to them, they couldn't help but agree it's time to act."

"Finally," Nika says.

"I couldn't agree more," Azarias says.

"But how is this moving slowly?" I ask. "This is pretty much what we've been fighting for since we've started talking to them."

Azarias rubs a hand over the stubble on his jaw. "That's where it gets tricky. I'm only authorized to show you some of our strategy. Not all of it."

"What?" I gasp. "How can we create an adequate attack plan if we only have *part* of the plan?"

"She's right," Matthias says. "We can only help provide intel if we know your resources, your training. Talionis is too great an enemy to go against without a clear strategy."

Azarias holds up his hand. "I know. Trust me, I know." His lips press into a grim line.

"Finnigan?" Max asks.

Azarias gives one nod of his head. "And Lorenzo."

Max and Thaddeus both frown at the name and exchange a look, but they don't ask Azarias to elaborate.

"Give me some time," Azarias says. "I'll get you the access you need. We just need one more vote in your favor." His assurance and the sternness remind me of Cai. He looks like he's about to say something, but after a shared look with Max, he stays quiet.

I want to spew out more questions and arguments, but it's no use. Azarias isn't the one stonewalling us. Reginald Finnigan is. And whoever this Lorenzo guy is. I have no choice but to trust Azarias will do as he said and get us the access we need.

"But first things first." Azarias rubs his hands together, his tone lightening. "It's time you see all of Eryndale. Tomorrow, we'll bring you into the planning process."

My mind whirls with everything, but relief loosens the tension in my shoulders. In an hour, things have shifted. Now we'll be accepted in this city, and they'll work with us to do what needs to be done to stop Ark.

All because of a letter from Cai.

But what about their trust of my mom? And how are we going to make any kind of plan if we don't have all of the information we need? Not to mention that Reginald has been so dead set against working with us, he believes all of Ark's plans are a lie.

Maybe Azarias will change his mind, but still. We know Talionis in a way none of them do. They need to understand that we are facing a clear and present danger.

"Levi, come on, bud," Azarias says, breaking into my thoughts.

The boy jumps up from his bug observation and scampers over. He tucks his hand into Azarias's and grins up at him.

"They are cute to watch," Nika says in a low voice near my ear. "But I'm still trying to figure out how that boy is his son. I mean, the man may be a little lighter than me, but there's no way some of his melanin didn't transfer to his kid."

I shrug. "Maybe he's adopted. Or he looks like his mom."

Nika shrugs. "Guess it doesn't matter. At least we can finally start moving forward."

I don't respond as we follow Azarias. I'm glad we can begin making progress, but I have more questions now than I had before. And I want answers more than I want a tour of the city.

TEN

Azarias leads us deeper into the refuge city than we've been. Since we've spent the past two days either in meetings or at the DeForts' house, we haven't seen much of Eryndale other than the path from the DeForts' to the central complex.

We cross a bridge and enter a section of the city that's clearly residential. Flower boxes adorn windows, toys clutter the entrances in front of some houses, and laundry hangs from lines strung between trees. Some of the houses are two or even three stories tall, others are one level but wide, with several support posts stretching down to the ground. It feels homey and seems to embrace me and invite me in.

Some of my edginess eases, and the overall calm atmosphere seeps into my soul. This is how I expected to feel when I entered Eryndale.

Children laugh and shout to one another, running back and forth on the ramps and clambering down rope ladders to their friends on the ground.

"Dad, can I go play?" Levi bounces back and forth on his feet.

Azarias ruffles his hair. "Sure."

He gives his dad a quick hug, mumbling a "thanks" into his stomach.

"Hey, Izzy!" he shouts.

A little girl around Levi's age turns at the sound of her name. Her springy hair and warm brown skin cause my heart to skip a beat. Her smile lights up her face at the sight of her friend and drives every warm feeling from me.

She's younger than Storm, and her hair is rich and dark instead of blond. But her smile. Her enthusiastic greeting of Levi. All of it reminds me of my young friend. A lump lodges in my throat, and a burning sensation pulses behind my eyes. I blink, and the threat of tears melts away. But the lump remains.

Levi and the girl walk away, both talking, hands waving animatedly. My eyes follow them, but my heart sees Storm sitting with me and Cade at the table, her expressive face telling her story as much as her words. The incessant chatter. Her laughter and endless questions. Her smile that wouldn't evaporate, even on the darkest days. The way she lit up the place that was my prison.

I blink again.

Storm is just as much responsible for me being here as Cade is. Cade took my bullet. Storm was the reason I started to fight. The reason I knew I needed to escape and do something to stop Demetrius Ark. But I couldn't save her.

Darker memories surface.

Storm sobbing after the first Warfare Scenario we did together. Her haunted eyes even when she was playing. Her tight squeezes begging me to come back soon.

I left her. I didn't save her.

What are they doing to her now?

A hand on my arm makes me jump. "Bria." Nika's concerned eyes find mine. "You okay?"

The others are several yards away now, and Azarias is leading them down a set of stairs to a lower level. I'm alone with Nika.

"I don't know." My voice cracks, and my hands tremble.

"Want to talk about it?"

I offer as much of a smile as I can muster. "When do I ever want to talk about it?" The smile fades. "We should probably join them."

Everyone else has gone down to the lower level except for Matthias. He has one foot on the first step, but he's looking back at us. I wave at him and force another smile. He waves back and heads down the stairs. My smile evaporates.

Nika and I walk, the creaking of the boards beneath our feet reverberating through my body. "I'm worried about Storm," I admit.

Nika doesn't respond for a long moment. "Understandable," she finally says.

"What are they doing to her?" The question bursts from my mouth. A question I know Nika can't answer. "And Cai . . ." I can't even finish the question.

She says nothing. Just squeezes my arm briefly. Nika is as familiar with the horrors of Talionis as I am. She knows Storm isn't safe, and it means a lot to me that she isn't offering lame platitudes to temporarily make me feel better.

I stop when we're close to the stairs, and she stops with me. "I'd go through Hell Week again or face Corporal Valarius's bullet, or die from an attack of wild dogs in the Ruins—I would do anything to save her. To know she's okay. To take her place." My words are disjointed, overwhelmed.

Nika turns me to face her. She places her hands on my shoulders. "We're not done fighting for her, Bria. I'm in this with you. We'll do everything we can to get her back."

"But what if we can't? What if it's already too late?" My questions hang in the air like a dense fog. I break away from Nika and jog down the stairs.

Once Nika and I catch up to the others, I force my focus onto the tour Azarias is giving.

I thought most of Eryndale was in the trees, but numerous buildings and areas fill the ground space as well. There's a school where kids are taught not only how to read and write and do math, but also how to garden, cook, build, and even how to defend themselves. A training area for scouts takes up a massive portion on the western side of the city. Azarias doesn't bring us into it now, but he promises to give us a full tour soon.

There's a farm-like area, with many gardens and a field showing sprouts of what will yield a harvest in a few months, along with cows and chickens and pigs and goats—and probably other animals.

We pass a building that begins on the ground, then spirals up into a huge tree.

"That's the Record Hall," Azarias says. "This is where we keep a full history of Eryndale and the Demise."

Azarias shows us so much that I almost can't take it all in. Eryndale is like another world. Mrs. DeFort pointed out a few things when she led us to our meetings with the C.A.E., and we saw a bird's-eye view when we first arrived, but this place is incredible.

As we near the center of the city, Azarias gestures up to a building near where we faced the C.A.E. "That's the map room. Well, that's what I call it, at least." He grins. "It's the Cartography Center. It's where they create all the maps and make plans for new villages and spheres."

Sounds like my kind of place.

"What's a sphere?" Bryson asks.

"Oh, right. You wouldn't know that. It's a hub town that's created as a larger base for us to work outward from to create new towns and—"

"Nika?" A female voice from behind us stops Azarias.

Nika's entire body goes rigid. She turns slowly, as though in a dream.

A woman several years older than us stands nearby, her mouth open partway, eyes wide. She takes a step forward, almost stops. Takes another step.

Nika draws in a sharp breath. "Kemena." Her voice cracks, and then the two women are running toward each other. They embrace, clinging to one another.

"I can't believe you're here." Kemena's voice holds a tinge of wonder. She pulls back and stares at Nika's face, wiping a tear from her cheek.

"Who is she?" Ari whispers to me.

"Her sister, I think."

We watch the reunion. Emotion swells in me, and a knot lodges in my chest. A deep ache to see my own loved ones. Will I ever get the chance to embrace them? To tell them I love them?

"I thought I would never see you again," Kemena says. She

tucks Nika's hair behind her ear, not unlike what I would do with Storm.

Nika's face holds pure joy, and she melts into her sister's embrace again.

It's almost surreal to see Nika in this way.

After a few moments, the two join the rest of us.

"This," Nika says, wiping a stray tear from her cheek, "is my older sister, Kemena." She clings to her sister's hand like a little kid, trusting, unwilling to let go.

"Hi," Kemena says.

She's beautiful, like Nika, with her dark skin and hair and deep brown eyes. Her hair isn't curly like Nika's, but braided into dozens of small braids that are twisted together on top of her head. The smile she gives is open and inviting, and there's a gentleness about her that almost makes me wish I could give her a hug.

I want to trust her, which is a strange feeling. Maybe it's because I trust Nika, and Nika clearly adores her older sister.

Azarias decides now would be a good time for a break from our tour. He tells us we're free to explore on our own, and he'll meet us at the DeForts' in a couple of hours to share what will happen tomorrow.

Everyone goes their own way, giving Nika and Kemena time alone to catch up. I step toward the Cartography Center.

"Bria, wait," Nika says. "Can you stay? Please?" She's still holding Kemena's hand.

I glance between the two of them, unsure if I really want to stay. As much as I hate to admit it, it's hard seeing my friend reunited with her sister while I wonder if I'll ever see any of my family again. But I also feel drawn to Kemena, and Nika rarely asks anything of me.

My eyes dart around. "Um, don't you want to be with your sister?"

"I'm not letting her out of my sight." Nika smiles, but it fades. "I want someone to help me tell her what I went through. What we went through." She looks at her sister, then back at me. "Who better to help me do that than my closest friend?"

Kemena's face echoes my surprise at Nika's words. "My baby girl made herself a best friend?" Her eyes fill with unshed tears.

Nika rolls her eyes and lets go of Kemena's hand to give her a light shove. "Come on, Kem." She groans. "Don't make it such a big deal." But a small smile twitches the corners of her mouth.

Kemena gives her a kiss on the cheek. "God sure has an interesting way of answering prayers." She walks over and embraces me.

My arms stay stiff at my side for a moment, then I hug her back, the ache in my chest exploding. It feels like hugging my mom. A tear squeezes past my defenses, and I pull back to swipe it away.

Kemena's face softens, and I turn slightly to compose myself. It's as though she can see my pain, my questions, my fears, even though she just met me. It's unnerving.

"Stay, Bria. Please," Kemena says.

I'm almost afraid of what these two sisters might bring out in me. But I find myself saying, "Okay."

"Perfect." Kemena links her arm with Nika. "Come on. I'll show you my favorite spot in Eryndale."

She leads us away from the bustling central areas of the city. She weaves in and out of the paths and sections of the city with familiarity.

"How long have you been here?" I ask as we wind our way around a building.

"Eight months and two days."

"That's specific," Nika says.

A small stream trickles nearby, and Kemena leads to a bridge to cross over it. "I've counted every single day since I lost you, baby girl." Emotions run over her words like the water running over the rocks in the stream below us.

This moment is personal, and I feel like I shouldn't be here witnessing it. But I'd make more of a scene if I turned back now.

"I started searching for you the day I woke up and found you missing," Kemena says. "I left Thornfield—even though our parents didn't think it was necessary." There's an undertone of anger that's different from what I've already come to expect from Kemena. "They believed the note. I never did."

"What note?" Nika asks.

Kemena exhales slowly, as though she doesn't want to relive the moment. "The note left by your bed saying you were tired of living in a small town and wanted to explore on your own."

"I never wrote any note!" Nika grinds to a halt as we step off the bridge. "I would never have left you like that. Not after everything."

Kemena's eyebrow quirks in a way so similar to how Nika's does that it takes me off guard. "Didn't I just say that?" she asks me.

I don't answer, but that seems fine with Kemena.

She turns her attention back to Nika. "I'm glad to see my little sister hasn't changed *too* much." She wraps an arm around Nika. "She still only half-listens to what I'm saying."

Nika lets out a long-suffering sigh. "Whatever, Kem."

Kemena laughs, a contagious sound that pulls a chuckle from me. Nika frowns.

"Anyway," Kemena says. We begin walking again. "I went to every town and village I could find searching for you, asking if anyone had seen you. No one had, but I also found in some villages other people your age had mysteriously disappeared. And some of the parents I spoke with showed me letters just like the one left by your bed."

A chill creeps over me despite the warm day. It was bad being taken by the soldiers, waking up in the forest and not knowing where I was. But I imagine it would be its own kind of horror to wake up and find your loved one missing, with no idea of where they'd gone other than a note.

It all reminds me of what Ava's parents told us when we were in Leddington. They'd found a note supposedly from Ava saying she wanted more than their small town had to offer. The fact that it wasn't true brought them comfort. Even though I also had to deliver the shattering news that Ava died in Talionis.

We walk down a worn path with tree branches crossing overhead, forming an arch.

"Then one day," Kemena continues, "I encountered a scout from Eryndale. Azarias." She pauses for a fleeting moment. "He was asking questions similar to the ones I was asking, and when

I realized where he was from, I insisted he bring me here and help me find you. I knew more was going on than I understood, that these kidnappings were bigger than just a few teens. It was clear I would need help to figure it all out and to get to you. I've been here ever since."

"How did you convince Azarias to bring you back here?" I ask.

"Kemena can be very, um, persuasive when she needs to be," Nika says dryly.

"Yes, I can, can't I?" Kemena winks. "And it's a good thing, because it got me here, which led me to you." She puts her arm around Nika and pulls her close.

We wander farther down the path, then Kemena steps off of it and into the trees. "We're almost there. I've wanted to bring you to this spot since the day Essie brought me."

We step over undergrowth worn down into its own path of sorts. Kemena walks toward a bush, pushes past it and some leafy vines, and is swallowed up. Nika and I stop and look at each other.

"Coming?" Kemena calls from the other side.

Nike goes first and I follow, pushing past the greenery. I feel like I'm about to enter the Ruins. Every time I would train with Cai, I would have to sneak away and crawl through the small vegetation-covered opening in the fence. I never want to be in that place again, but I would give just about anything to see Cai lounging on the branch of a tree, waiting for me on the other side of these vines and bushes.

Instead, I enter a haven unlike anything I've ever encountered.

The area isn't big, but every inch of it invites me in. An alcove hidden amid the trees and bushes. Vines and branches weave together in a purposeful pattern, creating walls that go at least eight feet high. Overhead is open to the sky above, with a few branches stretching across the opening like protective arms, concealing and guarding any who are within their embrace. Two benches are situated near each other, and a blue and green hammock is strung up across from them. Another hammock-like chair hangs from a thick branch, swaying in the breeze.

There are patches of flowers, well-tended, blooming, and bursting with color, and the scent of a nearby rosebush perfumes the air. Solar-powered lanterns are placed in various areas—some on stumps, others on the ground, a few hanging. I can imagine this space is warm and inviting with them glowing, even on the darkest of nights.

There's an almost sacredness here. A deep peacefulness.

Kemena busies herself plucking a weed, then she moves onto the rosebush and removes some of the dying flowers. Finally, she sits on a bench and leans back, pulling one leg onto the seat with her.

Nika and I haven't moved from the entrance. We both just stare.

"You can sit." Kemena smiles and gestures to the seats.

"Wow," Nika says, finding her voice. "I mean seriously, wow. This is amazing." She joins her sister on the bench. "How did you find it?"

The swinging chair seems to beckon me, so I settle myself into it. My feet brush the ground, and the soft fabric cocoons me.

"I told you. Essie showed it to me," Kemena says. "Not many know of this little place, and she likes to keep it that way." She leans forward, conspiratorially. "But I'm pretty sure she's made many havens like this one. At least, that's the impression I've gotten." She reaches out and plays with Nika's hair.

Nika leans against her, more at ease than I've ever seen her. Nika has always been strong, the one to take charge and say what she thinks. But with Kemena, she's almost childlike and clearly doesn't need to be in control. She rests in her sister's embrace, trusting her.

"Will she mind that you showed us?" Nika asks.

Kemena shakes her head. "No. She had faith I'd be able to share this place with you one day. Even when I would lose heart." Emotions bring Kemena's words to a brief pause. "I mostly come here to pray and to think. God's met me here so many times. Even when I didn't necessarily know He was meeting me."

Her face moves into a wry expression so like Nika, I can't

keep from smiling. It's interesting to meet the woman who helped shape my friend into who she is today.

We lapse into a comfortable silence. I almost welcome it, even as I wish I knew Kemena well enough to ask her some questions. What did she mean by not knowing when God was meeting with her?

Her words make me wonder if there are times when I haven't realized God was with me, maybe even when I've felt so alone.

I lean back against the swing and look up through the branches. *God, I hope You're with me when I don't feel it. But I have to be honest. I would much rather know You're there than feel like You're not, even if You are.*

I know God has saved me. I know I'm free from my sin. But it's hard for me to understand how He's supposed to be a part of my everyday life.

Kemena asks us to share what happened in Talionis, interrupting my thoughts. Time stands still in the peaceful alcove as Nika and I share with Kemena all we've been through. Some of the dark memories we relive seem to taint the surrounding beauty, threatening to wash over me and drown me. But then we share how Nika and I met on the first day, how we became friends. Learned to trust each other.

Kemena's eyes fill with tears as we talk about our friendship, and I almost ask why. But decide not to. If Nika wants to share with me more about her past, maybe I'll understand why it's such a big deal that she and I are friends. Then again, maybe Kemena's still emotional over having her sister back, and the tears have nothing to do with me or my friendship with Nika.

After a while, Kemena glances at her watch. "Looks like it's almost time for you all to meet with Azarias again. We should head to the DeFort's." She gives a dramatic eye roll. "Heaven forbid we keep the man waiting."

Mrs. DeFort is outside nodding vigorously as two men in their early sixties with tool belts strapped to their waists gesture to the outside of her house.

"Great," one of the men says as Nika, Kemena, and I approach. "We'll get started on construction tomorrow morning. Probably around seven. As long as Paul stops giving me more *ideas*." He shakes his head at the taller man, who smirks.

"I was just offering a suggestion," Paul says. "That's what brothers are for."

Mrs. DeFort laughs. "Watching you two work together is always an experience. Thank you, Bill and Paul. We're excited to have the porch installed. I'll be sure to have bagels and muffins for you and your guys."

Bill tucks a pencil behind his ear. "They'll be happy to hear that."

With that, Bill and Paul nod at us and leave.

"Oh, good!" Mrs. DeFort says when she turns to find us waiting behind her. "You girls are back." Her gaze flicks between Nika and Kemena, and her face softens. "I should have seen it. She's your sister." The words are directed at Kemena and full of emotion. Mrs. DeFort clears her throat and rubs her hands together. "I have a fun surprise for you. Come inside so I can tell all of you at once."

She bustles into her house. "You come too, Kemena!" she calls from the doorway.

The three of us exchange a glance, then follow Mrs. DeFort into her house. I'm not in the mood for a "surprise" but there's no way I'll disrespect Mrs. DeFort by saying that. Especially after all she's done for us.

We enter to find the rest of our friends lounging on sofas in the living room and Azarias waiting by the door. Matthias grins at me and pats the cushioned seat next to him. My face warms, but I join him.

Telling him I cared about him while we were running from Broche, right after I feared he would be taken from me forever, seemed like a good idea. But now . . . well, now I don't know what to do with the shift in our relationship.

Mrs. DeFort clears her throat, drawing our attention. Her eyes are lit up, and she seems barely able to contain her excitement. "Tonight, I've arranged for a party to welcome all of you to Eryndale. You have been mistreated and accused long enough. It's time you experienced what Eryndale is truly like."

Azarias blinks. "What?"

Mrs. DeFort waves off his question and heads to the door. "I have lots to do! The party starts in an hour."

Azarias follows her from the room.

A party? Seriously?

"There's a lot *we* need to do," I say to no one in particular.

Kemena snorts. "That's true, but once Emmi gets her mind set, there's no stopping her. Besides"—she wraps her arm around her sister and pulls her in for a hug—"it seems to me like you all could use a little fun and rest. Tomorrow will be soon enough to dive into planning."

"I don't want to go to a party," Shane grumbles.

Ari nudges him with her shoulder. "Oh, come on, grumpy. It'll be fun."

Shane's face softens, and a moment later, we're all filing from the room to get ready for the celebration. Although everything in me wants to ignore the invitation and dive into planning.

I approach the center of Eryndale as dusk falls. This is the last thing I want to do.

The other girls left before me, and I almost had to force Nika to leave. She could tell I wasn't interested in a party, and I doubt she's expecting me to show up at all, though I told her I would. Now just doesn't seem like a time for a celebration. There's too much at stake. Too many plans we need to discuss, too much of a risk in delaying.

Storm and Cai are in danger, and all I want to do is save them.

But, like Nika said as she sailed out the door, nothing could be done tonight. We might as well experience more of Eryndale.

So, here I am. Crossing a bridge as lights spark through the trees and the sound of music and laughter drifts along the breeze to me. I sigh, but force one foot in front of another and plaster on a smile.

People are milling around, laughing, eating, and clearly enjoying themselves. The camaraderie here is different from anything I've ever seen before, and I can't help but be drawn in. Tables are overladen with food, kids run all over shrieking after one another, and there's even a large area set aside where people are dancing to the lively music.

It's a beautiful scene. I only wish I could enjoy it more.

"There you are." Nika materializes next to me, and I jump. "I was about to come find you."

"I told you I'd be here."

"Mm-hmm." Nika takes hold of my arm and leads me through the crowd and to a table where others are seated and eating.

Kemena sits next to Azarias's son, Levi, her head bent down in concentration as the little boy spews words out of his mouth. His little face and body emphasize whatever he's saying, and Kemena laughs. Her laugh brings a smile to Levi's face, and he leans against her.

"Levi seems to like your sister," I say to Nika as we settle ourselves at the table, conversations whirling around us as fast as the couples and friends dancing not far away.

Nika pushes a plate of food toward me. "Got you some food before it was all gone. You're welcome."

I roll my eyes, but the tantalizing smells rising from the barbecued chicken, wedges of potatoes, and fresh salad make me happy I have a friend willing to look out for me. I take a bite, which seems to satisfy Nika.

"Yeah, Levi *loves* Kem," she says. "As soon as he saw her, he raced over and planted himself next to her. He's been talking to her ever since. I haven't even tried to get a word in." She shakes her head lightly. "It's funny though. I mean, Kem's good with kids, but I can't figure out why Levi seems so . . . attached to her."

I swallow the bite of chicken in my mouth. "Maybe she's friends with his mom."

"Maybe," Nika shrugs. "I am curious though. I'll just ask her later."

I take another bite to keep from smiling. Since reuniting with her sister, Nika hasn't let her out of eyesight for more than a few minutes. She even asked Mrs. DeFort if Kemena could stay in the extra bunk in our room—which Kemena chided her for. But Mrs. DeFort said of course and insisted Kemena bring her things over and stay at the house.

I can't blame Nika for wanting her sister close. Kemena seems great, and she's part of Nika's family. If I had a family member here, I'd be doing everything I could to spend time with them as well.

The music changes in tune, and Nika jumps up. "They played this one earlier, and Kemena promised she'd teach me the dance when they played it again."

Kemena glances over, catches Nika's eye, and nods, getting to her feet. She pats Levi on the head, and I hear her say something about coming back soon to hear the rest of the story. She waves Nika to come with her.

"Want to come?" Nika asks.

I shake my head. "Nah, I'm okay. I'll finish eating."

Nika shrugs. "Suit yourself. But you'd better get out there and dance at least *once* tonight. You need to have a little fun."

Before I can find a suitable retort, Nika glides over to her sister, and the two of them join in the rhythm of the music. I watch them while I eat, amused by Nika's attempts at first, and then impressed by her ability to catch on so quickly. The sisters spin and whirl and dance their way around the floor, along with dozens of others. It does look like fun. Maybe I should have taken Nika up on her invitation.

"Mind if I join you?" Matthias's voice behind me pauses my hand where it is halfway to my mouth.

I turn to look up at him, trying to decide on my answer. Part of me wants his company, and the other part wants to send him away. Though I'm not entirely sure why.

"Sure."

He grins his contagious grin and slides into Nika's vacated seat. My heart skips a beat as his shoulder brushes mine.

We sit in silence for a few moments, watching the dancing. I push my plate away with one finger, no longer hungry, and more than a little uncomfortable. Since when has Matthias been able to sit still and not talk? He's like the grown-up version of Levi.

"I like it here," he finally says.

I release a breath I hadn't realized I was holding and nod.

"It's different from any other place I've lived. Safe. Happy." His gaze never leaves the dance floor, but I watch him. He has a far-off look in his eyes, as though he's watching the dancing, but seeing something else entirely. Something that's drawing sad lines on his face.

The scruff of a beard lines his jaw, and his skin is even darker than usual from the longer days as spring edges into summer. He turns to find me staring at him, and his blue eyes connect with mine. My cheeks flush, and I hope it's dark enough to keep him from noticing. I want to turn away, but find I can't.

His mouth twitches. "Do I have something on my face?"

I face the dancers again. "No. Why?"

"Oh, so I'm just that handsome?"

It's like I can *hear* his eyebrows wiggling as he grins at his own joke.

My mouth twitches, and I look at him out of the side of my

eye. "Maybe yes." The flirtatious banter escapes me before I can stop it and immediately leaves me feeling embarrassed.

He gently takes my chin and turns my head to fully face him. "And you're gorgeous."

My heart leaps into my throat. I shift, but can't find the words to respond. I face the dancing crowd again, but hardly see them. What is this thing with Matthias supposed to even look like? Part of me wonders if I should pull away, so I can focus on what I need to do.

"Okay, okay, I get it." Matthias rests his elbows on the table and cranes his head to look at me.

"Get what?" I ask, suddenly terrified that he could read my thoughts.

He grins. That huge, ridiculous, grin. His white teeth sparkle against his tanned skin, and his eyes shine. "I'll let you dance with me."

In one fluid motion, he gets to his feet and holds out his hand to me.

"What?" I sputter. I stare at his hand, my heart racing like I'm about to enter a new Warfare Scenario.

He wiggles his fingers. "I know you wanna dance with me. Come on."

I look at his hand and then up into his face. "I'm fine."

The grin on his face slips a little, and some of the sadness I thought I saw earlier returns. "I know you are." His drops his hand.

The music changes, and a new lively tune fills the air. The self-assurance and confidence I'm used to seeing in him is gone, and he looks at me with a vulnerability that's terrifying. "Will you dance with me anyway? Please?"

Something in me shifts, and when he reaches out his hand again, I nod and take it. I rise, and the smile he gives me spreads warmth through my chest.

Even if it's the smart move, I'm not ready to pull away from him.

He leads me to the dance floor.

"Do you know this dance?" I ask. Everyone appears to follow the same intricate steps and movements.

"Nope." He bobs up and down with the music. "But I'm a fast learner." With that, he pulls me the rest of the way onto the dance floor.

The music seems louder here, the air itself pulsing with the beat, perhaps because the stage is closer. It's warmer as dozens of people dance around. Matthias releases my hand, face set in concentration as he kicks his feet, twirls, and attempts to follow the steps the others are doing.

A laugh bubbles up inside of me. He looks ridiculous, but he doesn't care one bit. He just throws himself more exuberantly into the dance.

"I think I'm getting it!" he shouts.

He grabs my hand, forcing me to dance with him. Before long, I'm laughing so hard I can barely keep myself on my feet, let alone dance with any kind of rhythm to the music.

Matthias spins me around, then tries to guide us to the left when everyone else is going right.

"Whoops." He quickly corrects our course. Then he does his own little jig that looks nothing like anyone else, but somehow fits with the beat.

He takes both of my hands and whirls us around in a fast circle. Others clear out of our way. And I laugh more, letting myself enjoy the moment.

Because I *am* enjoying this. I'm actually having fun.

Before I can overanalyze it, Matthias grabs me around the waist, lifts me off the ground, and spins me around. A squeal escapes, and I grip his shoulders tight. He laughs and sets me back on my feet.

The song ends, and everyone claps for the musicians. Matthias takes a bow. I shake my head, but the smile on my face is too broad to wipe away. He winks at me when he stands.

A new song starts up, and Matthias bows again, this time to me. "Another dance?"

I bite my lip and nod. Which earns me another grin. Then I'm swept away, by the guy I've learned to trust. But who scares me more than I have even admitted to myself. Because every moment I'm with him, he finds his way a little deeper into my heart.

It almost seems wrong to be having so much fun right now. When everything is ready to fall apart. Knowing Ark is hunting us. Fearing for Storm's safety. Wondering if Cai is even still alive.

But the laughter, the joy, the safety I feel right now dancing with Matthias, it doesn't feel wrong. It feels good. Right.

So I dance, song after song, with a boy I know so well and yet desire to know better, letting my mind forget everything that has tormented it for so long.

I'll remember it all again soon enough. The weight always comes back. But for now, this moment, maybe it's okay to let it go and have fun.

After four or five songs, Matthias and I take a break.

"Want some iced tea?" Matthias asks as I sink into a nearby seat. Sweat glistens on his forehead, and he's rolled up the sleeves of his shirt, exposing muscular forearms. But he looks happier than I've ever seen him.

"Sure." I smile at him, allowing some of my feelings for him to show.

The smile he gives me in return leaves me breathless. Or maybe that's just from dancing.

I watch him walk away, saying hi to far more people than I know. Laughing and joking with others waiting in line to get iced tea.

Matthias is a good guy. Despite his father and all the pain he's gone through in his life, he still knows how to have fun. How to care for others and make them feel seen.

"Bria?" The two young voices simultaneously saying my name makes my entire body freeze.

Blood pounds in my ears. This can't be happening. The sounds of music and laughter fade as I turn to the sources.

And I see them.

My twin eight-year-old brothers, Eli and Zeke, stand mere feet away from me. I leap to my feet as they race over and practically tackle me.

I drop to their level, hugging them to myself. They cling to me.

I pull away to look at them, but keep a hand on each boy.

"How . . . what . . ." I clear my throat and start again. "I can't believe you're here."

They grin at me, their identical faces exactly how I remember them, but more mature.

"I missed you," Eli says, his smile slipping.

"Me too," Zeke says.

I tug them back against me, emotions clogging my throat. My eyes burn. "I missed you too. So much."

"Who are these cute boys hugging my girl?" Matthias's good-natured tone breaks over us, and I shift to face him.

"She's not yours." Zeke pulls away from me and frowns up at Matthias. "She's *ours*."

Matthias sets two iced teas on the table. "My apologies." He crouches and reaches out a hand to Zeke. "I'm Matthias. What's your name?"

Zeke eyes Matthias for a moment, then shakes his hand. "Zeke." He nods at Eli. "And that's my brother, Eli." His eyebrows are drawn down, as though he's still trying to decide what to do with Matthias. "We're twins, and Bria's *our* sister."

Matthias shakes Eli's hand next. Both twins' faces hold the same skeptical look, but Matthias doesn't seem fazed.

He suggests we sit at the table, and I think I agree with him as I take my seat on the bench. Eli and Zeke crowd either side of me, pressing as close to me as possible. Which is exactly what I want. Matthias sits across from us and launches into a conversation with my brothers, but I barely contribute.

I just hold a boy on each side. It's surreal seeing my two worlds collide.

Matthias is talking to my brothers.

My brothers are *here* in Eryndale. They're safe. Ark can't get them. I want to ask them a thousand questions. Or start sobbing uncontrollably. But I need to stay calm for the boys, so I take a deep breath and reign in my emotions.

How is this possible? And if they're here . . .

"Where are your mom and dad?" Matthias asks. His tone is light, but I hear the deeper concern, and I want to hug him for asking the question I am afraid to put into words.

Eli puffs out his little chest. "They're doing 'portant stuff."

"Yeah," Zeke adds. "And it's secret."

I look down at Zeke. "What are they doing? Are they here?"

Zeke lets out a long-suffering sigh. "I told you! It's secret."

"But they're in Eryndale?" I press.

"No," Eli says.

I turn my attention to him.

"They had to go stop bad guys." His brow furrows. "I miss them." His eyes light up. "Now that you're here, maybe they'll be back soon!"

I don't know how to respond. The boys' answers just added more questions. I take a sip of the iced tea Matthias brought for me, which immediately leads to the boys wanting a drink.

Their constant taking of my food and beverages used to drive me crazy. But after all this time of wondering if I would ever see them again, I happily pass my glass over.

I catch Matthias's eye, and he reaches over and squeezes my hand where it rests on top of the table. I turn my hand so I can squeeze back.

Levi joins us a moment later, and it's clear the three boys are buddies, even though my brothers are a little older than Levi. They talk over one another, and the distraction is helpful. Otherwise, I'd be marching up to someone in the C.A.E. right now to demand to know where my mom and dad are and what they're doing.

Matthias rubs his thumb over the back of my hand, and I realize we're still holding hands. But I don't let go. He's focused on something the boys are telling him, and they're so happy with his attention, they don't seem to mind me sitting here quietly.

It didn't take long for Matthias to win them over. I think my brothers will end up liking him more than they do me before long. The thought makes me smile.

I shove aside my questions and focus on the boys. This moment is a miracle, and I'm going to enjoy it.

There are so many things to figure out, but one thing I've learned since being taken: moments like this are a gift. And I need to treasure them, not take them for granted.

ONCE MRS. DEFORT FOUND OUT ELI AND ZEKE ARE MY BROTHERS, SHE insisted we all walk them back to where they're staying with Azarias and Levi so I could see for myself that they're being well taken care of.

I'm not sure if Azarias appreciated the gesture, but he seemed fine with it. And when he said something about the boys needing to go to bed, Kemena silenced him with a look and a comment about them being fine and this reunion being more important than their bedtime.

I tucked both my brothers into their beds, kissed them good-night, and promised that I would see them tomorrow.

All of my friends were waiting outside for me when I emerged, and now we're walking the short distance back to the DeForts' house.

We're in Eryndale. They don't think we're spies anymore. And Eli and Zeke are here, safe from the danger of being taken by Ark.

It's almost surreal.

If Storm and Cai weren't still in Talionis, and if my parents were here with me, would I want to go back and stop Ark? Or would I just want to stay here and enjoy what I haven't experienced in a long time: peace?

I twist the chain of my necklace around my finger, and some of my joy fades. I'm not as brave and courageous as I wish I was. If not for Storm and Cai and the strange unknown about my parents' whereabouts, I think I'd be done fighting. Ready to forget Talionis and every nightmare that still haunts me and move on. I know that's wrong. But I have to acknowledge it.

"You okay?" Matthias asks, his voice low and concerned. He's stayed next to me our whole walk back, and we are nearing the DeForts'.

"Yes?" The answer is more of a question.

He stops, and I automatically stop with him. "Tonight was good, but also a lot to process. Which is okay."

A loose curl rests on his forehead, and I reach up to brush it back.

He inhales quickly, and a sudden awareness of how close I'm standing to him fills me.

I force myself to step back. "Thanks for everything tonight, Matthias. Dancing, talking to my brothers, being there for me. I needed it." The vulnerability in my words keeps me from looking him in the eye.

He ducks low until his gaze meets mine. "Thank *you.*" His jaw works for a moment, as though he's searching for words. "Bria, I—"

"Girl, you coming?" Nika calls to me from right outside the door to the DeForts'.

I move toward her. "Yeah. Be right there." I take another step. I know Matthias has more to say, but I'm not sure I'm ready to hear it. There's been too much to process in the past twenty-four hours already. "We should go."

He sighs, but nods. "Sure."

We walk the last several yards to the DeForts' house and enter.

"Goodnight, Bria." Matthias says before we part ways to go to our rooms.

"Night." I rush after Nika, feeling slightly ashamed. But also relieved.

Yup. I'm a coward. On more levels than I even realized.

TWELVE

It's late, but sleep eludes me. Too much has happened today, and I have so many questions. I rise carefully from my bed and ease down the ladder.

Maybe some tea will help. Mrs. DeFort did say to make ourselves at home, and the kitchen is far enough from the bedrooms. I doubt I'll wake anyone.

A light glimmers from the kitchen, and I squint against it. Nika sits at the island, hands hugging a mug of tea, cheeks wet. Guess I'm not the only one who couldn't sleep. I debate going back to our room, but then decide not to. If I was the one sitting there with tears on my face, Nika would come over and ask what's wrong. Probably make me talk about it.

Maybe I should try doing the same for her.

"Girl, I can hear your brain thinking. Just come have a cup of tea." Nika drags her sleeve over her face.

Okay then. I guess I'm not as quiet as I thought I was. I join her at the island.

She nods at a tea kettle on the stove. "Water should still be hot enough, and I found tea in that drawer." She points to a drawer near the stove.

"Thanks." I take a mug from the cabinet and set about pouring myself a cup of tea, searching for something to say next. Asking someone questions when they're clearly distressed isn't my favorite. I keep my back to Nika as I pour steaming water onto the tea ball in my mug. Then I take a deep breath and face my friend.

"Are you okay?" I ask the only question I can find. It's clear she's not great. But what else am I supposed to ask? I settle into a stool adjacent to her.

"Yeah." She traces her finger around the lip of her mug. "Just a lot to process in one day, you know?"

I nod, even though she's not looking at me.

She sighs. "I didn't expect the memories and emotions I'd feel when I saw my sister again." She looks up, a half-smile on her face. "Then again, I didn't expect to *see* my sister here. That was more than I could have ever hoped for." She takes a sip of tea. "Guess you feel the same way about Eli and Zeke being here."

I nod and take a tentative sip of my tea.

"I don't know if I would have survived without Kemena," Nika says. "My parents . . . well, they didn't really know how to be parents. Even though they had so many kids. We were just something for our mom to criticize. Yell at. Something for our dad to beat." The words are matter-of-fact. There's no pain in them, no sadness. "All they cared about is how our family looked to other people. Especially people at church. Heaven forbid anyone think we were anything less than perfect. We went to church every week, no exceptions. We'd fill up a row, and boy could we put on a performance. It didn't matter how my parents were every other moment of the week—when we showed up at church, they acted perfect. They smiled, said 'Amen!' when the preacher wanted them to, carried the family Bible." She releases a noise between a sigh and a groan of pain. "And they made sure each of us kids knew we better not say anything to make them look like anything other than wonderful *godly* parents.

"Every bruise we had was carefully covered, and we all knew we'd better smile or we would regret it when we got home. One time, one of my brothers laughed when an elder told him our dad was a 'great father.' The elder was confused, mentioned it to my dad. I'm sure Jesse didn't mean anything by it, but he got the beating of his life later that day. He couldn't even sit. I tried to stop my dad, but he threw me out of the way. I slammed into the wall, knocked something over. My mom told me to be more careful and not so klutzy."

I sip my tea, unsure of what to say or how to respond. Nika's home life is nothing like what I experienced. "I'm sorry."

Nika shrugs and takes a drink of her own tea. "It is what it is. I know it's by God's grace alone I didn't hate Him because of the hypocrisy of my parents." She shakes her head in wonder. "Somehow, I loved church. It was there I started to reach beyond my hurt and pain and *toward* the One who the preacher told me loved me. And, girl," Nika's voice is rough with emotion, "all I wanted was to be loved." She clears her throat. "But things at home just kept getting worse. Kemena moved out pretty much as soon as she could, and she would come over and check on the rest of us. She's the oldest, and we all adored her."

She lapses into silence for a moment, and I stay quiet, too, waiting for her to decide if she wants to continue.

"Worse stuff happened." A tear tracks down Nika's cheek. "And I spiraled. Thought I didn't matter. Even considered taking my own life."

I grip my mug until I'm almost afraid I'll crack the ceramic. The heat spreads through my hands, but it's nothing compared to the heat of anger coursing through my veins. I'm not sure *what* happened, but if it was enough to bring my friend to a point where she was that broken, it must have been bad. Part of me wants to ask her about it, but the other part is afraid to hear the answer.

It's hard for me to imagine Nika as anything but strong. I can't picture her so lost. So desperate. "How did you get past it?"

She takes a sip of her tea. "I found my parents' Bible, the one they only took out for church on Sundays, and I was *so* desperate. I opened it up and told God that if He was real, He had to prove it to me. And I started reading it. I'd wake up early, before everyone else, and read the Bible.

"Pastor John used to say, 'If you don't believe God loves you, just open your Bible and read for yourself what God said.' I wanted to believe him, but I was always afraid he might be wrong. My parents would talk about God all the time, but I never saw any real love from them. But . . ." She gives an almost imperceptible shrug. "Pastor John was right. And God answered my prayer. Not all at once. But as I read the words, some of it started to sink in. The more I read and began to understand things Jesus said, the more I realized He hated it when people claimed things about God, but acted in a very different way. And then there was Kemena. If you think *I'm* stubborn or persistent, you haven't seen *anything*."

"I can only imagine," I say with a wry grin.

Nika chuckles, and her face softens, some of the pain dissipating. "She hounded me during the time I was so depressed. Whenever she'd come over, she would make sure to spend time with all of us, but she started seeking me out and forcing me to spend more time with her than usual. It's like she had this weird sense that something was very wrong."

I trace my finger around my mug handle. Nika has definitely learned some of Kemena's skills in *that* area.

"She would pester me over and over. 'What's wrong, baby girl? You haven't been yourself. Where's your smile?'" Nika says each phrase in a high-pitched voice that sounds nothing like Kemena and would make me laugh if we were having any other conversation. "I lied to her over and over again."

Nika sighs. "I couldn't bear the thought that she would treat me in the same way my parents did: dismiss what happened. Ignore my pain. Tell me to just get over it. But she never believed me, no matter what I told her to get her off my back. And frankly, that terrified me far more. I knew how to handle people *not* caring about me. Having her care was scarier to me than my dad's beatings or my mom's indifference and annoyance."

Yup. Nika definitely learned a lot from her sister.

"One day she took me out of the house and on a walk." Nika purses her lips. "I didn't want to go, but she didn't give me any choice in the matter." She tries to look annoyed, but I sense a profound gratitude in her words. "As soon as we started down the trail, she told me we wouldn't be turning around until I told her what was going on. I wanted to be angry with her for telling me what to do. Annoyed. But all I felt was this overwhelming relief."

She pauses. "Kemena chased me, ran to where I was in the darkest, most painful moment of my life, and refused to leave me alone there. She showed me a picture of Jesus in her pursuit of me in the midst of my pain, her love for me even though I'd treated her badly, lied to her, and pushed her away over and over again. So I broke. Told her I wasn't okay, that I wasn't sure how to live. And it was such a relief. I think I'd wanted to let someone close for a long time, honestly. The more God softened my heart to Him, the more I saw I wasn't meant to handle this all on my own."

I sip my tea absently, the now lukewarm liquid running past an ache in my throat.

"We didn't get very far on our hike. Just sat on a boulder, and I sobbed in her arms. She took me back home, and the next day she brought me to her house. She knew I couldn't talk in our parents' house." Nika shakes her head. "I still don't know how she convinced my mom to let me come over. I was a little uncomfortable—talking about my feelings, trusting Kem with them. It was all new still. I wasn't sure how I'd be if she started asking me tons of questions. But she brought me out to the garden, and we sat in the dirt, pulling up weeds. She didn't push me. She was just there, you know?"

I nod.

"A few minutes into rooting out weeds, I started to dig out the painful things I'd buried. Once I started talking, everything kinda gushed out. Like it was all just waiting for an opportunity to finally emerge from the place I'd hidden it. Kemena listened as I talked. I told her I didn't think I mattered. That the hurt I felt was something no one else cared about. I told her I didn't think anyone loved me. And then"—Nika's voice cracks with the memory—"then she started to cry. For *me*. Something in me broke, and the tears I needed to cry for all I'd lost and the hurt I'd experienced poured out of me. Like, gushed, girl." Nika's eyes shimmer with tears now, but her words make me smile.

"Always knew you were soft under all that toughness," I say.

"Please. You're one to talk." We grin at each other, and I take a breath in the momentary lightness.

I sober again. "Did it help?"

Nika and I have lived very different lives, experienced different things, but a part of me understands the ache of brokenness she's talking about. The need for someone else to care.

Nika nods. She drinks down the last swallow of her tea and sets her mug aside. "Yeah, it did. More than I ever would have thought. It amazed me that someone would care, but Kemena did. She told me my pain broke her heart, but even more importantly, it broke God's heart. She wrapped her arms around me, pulled me close, and said, 'Baby girl, those things are lies. You are loved, and you matter.' She pointed me to God, helped me grow. Helped me heal. She *showed* me Jesus. And that changed my life."

We sit quietly next to each other for several moments. A clock on the wall clicks off seconds, but I don't look at it. It's late. But I don't want the conversation to end. Hearing Nika share so openly with me, seeing how vulnerable she made herself with Kemena, both call to something deep within me to do the same, and also terrify me completely.

"How did you end up going to live with Kemena?" I ask, more to get out of my own head than for any other reason.

She gets up and adds water to the kettle, then puts it to heat on the stove. "Kemena wanted me to move in with her right away, but I was scared to take that step and didn't want to leave my younger siblings. Things at home with my parents were still bad and started getting worse. They didn't like how I was changing." She empties her tea ball and then refills it with fresh herbs. "Everything started to get directed at me, even if I hadn't done anything wrong, from my dad's fists to my mom's hate-filled words. Eventually it was too much, and I couldn't stay anymore. So Kemena brought me to live with her when I was fifteen. Turned out to be the best thing for me."

The water in the kettle raps against the side in a boil, and Nika pours it over her tea. "My sister would hold me when I couldn't do anything but cry. When I didn't even have the words to say, she would sit with me. When I was angry, she would listen. And then gently correct me, which drove me crazy. She helped me talk, even when I didn't want to, and address the demons that haunted me."

She settles back onto her stool and wraps her hands around her mug. "I began to heal. But it wasn't always pretty. Healing . . . it can be painful. But it's good."

I nod, though the idea is scary. Digging up all the painful stuff . . . I've done it, at least to some extent, and I don't cherish the idea of going through it again.

THIRTEEN

"Hey, Wade, how's it going?" The shout rings through the room from outside.

I sit up straight in bed, heart pounding. What is going on?

Another man's voice calls out a response, and the two guys go back and forth.

My eyes are gritty with sleep, and exhaustion weighs on me. A glance at the clock on the wall shows me it's 0620.

Who is up—and shouting—*this early?*

The walls to the room shake as someone . . . hammers?

Kemena and Ari are both sitting up now.

I jump out of my bed as a new string of noises ricochet through the room. Hammering, some sawing, and another tool, I think. Whatever it is, the whole room is shuddering.

Kemena swings her legs out of her bed and looks at me. "Let me guess: The DeForts are getting some construction done?"

I nod.

"And the construction guys said they'd be here at what, seven?"

My forehead furrows. "Yeah, but it's not seven. Unless that clock is wrong." I nod to where it ticks away on the wall.

Kemena tucks a braid that fell out back into the twist on top of her head. "No, that clock is right. Bill, Paul, and their guys show up early wherever they go, period. They're fantastic workers and do better work than guys half their age, but they start early. And they start loud."

We grin at each other. Ari stretches, a big yawn escaping her. Nika is the only one who seems able to sleep through the ruckus on the other side of our wall.

"Your sister can sleep through anything," I say.

Kemena laughs. "You're right about that. But this is how you get her up every single time."

"She really doesn't like it if you put water on her." Ari shudders.

Kemena laughs a full-belly laugh. "Well, that works too, but so does this." She reaches over and tickles Nika right under her ear.

A second later, Nika's eyes fly open, and she scowls at her older sister.

"I can't believe you just did that to me." She sits up and crosses her arms over her chest. "You know I hate that."

"But it always works." Kemena smirks and bends down to give her a hug.

Nika pushes her away for a second, but quickly relents and lets her sister hug her.

Soon the four of us have changed and are exiting our room, since it's clear there's no going back to sleep.

I'm still exhausted from my late night with Nika and the celebration the evening before, but there's a lot to do today. Now that I'm up, hopefully I can see my brothers before whatever else Azarias has planned for us.

We file into the kitchen. Mrs. DeFort bustles around the room, stacking a plate with bagel breakfast sandwiches.

"The guys are out doing their work," she says, adding another sandwich to the already full tray.

"Yeah, we heard," Kemena says. "Did anyone ever mention to Bill and Paul that it would be nice if they could start a little later than 6 a.m.?"

Mrs. DeFort chuckles. "I know it's early, but they do the best work around, and I have been waiting for my porch for ages. I'm just happy Kassre finally said they could go ahead and put it up."

Her eyes sparkle as she turns her attention to us. "Bill's ideas are fabulous. And Paul suggested some adjustments yesterday that I'm just ecstatic about. They're using reclaimed wood and all kinds of gorgeous materials to make a stunning addition to the front of our home."

Nika yawns. "I would have slept through it and enjoyed seeing the finished project . . . if my sister hadn't rudely woken me up," she says under her breath, which has Kemena smiling and pulling Nika in for a side hug.

We help Mrs. DeFort finish loading the food onto the trays. There's a tray of breakfast sandwiches, one with fruit, and another with fresh muffins, bagels, and pastries.

Once everything is stacked high, she says, "Let's bring these out to the men."

I pick up the breakfast sandwich tray, and my stomach rumbles as the smell of eggs, cheese, and bacon wafts up to me.

"After breakfast, I suspect you kids will be meeting with Essie," Mrs. DeFort says as we make our way to the door.

"Why?" I ask.

"As the founder of Eryndale, she likes to speak with all new arrivals personally," Mrs. DeFort says. "And I'm sure she is very eager to meet all of you."

Her words leave me both excited and a little nervous as we enter the coolness of early morning.

The guys are outside chatting with the construction workers as they work on laying wooden boards over the beams they have in place. Apparently, the boys woke up and immediately went out to see what was going on.

Matthias stands close to a worker, the only one without facial hair, who is helping steady a ladder. Matthias shields his eyes against the sun with his hand, watching with a look close to awe as Bill secures the board in place.

None of the five men working can be under the age of 50, but they work like a seamless machine. Paul is off to the side, preparing the material, and Bill instructs the other three guys on what to grab and where to go, doing a majority of the heavy lifting himself.

"Ow!" an older man with a goatee yelps, and all the guys freeze.

Then the man who yelped starts cackling.

"Wade!" Bill shakes his head, but there's a smile on his face. "You're gonna kill me, man."

Wade laughs even harder and slaps his leg. "That gets you guys every time."

"One of these days you're gonna say something and none of us are gonna come help you," the oldest guy there says. He has a thick beard and a bald head, and he's short and wiry.

"Nah, you'll always show up." Wade reaches for a breakfast sandwich from my tray.

I stretch it closer to him.

He takes a massive bite, then tucks the sandwich into his tool belt and strides toward the boards laid out on sawhorses. He and Bill lift one of the longest pieces and work together to get it into place.

There is a cadence and rhythm about the way these guys work that is both beautiful and awe-inspiring, while also humorous.

They make jokes, laugh, and poke fun at one another. There's a lot of pointing, scrambling up and down ladders, and asking one another building questions. Sometimes they don't ask for things. They just clap until another guy hands them the tool they need.

And Wade yelps more than once about some kind of nonexistent injury.

We soon learn that the other guys' names are Joey and Fred, and the five of them have been in charge of construction in Eryndale for the last twenty years.

My friends and I eat and enjoy the show. When we said we could leave them to do their work, the guys insisted we stay. They seem to like having an audience.

This is what I always imagined Eryndale to be like: a place with friendship, where people can find their purpose.

Azarias shows up around 0700, along with Levi, Eli, and Zeke. The twins practically tackle me before I can get out of my chair.

It's still surreal to have my little brothers here and to know they're safe and okay. But it's also bringing up more questions than I know what to do with.

The boys settle next to me and we watch the construction crew together. The twins and Levi laugh every time Wade yelps, which just makes the man do it more.

"How long have you guys been in Eryndale?" I ask Eli.

He doesn't drag his gaze away from watching Wade and Bill shoulder a beam into place. "A while."

"How long have mom and dad been gone?" I try another question, this time nudging Zeke for the answer.

He lifts a shoulder. "I dunno." His eyes brighten. "But we got to ride the mechanical horses last week! It was so cool."

"Yeah." Eli crowds closer. "I went *so* fast."

I have no idea what mechanical horses are, but I nod. The boys go back and forth talking over each other about their adventure, but I have a hard time focusing. I want to drink in every moment with my brothers, but I'm also desperate for answers to my questions.

And the boys are too little—and too easily distracted—to give me the answers I need.

Azarias comes over. "Bria, can I have a word?"

The boys are talking with Levi now about going to watch the scouts train a dog named Ajax, so I nod and extricate myself from between them.

Azarias leads me a few feet away from everyone else. "You said my mom is your aunt."

I nod, even as the thought of Elena sends a bitter swirl through my stomach.

He looks between me and my brothers. "But you're Lily and Josiah's daughter."

"Yes. Our moms are sisters. Your mom lived with my family in Derbe."

He rubs the back of his neck. "Lily never said anything."

I cross my arms over my chest. "I never knew Elena had a son—or any family—until Cai realized the connection. My parents must not have known either." As I say the words, I wonder if they're true. It's clear my parents are more connected in Eryndale than I ever realized. I know less about them than I thought possible.

Azarias stares sightlessly at the construction. "Why didn't she come to Eryndale with your parents?"

"Because she's been working for Talionis." The words are sharp as they leave my mouth, and Azarias's gaze swings to me. But I don't stop. "She provided them with all the intel they needed to kidnap me and other teens in Derbe and force us into a new life." I gesture to where the boys sit. "When we were in Talionis, Ari was able to get access to files with lists of names for the next kidnapping Talionis was planning. Elena's name was listed next to my brothers' names, which means she recommended them for the next extraction from Derbe."

Azarias's face is drained of color. "Why would she do that?"

I clench my jaw. "Because she's a coward." Even I can hear the bitterness in my tone. I swallow it back and stare into Azarias's eyes. "When did my parents arrive in Eryndale? And where are they now?"

He hesitates. "I'll need clearance before I can answer your questions."

I want to argue, to insist he tell me *now,* but my brothers and Levi race over.

"Can Bria come with us to see Ajax?" Eli asks Azarias.

Azarias clears his throat. "Not right now." His tone is gentle. "You guys need to get to your chores for today, and Bria and her friends need to go see Essie."

"Can we come?" Zeke asks immediately.

Eli and Levi chime in, begging to join us.

Azarias pats Zeke on the head. "Not this time, little man."

Levi opens his mouth, but a look from his dad silences him.

"I'll take you to see her later today," Azarias promises the boys.

The frustration blooming in me at Azarias's lack of answer dissipates as I hug the twins and say goodbye. At least they're safe and I can hold them in my arms. And Elena isn't here.

I don't know what's going on with my parents or why no one will give me a straight answer, but at least I won't have to deal with the woman who betrayed me.

It's hard for me to leave my brothers, but I need to continue to make efforts to fight against Talionis. The twins might be safe, but Storm still isn't, and I have no clue what's happening with Cai.

Kemena offers to take the boys where they need to be. After a round of quick goodbyes, Azarias guides my friends and me to Essie's house.

We walk for several minutes, which gives me a little time to push my aunt far from my thoughts, before coming to the quaintest cottage I've ever seen.

It's not lifted up in the trees like most of the houses in Eryndale, but on the ground with a beautiful patio that I'm sure Bill and his guys built, and window boxes and shutters and flowers everywhere.

It's a haven, and we haven't even stepped inside yet.

Azarias doesn't knock. He just opens the door.

My friends and I hesitate for a moment, then follow him inside.

Essie greets us, her face wreathed in a smile as she beckons us into the room. "Come in, dear ones."

I immediately feel at home and like I've known her my whole life, which is ridiculous. But when she looks at me, it feels as though she knows me as well, like she can see into my heart.

Essie is much like Cai, her son, and I feel the comfort of knowing she will take care of us and listen to what we have to say.

My only hope is that this woman, the matriarch of Eryndale, can help us do what we need to do against Talionis.

The living room Essie leads us to is the cozy and spacious room of a grandmother. I never knew my grandparents, but I always imagined, if I had any, they'd have a house like this. Despite the comfort of the space, as I settle myself on a plush chair, I can't help but question what I want anymore.

Ark needs to be stopped, but do I want to be part of stopping him? Or do I just want to rescue Storm and Cai and get them away from him so I can find some semblance of my life again?

But that would require discovering more about what is going

on with my mom and dad, and no one seems to want to give me any answers on that front.

My muscles tense, itching to be used, pushed to their limits. The past couple days have been good for recovery, but I'm tired of being in meetings. I actually wish I could go for a run.

Talionis changed me. Even in the smallest of ways.

Now I'm used to days full of physical exertion, to the point where I would almost collapse by the end of the day. And I find I prefer it to meeting after meeting, conversation after conversation. My mind is too full to handle *more* details.

But I don't have a great deal of choice in the matter.

Maybe after this, I can ask Azarias about a way to blow off a little extra steam.

Reginald Finnigan enters the sitting room, scowling. "Took you long enough to get here," he snaps. "We've been waiting fifteen minutes."

I'm surprised to see him here, and any relaxation I might have experienced in the cozy space evaporates before I can grab onto it.

"Reggie," Essie says. "That is no way to treat our guests."

"Sorry," Reginald mutters, the scowl disappearing into an expression so similar to Eli and Zeke when they're in trouble that I almost laugh.

"Not to mention, we're *early* for the meeting," Azarias says, keeping his voice low. He shoulders past Reginald.

A moment later, Gabe and another man enter.

Now that we're all filling the room, it feels far less spacious than my initial impression.

"Welcome, new friends. My name is Essie." A smile creases her face, and every line seems to accentuate it, as though, despite the pain and hardship she's undoubtedly endured, her face has been lined by joy. Not bitterness. Not difficulties.

I can't stop the smile I offer her in return.

"You know Reggie, Azarias, and Gabe," she continues.

My friends and I nod.

"And this," she gestures to the man who entered with Gabe, "is Lorenzo. He's one of the heads of the S.O.C., and he asked to join us for this little gathering."

I recognize him from our meetings with the C.A.E. and S.O.C. He's older than Azarias and Gabe, with shoulder-length hair that's more gray than anything. Despite his age, he has an athletic build and there's an air of authority about him.

He nods in greeting as Essie introduces us, but his blue eyes are shuttered, and I can't get a clear read on him. It's almost unnerving to have him in the room for this meeting, though I can't put my finger on *why*.

"Now, let's get down to the reason I've asked you here," Essie says after the introductions are out of the way.

I turn my attention to her.

"Normally when I first meet with new arrivals, I talk to them about purpose. One of the goals of Eryndale is to ensure every person who enters our protection becomes a part of our city. Finds their purpose here." Her gaze flicks to each of us. When her eyes connect with mine, she adds, "And everyone has a purpose. A reason God created them and put them in this world." She moves her focus to someone else, but the power and conviction of her words plant themselves somewhere deep within my soul.

She folds her hands together in her lap. "Because of the circumstances we're facing and the threat of Talionis, I know you can't all be integrated into our life here. Not in the way I would like." Her worn brow creases. "But before you enter into planning out an attack, I wanted to speak with you all personally."

She pauses, and there's a weight in the pause that keeps me from so much as shifting in my seat.

"It grieves me greatly that we must rely on ones so young to assist us in stopping an enemy like Talionis." Her voice is low and full of emotion. "I would much rather the six of you put this dark experience behind you and enjoy the freedom of our beautiful city. But, although I don't understand it, I know there are times God has difficult things for us to press into. Even in our youth."

She tucks a wisp of her white hair behind her ear. "I'm sorry you faced the questioning you did upon your arrival, and I do hope you can extend some grace and understanding to the leadership here."

Reginald grunts his disapproval, but turns it into a cough when Essie looks his way.

"The C.A.E. was divided in how to move forward, and my vote will determine how much access you are given to the plans Eryndale has made against Talionis. Another matter arose yesterday that kept me from casting my vote then. I wanted you all to be here to hear it now." She looks at Reginald, then Azarias, Gabe and Lorenzo. "You will have full access to all our plans."

Relief courses through me at the trust Essie is placing in me and my friends.

Reginald's mouth drops open, and he sputters like a fish out of water. "W-what?"

Gabe's eyebrows shoot up ever so slightly, but otherwise he barely reacts. He's been on our side from the beginning, and I'm thankful he's here.

"Giving them complete access to our plans is . . . it's too dangerous!" Reginald says.

"I'm inclined to agree," Lorenzo adds.

Essie holds up a hand, and although Reginald's face is red and he looks ready to burst with more objections, he goes silent. Lorenzo's jaw bunches, but he too remains quiet.

"My vote *is* the deciding vote. And you both well know it." Essie stares at the two men with a stern expression that makes me squirm.

"Well, yes, but—" Reginald starts.

"I've made my decision." Her tone leaves no room for argument.

In this moment, I see how she was able to lead people. It's as though I'm catching a glimpse of Essie forty-five years ago. There's a firm, settled assurance about her. It's no wonder she could take charge and lead others to establish a place like Eryndale. Her strength and determination, woven together with her gentleness and kindness, make me want to follow her and trust her.

Lorenzo crosses his arms over his chest, catching my attention. Maybe he's unhappy with the situation, but his face remains unreadable. It's disconcerting to think he might not want us involved in all the plans. Especially since Thaddeus told us the scouts were on our side in this.

"My son"—Essie's voice breaks ever so slightly—"vouched for them. And I trust Cai."

My throat thickens at her words, and a longing to see my uncle fills me. To at least know he's alive.

She removes a handkerchief from her pocket and dabs at her eyes. "Now that we've settled that, I expect you all to have the access you need." Her gaze roams the room, settling on each person for a moment before moving on. "Time is of the essence in this battle, but you are each important. If you have any qualms or if there is anything you need, please know my door is always open to you."

She stands, and the rest of us follow suit. "Azarias and Lorenzo, please see to it that our guests have access to everything they need."

Gabe steps forward. "I'm happy to help with that." He ducks his head. "Your decision makes sense, and I want to aid them however I can."

Essie smiles. "Thank you, Gabe. But I need you and Reginald to remain behind. I have some things to discuss with both of you. And we will need to call the C.A.E. together this morning to inform them of my decision."

Azarias kisses his grandmother goodbye. Moments later, he and Lorenzo are leaving Essie's home. My friends and I head toward the door.

"Bria." Essie's voice stops me.

Her eyes are tender. "I have a hunch you're good with maps?"

"Yes. My mom taught me." An ache echoes through my body at the word "mom."

"That's not a surprise." She closes the small distance between us, reaches out, and rests her worn fingers against my cheek. The ache lodges in my throat like a weak dam about to burst. "You are like her, I think."

"How . . ."

"We'll talk soon, dear girl."

I stand still, not ready to leave. The room is silent. My friends are probably waiting for me outside, and Gabe and Reginald watch us from the other side of the room, but I don't look away from Essie.

She peers at me as though she sees right through me. Into my thoughts, my fears. I shift on my feet. I'm not uncomfortable. But I feel. . .vulnerable.

It's as though, with only a few words, Essie knows who I am. My fears. My hopes. As silly as it seems, I feel like she's holding my dreams within her weathered fingers. But that part doesn't terrify me. To my surprise, I trust her. I barely know her, but I trust her.

"I trust my son's judgment, and he spoke highly of you in his letter to Azarias." She pauses, her gaze intense and gentle. "But even if he hadn't, I would still be honored to have you as a part of Eryndale."

Something squeezes in my chest, and my eyes fill with tears. I blink them away, because there are others in the room. But I wish they were all gone, that I was alone with Essie. For some reason I don't understand, I know I could cry freely in front of her. And I *want* to.

A gentleness softens her eyes. "The two of us will talk soon."

I nod and attempt a smile, both eager for the conversation and a little afraid of it.

Essie wraps her hands around mine. They're soft and wrinkled, yet her grasp is firm and reassuring. "In time, you'll learn all you need to know."

"Shouldn't she go?" Reginald's voice shatters the sweetness of the moment.

Essie faces him. "Let her be." Her words are sharper than before.

Azarias comes back into the house, and Essie says goodbye to me.

I follow Azarias outside to where my friends are waiting.

How much does Essie know about me? Does she know about those I've hurt? What if she knows me as well as I know myself and understands how dangerous I am?

The questions bombard me as I leave the cottage, but I do my best to push them aside.

Now isn't the time for questions.
Now we need to plan.

FOURTEEN

Since Essie has given us clearance, Azarias instructed us to wait for him and Lorenzo in a private meeting room near the entrance of the Cartography Center.

I'm tired from my lack of sleep last night and the early morning wake-up call. Even after Nika and I went to bed, I had a hard time falling asleep. Our conversation replayed in my mind over and over. Pain infects everyone. In different ways, to different degrees, yes. But it doesn't discriminate. Nika's pain is something she still holds, yet it doesn't define her anymore.

I want that to be true of me as well. Our pain is different—I can't imagine what she's been through—but if God can work in her life and keep her pain from defining her, maybe He can do the same for me.

A yawn presses out of me, and I do my best to stifle it. Nika echoes one right after me. We share a look. I know we need to plan—it's what we've been fighting for—but right now, after everything, all I want is a nap. Maybe in that nice alcove Kemena showed me and Nika yesterday.

Azarias enters the room, his presence instantly taking over. He's a leader through and through, just like his dad. Cai. I miss him. The haunting question of *is he alive* whispers its all too familiar tune through my mind. I give my head a subtle shake.

"Thanks for coming," Azarias says, as Lorenzo follows him into the room.

"We're good at obeying orders," Matthias quips. "At least that's one thing Talionis taught us."

An amused expression flits across Azarias's face. "Eryndale's different. Every request is not an order. But I'm glad you're all here." He gestures to the chairs around a table on the far side of the room. "Let's sit. We have a lot to go over."

We do as he suggests, and my exhaustion melts away. This is what I've been waiting for. Getting Eryndale involved in the fight against Talionis is the only way I can see us defeating them.

Lorenzo stands off to the side. Although he's the ranking official, it appears he's letting Azarias run this briefing.

Azarias leans forward, elbows resting on the table. "Eryndale has known about Talionis since before it was built."

"What? How?" Matthias asks, half-rising out of his chair.

Azarias stares at Matthias until he drops back into his chair. His eyes rove around the room, finding each of us.

Something in me stirs. I want answers to Matthias's questions, want to understand what Eryndale knows. But more than anything, I'm confused.

"If you knew, why didn't you stop them?" I blurt out.

Azarias releases a breath. "I'm sure you all have many questions, and you will likely have even more as I talk. But please allow me to share the intel I'm able to share with you, and then I'll answer questions at the end. Okay?"

There's some nodding around the room.

"Years ago, when I was about fifteen, someone connected with Talionis met my father while he was on a scouting mission. This contact was not a believer in what Demetrius Ark was planning, and when he found out about Eryndale, he told my dad what those plans were. Together, they decided to stop him."

I chew on my lip. Cai never told me any of this. He knew about Talionis *before* he was taken captive?

"Our contact was on a recon mission, creating maps of the region to help Ark determine the best place to build Talionis and so he would know the state of the survivors in the North American region. My father and the contact decided to create a map hiding vital areas of the region connected to Eryndale, as well as the city of Eryndale itself, in order to mount a surprise attack to thwart Ark's plans. My dad brought in the best cartographer he could, and they designed a unique map."

"My mom," I say, forgetting Azarias wanted us to hold our questions until the end. But this isn't a question. It's a statement.

Azarias focuses on me, eyes narrowing. "What?"

"My mom created the map we used to get here. The map Ark had in his safe," I say with confidence.

"I'm not at liberty to share the details of our cartographer." An impassive look shields Azarias's face, and his eyes flick to Lorenzo.

I shift slightly. "But Essie just gave us clearance."

Lorenzo steps forward. "To know the details of our plans to attack Talionis. Not clearance for every secret in Eryndale."

I clamp my lips against further questions.

Okay. Maybe I was wrong. But then why did the leadership in Eryndale know about my mom? How fully is she connected to this place? I swallow hard. The twins said she and my dad were doing something important, but what does that mean?

Do I know my parents at all?

"Things were going well," Azarias says. "We had plans to attack Talionis while it was being built, to stop Ark early. Then my parents disappeared. Gone in a second. They left for a short trip. It was supposed to help solidify certain things, get details about Talionis. The contact would only communicate with my dad, so no one else went on the mission."

A dark frown mars Azarias's face. "I was supposed to go with them, but we fought, and I refused." He grips his hands together on the table.

Memories of sitting in the Ruins with Cai right after Ava died rush over me. I told him what happened with Ezri, and he told me about the last moments with his son. But why didn't he share with me the *reason* for the trip? Why didn't he tell me he knew about Talionis?

"Anyway," Azarias continues, "after my parents disappeared, we sent out scouts to search for them, but there was no trace.

Some of the leaders thought the contact double-crossed us. Others were sure a group of Raiders attacked them. The one thing everyone agreed on was that they were dead. There was no way my dad wouldn't return to Eryndale if he was alive."

Cai couldn't return because he was taken captive, but why didn't Aunt Elena come back? Why remain a Watcher in Derbe? Azarias's gaze connects with mine and the ache in his eyes makes me wonder if he's thinking the same thing.

He blinks and the look vanishes. "Everything was put on hold. We needed the details my dad was supposed to retrieve from his contact to plan further. We just didn't know enough to push on. Even though I wanted to. I was young, but I was . . . *persistent* in my desire to see something done. I couldn't let my dad's work fall to nothing. He and I didn't always see eye to eye." He rubs his neck. "But he was my dad, and I trusted him. And I knew he was right about Talionis. Demetrius Ark needed to be stopped. Over the years, I advanced as a scout, took over my own team, and have never stopped fighting to see something done to bring the city of Talionis down."

My chest tightens as the pain of Azarias's loss hits me. But his loss didn't cripple him or make him into someone like his mom. Despite not having Cai in his life for all these years, he's so much like his dad.

"When I heard about the kidnappings, teens missing from towns all over the eastern region, I knew it was Talionis. But some of the leaders here didn't want to believe me." He pauses. "We have established some plans to mount small attacks to weaken the infrastructure of Talionis, but we need more intel. And that's where you come in." Azarias rises to his feet. "If you'll follow me, I have something I want to show you."

We stand to follow him, but he pauses at the door, head bent toward Lorenzo as he whispers something I can't hear. Azarias nods, and Lorenzo leaves without a word to us.

Lorenzo is a little disconcerting. Maybe because he's making it so clear he doesn't trust us completely. But I don't have time to dwell on the scout leader.

The more important question is, who was the contact Cai had in Talionis?

He never mentioned anything like what Azarias just shared, and it almost feels impossible to think Cai knew so much about Talionis before it was built. My mind traipses over the soldiers and people I know in Talionis, but they all appear so loyal to their *Commander*. It's hard to imagine any of them betraying him.

Azarias leads us over a short bridge that connects the meeting room to the Cartography Center. My questions wash away, and a giddiness almost makes me skip forward. I love maps, cartography, all of it. And, in spite of everything going on, despite the threat we're facing that's growing stronger by the hour, I feel excited to enter the heart of Eryndale's Cartography Center.

This is the place I've dreamt of for years. I longed to be a scout, to travel around the region and create maps, and to have *this place* as my home base.

Azarias opens the door. I almost run through, but manage to keep myself from shouldering past my friends.

When we enter, my jaw drops.

The inside is open and massive, and it rises high above us. Maps of all shapes and sizes hang from the walls, and small miniatures of towns and villages are displayed on tables throughout the building. The models seem interspersed with some form of hologram tech.

It's like seeing the world from a transport.

Mountains, valleys, rivers, lakes, the ocean, towns, villages, even destroyed cities—all displayed in perfect proportions. Men and women move around the room, some adjusting the models, others on higher levels looking down and making notes. A few work out measurements as they bend over a map.

One woman appears to be adjusting the hologram over one area. She pushes a button and the river cutting through that model starts moving.

"Incredible." The word escapes my mouth. I wander to the nearest table, but can barely take it in.

Machines work around the edges of the room, their whir a soft backdrop to the work being done.

Nika steps up next to me. "This is amazing."

"4D Printers," Ari says, eyes lighting up. Her focus shifts to the woman I was just watching. "And holograms. Old ones. I wonder if I could help them update the software. Install some upgrades."

She moves toward the nearest one, but Bryson gently grabs her arm.

"You can check it out later," he says.

"This is our model of the North American region," Azarias says. "The cartographers constantly update it as scouts discover new places and establish new towns and villages. If you'll follow me."

He weaves his way around the tables, and I do my best to try not to stare at everything with my jaw flapping against my chest.

My eyes catch names of towns I've seen on maps of the western region. Little homes clutter the models, along with farms, shops, and even miniature animals. We pass the model of Eryndale, and it takes far more effort than I would ever admit to continue on. I want to study it, memorize it.

For the first time, I think I better understand Ari. This must be how she feels whenever she encounters tech she hasn't worked with before.

I pull my focus from the model to look at my friend. Her eyes are wide as Shane practically propels her forward to keep her from stopping at a 4D printer.

Azarias finally stops. "We believe Talionis is located in this region. But we've been unable to confirm, and we haven't been given the go-ahead to get close enough to check." The edge in his voice makes me think he isn't pleased about that reality. "Now that you're here, you can help us have a clearer understanding of what we're up against."

My friends turn to me.

"Bria's the girl you want if you're talking maps," Matthias says. "Not sure how she is with models—these are really cool, by the way—but she catches onto things pretty fast."

My cheeks warm at the compliment. I focus on the model and holographic image before me. It's different than looking at a map, but in some ways it's easier.

"Good," Azarias says. "You can work with Thaddeus. He's the

cartographer most involved in the Talionis proceedings. I'll get you clearance into the upper rooms. That's where the working model of Talionis will be fitted together once we have some information. You'll also be able to access pre-Demise maps that might be useful."

My brain spins as I try to process all he's telling me. "You mean I'll get to work here? With the cartographers?" My voice is high and way too eager, but I hold my breath and wait for Azarias's response.

"Yes. If you have skills in cartography, we could use your help here."

My heart skips a beat. This can't be real. How can a dream come true when so much is at stake? I nod to let him know I heard his words.

Azarias faces the model. "What do you think? Is this an accurate depiction of the location of Talionis? If we're off even by a small amount, it could impact our strategic planning."

I move closer to the model and lightly touch one of the perfect little trees. I turn slowly and take in the surrounding models, then close my eyes and imagine them in map form. By the time I'm looking at the temporary model of where they suspect Talionis to be, I'm chewing on my lip.

"You're close. But . . ." I tilt my head and glance at the towns to my left and the mountain range to my right. "You're too far to the west. And a little too far north as well. If I could see a map alongside the models, I'd be able to work with your cartographers to ensure it's in the right place."

I step back toward my friends and Nika and Ari grin at me.

"Impressive," Azarias says.

Matthias puts his arm around me and gives me a quick side hug. My heart skips a beat. "She's the best."

Even Shane nods his agreement.

"Welcome to my world," Thaddeus says, strolling over to us.

"Where're Levi and the twins?" Azarias glances past Thaddeus. "You probably don't want them roaming around in here unsupervised."

I crane my neck to see if my brothers are here, but their identical faces are nowhere to be seen.

Thaddeus winces. "The mere *thought* of them in here alone will now keep me up at night for the next three weeks." He groans. "Thank you for that."

Azarias smiles, as though well aware of how his words affected Thaddeus. "Well, you were supposed to be watching them. They were excited for your kayak ride today. Catch anything?" The teasing tone in Azarias's voice is surprising and also refreshing after the serious nature of the past hour.

Thaddeus rolls his eyes. "What do you think? And to answer your question, I left the boys with Kemena and came to meet you in here. Saw you heading this way and figured I'd be more useful than you."

"True enough." Azarias nods to me. "Bria can help you get a more exact location on Talionis." He shakes his head. "You were wrong about this one. Why you're master scout and our lead cartographer, I'll never know."

Thaddeus shoves him good-naturedly. Even though Thaddeus is decades older than Azarias, it's clear he respects and trusts the younger man.

Azarias glances at his watch. "I should go check on the boys. They can spend another twenty minutes here, but then they need to be shown the scout training facility," he says, directing his comment to Thaddeus.

"I'll get them there in time," Thaddeus says. "As long as you don't make me babysit again."

"Bro," Azarias says, raising his hands, "you *offered* to take them kayaking."

"I'll deny it til the day I die," Thaddeus grumbles, but his lips twitch.

Azarias chuckles as he leaves the building, and I wish I could go with him. I want to study the maps and stop Talionis, but even more, I want to be with my brothers.

Thaddeus faces us again. "Do you have any questions? I'd love to dive into readjusting the placement of Talionis, but I don't think we have enough time now to do it properly." He gazes longingly at the nearby model.

"I have a question," Ari says.

That's not surprising. But I am surprised she didn't just lead with her question . . . or questions.

Thaddeus turns toward her. "Sure. What is it?"

"Here we go," Nika mutters.

"Who's Levi's mom?" Ari asks. "And why doesn't he look anything like his dad?"

Thaddeus's eyebrows shoot up. "I didn't exactly mean *those* kinds of questions."

Ari's face reddens.

"Figured you'd ask me about the cartography of the region since Azarias is woefully unskilled in explaining any of this," he says.

None of us respond. I'm as curious about the answer to Ari's question as she is. But I'd never dare ask it.

Levi looks absolutely nothing like Azarias, and we haven't heard a single thing about his mom in the few days we've been here. My brothers haven't mentioned anything about her, and they're staying with Levi and Azarias. All three of the boys just talk about Kemena.

An awkward silence descends.

"Levi was adopted by Azarias," Thaddeus says. "His biological father is a Raider chief."

Levi being adopted isn't a huge shock, but Thaddeus's answer raises another question. "How did Azarias end up being able to adopt the son of a Raider chief?" I ask.

Thaddeus looks at the door and then back at us. "As far as we can tell, Levi's mom isn't around. But most of the scouts who have been out to the western villages and towns have encountered his father. He's one of the cruelest chiefs. He'll kill anyone to get what he wants. Years ago, we had him in custody, but he escaped." Thaddeus's nostrils flare at the memory.

"When Levi was three, his father brought him along on a raid. It happened to be at a new village Azarias and I were at with our teams. We fought them off, but Briggs, Levi's father, didn't want to give up as easily as the rest of his crew did. He and Azarias ended up in a one-on-one match on the outskirts of the village. Briggs was trying to kidnap a woman, and Azarias refused to let it happen. Levi was there, and as the two fought, the boy cried. He'd been crying the whole time. Briggs realized the rest of his crew had left, and he was about to leave. He told Levi to come with him. Yelled at him to. But the boy was inconsolable, sobbing. So he didn't. Briggs cursed him, told him he was no son of his. Not anymore. And then he got on his horse and rode off.

"Azarias went to Levi, and I've never seen anything like it." Thaddeus pauses, deep in thought. "He picked up the sobbing boy, whispered in his ear that he was safe, that he would be okay, and Levi clung to him. Wrapped his little arms around his neck and wouldn't let go. Azarias decided in that moment to take him in, and the kid became his from that day on."

Thaddeus presses his lips together, a fierce expression taking over his face. "They may not be blood, but I defy anyone who would tell me that boy isn't Azarias's son."

His words ring through the room, and my admiration for Azarias rises.

"Wow," Nika says.

Shane's face has paled, and he gazes out the window. Ari goes over to him, but when she touches his arm, he shrugs her off.

Thaddeus claps his hands together, startling me. "We should probably head over to the scout training facility. Don't want you to be late for your orientation with them." He strides toward the door, and we follow.

FIFTEEN

As a group, we make our way across several bridges to the scout training area. It feels surreal. Just two days ago, we were brought in as spies. Now we're about to get a glimpse of Eryndale's scouts so we can help them plan and assess how they'll fare against Talionis's soldiers.

Apprehension squeezes my stomach tighter. Being a scout is what I've dreamt of my whole life, but I'm afraid this will feel like I'm back in Talionis.

I glance over my shoulder, and my eyes connect with Matthias's. He offers me a reassuring smile, which settles and unnerves me. I smile back and face forward again.

If I look into his eyes for too long, all I'll want to do is be in his arms dancing like we were last night. Pretend none of the horrors of Talionis are real. Laugh with him and play with my brothers.

We reach the high-walled training facility. Malachi is waiting for us, and he nods a greeting to Thaddeus.

"Welcome to orientation," he says, focusing on us. "Since we already know each other, the S.O.C. decided you guys would train with my team."

Malachi brings us through the gate and into the complex. The air itself buzzes with activity. Seasoned scouts train new ones, and trained scouts are working out to stay well-conditioned for their next mission. It's sectioned into different areas for training, which is reminiscent of Talionis in some ways.

There's a physical conditioning area, weaponry training, and a huge section where Malachi tells us they do intensive trainings for scouts who will be sent into more dangerous regions.

"What constitutes a more dangerous region?" Matthias asks as we move onto a high bridge that leads us to a platform overlooking the intensive training space.

"The Northwestern Region is the most dangerous." Malachi tilts his head, and a line forms between his eyebrows. "Well, it was until Talionis, at least."

We leave the platform and head down a bridge that leads to a large building fifteen feet off the ground and supported by several trees and support beams. After a moment, I realize Thaddeus isn't following us anymore.

"I'm gonna give you a basic rundown of what scout training looks like. Since you've all been through training before, I expect you'll catch on quickly."

"I don't think we're training," Shane says. "Just assessing things so we can advise on how your resources will match up against Talionis."

Malachi quirks an eyebrow. "Seems like we've gotten different intel." He shrugs. "No matter. I need to show you around either way."

I was under the same impression as Shane, but I almost hope Malachi is right. It would feel good to push my body after these days of rest and meetings.

A group of five scouts passes us, laughing with each other and drawing our attention. I immediately recognize Jordyn and Moses. Moses and Malachi are probably a decade apart in age, but it's obvious the two are brothers. But Jordyn really doesn't look like either of them.

"Yo, bro!" Moses lifts his hand. "Have fun with the newbies."

"I'll have more fun than you're gonna have when Glacier gives you a beat down in HTHC, Retro," Malachi says, eyes sparkling.

"You know that's right," a slim young woman with short light brown hair with blond highlights says.

Moses gives an over-exaggerated grimace, and the others in the group laugh as they walk away.

We go up the stairs leading into the huge building.

"This is one of the hubs of our training facility," Malachi says. "The building is divided in half: one half is dedicated to training on building and construction in order to help the villages in the different spheres, both in their creation and in rebuilding. Whichever is needed. Bill, Paul, and their guys do a lot of the instructing there. The other half is for mission prep and mission debrief."

He opens the door to the building, and we file in. The entryway is narrow. Two doors are on the wall at the back of the entry, one on the left, the other on the right.

Malachi glances at his watch. "I'd like to take you into the Mission Center, but there's a prep happening right now. We'll start with the Construction and Rebuilding half."

He directs us to the door on the left, and as soon as we go through, the smell of freshly cut wood and the sound of tools running fills the air. The smells and sounds remind me so much of my dad that a breath catches in my throat. If I close my eyes, I could almost imagine I was at home, in his workshop.

Has my dad been in this shop? Worked with Bill and Paul and the other guys?

How much *don't* I know about my parents?

I release my breath and with it, all of the emotions threatening to flood me, and focus on what Malachi is saying.

He weaves his way around a table and waves at a woman who is putting together a window frame. We trail behind him, trying to take it all in.

A hand-carved sign that takes up most of the wall catches my eye: Follow God, do justice, love mercy, and walk humbly with Him. It's beautiful and the words call to something deep inside me. How many in Eryndale believe in God and live according to these words?

"All the scouts in Eryndale are divided into teams," Malachi says.

"Teams?" Nika asks.

Malachi looks back at us. "Yup. My team's the best. The Wild Dogs." He gives us a massive smile.

"Each team is like a family," he continues.

Shane stiffens at the word *family,* his mouth a thin line. Matthias's insight into his past after Shane and I had a huge disagreement on our journey to Eryndale gives me a little more compassion for him. I can't imagine what it feels like to have your family completely abandon you. The thought makes me want to find my brothers and hold them close.

"We're like brothers and sisters. Our lives' purposes are to help others, but we'll fight for each other—die for each other, if needed." The sound of hammering echoes in the background as though emphasizing each word. Malachi's face becomes serious. "I don't know much about your experience in Talionis, but I can't imagine it was like that."

He turns and leads us from the room.

The teams here sound different from our units in Talionis. But I know what it's like to have a friend give his life for me. Even in a place as dark as Talionis.

———

The prep in the Mission Center hasn't ended, so Malachi takes us to the dining area for lunch. Loud, energetic conversations reverberate through the room, although a few tables seem more subdued.

Malachi directs us to a table already occupied by the five scouts we saw earlier.

"Bria, Matthias, Nika, Shane, Ari, and Bryson: meet the Wild Dogs."

"Woot, woot!" a guy with massive muscles and tattoos lining his arms and almost every area of exposed skin says in a deep voice.

"That's Isaac," Malachi says.

"But we call him Hack," Moses interjects.

Isaac gives a tiny salute. He could almost look scary, but then he smiles, and it gives him a boyish appearance.

"You've met Karyss." Malachi gestures to her. "And you know my little brother and sister: Moses and Jordyn."

Moses half-rises out of his seat. "Dude. Why aren't you using our call-signs? Karyss is Lyrics, Jordyn is Gator, and I, of course, am Retro."

Malachi lightly shoves his brother back into his seat. "You're the only one who uses those names, little man."

"I'm as big as you now," Moses grumbles.

"Are family members normally on the same team?" Nika asks.

Malachi shakes his head. "Not always. But Jor started training young, and mom said she could only go out if she was on my team."

"And they would, of course, be lost without me," Moses adds, a smug expression on his face.

Jordyn elbows him in the stomach, and Moses deflates with a grunt.

"I don't get lost, and I'm excellent at navigating, so I'm the team navigator. That's why Retro calls me Gator." Jordyn's face splits into a self-satisfied smirk.

Malachi points to the last person. "And this is Glacier."

"Hey," Glacier says. "Ignore Retro as much as possible."

"Not nice!" Retro complains.

Glacier nods to the open chairs. "Take a seat."

"What's on the menu today?" Malachi asks as he slides into a chair next to Retro.

My friends and I fill in the remaining seats at the long table, and Matthias has to grab a chair from another table to squeeze in. Right next to me. My stomach flutters as his shoulder brushes mine and I force my attention to the conversation at the table.

"Who knows?" Isaac shrugs. "Cook was in a mood today. Maybe because Retro was giving him such a hard time about the rations he sent with us on the last mission." He flings a balled-up napkin at Retro, who catches it and tosses it back.

"Look," Retro begins, straightening in his chair. "It's a matter of principle. Wolf told me his unit was given *fresh* bread in their last mission's rations. Ours was a little on the stale side." He holds up his hands in front of him. "I'm just saying."

"Our bread was fine," Karyss says. "You're just picky."

Others agree, throwing jabs at Retro. There's an easy camaraderie. Malachi is right. It feels like I sat down for a meal with a family.

Someone shouts, "Table 13!" from the kitchen.

Retro jumps up. "That's us."

"If Cook put something gross in our food, I'm gonna kill you," Glacier calls after him as Retro goes to retrieve lunch.

He returns moments later with a tray of plates loaded with sandwiches, carrot sticks, and thinly sliced potatoes baked until they're crispy. He sets a plate in front of each person with a flourish, but ends up with one short.

"Huh," he grunts. "I'm sure I told Cook the right amount." He shrugs. "Guess I have to get another plate. Feel free to start eating without me," he says with a pointed look at Malachi, who is already halfway through his sandwich.

Malachi smiles around a mouthful of food, and Retro glares at him before he saunters away to get his own meal.

I pick up one of the thin strips of potato and try it. The salty crispiness dances on my tongue. I grab another. Conversation stalls as everyone eats, and after a few minutes, Retro returns with a plate of food and plops down in his seat.

"Cook needs to chill," Retro says.

I look at Nika, my eyebrow raised. What does *chill* even mean? Nika shrugs, face scrunched in confusion.

"I only told him it's okay to change things up, you catch my drift?" Retro elbows Jordyn to get a response, but she rolls her eyes and continues to eat.

Matthias mouths, "What?" to me, and I shake my head.

Retro picks up his sandwich as my friends and I watch him in stunned silence. He takes a very large bite, but almost immediately stops chewing. His nose wrinkles in disgust, then he removes a wad of paper from his mouth.

Isaac spews water out of his mouth, choking in laughter.

"Serves you right," Jordyn says. "You need to learn to stop telling people how to do their job."

My friends and I join in the laughter with the rest of the table.

Retro opens his sandwich and complains as he removes more paper. After examining every inch and deeming it "safe," he reassembles it and eats.

When the others get into a conversation, I lean toward Glacier. "Why does Retro use such strange words and phrases?" The more the guy talks, the less I understand him.

Glacier gives an exaggerated eye roll. "That's the reason we call him Retro. Every time he hears a phrase or word that used to be popular before the Demise, he clings to it and starts using it. As much as he can. He loves old toys and gadgets too. Don't even think about getting him started talking about yo-yos—at least not while I'm around."

"What's a yo-yo?" Ari asks from the other side of Glacier.

"Did someone say yo-yo?" Retro's voice rises over the other conversations at the table.

"Oh no," Glacier groans, dropping her head into her hands. "Here we go."

"What's a yo-yo?" Matthias repeats the question.

Retro's mouth falls open. "You don't know . . . this is awful. I have to remedy that."

"Please no," Karyss says. "Remember the rule. No yo-yos at the table."

Retro presses his hands together in a pleading gesture. "But this is an emergency." He waves at us. "They don't know what a yo-yo is!"

"You might as well let him show them now," Malachi says. "Or you'll hear about it until you do."

Retro gives a toothy smile, bobbing his head up and down.

"Fine," Karyss and Glacier say together.

I can't decide if I should be curious or afraid, based on the girls' reactions, but I don't have time to think about it.

Retro catapults up from the table and pulls a circular object from his pocket. He unwinds a string from the top of it, places it on his finger, then throws the circle to the ground. It spins down, then right back up to his hand.

"This," he throws it down again, and this time it stays down longer before he pulls it back up, "is a yo-yo."

"Cool," Matthias says.

Karyss slams her hand on the table. "Don't encourage him."

Matthias's eyes widen, and he nods.

"It's *super* cool," Retro says. "Watch this."

He throws the yo-yo to the ground, then makes quick work forming the string into a triangle and swings the yo-yo through it. He releases the string and pulls the yo-yo up into his hands.

I can't stop myself from being a little impressed. He kind of makes it look fun.

But then he spends the next fifteen minutes of the lunch break demonstrating more tricks and giving us the history of the yo-yo as he knows it. By the time Malachi is telling us we need to continue orientation, I can understand why Glacier and Karyss didn't want to give him any opportunity to talk about the toy. I wouldn't mind trying it sometime, but I don't know if I want to get Retro started on it again.

"We'll meet up with you guys later," Malachi says to the others as me and my friends get up and prepare to follow him.

"Sounds like a plan, man," Retro says.

Jordyn rolls her eyes, but there's a smile on her face. Retro's silly, carefree nature reminds me a little of Matthias when I first met him.

The thought has me searching the faces around me until I find Matthias. A step behind me. He winks. Like he knew I was looking for him. Warmth spreads through my chest, and I shift my focus to Malachi as he answers Shane's question about physical conditioning for the scouts.

I care too much about Matthias. And I'm afraid my distraction could be more dangerous than I realize.

THE TREES THICKEN AS WE FOLLOW MALACHI DOWN A BRIDGE HIGH above the training area.

We arrive at a broad platform. Several older men and women are there, talking in hushed tones and pointing out different things on the ground below. Malachi leads us away from them and to the far right corner of the platform.

He goes to the railing. There's shouting below, and I glance down to see some kind of fight happening.

"This," Malachi says, his voice low, "is part of the training scouts go to in preparation for fighting off Raiders."

A small group in black is about to enter the mock-up village. Scouts exit the village and approach them, shouting warnings. They stand with their feet apart, weapons drawn.

"This specific training is—or was—the most common." He points to the scouts. "Most often, scouts face the Raiders head on, announcing their presence and trying to prevent a fight from breaking out or the Raiders from entering the town they're protecting."

The "Raiders" below continue their advance, and a scout fires a warning shot.

New Raiders pour in from other angles, and a fierce battle ensues, with some fighting with swords and hand-to-hand combat, and others shooting guns that leave colorful marks on those they hit. The weapons aren't nearly as advanced as what Talionis uses, which leaves me uneasy. We're going to need an incredible plan if we have any hope of defeating an enemy as well-equipped as Talionis.

I study the formation of the scouts, the ways the Raiders are attempting to infiltrate, and can't help but see flaws on *both* sides.

Which is thanks to Major Vasco and his intense Warfare Scenarios.

"Now," Malachi says, drawing my attention, "we've begun new training."

A whistle blows, and the fighting below us stops. A training scout goes over ways for the scouts to improve. Part of me wants to go down and add my thoughts, but since my friends and I just got cleared to be here, I doubt they'd appreciate that.

"What type of training?" Nika asks.

"Covert ops." Malachi crosses his arms over his chest. "We use small, mobile groups working together to coordinate small-scale attacks and skirmishes. The goal is to exhaust the enemy and spread them as thin as possible. It's what we plan to use against Talionis."

"But that will take time," I say, panic clawing at me. The one thing Storm and Cai *don't* have is time.

"Why covert ops instead of an all-out attack?" Matthias asks.

"Based on the little we've seen and know of Talionis, we don't have half as many battle-ready men and women as they do. Let alone the weapons and tech." Malachi's mouth forms a grim line. "A full-on attack would be suicide."

The words land on my chest like a downed Talionis transport crashing on me.

What Malachi is saying makes sense—and it tracks with what I just witnessed in the training below. But without even hearing all of Eryndale's plans, I know the tactics they're preparing for will take time. Weeks, probably *months*. And I can't wait that long to rescue Storm and Cai.

CHAPTER

SIXTEEN

I fling a knife at a makeshift target and allow myself the satisfaction of hearing it stick with a *thud*. After our orientation finished, Malachi told us we could explore the compound on our own for a bit.

Ari and Bryson went to check out the tech center to see what help they could offer there. The rest of us found the weaponry station. When I discovered knife-throwing lanes, I asked if I could check out some knives.

My mind is overwhelmed, and I need to move. Do something I can control and understand.

Having the knife belt strapped to my waist is comforting. I hadn't realized how much I missed the familiar weight and smooth handles of my knives until strapping it on.

One more thing I didn't know I had until I lost it.

I grit my teeth, pull another knife from my belt, bend low, and send the knife soaring toward the target, releasing some of my pent-up emotions with it. The knife sticks in the center, next to the other one.

When Cai first taught me how to throw knives, I never expected it would become something I was not only good at, but something I almost *need* to do. I take a breath, pull a knife, and throw it with speed and accuracy.

I know how to do this. It's familiar and almost makes me feel connected to Cai. I close my eyes and picture him standing near me. Correcting my stance. Instructing me on how to throw better. A smile plays at the corners of my mouth, but it can barely hold itself in place.

I miss him.

There has been no word about him, that I know of. Maybe Ari will find something out now that she'll have access to Eryndale's tech.

I'll ask her to carefully dig into whatever she can to get answers about Cai. And Storm.

An ache winds itself like a rope around my chest.

I squeeze the hilt of a knife. I open my eyes and throw the blade with more force than necessary, wishing I could throw my painful emotions and pulsing fears with it. The knife lands closer to the edge of the target, and there's a loud *crack!* as the board splinters.

"Strong arm."

I turn to find Max watching. "Thanks."

He strolls over. "You have quick reflexes and good instincts."

I roll my shoulders and rub my thumb over the hilt of the knife still clutched in my hand. "Thanks. Talionis was good for something, I guess. But the knife throwing is Cai."

Max nods. "You'd make a good scout."

My shoulders tense. I always dreamed of hearing someone tell me I'd be a great scout. Maybe one day I actually could. But now, there are far more pressing matters. I swallow the apprehension and fling the knife toward the target.

"And I'll make sure I'm never the target when you're throwing knives," Max adds.

I turn to respond, but my breath dies in my throat. There's a smile on his face, but then he cocks his head slightly, his deep brown eyes studying me. So much like Cade. I drag my gaze away. I need to tell him the truth.

Max rests a hand on my shoulder. Sympathy and pain mix in his eyes. "I know what happened. To my brother."

His words are enough to shred the final bits of my emotional resilience. Tears spring to my eyes and cascade down my cheeks. I'm not sure who told him, but I'm relieved I don't have to tell him everything. "Max, I'm sorry. I . . . I didn't know he would take my place." I draw in a shuddering breath. "He shouldn't have died. It's my fault." The tears continue to fall, and I don't stop them.

I miss my friend, and I wish I could take back the choices I made that led to his death. I may have led Storm away to protect her, but it was all done out of fear. Because I couldn't imagine trusting my friends to do their part. And in the end, my actions didn't protect Storm. She's still in Talionis, under Ark's dangerous watch.

And Cade is dead.

Every word I try to form falls flat before I can voice it. How can I express both my sorrow *and* my gratitude toward Cade?

Max reaches into his pocket and pulls out a handkerchief, which he hands to me.

"Thanks," I mumble, sopping up some of the tears.

"Matthias told me." Tears glisten in Max's eyes, but they don't leak. "I know where my brother is, and I'm proud of him." He turns his focus away from me and swallows hard. "I'll miss him until the day I die, but I *know* I'll see him again." Max's eyes find mine. "Cade wouldn't want you to hold on to your guilt. He's completely free now, and God used his death to capture your heart. It's what Cade wanted."

I wipe my face again. "I miss him. He was a good friend."

A tear forces itself out of Max's eye and tracks down his face. "Yeah. You know, Jesus said, 'Greater love has no one than this, than to lay down one's life for his friends.' Cade did that." Another tear falls. "My brother is showing me by his death what it really looks like to love like Jesus." He rubs his face against his shoulder. "I hope we can be friends, Bria."

A weight falls off my chest, making my next breath easier to take. Max doesn't hate me. He knows I'm responsible for his brother's death, but instead of anger, he's offered me kindness. Comfort.

"Sorry I didn't tell you sooner," I say.

"I wish you had said something, but I understand it must

have been hard to know how to bring it up." Max smiles, removing any sting his words might have had. He walks toward the target, and removes the knives. "How about we see which of us is better with these things?"

"Okay," I say. I'm ready to move forward now in a way I haven't been for a long time.

CHAPTER

SEVENTEEN

"Bria." Mrs. DeFort's quiet voice beside my bed wakes me instantly.

I sit up, concern flooding me. Why would Mrs. DeFort wake me in the middle of the night? "What's wrong?"

The shadows of the room shroud her face. "Get changed quickly." Her voice is calm, which contradicts her urgency in waking me up.

I open my mouth to repeat my question, but she moves on to wake Kemena. Apprehension tightens my shoulders, but I obey Mrs. DeFort's order.

Within a few moments, all four of us are awake. Mrs. DeFort exits the room, telling us to meet her by the front door as soon as we're dressed.

"What is going on?" Nika whispers to me as she ties the laces of her boots. "And why does it have to happen in the middle of the night?"

I shrug. "I don't know. But it's making me a little nervous."

The four of us exit the room and head to the front door. The guys are dressed and waiting there with Mrs. DeFort and Malachi, Moses, and Jordyn.

"Let's go," Malachi says.

Before any of us can say a word, he opens the door, almost disappearing into the darkness.

Mrs. DeFort shoos us after him, shuts and locks the door to her house, and follows.

This all feels ominous. Why did they wake us up? And where are we going in the middle of the night?

The inky darkness makes it difficult to see much of anything. I miss my lenses. Although I got sick of the green tint, being able to see while traveling at night was a huge advantage. And it removed some of the stress of wondering what—or who—might lurk in the shadows.

My friends and I stay close to Malachi and Jordyn, and Mrs. DeFort and Moses remain at the back of the group. They lead us down pathways, over bridges, and toward the scout training area. None of us say anything. We just creep through the trees after them. I have no idea what time it is, but it's late. There are no lights on in any of the houses or buildings we pass. The faint glow of lights along the path is all we have to see our way, and looking out over the edge of the bridge we're walking on leaves me feeling almost dizzy. I can't see the ground. It's like a black chasm.

And it doesn't feel like a good sign for whatever we're about to face.

Ari pulls out a piece of tech. Where in the world did she find *that?*

"Put that away." Mrs. DeFort's tone reminds me of my mom reprimanding me, and it's enough for Ari to instantly obey.

Malachi glances back sharply at the words from his mother, but turns around when he sees Ari obeying the command. His shoulders seem to tense even more. Whatever is going on has him wound tight.

Are we heading into more trouble?

The scout training facility is not far ahead now. Lights glow near the gates, but Malachi turns and leads us to the Cartography Center. It appears dark and empty, at least from the outside. Malachi pulls a key from his pocket and unlocks the door. We enter the building to an equally dark entryway, and Mrs. DeFort closes the door behind us and locks it before Malachi moves forward.

He directs us through a door and into the main area. I squint against the light, then take in the room filled with fifteen or so people.

It's an interior room with no windows, keeping the lights from spilling out and alerting anyone who might pass. I take in the others who are here and find I recognize most of them. Thaddeus is bent over the model where he and I worked earlier to build a replica of Talionis.

Max and his team are here, and so are the rest of the Wild Dogs. Essie stands off to the side near Azarias. Bill, Paul, and their guys lounge on stools, looking a bit tired. Their early morning starts must make late night secret meetings difficult.

Lorenzo is here, which makes me feel a tad uneasy. Maybe it's the scowl on his face as my friends and I file in.

There are a few people I don't know, but I don't focus on them. I'm too on edge. Something about the way everyone here seems to be fully alert, tense. Ready for action.

It doesn't bode well.

"Sorry for the late night meeting," Azarias says, wending his way to the center of the room. His eyes land on me and my friends.

Without much thought, we've all gathered together. I suppose there's something comforting in knowing we're not in this alone. Whatever *this* is.

"There are things you don't know," Azarias says. "Plans very few know about—even among the leaders of Eryndale. About Talionis."

As soon as he says the name of the city, bumps rise on my arms. I had a feeling it was about Talionis, but now I know. I'm eager to hear what he's about to divulge, but also terrified for a reason I can't identify.

Then it hits me.

I've wanted to act, to do something to save Cai and Storm. But acting against Talionis will mean leaving Eli and Zeke, and I don't know if I can bear to do that.

Lorenzo clears his throat, grabbing my attention. "Not everyone is comfortable with all of you knowing this information." He frowns at Azarias. "Nevertheless, circumstances supersede fears at times. But"—he focuses on my friends and me—"if any of what we're about to divulge becomes known by someone not in this room, there will be consequences."

"Really, Lorenzo." Mrs. DeFort crosses her arms over her chest. "What exactly have these kids done to break your trust?"

Lorenzo doesn't respond, and it takes more muscles to keep my face a mask than I would ever want to admit. Lorenzo is one of the highest ranking scouts in Eryndale, and it's clear he doesn't trust us.

Which makes me less inclined to trust him.

He nods at Azarias as though giving him the go-ahead to continue.

"As you have seen," Azarias says, "there are those in Eryndale who are very outspoken against anything being done to stop Talionis. They believe such a fight is not one Eryndale needs concern itself with. But they are wrong. As I'm sure all of you would agree.

"The trouble is, we fear there is a deeper reason for some of them to stand against an attack. A reason that would not only harm the villages Eryndale seeks to protect, but also Eryndale itself. We think we have a spy in our midst. That he or she has been here for years, delivering intel to Talionis secretly." He hesitates, his jaw clenched. "We think it's the reason my father was taken fifteen years ago."

My entire body goes hot, then cold. A spy. In Eryndale. When Catori hinted at this possibility, it was unnerving. But hearing it confirmed from Azarias brings the reality crashing in.

"Because of our suspicions, we have gone to great lengths to keep our most detailed plans secret, only known by a small group. Every person here has been vetted. Every one is trusted." Azarias focuses on Max. "You can give them their belongings."

Max, Enya, and Zoe grab our packs and bring them to us.

Ari snatches her pack from Max with a gasp and clutches it to her chest.

"Please make sure everything is there," Azarias says. "Unfortunately, it's far safer for each of you to have these items than for them to be held by the C.A.E."

All of us go through our packs, Ari laying out each item and mumbling to herself as she reviews and checks over her precious tech. It would be funny to watch if not for the gravity of the moment.

The others are silent as my friends and I check our packs. I open mine to find everything more of a mess than I'd have liked. Clearly, someone went through it and didn't care about putting it back in any kind of order. I sort through it, finding some clothes and personal items that belong to different friends. The six of us reorganize everything until we all have our own stuff. Everything is here.

Ark's letters, notes with his plans, the encrypted files, his key. All the items I stole from his safe.

But what brings me the most relief is seeing Cai's Bible. I caress the worn leather, releasing a small sigh.

"I'm missing a screen," Ari says.

She has her pack as well as Shane's and Bryson's open in front of her, with tech littered all over the ground. She hovers over it all like a protective mama bear. With the amount of items before her, I'm surprised she would even realize there's a screen missing.

"Oh, here!" Malachi pulls the screen from his pocket. "I've been holding onto it for you since you used it at my parents' house." He passes it over to Ari, and I'm almost afraid she'll cry in relief.

The rest of us confirm that everything is here.

"Good," Lorenzo says, his voice low and raspy. He nods at Azarias. "Best to continue."

Azarias nods to the map in front of me. "This map was made by one of our best cartographers, and my father commissioned it to be done for his mole in Talionis. Certain villages were kept off the map—namely the Center Villages of each sphere."

The fact that Azarias isn't acknowledging that my mom was the cartographer who made the map makes me question my assumptions. It seemed so clear when I was studying it while we were on the run. But maybe my overtired brain saw things that weren't there. Disappointment threads its way through my body. If my mom didn't create the map, then who did? And where are my parents *now*?

At least I figured out one thing. The Center Villages must have been the ones I thought might be missing on the map.

"Kemena and I met while I was investigating what I suspected was Talionis. Her information about her sister"—he nods at Nika—"confirmed my suspicions. Our group soon uncovered more that revealed how compromised things were. There were spies for Talionis everywhere. In almost every town and village in the east, at least as far as we could tell." He swallows hard and his gaze connects with mine. "From what you shared, my mother was even compromised."

I clench my jaw at the reminder of my aunt, and incline my head in agreement. No one else seems surprised by Azarias's admission, which must mean he already told them about our conversation.

Azarias looks toward Essie.

"Go ahead," she says.

"We were able to smuggle someone into Talionis through our inside person. The goal was to have them work together to leak intel out to us."

"Who's your inside person?" Matthias asks, confusion written on his features.

Azarias tilts his head slightly. "Not even everyone in this room knows that person's identity, and it's important we keep it that way. If he or she becomes compromised, much of our mission is at stake."

Matthias opens his mouth to argue, but Essie gives him a small shake of her head, and it is enough to quiet him. The woman has a gentle but firm way about her that makes her easy to follow.

"Where are my parents?" The question bursts from my mouth. "My brothers are here, so that means my mom and dad must have come at some point. How do they fit into all of this?"

Azarias drops his gaze, and as I look around the room, I find no one else wants to look at me either. Until I focus on Essie.

Her face softens. "I wish we could tell you. But their activities are classified, and *everyone* must be in agreement before someone new is read in on their operations."

I look at Lorenzo, and he's staring at me. He must be the one behind keeping this information from me. My jaw trembles as I search for words to insist they tell me what's going on. Where my mom and dad are.

A shadow filters over Lorenzo's face. "We don't want their safety compromised."

"I'm their *daughter*." I spread my arms out. "I deserve to know what's going on with my parents. Do they even know I'm alive?"

Essie comes over and takes my hands in hers. The gesture is too sweet, too tender to take place alongside of all the frustration and anger I feel. But I don't pull away. I respect Essie. Even if I don't understand the decisions she's making.

"Please trust us, Bria." Her words are soft, but passionate. "There's more we need to share tonight."

My hands tremble in hers. I want to argue. To insist upon knowing what's going on. To finally have someone define what "important" mission my mom and dad are on, or at least answer my question about whether or not they know I'm alive. But I nod my agreement.

Essie gives my hand a final squeeze before telling Azarias to continue.

"We thought we'd have a little more time," Azarias says, "but Talionis's attacks on villages continue to be fierce. Teens and kids are being taken every day. We've found some of our counter measures are working to keep them safe, but we can't delay any longer. We need to act. As soon as possible."

I nod in agreement, even as the very idea of heading back toward Talionis causes my heart to race.

"The problem is," Thaddeus jumps in, "that this means bringing all of Eryndale leadership into the plans. Including whoever the spy might be."

"Do you have any suspicions about who it is?" Matthias asks.

Azarias shakes his head. "No. They've done an excellent job of concealing their identity."

Lorenzo steps forward. "We're worried it might be more than one person." He crosses his arms over his chest. "At this point, we will keep our most critical plans within this circle only. But we need numbers in order to attack, and attack well. Whether we like it or not, the dangers moving forward are much higher than we wanted them to be. But we can't risk Demetrius Ark succeeding in his plans, especially considering they seem to be more nefarious than we realized."

He's right, but my confidence in our ability to stop Ark is diminishing. Especially considering there's a spy in Eryndale.

"We are going to organize teams of scouts to go to villages in all the spheres we can reach. The teams will work on gathering as many as possible to be a part of our attack against Talionis. The more units we can have sabotaging Talionis, the higher our likelihood of success." He paces. "There are risks even in this. The Raiders have moved farther east than ever before. Soldiers from Talionis are crawling through villages and towns searching for all of you. And Ark is growing more desperate to find you. Which makes him all the more dangerous."

I nudge my pack with my foot, wishing I could undo the moment when I stole all of Ark's items. How different would things be if he wasn't so desperate to find us?

"We would like to send all of you out west with Max and his team and the Wild Dogs. We know you'll be safe with them, and less likely to risk being seen or captured by soldiers from Talionis. However, there are dangers of attacks from the Raiders. You'll travel by Skinter Blades and Suits."

"Wait, what are those?" Nika asks.

For the first time tonight, the hint of a smile plays around Azarias's mouth. "That might be the one thing you actually enjoy. The Wild Dogs will get you oriented with them over the next two days before we send you out to the villages. In those days, Bria will work closely with Thaddeus to ensure the map is as accurate as possible."

Over the next hour, Azarias, Lorenzo, and Thaddeus share details about the developing plans.

My friends and I provide as much information on how to breach Talionis as we can. And we explain what we found in the files from Ark's safe as well, since our Talionis training gave us clearer insight into what's happened in the rest of the world. Information none of those in Eryndale were previously aware of. When we explain how we're trying to crack the encrypted files to find out why Ark would go through such lengths to protect the information, even Lorenzo agrees that should be a top priority. He assigns a few people to help Ari with the encryptions.

The convert ops strategies they're planning to employ feel like they'll be too slow. But I don't have any clear alternatives to suggest.

Ari gasps, drawing everyone's attention. She's moved away from the rest of us and is working with her tech.

She looks up, and dread fills me an instant before she says, "There's a new message."

CHAPTER

EIGHTEEN

The room is silent.

Lorenzo nods at Ari. "Play it."

I want to say no, to run from the room, to flee these problems once and for all and hold my brothers close to me. But I can't.

Ari presses play.

Matthias is closer to me now than he was a few moments ago, and I reach for his hand.

It doesn't matter to me if romance is silly or foolish or if this is the worst time for anything to go on between the two of us. At the moment, I'm just thankful he's here by my side, comforting and supporting me as we face once again a threat that neither of us can seem to overcome.

The hologram springs to life, but it's not Ark.

It's Storm and Cai.

My breath catches in my throat as Matthias squeezes my hand tighter.

Cai is alive.

At least in this footage he was.

He crowds close to Storm, his face beaten and bruised. His beard is patchy, and his left eye's swollen.

But he's there, he's breathing, and his eyes are still Cai's eyes. They still look like they understand far more than anyone could ever understand. And there's a strength and defiance in them that causes me to breathe easier, despite knowing he's under Ark's cruel grasp.

Storm's face is blotchy from tears, her blond poof of hair pulled back into a ponytail and making her look older than she should.

The hologram pans to Ark. "As you can see, we are still waiting for you to return."

His voice is calm, but there's an edge underneath it that pokes at me, prodding me to act, to do everything he says—or else. His cool eyes stare at us. His handsome features school into a perfect mask, yet look like they're ready to shatter at any moment. Like he's tired of this game we've been playing.

"I've waited a long time." He paces, and I recognize his office.

Storm and Cai are in a different room, but the hologram breaks back and forth between the two images.

Colonel Keenan Valarius enters and stands beside Ark.

Matthias squeezes my hand again, and this time, I squeeze back, letting him know I'm here for him as much as he's here for me. I won't let him face his father alone ever again. Even if it's just an image of him.

"Everything's ready, Commander," Colonel Valarius says.

"Good." Ark once again gazes into the screen.

A chill runs down my spine.

The hologram shifts into a closer view of his face.

"You have one week," Ark says, "or there will be destruction rained on this region unlike any you have seen before. At this point, I suspect you've gathered some who might help you. Tell them that if they stay on your side, they will face far more damage than they could have ever comprehended. We know there's more to this region than we first understood. I suspect there's a traitor in my midst, and that person will be dealt with." His lip twitches, but he keeps his mask in place. "But for now, know this. Everything you do from here forward jeopardizes more lives than you are attempting to save. And the two you care about most?"

The image pans back to Cai and Storm.

"They're in more danger than any other. Because I won't kill them, Bria. I will let them suffer. And that suffering will produce more harm in your life and theirs than you understand." He pauses to let his words sink in. "So choose now. Will you act? Will you return? Will you deny yourself and your freedom in order to save those you claim to love?" Another weighted pause. "Or will you continue down this path that will bring destruction?"

My heart aches, ready to explode with the pain of not knowing what to do. How to handle this impossible situation. With my free hand, I grip my necklace. Then quickly release it as memories rush in of Ark returning the treasured item to me with a new chain. Forever intertwining himself with the last gift I ever received from my brother.

"Shane, you are a worthy recruit."

Ark shifts the focus of his message, and I feel more than see Shane tense nearby.

Ari holds his arm, as though keeping him standing.

"It has destroyed me," Ark says, "to see you turn this route, become someone I know you're not. Come back." He reaches out a hand. "Find your place in Talionis. I have not forgotten you, my son."

The look on Shane's face is impassive, and I can't tell if Ark's words are making an impact or making him angry.

Maybe a little of both.

And I can understand. From the little I know about Shane's past, he's gone through a lot. And he excelled in Talionis. It was probably the first time in his life, he felt accepted, like he could succeed.

I only hope he can feel as accepted here in Eryndale, and not be drawn back in by Ark's lies and empty promises.

"And Nika, Ari, Nalani, and Bryson: I know some of you have chosen this route with Bria. You are more malleable, more ready to hear what she has to say and believe her lies."

I'm shaking now, angry that Ark could paint me in this light. Act as though I would betray my friends and be a traitor to them.

But it's another move, another manipulation. Another way he can get to me, cause me to turn back, and give him the items he's desperate for.

"You all can return, even Bria. I will accept you back and allow these two, who you love so much, to have their freedom as well."

Once again, an image of Cai and Storm. This time, I see their hands are bound. Storm's wrists are bloody from the bindings. Then I notice her arms. They're toned, muscular. Which means they're training her still. The tormented look in her eyes tells me that as much as the strength in her little body.

But they're also torturing her.

How can I stay back? How can I leave them there?

But how could I leave my little brothers in Eryndale after just finding them again?

I need to do something. But what?

"Come back, all of you."

I suddenly realize I'm not sure what Ark has been saying for the past minute, but it's probably just the same as it was before.

All lies.

"Matthias Valarius," Ark says. He tilts his head to the side.

Colonel Valarius stands behind him, mouth clenched and eyes narrowed.

Ark clicks his tongue. "You surprise me. So talented, so gifted. You could be like your father. You could be great in this city."

Colonel Valarius's shoulders straighten at those words. His face shifts. Unconcealed hatred for his son replaces his typical calculating look.

"Yet you act like your mother. Emotional. Moved by extremists' words. Ready to follow an empty faith rather than pursue greatness in this city." Ark's face darkens, his cool mask slipping for an instant before he reins in his emotions. "We have a lot for you here. Come find your place in our ranks. Be who you were destined to be."

I tighten my grip on Matthias's hand, seeking his support as much as trying to give him mine.

Ark sits behind his desk. "And now, to those who are watching this, who have never met me: these traitors speak lies. I would like to see you experience the truth of Talionis. The excellence of my plan for you. Turn the recruits in, and you will be rewarded beyond your wildest imaginings." He presses the tips of his fingers together. "But know this. If and when I need to show you all that I am capable of—my power, my strength—you will bow before it. You can choose: come and join me now, experience all I have for this region, all I can do for this desolate landscape that was once America."

Again, the screen pans in, focusing wholly on Ark and dimming and muting the area behind him. "Or you can experience the consequences of traitors."

He tilts his head, eyes shifting back and forth like he's considering something. "Two weeks, Bria. I will be generous and give you a little more time. I don't know how far you've traveled, but undoubtedly you need time to return. You can turn the tracking on this device back on. Ari, I know your skills in this area will allow you to do that. Or you can travel back on your own. Return, and return within my timeframe, or face the consequences."

The hologram goes black, filtering back into Ari's screen.

A deep silence permeates the room as all eyes focus on me and my friends. A sickening sensation twists my gut as I look at Azarias, Thaddeus, the DeForts, Max, Lorenzo. Everyone else here.

Even Essie's eyes hold a shadow of something that almost scares me.

"Are you going to turn us in?" I ask, suddenly afraid that in this place where I thought I'd find refuge, I'll instead be sacrificed to preserve the life they've built.

Because for one life, is it worth risking everyone else's?

"No," Azarias says, his word sharp, breaking through my thoughts. "But keep your items close and prepare, because I know that what comes next is going to be difficult."

He looks around the room at the others in this underground meeting. This secret sect within Eryndale that's fighting to stand against Talionis. Despite traitors within the refuge city. Despite those who claim it's too dangerous.

I respect every person here because they're standing for what's right, in spite of possible consequences. But will they continue to stand?

"We have to show the C.A.E. and the S.O.C. this hologram," Lorenzo says.

"Nah, that's a terrible idea," Malachi speaks up. "Seriously, man, you can't do that."

Others chime in, agreeing with Malachi, arguing against doing anything further with the hologram message.

But Max has that look in his eyes that reminds me so much of Cade.

"Lorenzo is right," he says, breaking through the cacophony in the room. "We can't keep this from them. If Talionis's threats are sincere, and I suspect Ark does not make empty threats, then we need to prepare the region for whatever might come."

"It's going to change things," Azarias says.

"True," Thaddeus agrees, "but we need to act, and we need to act immediately."

"Prepare the scouting units we can trust," Lorenzo says to Azarias. "I want them ready to begin covert ops as soon as possible. Max, you and your team will need to leave at first light and go west. Mobilize anyone you can to come join us in the fight. We can't afford to waste a single moment."

Max and his team nod their agreement.

"First thing tomorrow morning," Lorenzo says, "I'll convene an emergency hearing and show the hologram to the C.A.E. and the S.O.C." He turns to Essie. "Are you okay with that?"

"Of course." Her voice is tender and a little broken.

Then it hits me. She just saw her son. And Azarias just saw his father for the first time in years.

They know he's alive, but he's not alive in the way they'd want to see him. Not alive in the way I'd want to see my mother and father.

All I want to do is hold Eli and Zeke, kiss them, let them wiggle under my embrace and my affection, and just know that they're here. They're alive.

I can't wake them right now, but first thing in the morning I'll do just that.

"Honor God," Max says, demanding my attention.

"Do justice, love mercy, and walk humbly with Him," almost

everyone else responds with the same phrase I read in the scout training facility. Like it's their mantra.

Max and his team leave, and I wonder if I'll ever see Cade's brother again.

I focus on the rest of the room. "What happens next?"

"We'll find out tomorrow," Mrs. DeFort says, some of her bluster subdued in the face of all she just saw. "For now, everyone needs to get some sleep."

Several of those who were in the underground meeting last night are in the room where we stood before the C.A.E. when we first arrived. With the Scout Oversight Committee here as well as other prominent members of Eryndale's society, the room feels stuffy and overcrowded.

The day is warmer than others, despite the early hour of the morning. Although I only got a couple of hours of sleep last night, I find I'm not tired.

Lorenzo began the meeting by informing all those gathered that he wants to send my friends and me to the west to gather more who could come train and fight against Talionis. It makes sense to gather more, but now I'm not sure I even want to be involved.

As soon as the sun broke the horizon, I went to Azarias's house to see my brothers. They were barely awake, which meant they were willing to snuggle with me on Azarias's porch. Holding Eli on one side and Zeke on the other, knowing they're both safe —it was almost enough to make me forget everything I've gone through.

Almost enough to make me want to ignore Talionis for good. Stay in Eryndale and take care of the twins.

But Storm and Cai are still in Talionis, being held by Ark as leverage. And I have thirteen days before Ark turns the full force of his hatred for me against them.

So I need to act, even if the idea of leaving my little brothers tears me apart.

The hologram of Ark plays to a silent room. The men and women gathered are hushed, but shift and cast glances to one another that leave me uneasy.

Azarias shuts off the hologram, and the silence in the room remains.

Watching it again didn't make me feel any better. Anxiety claws at me, begging me to act or run and find my brothers, pretend none of this horrible reality is real. Do anything except stand here and *wait*.

"Well, what are we going to do?" Gabe asks. His charisma and dynamic personality seem to draw every eye even before he started speaking. "It's clear it's time to do something."

"Acting now would be foolish," Reginald chimes in. "Let's just turn them over." He waves his hand at me and my friends. "Give Talionis back what they want. We have to protect the region. It's what Eryndale does."

"No," Azarias says firmly. "Eryndale stands against injustice. That is who we are. That is what we do."

"I'm not willing to risk the lives of so many for a mere few," Reginald sputters.

Several others chime in with their agreement.

"How could Talionis know about us, anyway?" Reginald says. "How does Demetrius Ark know that they have others they're talking to?"

"It makes sense that they would," Gabe says. I'm not fully sure what to make of the man, but I'm thankful he's on our side. "After all, the fugitives have been away from the city for a couple of weeks now. Why wouldn't they have gathered allies along the way?"

"I don't like it." Reginald hefts himself to his feet. "And you want to send them out west? You want to expose other villages and draw Talionis to those who have been safe so far?"

"They're not safe if they're under attack by the Raiders," Lorenzo says.

"The Raiders are an enemy we know how to defend against," Reginald says. "Talionis is *not*. They're stronger, more powerful."

Azarias nods. "You're right. Which is why we need them to encourage others to come and help us in this fight."

"This fight?" Reginald shouts. "What fight? I don't recall voting on any tactical deployments." The man's voice rises to an irritating squeal that sets my teeth on edge.

"It's time to deploy the covert ops strategies," Lorenzo says.

Several members of the Scout Oversight Committee chime in their agreement.

"It's what we've been preparing for," Lorenzo says. "And it's time our teams went and did what they can do."

"It won't be enough," Reginald argues. "And we can't force teams to enter into what will very likely be a suicide mission."

Others who have been wary of us nod in assent.

This can't be happening.

They can't be ready to turn us over . . . right?

The doors behind us burst open, and two scouts straggle in. Their clothes are dirty and ragged, and their shoulders are stooped. It looks as though they've been traveling for days.

"We have news," one of them says. She stands tall despite her ripped clothing and the blood caked to her face from a cut on her forehead.

Lorenzo rises from his seat near the center of the room. "Report."

"We were in one of the Center Villages, a village Talionis shouldn't know about. And the soldiers came." She steps forward. "The one leading them was vicious. He had golden eyes." She presses her palms against her eyes.

She encountered Laban. And after we pushed him back, I can only imagine how terrifying he was.

The scout continues. "They raided the town for any teens and kids there. Destroyed fields. Left the town desolate. I don't even know how they found it." Her voice cracks. "They shouldn't have known it was there," she repeats.

I recognize the hollow ache in her eyes. She witnessed something horrific. Something she can't begin to know how to process.

And it was at the hands of Laban Meritas.

She gestures to the young scout with her. He hasn't picked his gaze up from staring at the floor in front of him. "We're the only ones left of our team."

As soon as she finishes, it's as though every person in the room starts talking at once. The volume increases to a high level, with the accusations against us ringing clearer than anything else.

Lorenzo instructs Malachi to take the scouts and debrief them fully, and Thaddeus leaves the room with him. I suspect he's going to the Cartography Center to figure out how Talionis could have discovered these places.

But it's Talionis.

Their technology is better than anything Eryndale understands. Ari could probably shed some light on the matter.

But right now, what catches my ear is Reginald, even though he's talking quietly to those around him. I strain to better hear what he's saying.

"...spies...impossible for them to discover these places."

The room goes quiet, as though everyone is beginning to put together a piece of a puzzle that's not even there.

"This is your fault." Reginald's eyes scan me and my friends. "Our Center Villages have remained safe for all the years Talionis has been in the region. And yet, now they're under attack. Because of you." He shoves himself to his feet. "They're spies." He points a finger at us as spittle spews from his mouth at the force of his words.

Gabe stands as well. "What happened is terrible," he says, keeping his voice measured. "But are we really ready to give them over? To assume that they are spies? There must be something else we can do."

"Give them a chance," Lorenzo says, and his words almost surprise me. He hasn't seemed sure about trusting us before, but maybe last night changed things. "Send them out in two days' time with the scouts who are going to be working in covert ops against Talionis. If they train, if they fight with us, then"—he lifts his hands, palms up—"we know they're not spies. And if it's clear Talionis knows more than they should about wherever their group is, then we turn them over."

His words break over me like ice water. I want to do something to save Storm and Cai, but his suggestion will put me and my friends in the position where everyone we're supposed to be working alongside will be watching for a moment when we fail. All so they can turn us in for the false peace Ark is offering.

There's murmuring around the room.

Azarias steps forward. "We can't put them right back near the city that wants them. That would be foolish. And we know we could use them out west. They could help us gather forces."

"There are others who can gather forces," Lorenzo says. "Max and his team are already on their way to do just that."

Reginald's lip curls. "I still don't like the idea of deploying *any* teams to fight against Talionis."

Several people start talking at once, some agreeing with Reginald, others insisting action be taken immediately. My brain races as I attempt to process everything that's happening, but it feels like I'm navigating a Kill Zone in Talionis, desperately hunting for the path through that will keep me from getting hit by dozens of training bullets.

Essie stands from her seat in the center of the room, and the arguments cease. "We all know something must be done. And soon. But what we are facing is incredibly dangerous."

A woman from the S.O.C. who I don't know raises her hand, and Essie nods for her to speak. "I suggest a two-fold approach to moving forward with the covert ops: teams must volunteer to go, and then they must pass rigorous evaluations to ensure they are capable of such a dangerous mission. Only those who pass will be sent."

"An excellent approach," Essie says. "All in favor?"

Almost everyone raises their hands.

Reginald sniffs. "Fine. But then one of those teams must be willing to work with them." He points to us with as much disgust as if he was gesturing to bags of week old garbage. "If a team is willing to be tied to them, then the fugitives can do as Lorenzo suggests. They can fight alongside our scouts and prove their loyalty or expose themselves as traitors."

His eyes lock on mine. "But they cannot stay within our city or enjoy the safety of traveling west as kidnappings and looting and destruction of towns and villages continue to the south and east." He tilts his chin up. "If no one will risk working with them, then I move they be bound as traitors until we can return them without exposing more of our resources."

My friends and I look at each other. The weight of everything that's happening pounds through my temples.

"You can't expect so much of them," Mrs. DeFort says from near the back of the room. "They're just teens."

"Yet they have fought like soldiers." Reginald crosses his arms over his chest.

"They haven't been trained for the covert ops," Azarias says.

Reginald sneers. "Somehow they've survived all that's come against them. If they're so great, so *talented*, then let them fight for us and let us see what we can do against this city you claim we need to go to war with."

Azarias and a few others protest some more, but after a few minutes Essie brings the arguing to a halt and calls for another vote.

My stomach twists as more hands are raised in favor of Reginald's suggestion.

The meeting wraps up several minutes later after the leadership determines to take the next few hours to find out if any scout teams will volunteer to work with us.

My friends and I go back to the DeForts' house, Mrs. DeFort muttering the whole way about how unfair all of this is, how cruel Reginald is being, and how senseless these leaders are if they think they should send mere children back to a city like Talionis.

But when we enter the house, she leaves us alone in the living room, shutting the door behind us.

Nika faces me. "What do we do?"

"I can't believe they think we're spies," Shane says before I even open my mouth to respond to Nika. "How idiotic!" He throws his hands in the air and paces around the room. "After everything we've shared, everything we've done to run from Talionis, how can they—" He grunts out frustration, not even finishing his sentence. "At least in Talionis it was clear what you had to do to make them happy."

Ari goes over to him, but he shrugs her off.

The look of hurt in her eyes is quickly replaced with resolve as she strides back toward us. "Can we get out of this?" Ari directs her question to me. Like we're in the middle of a Warfare Scenario or heading toward a Kill Zone, and I need to make a decision about how to get us all through alive.

"If a team will choose to train with us, we might have a chance," I say, forcing my mind to focus on strategy.

Not on the fact that I'm going to be forced to leave Eli and Zeke behind, and I may not even have the chance to fight to save Storm and Cai if none of the highly trained scout teams will work with us.

Ari's lips twist to the side. "I can use the tech that I have to come up with ways to fight Talionis, to get inside their intel and their server frames, even, if we're close enough. If we go, I might be able to do some damage."

The room falls silent after Ari's words. Because the reality is, we might not get that chance.

Why, God? Why does it have to happen like this?

I don't want to fight Talionis in this way. With people who aren't willing to trust us.

I know Talionis is evil. I know what Ark's planning is wrong.

But suddenly, all I want is my family and friends here in Eryndale together. Safe.

Whatever Ark wants to do in another part of the world, who even cares anymore?

If I can get Storm and Cai and find my mom and dad and bring them here, that would be enough. And yet, that's not even an option when it's clear so many here don't trust us.

We can't stay. I can't keep my friends safe.

I look at Ari and Bryson. They weren't elite recruits. Bryson's in shape because he's a runner, and he and Ari are both brilliant with tech, but covert ops? Sabotage? Can they handle that?

Fighting is the answer. It's what we came here to prepare to do.

I don't know if we'll even get the opportunity, and if we do, who am I going to lose next?

CHAPTER

TWENTY

There's a knock on the door, and Azarias pokes his head in. "After you left, the council talked some more," he says. "I need you all to come with me."

The somberness of his words does nothing to ease the tension twisting inside of my gut. Even if a team of scouts agreed to work with us, I don't want to do this. I don't want to go back to Talionis unless it's to rescue those I care about. I don't want to fight and try acts of sabotage and covert ops strategies that I don't understand in order to stop Demetrius Ark and his plans.

It's all beyond me, and I'm physically and mentally and emotionally exhausted, but I follow Azarias from the room along with the rest of my friends.

We go through the city, much of which is becoming familiar. Kemena joins us and whispers something to Azarias. He tilts his head at her, and the two seem to communicate without saying much of anything. Then we continue our walk.

We enter the Cartography Center, and Azarias leads us to a back corner of the space and into a private room. Lorenzo, Malachi, and Thaddeus are in there, along with a couple of other scouts I recognize from the meeting the night before.

As soon as the door closes, Lorenzo says, "We have a bit of a situation. Because of Reginald Finnigan's motion, you must travel with a team of scouts who volunteer to train and fight with you." He hesitates. "But very few of our teams are willing to take on a group the C.A.E. considers to be 'high risk.'"

"Why would you put us in this position?" I ask, some annoyance leaking out. If he hadn't offered his *suggestion,* we wouldn't be in this position.

Lorenzo studies me, his face expressionless. We stare at each other for several moments, and I wonder if he'll respond.

"As soon as I heard Addie give her report, I knew there wasn't another option." Lorenzo grips the back of the chair in front of him. "We need to move against Talionis, and there isn't time for people like Finnigan to play judge. Plus, we could use your help on the front line. You know this enemy better than any of us."

I don't like that they've put us in this situation, but his reasoning makes sense.

"It's dangerous," I say, "and not all of us are as equipped for this as others." The words are awkward and weighted as they come out of my mouth.

"Bria's right," Shane says. "Even if a scout team agrees to work with us, some of us should remain behind."

"I know I'm not an elite recruit," Ari pipes up. "But I am skilled with tech. I could be an asset. Really."

Her eagerness and words twist me, and I fear once again for the threat she'll be facing if she is part of the attack against Talionis.

"Unfortunately, I don't see a way forward where any of you are allowed to remain behind," Lorenzo says.

My stomach drops, but I don't argue. Shane's jaw tightens and he runs a hand through his hair.

"More scouts came before the leadership after you all left," Lorenzo continues. "It seems the Raiders must be working with Talionis in coordinated attacks against cities and towns. The devastation they are wreaking is nearing irreparable damage. One scout claimed a girl who was half-robotic was responsible for kidnapping eight teens and killing or injuring every person who stood against her." He keeps his face impassive. "We've debriefed some of the scouts, and we are trying to intercept them before they stand before the entire council. We don't want whoever is our leak knowing all the details of what we know.

Although we're sure he or she has his or her own source of intel."

"How did Ark even know how to connect with the Raiders?" Matthias asks. "It doesn't seem likely that he would have had the resources to reach out to them."

"We suspect Broche gave him contacts with them," Azarias says. "The man will do anything for money. From what we've seen of Talionis, there's plenty to be had through working for Demetrius Ark."

"I thought Broche was out of the picture," I say. "We messed him up pretty bad, and his top lieutenant, J, left after our battle with him."

Lorenzo rubs his jaw. "Could be, but based on the way Talionis soldiers and Raiders are coordinating their efforts, someone must have connected the two, or Ark made that connection through one of his soldiers in a city." He looks at each of us. "However it happened, we must do something as soon as possible." He rests his forearms on the top of a chair. "The option is either for you to be looked at as spies by more of the scouts and leadership here than I'd like to admit, or for *all* of you to train with our scouts and help us stop Demetrius Ark."

I loop my finger around the chain of my necklace, desperation clawing at me. "And that's assuming one of your teams will even work with us."

"Right," Lorenzo says, his voice grave.

Malachi clears his throat, drawing everyone's attention. "The Wild Dogs would be proud to train and fight alongside of all of you."

Some of the tension in my shoulders eases. Until I catch sight of Lorenzo shaking his head no.

"That's not possible," Lorenzo says. "Your team has scouts on it that are far too young for such a dangerous mission."

Malachi crosses his arms over his chest. "I have one of the best teams in Eryndale. They're passionate, strong, and work well together. And they just passed their last evaluation with perfect marks. You know they can do this."

Thaddeus grips the back of a chair. "Your mom is never going to let Jordyn go on a mission like this. She's barely okay with her being a scout."

"Then Jor will stay behind," Malachi says.

From the little I've seen of Jordyn, I doubt she'll be okay with that.

"But she's your navigator," Azarias says. "And we don't have another one we could place with your team."

Malachi's lips set into a grim line. "I'll talk to her and my mom. But if this is the only way we can help them"—he gestures to me and my friends—"and stop Talionis, then I don't see another option. We can't just give Demetrius Ark what he wants."

The room goes silent for a long moment, and I'm almost afraid everyone will hear the pounding of my heart. Jordyn's no older than sixteen, and I don't want her to have to face Talionis. But it sounds like the Wild Dogs are our only hope of not being sent back to Demetrius Ark by Reginald Finnigan and everyone else in Eryndale who's afraid of us.

"All right." Lorenzo nods. "But your parents will need to clear her to go, and your whole team will need to pass the evaluations the C.A.E. and S.O.C. have ordered for teams undertaking this mission. If either of those things don't happen, I won't approve the assignment."

"Understood," Malachi says.

Lorenzo dismisses him.

Once Malachi leaves, Lorenzo focuses on my friends and me. "We'll have you begin training with the Wild Dogs today. I know Emmi and Kassre DeFort well. They won't like their daughter doing something this dangerous, but if she can pass the evaluation they'll let her go if she wants to. The last thing they'll want is to see the six of you sent back to Talionis." His forehead wrinkles. "I wish there was a better way, but I don't see it."

He turns to Thaddeus and Azarias. "The sooner we can get them equipped to leave, the better. We have thirteen days left on Ark's timeline, and we need to do whatever we can to bring him down before he hurts Cai and that little girl."

The mention of Cai and Storm tightens my gut again. "Can we just send in a rescue team for them?" I say. "Once we're close enough, I could go in with a small group. We could set up a quick insertion that allows us to—"

"No, it's not an option," Lorenzo says, cutting me off. "I wish we could, but the leadership won't go for it. And right now, we need to do exactly what they want, or we'll lose our opportunity to fight Talionis. If we go against our orders, we risk losing the chance to stop Talionis at all."

A thousand arguments perch on the tip of my tongue, but the look on Lorenzo's face, and on Azarias's and Thaddeus's, for that matter, tells me there's no point in voicing a single one.

He turns to one of the other scouts in the room, who is probably close to Malachi's age and who I recognize from the underground meeting. "Wolf, can you bring them to the Wild Dogs? We'll have them undergo some maneuvers today and evaluate all of them tomorrow. And make sure to get them trained on how to operate the Skinter Suits. If possible, I'd like them to leave with the teams heading out in seventy-two hours."

"Skinter Suits?" I say. "What are they?" This is the second time they've been brought up, and the scouts didn't answer when Nika asked about them before.

Azarias smiles. "A faster way to travel."

TWENTY-ONE

Although Mrs. DeFort isn't happy, she and Kassre both agree to allow Jordyn to travel with the Wild Dogs if she can pass the physical conditioning portion. From the little I overheard of Mrs. DeFort's conversation with Azarias and Lorenzo before I was called away to train, it sounds like she has several other conditions she insists upon being met as well.

We spend the rest of our day running through conditioning drills while older scout overseers observe us and make notes on our physical fitness. It reminds me of Talionis, which is unnerving, but the scouts don't yell like the soldiers did in Talionis. And I feel relief as I push my body harder than I have in days.

We run through different training circuits, are tested on speed, strength, and agility, and work with the Wild Dogs on their advanced conditioning. Based on the raised eyebrows I've seen from Lorenzo more than once, the scout overseers are impressed with both me and my friends and the Wild Dogs.

Well, most of us.

Ari is . . . struggling. Physical fitness was never her strong suit.

It's not long before Lorenzo pulls her. The two of them talk off to the side for a few moments, which distracts me while I'm doing push-ups.

"Keep it going, Bria," Malachi says. "I need another ten from you."

Although Malachi isn't demanding like Laban or Sergeant Valarius, I obey the command.

I do ten more pushups, spring to my feet, and wipe sweat from my forehead. I nod toward Ari. "Why did Lorenzo pull Ari from training?"

Malachi follows my gaze to where the two are still talking. "He's probably trying to determine what she can do that will keep the leadership happy. They don't want any of you remaining behind, but if she can't pass our training measures, the S.O.C. won't allow her to leave."

I'm about to take a drink of water, but freeze. "What would that mean? Would she be allowed to stay?" Although I know Ari wouldn't like being told she needs to remain behind, it would bring some relief to know she was safe. And I know it would make Shane happy, since none of his protests about her needing to stay behind have helped convince anyone.

Malachi is silent for a long moment. "With the way everyone is overwhelmed right now, I don't really know. The newest reports from the scouts returning from missions has everyone on edge, and the leadership insisted you all go."

Before I can find a response, Lorenzo and Ari make their way toward us.

"I'm going to take Ari over to see Brandi," Lorenzo says to Malachi. "We'll get her equipped for a tech position with your team. With her and Isaac both handling tech, they should have additional time to work on breaking through Ark's encrypted files."

Malachi gives a quick nod. "Good plan."

Ari beams at the mention of tech, and I smile. But as soon as I go back to the circuit the Wild Dogs are running through, my smile dies. Ari won't be physically fit enough to be on a highly trained military unit in three days.

Which means having her as part of the team will put her in harm's way. Even if she is handling more of the tech side of things.

I step up to the starting line of a quarter-mile track and wait for the scout overseer to signal me to start. As soon as she gives the go-ahead, I sprint forward with as much speed as I can muster.

If they insist on Ari coming with us, that means I'll need to be in as good of shape and as mentally alert as possible so I can keep my friend safe.

Despite how close we'll be to Talionis.

After dinner, my friends and I meet Malachi and his team at the scout training facility. We've pushed hard all day through various trainings and evaluations, but our day isn't over. Tonight, our final evaluation will be a maneuver where the team lies in wait until soldiers attack a village. It's designed to draw the soldiers into a trap, where they believe the village is unprotected, thus allowing the element of surprise. During the attack, some of the team will hit the transport and render it useless.

They don't have any working transports to use for training, but according to the Wild Dogs, the lead tech innovator in Eryndale—Brandi—has worked with the engineers in the city to build a lifelike model.

I'm not relishing the idea of seeing *anything* that looks close to Talionis tech. But I'd better get used to it, because, assuming we pass this evaluation, we'll be facing Talionis soldiers by the end of the week.

Will any of those soldiers be recruits I trained with?

The question whispers through my mind and the rifle I'm holding seems to get heavier as we enter the outdoor village mock-up for the first time. Shadows cloak the buildings and streets, and I focus my attention on them rather than the question I'm not sure I want an answer to.

"Here's what we're gonna do," Malachi says. "We'll divide into three groups and keep watch over the different sectors of the town. Communicate through the—"

"Walkie-talkies," Retro says.

"Comm system," Malachi continues, spearing his brother with a look. "Any kind of movement, any sign of an attack, sound the alert, and be ready to fight. The tech unit"—he focuses on Ari, Isaac, and the three scouts with them—"will hit the transport."

There are nods of agreement.

Malachi keeps his focus on Ari. "As discussed, we won't be using any Talionis tech in this maneuver or once we're deployed. Understood?"

Ari stares back for a few seconds, and I can feel her looking for an argument that will convince Malachi using the tech is okay, even though the order comes from higher level scouts than him. But she finally nods her understanding. Which tells me she's argued her points more than once already.

"All right, let's do this," Malachi says.

My pulse thrums and adrenaline courses through me.

Malachi divides us into three groups, and I end up with Nika, Bryson, Karyss, and Glacier. We head to the east, and my eyes adjust to the darkness. It's strange being out at night without my lenses, but I don't miss the green hue over everything.

Ari brought the lenses to Brandi, and, according to Ari, the two spent a decent portion of the day trying to determine if they could recreate the lens using tech in Eryndale. Ari wasn't sure if they'd have it figured out and done before we leave, but she was excited about helping Brandi with it when we return.

Her optimism and confidence in our ability to defeat Talionis and all return to Eryndale is admirable.

God, why can't I be that confident?

"How much do you want to bet Ari still finds ways to use Talionis tech?" Nika asks as we jog behind Bryson, Karyss, and Glacier.

"My guess is she'll at least smuggle it out with us," I say.

Nika groans. She and I were furious with Ari when we discovered how she left behind supplies in the Ruins outside of Talionis in order to pack way more tech than we ever thought possible. But it turned out to be useful.

We round a corner, entering deeper into the mock town.

Ari spent all of dinner talking about her time with Brandi and the technological advances the woman has made for Eryndale. She discussed everything from mechanical horses that run like real horses—which are apparently used by the Raiders, but Brandi and Catori reverse-engineered a stolen one to design a fleet for scouts—to the cloaking technology Brandi invented to keep Eryndale hidden. Both Eryndale's entrances and views from overhead are masked and invisible unless you know exactly what you're looking for. Ari was practically glowing while she talked about it all. Even though most of it went over my head, I'm glad there's something good happening in all of this mess.

A piercing shriek cuts through the air, grounding me in the moment.

The five of us come to a halt. I bounce on the balls of my feet, ready to run in whichever direction needed.

My mind zips over what I know of this village. Our team isn't where we should be, but I suspect Lorenzo ordered the soldier attack early on purpose.

My instinct is to take charge, direct those with me, and come out of this maneuver successfully. But I stay quiet.

This time, I'm *not* in charge.

Karyss signals us to move forward, and we spring into action and race through the darkened village.

No lights are on, but the paths are easy to follow. Bryson, Karyss, and Glacier stay in the front, and Nika and I are close behind.

My heart pounds in my chest in anticipation of what's to come. Every dark scenario I went through in Talionis thunders through my mind with each pounding of my feet against the ground. Just like those scenarios, this isn't real. It's not an actual attack.

We aren't about to face Talionis soldiers.

But it all feels real. Far too real.

The three in front pick up speed, and I increase with them. We pass through the center of the fake village, and the sounds of fighting grow louder.

Karyss twists back to look at us as we near the other end of the village. "We'll go left, you two go right, and we'll flank them as they approach. Malachi and the others will draw their attention. Wait for my whistle before you attack. Okay?"

Before either of us respond, the three of them break left and disappear into the darkness. We sprint right. Torches are flying through the night, carried by men and women on strange, metal horses. The crack of gunfire pierces my ears.

Nika and I duck into an alcove, hiding in the shadows as we wait for Karyss's signal.

"This feels too much like a scenario," Nika mutters.

"I know."

"And what were those metal horses?"

I shrug, even though she can't see me. "Maybe the Raiders? Lorenzo did say they're working with Ark now. They might have incorporated them into the maneuver. It's what I would do." Even as I say the words, I realize it's true.

If I was the one trying to prepare small tactical teams to go up against Talionis, I would throw everything at them that I could in each maneuver they went through. It's the only way to adequately prepare for what we're about to face.

The fighting draws closer, and my body tenses as I get ready to enter it. I've been trained for this. Whether I like the reality or not, I'm a soldier.

Nika and I stay silent now that there are enemy combatants nearby.

A crash thunders to our left. We don't move. These are the moments our elite training becomes evident.

Karyss whistles the signal.

I sling the rifle from my back into my hands. It uses small balls of paint instead of bullets, but the weight is familiar. And far more comfortable than I'd like it to be.

"Let's do this," Nika says, rifle in her hands.

The battle for the village is far more intense than I anticipated. As I suspected, we face a mix of both Raiders and Talionis soldiers. I shoot at one. The bullet hits her arm, bursting in a spray of orange paint and drawing her attention.

Pain flashes across her face, but it's almost immediately replaced with anger. She rushes toward me, and I take aim and shoot again. This time I miss, and now she's right on top of me. I have a moment of wishing for my knives, even though this battle isn't real. The thought vanishes as the woman kicks the gun from my hand, and I'm forced to engage in hand-to-hand combat.

This isn't supposed to be real.

It's a training exercise.

But I'm not so sure anyone told her that. The first blow she lands on my side knocks the air out of me. I recover quickly. I smack my elbow into her jaw, but not with all my force. She delivers a right hook across my face.

Seconds later, she flips me onto my back.

Okay. That's enough.

If she's leaving me with bruises, I'll return the favor. I flip myself back to my feet and rush her. Her eyes flash with surprise, then excitement. I land a hard kick into her stomach and follow up with a sequence of punches and jabs. She blocks a few, but most of them find the target I was aiming for.

Shouts and the grunts and cries of fighting echo in the air. Blood trickles from a cut above my right eye. Soon, I'm able to get the woman on the ground. She pulls out her red scarf, signaling she's down and out.

"A little help over here!" Nika calls out.

I twirl and see her surrounded by three of the Raiders. My gun rests on the ground nearby. I grab it and fire it at one of them. It hits the man in the back, and he falls to the ground, orange paint staining his shirt. Moments later, he pulls out his scarf.

The other two look at me, and I take aim again. When I pull the trigger, nothing happens.

I grit my teeth, toss it aside, and run toward them.

Their focus on me is enough to allow Nika to disarm the one. The other fires his gun, but I duck into a roll, and he misses.

I kick out his legs from under him, and he loses his grip on his weapon.

Together, Nika and I gain the upper hand, and it's not long before we're joining in the fray with Karyss and Bryson.

The fighting continues for what feels like hours, and it's brutal. I take many hits, but give my share as well.

This will be different from a Warfare Scenario in one awful way: I'll be coming out of this training with more than one bruise.

It's hard for me to believe they want us *injured* days before we head back toward Talionis, but there's no time to ask about it now.

One of the Talionis soldiers gets past our line of defense, and Malachi and Retro chase after him. It distracts me long enough to get my feet swept out from under me. I land with a hard thud, but before my attacker has the chance to finish me off, Matthias is there.

A whistle rings out in three quick bursts. The Raiders and soldiers who aren't on the ground with a red scarf retreat, and Karyss rallies the rest of us together once they are gone.

"Debrief time," she says, once we are all together. "Where's Malachi?"

No one answers for a moment, so I speak up. "He and Retro went after a soldier who got into the village."

Karyss nods at Glacier, and she and Jordyn jog into the village. A few scouts bring over some lanterns and lights, brightening the area. And revealing more than a few scrapes and red marks on the Wild Dogs and my friends. I'm not the only one who will be sore tomorrow.

Matthias is a few feet away rotating his shoulder, but the grin on his face as he talks to Isaac eases any fears that he's seriously injured. As though he can sense me watching him, he glances over and gives me a smile that makes me forget the pain of my scrapes and bruises.

Glacier and Jordyn return after a few minutes, Malachi, Retro and the fake Talionis soldier with them. The uniform isn't an exact match to what the soldiers wear, but it's close enough to make my shoulders tense.

"Not bad for your first round," Lorenzo says as he joins us. "Although I wouldn't qualify the defense as a complete success. A soldier got through your ranks, and he murdered two villagers before Malachi and Moses stopped him. And he radioed out, giving details of your operation that must be kept secret."

Lorenzo's eyes flicker in and out of shadows as he turns to look over the group.

My lungs burn as I hold my breath, waiting to hear if we did enough to pass the evaluation.

"Overall, the twelve of you showed excellent team work,

technical ability, and physical prowess." Lorenzo pauses. "You passed."

The tension over the group breaks and I blow out a long breath.

Lorenzo rests his hands on his hips. "When we're close to Talionis, the attack will be far worse than this. I want everyone working on hand-to-hand combat and doing training at the armory as much as possible before you leave. You need to be at the top of your game. For tonight, get some rest. You did okay."

We leave the training grounds, and I rub the back of my neck.

"I didn't think they'd actually *hit* us," Nika grumbles, lightly pressing her cheekbone. "Thanks for having my back."

"You've always got mine. Happy to return the favor."

She smiles, then winces.

As we walk away from the training grounds, one thought pulses in my mind. Lorenzo is right. The attacks will be far worse once we're closer to Talionis. But how are we going to face them when we only have two days left to prepare?

TWENTY-TWO

Something is happening. Even as I finish the training with the Wild Dogs and my friends, I can tell. There's a buzz in the training area. I don't know if it's good or bad. But with the glances in our direction, I'm inclined to think it's bad.

Malachi's dark gaze assesses the groups gathering. He rubs the back of his neck. "That's enough for now. Clean up. I'm going to find Azarias."

Everyone else heads to the towels and to grab water, but I jog to catch up to Malachi. "What's going on?"

He glances at me. "Don't know."

"Can I come?" I ask to be courteous, but I'll follow him no matter his answer. I want to know whatever the bad news is right away. Not wait to find out.

"Sure."

Malachi taps a scout I don't know on the shoulder. "Pedro, have you seen Azarias?"

The man eyes me, then focuses on Malachi again. "He's probably busy."

The words are cryptic, but Malachi waves them away. "Bria's fine. She's training with the Wild Dogs."

Pedro folds his arms over his chest. "Doesn't mean she gets to know everything happening."

My curiosity dims as the reality hits that other scout teams don't want any association with me and my friends. It should have been clear after Lorenzo told us none of them would volunteer to train and fight with us, but seeing Pedro's open hostility leaves me wishing I could be anywhere but here.

At least the Wild Dogs were willing to make us part of their team.

Malachi's eyes narrow. For the first time since I've met him, I think I'm about to see him lose control.

"Where is Azarias?" He grinds out the words, and the way he says each syllable confirms I *never* want to be on his bad side.

Pedro steps back, but he straightens his shoulders. "I have to go." With that, he strides away.

"Fool," Malachi says. "Come on." He walks at a fast clip, and I almost have to jog to catch up to him.

I stay silent as Malachi weaves his way around clusters of scouts, my heart hammering in my chest. An ominous foreboding swirls in my stomach like a storm brewing over the sea. The easy, light atmosphere of the scout training grounds is gone. Instead, there's a tension. And I don't like it.

Did Ark do something *more* drastic? Has new information come to light? Or is Reginald Finnigan's hatred of me and my friends infecting more and more people?

I swallow the bile rising in my throat and exit the training area right behind Malachi.

"I don't know why some people insist on believing lies and rumors," Malachi says.

The statement surprises me out of my own thoughts, but I don't respond.

"How are we supposed to accomplish anything if that's the basis members of our city are functioning on?" His pace quickens, and his shoulders are taut.

"Fear twists things," I say, and almost stop short.

It's like I needed to speak those words to *myself.* Weird.

Malachi lets out a sigh. "You're right." His steps slow a little, and he gives me a look. "I'm glad you guys are fighting with us."

A wave of emotions slaps me in the face. Part of me wants to be angry with everyone in Eryndale, hate the fact that people like Reginald won't believe us. But there are those who are different, who act the way I expected those in Eryndale to act. People like the Wild Dogs, Essie, and the DeForts who treat us with kindness and acceptance.

"We'll check here first," he says, and I realize we are at the Cartography Center. "If Azarias isn't here, he's either in a meeting with the C.A.E. or went out on a mission."

"A mission? Now?"

Malachi doesn't respond. We enter the Cartography Center, and, after a quick search, don't find Azarias. The trek to the central hub building is quiet, and I do my best to keep my mind reined in.

We burst through the doors. More unease washes over me, but I push it off as bad memories. Too many meetings before the C.A.E. where they didn't believe us. Too many times recounting everything we went through in Talionis. I give my shoulders a subtle shake and follow Malachi through the building.

Voices are coming from the center, where we had our hearings before the C.A.E., and Malachi heads in that direction. There's a determined look on his face, and it's clear he doesn't care who is in that meeting.

We're about to join them.

He strides to the doors and doesn't hesitate before opening them and stepping through.

I pause, but a voice catches my ear.

No. It can't be.

I follow Malachi, my heart thundering in my chest, breath coming in short bursts. Maybe I'm hearing things.

A small crowd is gathered in the center of the room, and I recognize several of the men and women as part of the C.A.E., but I don't see the source of that voice. Everyone turns to stare at us as the door bangs closed.

"What are you two doing in here?" Reginald Finnigan's voice grates against me like sand. "This is a private meeting."

"There is no reason they can't be here," Azarias says. "Malachi is one of the most trusted scouts in Eryndale. And Bria is training to travel with us back to Talionis in just under thirty-six hours."

"She hasn't been cleared for this level of intel," Reginald

blusters. "And she's being sent to *prove* her loyalty. Not because we trust her."

"She has insights that might be helpful," Gabe interjects. "After all, she knows Talionis better than any of us."

"I'm not sure she should be here either."

There's the voice again. Clear as the bubble-like walls of a Talionis transport. A flush of heat envelopes my body, and I stiffen, turning slowly to face my aunt.

Elena stands to the left behind Lorenzo, nearer to Azarias. She is thinner than I remember, but the look on her face is far too familiar.

The look of reproach.

I want to scream at her, throw something, but the only thing that cracks through my mouth is, "Why?" The word is weak, limp. Broken. Not at all how I want it to sound and far more vulnerable than I wish it was, but it hangs in the air.

She drops her gaze from mine, but doesn't respond.

I clear my throat. "Why? Why did you do it?" This time, the words are stronger. "I went through *hell* because of you."

She doesn't look up.

"Do you even care?" My eyes burn, threatening tears, which is the last thing I need. I draw in a breath, then another.

I spin toward Azarias. "You know what she did. She can't be trusted."

Azarias's lips press together, and he nods to Elena's hands. For the first time, I realize she's bound.

"I know." The pain in his voice cuts through me.

I can't imagine how I would feel if I discovered my mom was actively helping an enemy like Talionis.

Reginald clears his throat so loudly it must hurt. "It makes no sense to me why we would believe a fugitive we don't trust over Elena. She's Cai's wife!"

I step toward Reginald. "She has actively worked alongside Talionis for years. She's the reason I was taken." Based on the fact that Elena is bound, I know at least a few people in the room believe what I told Azarias.

"Talionis can make people do uncharacteristic things." Elena hangs her head as she says the words.

Air wheezes from my constricted lungs. Does she regret what she did for Talionis? What she did to me?

Reginald scowls. "What happened in the past is not nearly as important as what's going on now. These blatant attacks against towns under our care make it clear to me that going against Talionis is *foolish*." Reginald slams his fist into his palm. "They would destroy us, I have no doubt. And our underground contact is out of communication." His arm cuts downward. "No. The safer and better option is to return what they need and leave them in peace."

"In *peace*?" Azarias gasps. "Are you serious? They're kidnapping teens from villages, forcing them to fight for a cause that has *nothing to do with them*, and you want to leave Talionis alone?"

Reginald's face flushes red.

"They're more dangerous than you realize, son," Elena says, drawing everyone's attention. Her head is held high now, shoulders straight in spite of the ropes binding her hands. "And they have people everywhere. Watchers, they call them. Any plan of attack you create will likely be made known to Talionis before you can ever carry it out."

How does the woman sound so haughty and superior after everything she's done? I stride to her, and her eyes flicker with a mix of fear and stubbornness. She's my aunt. My mom's sister. The two of us have fought on more than one occasion, but in the end, I always trusted her. I believed she cared about me.

Not anymore.

I stop when I'm closer to her than I need to be. "You would know, wouldn't you?"

She takes a small step back. Her face pales, her mouth springing open. "Bria, I—"

"I don't care what you have to say." I turn away from her, surveying everyone else in the room. Lorenzo, the leaders of Eryndale, Essie, Azarias, Malachi. A few of them I trust already, others I barely know, but one thing is clearer in my mind than ever before. "Whatever plans you make here, don't let this woman"—I jab a finger in Elena's direction—"sway your decisions. She can't be trusted. Just her being here puts all of us in more danger."

No one responds, and I don't care. I can't stand here in this room anymore listening to arguments and people fighting over decisions that need to be made, especially if they're going to listen to my aunt.

And I can't be in the same vicinity as that woman any longer.

She's bound, but it's far too evident that some—like Reginald Finnigan—don't believe she should be.

I leave the room. Lorenzo calls after me, but I ignore him. I need time and space to process my emotions, and hearing Lorenzo question me again—after everything I've already been through—will do nothing but make me angry.

My steps slow as the door slams behind me.

Eryndale is still standing, and Elena knew about it. So why didn't she tell Talionis?

I want to shake the question away, but it clings to me like a leech. Maybe exposing the refuge city is her next move. The thought sends a chill over me that doesn't fit with the warm air as I exit the building.

For now, she's bound and will be, hopefully, kept under watch.

She doesn't want Eryndale to fight against Talionis.

Which means that's exactly what we need to do.

Elena has already been the reason for my life shattering once. I refuse to allow her to have a hand in determining what I do next.

TWENTY-THREE

I stride away from the center building with no clear direction in mind. Frustration billows through me, pushing me forward like a sail on a windy day.

With everything going on, the last thing I needed was to see Elena. Seeing her, hearing her voice, brings back to the foreground all she did to me.

And, despite the fact that she turned me in to Talionis, that she was preparing to turn my *brothers* over to Demetrius Ark, she still has the audacity to speak to me like a child. Scold me. Act like she knows best. Even though she was *bound!*

I clench my hands into fists, ready to hit something. Throw something. I want to scream. Or cry. Too many emotions rage through me.

"Hey, I've been looking for you." Matthias strides toward me. His smile dies as he looks at me. "What's wrong?"

I shove my hand through my hair. "My aunt's here."

His eyes widen. "Yikes. Do they know she's dangerous?"

"Yeah. They have her in custody, and Azarias knows what she did to me. I don't think he'll let her free, even though she's his mom. But Reginald Finnigan thinks everyone should trust her more than me."

He catches my hand in his. "At least they know who she is. We can't control what happens next, but there's enough evidence to show she can't be trusted." He gives my hand a light squeeze. "Right now, you need a distraction."

He pulls me to a nearby bridge, and I let him, thankful to have him close. There are moments when I'm not sure what to do with the changes in our relationship. But right now—after seeing my aunt, knowing we're heading back to Talionis, racing against Ark's clock to save Storm and Cai—I'm thankful I can hold his hand. Know that he's more than just my friend.

My cheeks flush at the thought, and he squeezes my hand like he can read my mind.

"Where are you taking me?" I ask, realizing we're in a part of Eryndale I haven't been in before. "I'm not sure I can handle any more surprises today."

He glances back at me with a soft, understanding smile that steals my breath. "I wish I could have been there with you when you saw her."

His words make my heart skip a beat. Or maybe it's the fact that we're climbing a set of stairs.

"So . . ." I let the one word hang in the air.

"We're going to check out the Skinter Suits. After you left with Malachi, Retro told us we would train with the suits for the rest of the day. I didn't want to go without you, so I came to find you."

I don't know how to respond, so we lapse into silence. Our footsteps click as we climb the bridge's stairs, then we reach the top. There aren't many bridges or buildings up this high, and I haven't actually been at this level yet. It's almost dizzying, but the view is spectacular.

"Have you been up here before?" I ask.

Matthias shakes his head. "No, but I got directions from Retro before I went looking for you." He pauses and turns in a slow circle, pulling me with him. "Quite a view, huh?"

I nod and turn to find him focused on me. My pulse beats in my throat at the emotions in his eyes. Part of me wants to look away, but the other part wants to stare right back.

"There you guys are!" Ari calls from a nearby building, breaking through the moment.

We face her, and I let go of Matthias's hand.

"You have to see all this stuff." She gestures into the building. "It's amazing. I mean, I can see several areas for improvement immediately, but still. Some impressive stuff in here!"

She disappears back inside, and Matthias and I walk the short distance to the building that doesn't appear to be large enough to house much.

The door jingles as we enter, and my mouth drops open. Strange outfits that appear to be some kind of bodysuit with small solar panels are arranged all around us, and shoes with wheels on them line a wall of shelves at the back of the building. There's a wide, open floor with scuff marks in the center of the room, and the space is much bigger inside than it looked from the outside.

Nika and Kemena are here, as well as Retro and Ari. Ari is on the floor surrounded by pieces of tech.

"Sup homeys!" Retro greets us.

I'm about to ask where the rest of my friends and the Wild Dogs are, when a wiry middle-aged woman bursts from the back room, one of the outfits in her hands.

"Ah. More people." She grins at us before standing on tiptoe to hang up the outfit. Once it's settled on the hanger, she faces us. "Ya's haven't been here yet." Her short hair sticks out at every angle, and dark-rimmed glasses perch precariously on the tip of her nose.

"They'll need your basic instructions, too, Brandi," Kemena says. "These are the other two we mentioned."

This must be the tech developer Brandi who Ari has talked about.

Brandi hustles over to us. "Sure, sure, sure." She reaches out a hand, and I take it. Then she pulls me closer and spins me around, looking me up and down.

I throw a wide-eyed look at Nika and Kemena, but they're both just grinning. Some warning that the woman is a little strange would have been nice.

Brandi mutters words to herself that make little sense. ". . . small sized arm span, extra reinforcements, rugged blades . . ."

"Uh, nice to meet you," I say, but the words seem almost laughable. "So, how do these things work?"

Brandi drops my arm and focuses on Matthias as though she didn't even hear the question.

The door jingles again, and Azarias enters, but Brandi doesn't appear to notice.

Matthias spreads his arms and spins for her, mimicking what Brandi made me do.

She nods, muttering more nonsense, turns away, and heads into the back of the shop. "Ari, help me grab some gear, will ya?"

Ari jumps to her feet and hustles after Brandi, launching into a conversation that includes words like "velocity" and "electric charge." I'm not even sure I *want* to understand. I raise an eyebrow at Kemena and Nika, and they both laugh.

"That's just how Brandi is," Azarias says. "Give her a minute. She can only handle one task at a time. Super focused. But let me tell you, the woman can figure out just about anything if you give her long enough . . . and don't interrupt her." He shudders, but there's affection in his tone.

"Are you doing a run?" Kemena asks.

"Nah," Azarias says. "My, uh, mother is here. In custody."

My body tenses at the mention of Elena, but his confirmation that she's actually in custody brings a small relief.

Kemena rests a hand on his forearm. "You okay?"

"I'll tell you later." He nods to the back room. "I'm here to get things ready for the mission, and I need to go over with Brandi everything we need from her."

Kemena nods, then silence descends. I'm glad Azarias isn't going into details now. I don't want to relive what just happened with my aunt.

I want to train. And be distracted.

Although, based on the way Nika is staring at me with eyebrows raised, I'm sure I'll be sharing what happened with her sooner than later.

Brandi bustles back into the room, arms so full I can't see her face.

"Now here," she says, voice muffled by the pile in front of her.

She lays the gear on the ground. Ari is close behind her and drops her pile next to Brandi's. "We'll suit you's up and give you some basic lessons." She arranges the gear, pointing at each item. "You've got blades, suit, helmet, and I added in some extra padding. For your first fall. Can't have it hurt so much you don't try again."

"What?" I sputter, exchanging a dumbfounded look with Matthias. *First fall?* What exactly am I getting into?

Brandi doesn't answer my question. She's muttering to herself again, and Azarias looks like he's about to burst into laughter at any moment. He seems almost relieved as I am to have a distraction from what just happened.

Brandi spins and leaves the room again, calling back for us to "wait just a minute" before we get the gear on.

"Make sure they have what they need to start with a jump," Azarias calls after her.

"Sick." Retro pumps his fist.

Brandi pokes her head back out the door, eyes sparkling in a manic way. "You want 'em to start with a jump?"

"Yeah. Gotta get them ready for the mission."

She stares up at the ceiling, mouth working but no sound coming out. "Okay, okay. Not traditional training, you know? But I like. I like it." She disappears, then reappears a moment later. "C.A.E. is okay with different procedure?"

Azarias shrugs. "Probably."

Brandi blinks, then disappears again.

"Why would she ask that?" I ask, feeling more hesitant about this endeavor with each passing moment.

"Because *no one* starts with a jump," Kemena says. "A jump. Seriously, Azarias? The others are doing it the traditional way. They're all down there practicing."

He lounges against the wall. "You know a jump's the fastest way they'll learn. Plus, it's not technically dangerous. They'll have enough protective gear."

Kemena quirks an eyebrow. "The C.A.E. is going to say it's too much of a risk."

"They need to learn before we leave. You have Nika up here to do that, don't you?"

"Well, yeah, and I—"

He pushes off from the wall and stalks toward her. "I wouldn't risk anyone's life. They'll be fine. Trust me."

"You know I do."

Her words stop Azarias in his tracks and a genuine smile softens his features. Somehow I feel like she's talking about more than just us jumping.

"To clarify," Kemena says, "I wasn't saying I thought it was too risky. Just that not everyone else will like the idea."

Azarias's cheeks redden and I hear a muffled "sorry" before Brandi reenters the room.

She approaches me again, surveying me like Ari does a new piece of tech. I almost huff out a laugh when I realize Ari is looking at a blade with the same narrow-eyed assessing expression as Brandi.

Brandi feels my biceps, which is an uncomfortable moment, then gives a nod of approval. "She's strong. Should be fine. Yup, just fine. Just fine."

Nika snorts.

I shoot her a look. Why does it feel like everyone else is in on a secret that I'm about to discover in the hardest possible way?

"Put this on first." Brandi shoves a full bodysuit into my arms.

The fabric is different from any I've felt before. Almost stretchy and rubbery. I stand there holding it for a moment.

She blinks at me, her eyes magnified behind the thick lens of her glasses. "Well, off you go. Put it on."

"Yeah, Bria. Off you go," Nika says, laughter almost choking her words. She and Kemena are already wearing the same type of outfit.

Brandi whirls to Matthias, shoving a suit in his arms.

Part of me is tempted to demand someone show me how these things work before I put the suit on, but I'm intrigued. And I don't want to look weak in front of Azarias. He's been our ally from the beginning, and I need him to trust me as we head into the fight against Talionis. And with the information I've shared with him about his mother.

I pull the stretchy fabric over my clothes. It takes a minute to get it in place, and Nika and Kemena offer some assistance. Apparently, Nika has been here with Kemena already.

Once it's on, Brandi walks around me, finger tapping her chin.

She pulls at the fabric on my shoulders. "Good fit, good fit." Then she bends down and grabs another suit. This one has small hexagonal mirrors covering it. When she drops it into my arms, I'm surprised at how heavy it is. "Now this."

"What *is* it?" I ask.

"The charging and velocity control layer," Ari says without looking up.

"Yup, yup. Exactly." Brandi nods so vigorously, I'm almost afraid she's going to knock off her glasses.

I feel like I'm back in Talionis listening to another one of Mandeville's lectures on technology. Although he oversees all of Ark's technology and is the head tech instructor for the recruits, he doesn't have the gift of teaching. At least not someone like me who grew up without any technology. Everything he said went over my head, and Eryndale hasn't seemed to change me in that area.

Brandi opens her mouth like she's about to explain more, so I say, "Oh, makes sense."

Her mouth snaps closed, and she nods.

It's like looking at Ari twenty years from now. A small smile presses at the corners of my mouth as I slide into the second layer. Matthias does the same with his outfit.

Once I'm in the second layer, a thin film of additional fabric pools at my sides. "Is this suit okay? Looks messed up."

Brandi's mouth drops open. "I would *never* give someone a defective Skinter Suit. I don't *make* defective Skinter Suits. Heaven forbid." She blinks at me and mumbles something under her breath. Then she attaches the extra fabric on my sides to my arms. "These are for velocity. Azarias said you were starting from the air."

I lift my arms, and the film makes it look like I have wings. Very strange wings. Goosebumps rise on my arms under the many layers of gear. What did I get myself into?

Next, I put on the blades, which are essentially boots with

thick springs attached to dense, rubbery wheels lined up in rows on the bottom. Finally I pull on a helmet with a shield that comes down over my face and displays a higher level of tech than I anticipated.

Nika and Kemena show Matthias and me how to move in the blades on the open floor while we watch from the bench. Kemena glides one foot, then the other, moving around the shop with the ease of experience. Nika makes similar movements, but hers are less fluid and natural than Kemena's.

"Now you try." Azarias offers a hand to help me up.

I stay planted on the bench and stare down at my blades. "Give me a second."

Matthias gets to his feet and wobbles a bit, his eyes wide. "This feels weird."

I clutch the bench and stay seated.

"You'll be fine." Kemena glides over to me. "It takes a little practice, but you'll get the hang of it. Trust me."

I bare my teeth in what should be a smile, but feels far more like a grimace. I get to my feet, and they almost fly out from under me. I try to whirl my arms to keep from falling, but the extra fabric doesn't allow me to.

Azarias and Kemena both grab hold of me and steady me, and Brandi is by my side in a flash—though I'm less confident it's to make sure I'm okay. My guess is she's more concerned about her gear.

"First time on your feet is always a little odd," Azarias says.

"And second time," Nika calls over.

"Thanks for the warning," I say.

Kemena pats me on the back. "Now just do it like Nika is: left, right, left, right." She holds onto my arm and forces me to move with her.

Matthias is moving awkwardly around the room, using anything he can grab onto to keep himself standing. Retro skates over to help him, and the two crack jokes back and forth.

I tune them out and focus on the movement.

After a few minutes, the motion feels less stiff and almost . . . enjoyable. Maybe I could get used to Skinter Blades.

"This isn't so bad," I say.

"Great." Kemena releases my arm.

I'm not sure what happens next. The blades seem to have a mind of their own. I attempt to maintain the rhythm I had, but my balance is off.

Seconds later, I'm on the ground.

Nika laughs, gliding over to me. "Even with that less-than-graceful fall, you still look better than Ari does on the blades."

"Hey! I'm not *that* bad!" Ari says, looking up from a screen she has balanced on her lap while she holds a blade.

I smirk, the thought taking my mind off the embarrassing spill. "Then show me. Why aren't you practicing?"

"Because I'm helping Brandi," Ari says, distracted by the tech in front of her.

I get up, and Brandi hustles over. She spins me around, her hands checking over the Suit. "I thought you said she was starting with a jump?"

"She'll be fine," Azarias reassures her.

This whole "jump" thing is sounding more and more intimidating. "Maybe this 'lesson' is enough for today."

"Oh, come on. You're fine." Kemena pats my arm. "We're leaving soon, and you need to be ready to use the gear."

Nika skates around us. "And falling didn't hurt, did it?"

Shock passes over me. She's right. It didn't hurt at all. I guess the suits are sturdier than I expected. With a deep breath, I push away from Kemena and glide forward. Left, right. Left, right. The sooner I master this, the sooner I'll be ready to leave. To head back to Talionis and find a way to save Storm and Cai.

The rhythm of the movement becomes more natural and almost fun.

"They're ready," Azarias says.

"Okay." Brandi pushes a button by a wall without any clothes on it.

Two of the panels move outward until they're flush against the outside of the building. A small platform extends from the interior to the outside and overlooks a field that stretches out to raised pathways a hundred yards away.

My heart beats in my throat. "Jump" is making more sense, and I really don't like the idea. "Um, I think I'm supposed to be somewhere else. Help Thaddeus with something." I glide backward and away from the opening. I bump into someone, bringing me to a stop.

"Nope. Thaddeus is fine, and this part is fun." Azarias gives me a gentle push back toward the opening.

I shake my head. "I really think I'm good for today."

Nika folds her arms over her chest, which looks awkward with the fabric pooling around her arms. "You survived Talionis, *escaped,* and you're telling me you're afraid of a little jump?"

Matthias rolls up next to me. "We'll do it together." He smiles, but seems unsure, which does nothing to ease my uncertainty.

I clench my jaw. "Fine. What do I need to do?"

A smug look etches itself on Nika's face, but I turn my attention to Azarias.

"Good." Azarias nods once. "You're going to skate to the landing. Start farther back and build as much speed as you can, then jump off. Don't hesitate. It'll make it a thousand times worse than if you just leap off."

"Yeah," Retro says. "And if you wanna gain momentum in the air, keep your arms tucked at your sides."

"No, no, no," Brandi interjects. "First time jumpers always start with their arms out." She steps forward. "You do as Azarias said, but as soon as you leap from the platform, throw your arms out straight from your body. The Skinter Suit is designed to catch the air. It'll allow you to glide over the field and onto the ramps over there." She points to the raised walkways. "As you near the ramps, let your blades drop, and they'll hit the platform. Your momentum will propel you forward."

"Fine. Do it the boring way," Retro says. "But once you hit the platforms, if you want to go faster, just skate the way we showed you."

"They'll go plenty fast the first time if they just glide," Brandi argues.

"I'll glide." I'm not entirely sure what she means, but Retro seems to have a greater confidence in my ability than I do.

"You'll be fine," Azarias says. "The suit will carry you. Lean to the left or to the right to guide it, and when you get near the ground, let your feet hit first. The blades will absorb the pressure of the fall, and the momentum will allow you to speed forward. You'll start by traveling along the raised platform, but after a few rides along that, you'll be good to travel through the forest."

He must see my stunned expression, because he adds, "It's not as hard as it sounds."

Retro stretches his neck. "I'll show you newbies how it's done." He wiggles his eyebrows, then slides the shield down over his face.

Retro backs up to the farthest point away from the landing, then rushes forward, his blades whirring with energy. He launches off the landing, careening into the air, and my heart leaps. Keeping his arms at his side, he flies forward at a shocking speed. Then he throws his arms out and lifts into the air. Seconds later, he hits the raised walkways and skates out of sight.

"Better close your mouth before something flies into it," Nika says.

I shake my head. "That was crazy."

"He didn't do it the right way," Brandi says. "But decent form. Okay, okay. You." She swats a hand toward Nika. "Go on and do it like you did last time. Just like I told them, you hear?"

"Yes, ma'am." She looks at me. "See you down there."

She skates to the back of the room and rushes through the opening like Retro did, but as soon as she is in the air, she throws her arms out wide and glides down to the ground, still moving quickly but not nearly as fast as Retro. When she hits the ramps, she glides away.

"I'll go next. I've got this," Matthias says.

"I thought this was your first time too," I say dryly.

Matthias shrugs. "Confidence makes a difference, right?"

"All right, hotshot." I wave my hand at the opening. "Go ahead."

He skates off the platform, his movements a little jerkier, then he follows Nika's lead, throwing his arms out as soon as he leaps off. He bounces when he hits the ramp, and moments later, he's out of sight.

"Huh. Not bad." Brandi shoves me in the back. "Now you."

Indecision paralyzes me for a moment, but I take a deep

breath. Nika's right. I survived Talionis. Endured intense physical and psychological difficulty. Why shouldn't I be able to use Skinter Blades?

I slide the shield down, back up to the point the others started, inhale, exhale, and skate forward. I move as fast as I can, and the blades whir under my feet, moving me faster than I expected.

When I hit the platform, I don't have a choice about whether or not to jump. The blades are taking me off. In a blink, the platform is gone, and only air is beneath me.

My heart lurches in my throat as the ground comes closer with every rapid breath. I careen through the air, panic flashing through my mind like sirens in a scenario.

"Throw your arms out!" Brandi's voice resounds in my ears, and I register the comm system in the helmet a second before I do what she told me to.

As soon as I spread my arms, my entire body jerks up. I glide forward, and a laugh escapes. A real, out loud, laugh. This is incredible. I'm *flying*. This is the most amazing thing I've ever experienced.

"Whoo!" I shout.

The ramp comes into view, and I let my feet drop. The wind rushes past, but the helmet keeps me from feeling it. My blades hit the platform.

I bounce back up into the air, hit again. I glide several feet, then the blades shoot out from under me, and I tumble head over heels down the platform, off of it, and into a bush.

Air gushes out of me, and I stay still, waiting for the rush of pain I'm sure is about to come. But it doesn't. Slowly, I get to my feet, using the bush to keep me steady.

Nika and Matthias rush over to me. I push the shield up and feel the smile splitting my face.

"That was amazing." A laugh runs out of me.

"For real!" Matthias says. "Who's up for round two?"

Nika and I follow Matthias back toward the building we just leapt from. The longer I use the blades, the more comfortable I become, and the activity is a welcome distraction.

The past couple of days have been so full of trainings that I haven't had much time with my brothers, so when Azarias leaves and comes back with them and Levi later in the afternoon, I'm thrilled. They squeal with delight watching me and my friends soar in our suits and race along the platforms.

It's almost enough to make me forget that Elena is in the refuge city, and Storm and Cai only have twelve days left on the deadline Ark gave us.

Almost but not quite.

I round the bend on the raised pathway, and then turn around, skate to my brothers, and give them a hug.

CHAPTER

TWENTY-FOUR

I leap over a hurdle in the obstacle course I'm going through. Our final test before leaving first thing tomorrow morning.

The past day and a half have been a blur of training, planning with Thaddeus, and meetings with the Wild Dogs and other scouting teams who have passed the mandatory evaluation to fight Talionis. The days are long, and I fall into bed exhausted each night.

But I've taken every spare second to be with Eli and Zeke. There have been a few times when the boys were almost annoyed with me for interrupting their fun with their friends, but overall they seem as eager to be with me as I am to be with them.

Especially because they know I'll be leaving again tomorrow.

I drop to the ground and crawl through a small tunnel, pushing myself harder, faster. Anything to keep from thinking about the tears in the twins's eyes when they begged me not to leave.

As I come back into the sunlight, I catch a glimpse of Azarias and grab onto a new train of thought. He doesn't seem to know what to do about having his mom back, and I don't think he's even brought Levi to meet her. From the little Kemena mentioned, it sounds like he and his mom never had a great relationship. With everything she's done, and with all Azarias needs to do as we prepare to head to Talionis, it seems like he's pulled away from her.

Can't say I blame him.

Lorenzo and Thaddeus debriefed me, Nika, and Ari about what we know about Watchers, and confirmed with each of us individually that Elena's name was, indeed, on the list of names Ari decoded.

Thankfully they believed us, and now Elena is kept under constant guard and is being watched as a potential spy. Which is a small consolation.

I use the rope dangling down a wall to hoist myself up. My muscles burn, and I press into the exertion. Nowhere feels safe. Or like home.

By the end of the week, I'll be much closer to Talionis than I ever wanted to be again. But with only eleven days left on Ark's timeline, I know it's where I need to be if I have any hope of saving Storm and Cai.

I race to the end of the track to finish my portion of the race and stop in front of Malachi, sweat dripping down my face and back.

The other Wild Dogs and my friends are coming in as well, at different intervals and times.

Ari, as usual, is the last to arrive, huffing and puffing, arms flailing about as though she's hoping to grab onto the air itself to help pull her to the finish line. I wonder if she regrets hiding her actual stats while we were in Talionis by changing the tech on the back end.

Once we're all there, Malachi nods his approval. "You guys are looking good. Grab some water, and let's move to the shade."

I grab a cold water bottle and drink half of it as I walk toward the shaded area Malachi indicated.

Malachi rests his hands on his hips. "We're ready to ship out in the morning, but this will be the most dangerous mission we've undertaken together. You all know that." He paces as he looks each of us in the eye.

Overall, my time in Eryndale hasn't been good. Nothing like I expected it to be. We're still under suspicion, still looked at like we're the enemy by so many in the refuge city.

But this team of scouts is different. When no one else would, they volunteered to enter into a perilous mission in order to keep us from being turned over to Ark.

I look over the group. Retro, Jordyn, Karyss, Glacier, and Isaac intermingle with Nika, Ari, Shane, Bryson, Matthias, and me. My friends.

And I would give my life for any of these people.

"There will likely be casualties," Malachi is saying.

The words snap my attention, twisting at my heart. And leaving a rock in my gut that I don't know what to do with.

"But we will do our best to avoid putting anyone in unnecessary places of danger." Malachi turns his focus to the Wild Dogs. "You all know this is voluntary. None of the scout teams entering this battle are fighting because they have been assigned the task. You've passed the evaluations. You're up for this. But if you don't want to go, now's your chance to say."

"We aren't gonna leave our buddies when they need us most," Retro says, throwing an arm around Shane. "We're the Wild Dogs, and we're going to fight."

Malachi lifts his eyebrows, but I think he's proud of his little brother. "This is different from what you guys have done before."

The way he says the words leaves me wondering what Malachi has faced that's different from the others on his team.

"We've fought Raiders," Glacier says, "and they were no walk in the park. I think we should be okay with this." She flicks her short blond-streaked hair out of her eyes. "It's different from other things we've done, sure. Not the normal battle operations. But we all understand covert ops now more than we ever thought we would. Moses is right. We're not leaving the rest of our team to fend for themselves."

"Yeah," Jordyn interjects. "We know the threat Talionis presents, and we're not interested in sitting by and watching them take over and destroy what we've worked for our whole lives. We have to fight." Her words are fervent—almost surprisingly so.

She's the youngest of the group by far, and I know Mrs.

DeFort is upset she's going on this mission. But since Jordyn passed the evaluation with the rest of us, and she's the only available navigator, she's coming. Mrs. DeFort has made several demands to ensure her daughter's safety—including us reconnecting with Catori so Jordyn can remain with her once we're close to Talionis—and she also made it clear to me and my friends that she knows Jordyn going is what must happen.

Over dinner last night, Jordyn shared that the DeForts adopted her, and that Catori and Micah brought her to their family almost ten years ago. No one went into more detail, but I wonder more about the history there.

Malachi nods once, the hint of a smile on his lips, like this is the answer he was expecting.

"We aren't leaving our boys to go out by themselves," Retro chimes in.

Nika lifts her eyebrows at him. "Your boys? There's three guys and three girls, dude. What are you talking about?"

Retro grins. "Just an expression, dear, just an expression."

"Boy, if you call me dear one more time." Nika steps toward Retro.

He backs off quickly, but the grin on his face reminds me of an incorrigible little brother, although I think he's older than all of us.

Is this what it would have been like if my brother Ezri hadn't drowned?

"There's one more thing we need to discuss," Malachi says, the somberness in his tone catching all of our attention. He glances around and doesn't continue talking until another team passes by us. "The six of you have to go before the Eryndale leadership one more time."

My shoulders tense. "We're doing what they want. We passed their evaluations and we're fighting Talionis. Why do they need to see us again?"

Malachi shrugs. "I'd say it's customary, but it is a bit unusual. I think they want to make sure you know your place, that you're all ready to actually do everything you're supposed to do from here forward."

My friends and I exchange looks.

Fighting Talionis, doing what we're doing, was supposed to be a team effort with those in Eryndale. Not something that made us feel like we were less than or traitors.

"Fine," I say. "When are we meeting them?"

Malachi glances at his watch. "In five minutes. We'd better get going."

I STAND BEFORE THE LEADERSHIP OF ERYNDALE ONCE AGAIN, FEELING A little underdressed in my training gear and with hair plastered to my forehead from the workout we just did.

But part of me appreciates that I don't look put together for the group we're facing.

This is who I am. A girl who fights, who trains hard, who is physically conditioned for battle.

I hate what Talionis made me into, but I stand before the Eryndale leadership knowing I can defeat enemies, knowing I can strategically see ways around impossible situations.

It will be weird going into battle against those who trained me and, probably, those who trained with me. Fighting them with tactics that they taught me. My mind drifts to Major Vasco and his strategic skill in Warfare Scenarios. He praised me regularly for my ability to see through various situations, to find ways to defeat scenarios and bring back most of my team alive.

Most. Not all.

As the scenarios got harder, the enemies we faced got stronger. And I wasn't able to defeat them as well as keep my people alive.

And no scenario ends unless you defeat your enemy. Or your enemy defeats you.

My mind snaps back to the present as Reginald Finnigan clears his throat and brings the meeting to order.

"I still don't like that you are representing us in this fight," Reginald says. "But I have been outvoted."

His gaze shifts around the room. "I wanted to go on record one more time to say that if anything happens, if there's any so much as hint that you are betraying us, there will be consequences." He leans forward. "You *will* be turned over to Demetrius Ark."

"Are you threatening them, Reginald?" Malachi asks, arms crossed over his chest. "They've done everything you've wanted. They've trained and passed all of their evaluations. They're going to Talionis. We're putting them back at the center of the worst experiences any of them have ever gone through without the full support of this council. You put them in a position that's forcing my little sister to go on a dangerous mission. And now you want to threaten them."

"Hey, hey, let's calm down." Gabe stands, and I feel a small amount of relief. Gabe has been vocally supportive from the beginning, and the last thing we need right now is Malachi disciplined for speaking out against the C.A.E. "We just want to know that we're all on the same page, same team."

Gabe spreads his hands out as though smoothing the tensions that coil around the different individuals in the room. "I think this is going to go well. I think we have a shot at stopping Talionis." He pauses, tilting his head to the side. "There is one more thing we wanted to discuss with you. A slight change in plans that I think is going to aid us in the battle we have before us."

Azarias, who has been silently standing near the back of the room, strides forward. "I was not informed of any changes to the plans."

Gabe tucks his thumbs into his pants pockets. "There are still those who are uncomfortable with our new friends." He pauses as though unsure of the exact way to phrase his words. "I don't agree with it. I think it's dangerous to force people you don't trust into battle. But to show everyone my confidence in you and your team, and to help support the endeavors being made against Talionis, I will be going with you."

Azarias's jaw clenches, and Malachi's nostrils flare.

"We don't need someone from the C.A.E. coming," Azarias says.

"Nevertheless," Gabe intones, "I will be joining you."

"You haven't been trained," Azarias argues. "It's ridiculous—

foolish—for you to come with us, and you know it as well as we do."

Gabe lifts his one shoulder in what I think is supposed to be a self-deprecating gesture, but fails in the face of his confident nature. "I don't like it. I said that already. But others here?" He waves his arms around the room. "They will feel better if I am present with you."

There are some nods and murmurs of agreement.

"I've already approved this," Lorenzo says from behind us.

I'm not even sure when he arrived.

Azarias clenches his jaw.

"I'll stay behind the battle line," Gabe says. "Out of harm's way, of course."

"Of course," Malachi mutters under his breath, the sarcasm in his tone almost surprising.

It is frustrating that the C.A.E. is sending someone with us, but I'm glad it's *Gabe* and not Reginald.

"I will be there to send field reports to the council," Gabe says.

Azarias looks like he's going to argue, but Essie stands.

Her soft, weathered face looks wearier than it has any other time I've seen her, like she dreads what's about to come. "I have seen battles. I have seen destruction. And what ruins countries or towns or communities is not always the enemy, but the division that comes from within." She links her weathered hands in front of her, looking between Azarias and Gabe, then at Reginald, Lorenzo, and Malachi.

Her eyes even connect with mine, before going around the room and gazing at the different members of the council, and my friends.

"We cannot have division," she says. "I understand this is a scary situation, something none of us want to experience or go through." She releases a low sigh. "I created Eryndale because I wanted a place of rest and peace. I didn't want to see my grandson trained for battle, my son taken by mercenaries and soldiers. But here we are, and now together, we are going to fight."

She focuses on Azarias. "Azarias, if it makes the council feel better for Gabe to join you, I urge you to invite him in willingly. As Lorenzo said, he's already agreed to this. Please do not fight." She turns to Gabe. "And Gabriel, if you are going, then I expect you to listen to Azarias. He is the one trained for these things, as you well know."

Gabe gives a nod, ducking his head as though in humble submission. Although I wonder if Gabe would submit to anyone in reality. He strikes me more as someone who gives orders rather than takes them.

"Of course," he says. "I will endeavor to submit to those who understand battle far better than I."

Essie nods once, then she focuses on my friends and me again. "I do not want to send all of you back, but the C.A.E. has voted and the decision is out of my hands." Her eyes connect with mine, and I want to run to her and give her a hug, let her hold me like a grandmother would.

But I stay where I am.

"Bria, Elena claims there was more going on than you understand. We will continue to debrief her over the next days and weeks, but please know we have heard your concerns, and they're not being taken lightly. She will remain under guard."

I nod.

At least Essie isn't letting my aunt's lies sway her thinking. But the reality is, because of what Elena did, I was forced to become someone different. As much as I long for the life that was stolen from me, I could never go back to Derbe and pretend everything is fine. I am forever scarred, forever changed, both in good ways and in bad.

Thinking of home brings me to thoughts of my mom, my dad. My chest aches.

I don't know where they are or how they're doing, and I long to see them again. To know they're okay.

Essie has continued talking, but my mind struggles to focus again.

Before long, the council dismisses us.

We're to go back to the DeFort house, pack our things, and prepare to ship out first thing in the morning.

We'll be traveling by Skinter Suits until we arrive at the river.

There, Catori and her crew will pick us up again to travel back toward Talionis. Back toward the place of my fears. Back toward the place that holds those I love.

I'm ready to go back, as much as I don't want to. Because by going back, I finally have a chance to do something, to stop the evil being perpetuated by Demetrius Ark.

But even more, to rescue those I love.

TWENTY-FIVE

I check my pack one last time, even though I've already gone through it twice.

Everything is there. Changes of clothes, the items I stole from Ark's safe, Cai's Bible.

Nika and Kemena talk quietly on Kemena's bed. Although she isn't technically a scout, Kemena has trained with the scouts and she's coming with us. Even if the C.A.E. said she couldn't come, I don't think it would matter. There's no way she'll let Nika out of her sight now that they've been reunited.

Ari is prepping her tech to go. Loads of tech. She's not supposed to use Talionis technology, but it's not stopping her from packing it. Between that and the new items she has from Brandi, I'm not sure how she'll carry the pack. It will, undoubtedly, end up being carried by someone else.

We'll be ready to go first thing in the morning. I already said my tearful goodbyes to Eli and Zeke earlier this evening. Soon, we'll head to the last meeting for final preparations with the other scout teams who will be deploying next.

We just finished dinner with Mrs. DeFort, Retro, Malachi and Jordyn. It was an emotional affair. Mrs. DeFort is anxious about all of us leaving, but the fact that we're connecting with Catori seems to ease some of her fears.

Now that I know the DeFort family, I want to know more

about Catori's husband, Micah, as well. Whenever his name has come up, there's been a deep sadness.

It's hard enough to lose a loved one, but to not know if they're alive or dead . . . that brings an ache that's nearly debilitating. An ache I feel anytime I think of my mom and dad.

A rap sounds on our door, then Mrs. DeFort opens it and pokes her head in. "Time to go, my lovelies."

We follow her from the room. Jordyn is in the hall, and the boys trail out of their own room behind Malachi and Retro.

Matthias comes up next to me, puts his arm around my shoulder, and gives me a light squeeze before letting go. "We're going to be okay. We've got this."

As much as I want to smile back and believe him, I'm not sure it's true.

We crisscross through Eryndale to the scout training area.

We enter the mission prep center to find the room filled with people. I recognize some of them.

Bill and Paul and their guys are present for this meeting. Although they're not part of any scouting teams, they'll be traveling toward Talionis as well. They're responsible for designing various secret compartments and hidden rooms for the W.U.N. and E.U.N., and Lorenzo and Thaddeus want them close to help with troubleshooting any issues that might arise with smuggling people out of Talionis's reach.

Apparently, Bill and Paul are the ones who taught Cai how to design hidden compartments and spaces. The guys are impressive.

Lorenzo starts off the meeting, and we go over the details of what we know.

There will be five scouting teams going out from Eryndale tomorrow and heading toward Talionis, all taking different routes. All setting up positions at different points outside of the city in order to sabotage and prevent them from pinpointing where the threat is coming from. Most will travel by Skinter Suits, but one team will use the mechanical horses.

"We will be utilizing small insertion tactics," Lorenzo emphasizes. "No direct contact with the enemy, if we can help it.

Find ways to sabotage resources, cause confusion, and debilitate them."

He continues going on, and I half-listen.

I've heard it before, and I understand these are the tactics everyone has been preparing for. But I'm hoping that once we're close, I can convince him to let me enter with a small team. Save Storm and Cai.

We go through the plans with Thaddeus showing us on the maps that he brought in how we're going to be traveling alongside the other teams.

I look around the room, a weight settling in my gut. In reality, this is probably the last time all of us will be in the same room together. It's unlikely we'll be able to stand against this enemy without fatalities.

Ark will stop at nothing to get back the items he wants. He'll stop at nothing to accomplish his cause. And it doesn't matter how many lives are lost. Not to him.

My hands shake at the thought of going back, of facing this man who I fear and hate. But fear doesn't matter.

I must return to Talionis.

"Having Gabe as part of this will complicate things," Azarias says.

Lorenzo inclines his head. "I know. But it was acquiesce on this matter, or have our entire timeline delayed."

"He didn't even show up for this meeting." Azarias's nostrils flare. "He'll get in the way."

"I'll ensure he doesn't," Lorenzo says, his tone brooking no argument.

Azarias steps back, yielding to Lorenzo's leadership.

Lorenzo brings the tactical portion of the meeting to a close, and Essie moves to the front of the group. Once again, her class, strength, and character in the face of everything impresses me.

"I don't know if I will see all of you again on this side of eternity," she says. "It pains my heart to know we are sending so many of you to what very well may be your deaths. The C.A.E is aware that I am against teens being sent on this mission, but their decision stands." She pauses as though to gather herself.

"But I know most of you have chosen to follow God, do justice, love mercy, and walk humbly with Him."

As she says those words, several in the room mouth them along with her. Their mantra. A passionate belief. One that infuses their lives and orders their steps.

God is so real to those present. So real to those who are looking for a way to stand against evil. To overcome it by doing the right thing. And I want to be named in that number.

There are a few here who I'm not sure believe in God, Thaddeus being one of them. He has seen so much, respects all of their beliefs. But any time God is brought up, he makes himself scarce or ducks his head like he is now, looking like he wants to be anywhere but in the room.

It's strange.

He's such a large part of Eryndale. Such a strong man and leader in so many ways. A good guy. But it's as though he knows if he follows God, he must give Him everything.

And I wonder if he's ready to do that.

Sometimes I wonder if *I'm* ready to do that. To completely trust God with those I love and care about.

But I've given my life to Him. I've trusted Him to save me.

How can I do anything but also trust Him with the lives of my family, my loved ones, my friends?

Essie continues, "Before we go, I'd like to take some time to pray, to commit this work to God. I know not all of you wish to partake in that. And I understand. You may leave now. The tactical portion of this meeting has concluded, and you know what is coming. Our prayers will be with you, whether you are ready to receive that reality or not."

Her words could almost be offensive, but Thaddeus and the ten others who stand to leave the meeting don't seem at all upset. It's as though they've heard them before. Like they appreciate it, but they don't want God to be part of what they're doing.

And Essie allows that. Indeed, she seems to respect that the decision is their own.

It's strange to see the contrast between those here in Eryndale who truly have a different way of thinking and living compared to those in Talionis.

In Talionis, the beliefs of the city were thrust down the throats of every teen who was brought in. None were given free will or a chance to determine what they wanted to do themselves. Every single one of us was to listen, fall in line, obey, and believe the rhetoric that was being preached.

But that's not how it is in Eryndale.

There is choice. Free will. Opportunities to determine the course of one's life.

In it all, Essie's heart and the heart of those who I respect here seems to be to equip and encourage every person to walk in their strengths and find their place in the community.

I want to be a part of that community, but yet I still don't feel like I really belong. Probably because I'm still being treated like a traitor.

Once those leave who are less comfortable with prayer, Essie goes to her knees on the floor.

Shane shifts uncomfortably, and Bryson and Ari exchange looks. I don't think any of them know God or want much to do with Him. Something in my chest squeezes.

I've never thought of it before, of what would happen if I lost one of them, of their eternal destinies. What was it like for Cade? He was more mature in his faith. He understood God in a deeper way than I have yet. And he was willing to give his life for mine because he knew I wasn't ready for the eternity I would face apart from Jesus.

I'm willing to give my life for them, but am I as willing to talk to them about my faith? About how God has saved me?

Before I can think too hard on it, Essie begins to pray. "Dear Heavenly Father, you see the enemy before us. You see that he is stronger, mightier than we can understand. But You are greater. With three hundred men, you defeated thousands. You put to flight armies in the millions against troops who had few in number. You worked miracles—all for Your people. And once again, we ask that You would work a miracle. We do not ask assuming You will do it all. We ask putting ourselves in Your hands, willing to offer our lives to fight against this evil, willing to go to the death in order to do what is right."

My heart pounds in my chest as Essie prays, resonating with her words.

"And we ask that You would enter in, that You would equip us for all we are going to face. There is evil in this world. It is broken, and we know that evil is perpetuated by us in our own sin. And so, if there is anything in this group, in our hearts, in our lives, that is not right before You, I pray that each would surrender and seek Your forgiveness before entering this battle. Because we need to be right with You, our Father, before we find that we can fight evil ourselves.

"So, I commit each of these men and women to You. May they fight the good fight of faith, take hold of the sword of Your Spirit, and stand against the wiles of the devil. He walks about like a roaring lion, seeking whom he may devour, but we are here to resist him. We are here to be steadfast in our faith. We are here because You have put us here for such a time as this.

"Heavenly Father, take this group of consecrated individuals, and may they be Your warriors in a battle that is fierce, knowing that we are more than conquerors in Christ. Though Talionis may seem to win for a time, in the end, we know You will ultimately be victorious. And it is in Jesus' name we pray, amen."

As she says "amen," the word is chorused through the room.

Her words flood my heart.

Words I would never even have thought to pray before. Words that hold truth and weight and meaning that is beyond my understanding.

A few others pray as well, but my heart and mind can't pull away from the words of Essie. This elderly woman, whose faith is so deep, so rich, that it is almost intoxicating. Like a fragrance that would smother me with its sweetness, yet that I don't want to walk away from.

It is life.

This woman exudes life.

Despite all of her years, despite all of her hardship and pain, there is joy and life in this woman that I wish I could know better, but who I'm leaving tomorrow.

It breaks my heart a little, yet I also recognize that God has allowed me to encounter her right now.

Her words about being right with God whisper through me.

Lord, I pray in my own heart, *I don't know if I'm all right before You. I know I've messed up. Please forgive me for the things I've done that have been wrong, for the way I've talked and acted, for the bitterness toward my aunt.*

Even as I pray the words in my heart, my stomach twists.

I'm still angry with Elena, still furious about what she did and how she's treated not just me, but others as well. She betrayed me, and she doesn't seem to care.

But Jesus Himself was betrayed.

He gets it.

And so, I commit my bitterness and my lack of forgiveness to Him, desperately hoping He can help me overcome it so that I can be who He wants me to be.

After several more prayers and long moments of silence, Essie closes in a final word of prayer, a quick benediction.

"The Lord bless you and keep you, the Lord make His face shine upon you and give you peace."

My cheeks are wet when we're done, and I quickly run my sleeve over my face. My throat feels raw from holding back suppressed emotions. But there's a part of me that feels a lightness I can't explain. A fullness in my spirit that feels as though I've drunk of a river and could keep drinking more.

My faith is new.

This God I serve is one that I am only beginning to understand, and somehow, I know I'll never fully understand Him. But in it all, I am ready to follow Him wherever He might lead.

Essie prayed things that I still don't fully get, but that's okay. I want this faith, more than anything else, to define my life. Because those whose faith defines their life have been the ones that have *changed* my life.

We leave the meeting and trail back to the DeFort home. There's silence over our group.

Nika and I exchange a smile. She's brimming with a fullness that I understand deeper in my soul than ever before.

I glance toward Matthias. There's a settledness to him, an assurance. I'm thankful he's in my life. With little thought, I reach for his hand.

He gives me a quick look of surprise, then interlaces his fingers with mine and squeezes. Heat fills my cheeks at my boldness, but I want the connection with him.

I want him to know I care about him.

When we arrive back at the DeFort house, he doesn't let go of my hand until the last possible moment. As I'm about to enter my room, he pulls me in for a quick hug, kisses the top of my head, and says goodnight in a husky voice that sends shivers down my spine.

I slip into my room and ignore Nika's sly smile as I climb into my bed.

We are going into battle. We are fighting tomorrow against an enemy who is stronger than I even understand. But I feel content and ready in a way that I never have.

"Okay, God," I whisper the prayer in a tone so low I can barely hear it myself. "I'm ready."

And with those words, I fall asleep.

TWENTY-SIX

We are up and ready before dawn the next morning. I stand outside the DeForts' home and stare up at the structure that has become a haven for me. Even with the uncertainty we've faced in Eryndale, the DeForts have been a compassionate, loving family.

Although I've known them for less than a week, I feel like part of their family.

Jordyn and Moses are with us, and Mrs. DeFort bustles out and passes sacks of food to each of us. She takes time to fuss over every person she stands in front of.

"Now don't forget to eat and stay well hydrated." She licks her thumb and wipes at a smudge on Matthias's cheek.

His eyes widen, but otherwise he doesn't move, and a small smile etches itself on his face.

She comes in front of me. "Do you have everything you need, then? All the supplies, everything?"

"Yes, ma'am," I say.

"Oh, now come. No formalities. We're family now." She pats my cheek like I'm a little kid, which leaves me wanting to grin, just like Matthias did.

Malachi strolls forward. "All right, everyone ready to head out?"

We nod and give a course of agreements.

Mrs. DeFort, without any further ado, pulls me into a hug.

At first, I don't know how to respond. Then my arms circle around her, and I let her hold me for a moment.

It feels like hugging my mom.

Soft and warm and caring.

Mrs. DeFort and my mother are very different from one another, yet they possess the same maternal care that I didn't know I longed for until I didn't have it.

She moves on and gives a hug to each of my friends. Shane is the stiffest, but she holds on until he relaxes into the embrace and hugs her back. Somehow, I think being with the DeFort family has been a balm to his soul and given him something he never had before. A home.

"Wait. Before we go," Retro says, "I have a little gift for all of you. It's totally rad, and I don't want everyone else to be jelly."

I'm not sure if I'll ever get used to his strange way of talking.

He hoists a small bag into the air. "You're all the lucky winners of . . ." He digs his hand into the bag and pulls out a yo-yo. "Your very own yo-yo!"

He passes yo-yos out to each of my friends, skipping his sister because she "already has one, but doesn't appreciate how great it is."

I'm the last person he comes to, and he half-bows as he presents it to me.

I stare at it, not really wanting something so ridiculous adding weight to my pack. "Um, shouldn't we get going?"

"Yeah, yeah, yeah." He waves his hand as though batting my words away. "We will. But first, here you go." He pushes his hand with the yo-yo closer to me.

"Just take it," Jordyn says. "He won't give up until you do."

Retro wiggles his eyebrows. "Because I'm tenacious."

"No," Malachi says. "It's because you're *annoying*."

Moses puts a hand over his heart. "Ouch. Mom, can you believe he said that? To your *favorite* child?"

Mrs. DeFort shakes her head and goes back to fussing over Jordyn.

Moses leans forward conspiratorially. "Malachi's just jealous of my charm and many talents."

I can't help but smile, and I take the yo-yo from him. He takes another from his pocket and throws it to the ground, letting it hang there for a moment.

"Come on, guys. Everyone try," he encourages.

A few of my friends do as he asks, then Malachi is shooing his brother out of the way and leading us through the darkened paths of Eryndale.

Buildings come to life around us. Lights turning on in homes, lanterns flickering in front of houses, walkway lights dimming as the sun comes up and shines its brightness over everything.

I'll miss this place, even though there's been mixed emotions while I've been here.

We head to the training facility where we'll meet up with the rest of the Wild Dogs and the other scouting units who will leave at the same time as us.

When we arrive, Gabe is there, looking uncomfortable in his Skinter Suit and wearing a pack that is so small it can in no way carry everything he needs.

Azarias stands nearby, frowning as he stares at the man who has to travel with us.

Lorenzo and Thaddeus are suiting up and checking the comm units. Although they're older scouts and members of the S.O.C., they'll both be coming as well.

Thaddeus will go to a certain point and set up a staging site. It will be several miles away from Talionis, but will provide all scouting units entering the covert ops zone with intel, supplies, and reinforcements as needed.

Lorenzo's going with Thaddeus to establish the staging site, but then he'll be reconnecting with us. Which I guess is okay. We've had mixed interactions with the scout leader, and I'm still not sure where we stand with him. Although he has allowed us to be involved in the underground, he's clearly the one who is insisting information be kept from us.

Once we're out of Eryndale and away from the potential spies and leaks within the refuge city, maybe he'll be more open with intel.

"You have to wear it like this," Lorenzo mutters to Gabe as he adjusts the extra fabric of the Skinter Suit. "Stop fidgeting. If you don't have it on exactly right, you're not going to catch the velocity you need, and we don't have time to come back and help you start off again."

Gabe's mouth pinches into a line, but he gives a curt nod.

Somehow, I don't think he's used to doing anything he's not perfect at, so this should be interesting.

Retro greets Glacier, Karyss, and Isaac in his usual rowdy manner. Malachi shushes him.

"Dude. There's no one in this area that's still asleep," Retro says.

"Yeah, and that's because you with your loud mouth have been talking since 5 a.m.," Malachi shoots back. "There's no way the C.A.E.'s going to be happy if we cause a ruckus before we head out."

"The heroes of Eryndale deserve an elaborate send-off," Retro smirks. "I'm just trying to help everyone understand that."

Jordyn elbows her brother in the side. "You're being ridiculous. Mom's going to be so upset if she finds out you woke up half of Eryndale."

Retro's eyes widen, and for the first time, I see a hint of fear. Not at the prospect of what we're facing before us or of the battle with Talionis, but with the possibility that his mother will be upset with him.

A small chuckle escapes.

Jordyn heads over to Lorenzo and Thaddeus with the other navigators to get the coordinates for our team's route. Since navigation is so tied to cartography, it's a role I think I'd be able to fill if I'd had time to learn. But it's also tied to the technology in the Skinter Suits and I know it would take me a while to pick that up. Although young, Jordyn is confident in her abilities and, according to Malachi, one of the best navigators in Eryndale.

Within a few minutes, she is back and our coordinates are programed into our helmets. The other scouting teams shake hands with us, and we prepare to head out.

We will head directly east, then south.

Other teams will go in a different direction, all of us preparing to settle into the slots we were given in order to fight against Talionis.

"Avoid entering towns as much as possible," Lorenzo says. "Scouts and members of the E.U.N. have sighted soldiers in nearly every town we'll be passing, and we don't want them to have any idea of our resources, tech, or abilities to fight against them. The greater surprise we can bring in our first attacks, the better."

"Understood, sir," different scout leaders say as they nod in agreement.

"All right, we know we have to make good time," Azarias says. "Go swift, go fast, be safe."

The other scout teams sound off. One group mounts mechanical horses and heads out of the city. The whir of the horses rings in my ears, and I watch, fascinated as they move in rhythm like they're real animals. Each joint shifts as though muscles pulse within the frame.

A truly incredible piece of equipment.

Ari stares after them, and I can see her mind spinning as she tries to figure out how she could get her hands on one. She's been asking to work with them since she first saw one the other day, but we haven't had time.

Our own training has been too intense, and there wasn't a need for us to work with them since we're using the Skinter Suits and Blades to travel. So, Ari has trained with the Skinter Suits with the rest of us, bugging Brandi with information requests time and time again.

Another scouting team climbs to a high level so they can take off in their Skinter Suits to head southwest.

My team makes our way toward the southeast platform we'll be taking out of the city.

"Bria!" Eli's voice catches my attention, and I turn.

My heart seizes in my chest. I'm leaving, and the thought of possibly never seeing him again steals through me. At least I have one more opportunity to see my brothers.

I break from the team and jog over to where he and Zeke stand with Mrs. DeFort and Levi. She'll be caring for the boys while we're away, but I wasn't expecting her to wake them and bring them here after sending us off this morning.

Levi scampers off to where Azarias and Kemena are talking

and practically leaps into Kemena's arms. Kemena and Azarias will be traveling with our team, and Levi has been as upset about their departure as the twins have been about me leaving.

I crouch to the ground, and my brothers give me bear hugs.

"You two be good, okay?" I say.

They lean back to look at me. Eli grins, and Zeke makes a face at me. I ruffle both of their hair and pull them in for another hug. They squirm a bit, but their little arms circle around me and squeeze me back tightly.

Their mouths pull down, and tears form in their eyes.

They may not have been taken by Talionis or experienced the horrors Storm has, but I've learned that loss comes in different forms. And no matter how it comes, it's painful. My brothers lost me for months, didn't know if they'd ever see me again, and they've been separated from my parents for a long time as well.

These two kids have experienced difficulty in their young lives, and I resolve to fight as hard as I can to keep them from experiencing more difficulty in the months and years to come.

"Bria, let us go," Zeke says.

"Yeah," Eli echoes, shoving his hands against my side.

I hold them tighter for a moment, shake them a bit, then let go and step back with a grin.

"I'll miss you guys." As I say the words, a thickness forms in my throat. I push aside the desire to cry and breathe in deeply. "Listen to Mrs. DeFort, and try not to get into too much trouble, okay?"

They nod soberly.

I look at Mrs. DeFort. "Thanks for taking care of them."

"Of course, dear. That's just how we are," she blusters, but the sun catches the sheen of unshed tears in her eyes.

The team is several yards away from me now.

"I'd better go." I point with my thumb in their direction.

Mrs. DeFort nods. "Yes, you must. God be with you. Tell my husband to be careful."

I suspect she's already communicated that message to Kassre in whatever way she can, but I agree.

I give the boys each a quick hug, then jog to catch up to the rest of my team.

Nika gives me a questioning look when I return, and I smile at her. Hopefully *I'm okay* is the look I relay to her, but in reality, I'm not sure if I am.

The peace I felt last night, the calm settledness as Essie prayed, is nowhere around me now.

I wish I could see the older woman one more time, ask her to instill some of her wisdom and staid nature inside of me, but I can't.

It's time for us to leave.

Conversations murmur around me as the final preparations to leave come together. Brandi bustles around like a mother hen, ensuring everyone is secure and ready to go.

"All right, time to head out," Azarias says, commanding everyone's attention.

Anticipation whirs through me. It's time to leave. Time to act. And right now, I *need* action. There are only ten days left on Ark's timeline. Thinking and planning and preparing—they're all important, and I know that. But my brain is too congested with emotions and information to continue in those activities. I'm ready to travel, to fight.

Especially after the emotions of leaving my baby brothers in Eryndale.

Thankfully, I haven't seen my aunt again. I'm not ready to face the onslaught of anger and resentment that come from being in her presence.

"We'll travel as a group for several miles until we hit Sphere Two, then we'll split up: Wild Dogs will go with me and continue southwest before turning east. Alpha Team will go with Thaddeus and Lorenzo southeast. Three other teams left late last night, and we have several teams in the field. We'll keep in contact and give regular reports on how things are going. There will be no engagement with the enemy until all teams are in place." Azarias pauses, and the early morning sun glows from behind him. "There is always one exception. If a life is in danger —whether from Talionis soldiers or Raiders—we will fight. No life is unimportant. Now"—he shoulders his pack—"let's do what we were made to do."

There are some hoots and shouts of agreement from the

crowd and an overall air of excitement. Then, with one voice, the scouts say together, "Do justly, love mercy, walk humbly."

The words resonate through me and fill me with energy and enthusiasm. I am caught up in the sudden realization that I'm a part of something much bigger than myself. A thrill spirals through me, pushing aside my fears and anxiety.

As everyone lets out a loud "Whoo!" I shout with them.

Something in me releases, and when the scouts throw their shields down over their faces and race toward the jump-off point, I do the same. The sound of blades whirring fills the air like a transport engine revving up. Then I leap from the platform, and I'm soaring with the others.

"*Private comm with Nika,*" Brandi's recorded voice sounds in my helmet.

"This is so incredible," my friend says, and I can hear the laughter and joy in her voice.

"Race you to the first checkpoint," I say, tucking my arms against my side to gain speed.

"You really want to lose to me *again*? Okay, girl. You're on."

I don't bother looking through the crowd to find her. It would just waste time. Instead, I let myself soar, wind whipping around me, the warmth of the sun spreading across my face. And I forget the pressures of everything else.

As the ground comes closer, I spread my arms, and the wind catches me. I glide to the ground, letting my legs drop, then take off as soon as my feet hit. I thrust my legs back and forth, letting the momentum from the jump propel me forward as I continue to gain speed by skating. The navigation system in the helmet registers the path I need to take through the trees, and I follow it with ease.

It took a little getting used to, and the first tree I collided with wasn't thrilling, but it also wasn't as painful as it could have been. The more I practiced with the Skinter Suits and Blades, the better I became, even though I only had two days to learn. And now, I'm at the front of the group with a handful of others, one of them being Azarias—which I can tell from the blue streak on his Skinter Suit.

We race through the trees for over an hour, my blades

bumping over the undergrowth without any issue. Occasionally, when we go down a hill, I have enough speed to glide above the earth for a stretch. Those are my favorite moments. My mind springs back to a time weeks ago when I was in the Ruins, watching a bird soar high in the air, wishing I could fly.

And now I am.

Incredible.

"All-comm announcement from Scout Leader."

"First checkpoint in half a mile," Azarias says over the comms. "Prepare to stop."

I'm reluctant to stop, afraid the lack of distraction will allow everything to slam into my heart and mind again. But the stop is necessary. It's where our two groups will split. Plus, Jordyn has to program the next checkpoint into our helmets and we need to open the solar panels to keep our suits fully charged.

Lifting my arms, I stop the skating motion and allow myself to glide forward. The half mile passes in a few minutes, and I lean back on the heels of my blades and come to a stop.

"Send private comm to Nika," I say.

"Private comm sending," Brandi's recorded voice comes over my ears.

"Looks like I win," I say.

Nika skates over and slides up her shield. "We got here at like the same time."

I push up my shield and grin at her. "That's something someone says when they *lost.*"

She rolls her eyes and stops next to me. "Please. I was just saying that to make you feel better about yourself."

We both laugh. For the next few minutes, it's just us and a handful of scouts. Then the others begin arriving. All of our team is here before Alpha Team, which is thanks to Jordyn's skill in programing the best path for us to take.

"Oh, there's Ari." Nika nods at a person careening toward the checkpoint without an ounce of accuracy. "For a girl who loves tech and can use just about anything that is tech related, she really hasn't gotten the hang of these suits."

"Probably because they require some athleticism," Bryson mutters, approaching us.

There's a bing in my ear, then Ari's voice comes over everyone's comms: "*Hey, guys. Can you help me stop?*"

"Not again," Bryson and Shane grumble.

The two guys stand shoulder to shoulder, arms extended. Ari slams into them, and the three roll backward for several feet, until they hit a tree. They end up in a heap on the ground.

Ari rolls off the pile and pulls her helmet off as Nika and I skate over to them. She's smiling. "That was better than last time, don't you think?"

Bryson and Shane share a commiserating look and get to their feet. Shane reaches down to help Ari up, and they both roll slightly as she stands.

"You two have definitely gotten the hang of these suits," Kemena says to me and Nika, coming to a stop near our small gathering. "You shot off almost as fast as Azarias." She lowers her voice. "Next time, work together to beat *him*. Would do the man some good to see he's not the best at everything."

"What is with you and Azarias?" Nika asks as she settles herself onto a fallen log.

"Girl, nothing," Kemena says. "He's just irritating."

"I haven't seen him be *that* irritating." Nika purses her lips and taps a finger against them. "You know, you're acting just like Bria did with Matthias."

"Talking about me again?" Matthias asks as he skates over. He stops next to me, probably a little closer than he needs to be, but I don't mind.

Kemena busies herself with her pack, and I wonder if Nika might be right. Maybe something *is* going on between Kemena and Azarias.

Everyone sets out the solar chargers and takes a break to eat something from their pack. We'll only be stopping for thirty minutes. Enough time to give a decent charge to everyone's suits, but not lose too much daylight. Jordyn and the Alpha Team navigator are busy entering everyone's coordinates for the next leg of the journey.

I scan the sky, searching for any signs of transports. Memories of them coming upon us as we traveled to Eryndale steal over me. Hiding, praying they would pass. Facing Laban.

Right now, the skies are mercifully clear. According to Thaddeus's reports, there haven't been many transports in this vicinity. Which is good.

We have two days' journey until we hit the river and meet up with Catori. I glance around at the group that will be traveling on the boat and almost cringe. It's going to be a tight fit.

There are six of us, plus the six Wild Dogs, Kemena, Azarias, and Gabe.

Seems like *way* too many people.

But my friends and I are excited to see Catori and Davey again, and Moses and Jordyn can't stop talking about getting to spend time with their sister-in-law. Although it will be tight, hopefully it will be a good time.

"All right, everyone," Lorenzo says from on top of a large boulder, breaking into my thoughts. "Finish up your snacks, close up your solar chargers, and get your gear together. We're heading out. Wild Dogs, be safe, and God be with you."

He and Azarias clasp each other's forearms.

My heartbeat kicks up in my throat. We're one step closer to Talionis, and all I can hear in my mind is *ten days left*.

TWENTY-SEVEN

We travel hard for the rest of the day before making camp for the night. By the time we're settling around the fire and breaking out the food Cook sent for us, my entire body is stiff. I didn't realize the Skinter Suits and Blades required so many muscles to work. But it could also be from the sheer length of the day.

Gabe groans as he pulls off his blades and slumps against a tree. When he pulls off his helmet, his normal swooshy hair is flat, adding to his exhausted appearance. He shifts so his back is to the rest of us and lies down.

It's strange that the C.A.E. would send him along, but I'm glad we don't have to deal with Reginald anymore, at least.

Beef, carrots, and potatoes reheat over the flames of the fire, and two scouts pass out rolls. The aroma of the food cooking wafts through the air, and my stomach rumbles. I ease myself onto a log and release a sigh.

We've gotten as far as we were supposed to today, but there were scars from Talionis everywhere we traveled. We never went close to an occupied village, but there were signs of transports landing in fields, leaving burn marks. At one point, Azarias took us through a village soldiers from Talionis destroyed. There was silence on every comm unit as we went.

I'm not entirely sure why Azarias brought us there. Maybe so the Wild Dogs would see that the enemy we are facing is fierce. Evil.

Whatever his reason, the sight brought back more memories than I care to think about.

Nika flops down on the log next to me. "I'm beat. And hungry. I hope that food is ready soon."

"Same."

She nudges me in the side, then tilts her head to where Kemena and Azarias stand at a slight distance from the camp and appear to be arguing.

"I don't get the two of them," Nika says. "Kemena isn't rattled by much of anything, but she gets annoyed with Azarias *all the time*."

I watch them for a moment. "Maybe it's the stress of everything going on?"

She sighs. "I don't know. Whenever I've asked her about it, she doesn't say much. I questioned whether I should trust Azarias at first. But then she got all upset at me for even *suggesting* that. Said he was a good guy. Just stubborn."

"Dinner!" Retro bellows from his place tending the food by the fire. "And it smells *delightful*, if I do say so myself."

"No one needs your commentary, dude." Isaac chucks a twig at him. "Just serve it up."

"Is that any way to treat the guy making your dinner?" Retro plants his hands on his hips.

Glacier gets to her feet and goes to the pan of food. "You heated it up. Cook made it."

Retro sticks his tongue out at her, but doesn't respond.

A few more lighthearted jabs are thrown his way as the group dishes up the food. When it's my turn to be served, Retro adds food to my plate, but keeps it just out of my reach.

"Um, can I have that?" My stomach growls again, and I'm too tired and hungry to be embarrassed, even though Matthias is standing right behind me.

"First," Retro says, "how about you show me a trick with your new yo-yo?"

"How about you give me my plate before I hurt you?" I say in an overly sweet voice.

Nika snorts from beside me. "I wouldn't push it with her. Bria's dangerous enough when she's *not* hungry."

"Aw, come on," Retro whines. "Just one trick. It'll be fun. I promise."

I hold my hand out for my plate. "Food, Moses. Now."

He frowns at my use of his real name.

"Bria, I'll hold him while you punch if you want the backup," Isaac calls over, almost coaxing a smile from me.

"Yeah, and I've always got your back," Matthias says.

"Hey, no fair!" Retro says. But he passes over my plate.

I smile as I head back to my seat.

"Please tell me you would have actually followed through and hit him or something?" Glacier asks.

"She so would have," Nika responds for me.

"I would have enjoyed *that* show," Glacier says. "Retro needs to be knocked down a peg or two."

Retro dishes up his plate last and goes to sit down. "I'm absolutely delightful, and my personality is sparkling. Just ask my mommy." He grins the most absurd grin I've ever witnessed, and I almost spew the water in my mouth.

Laughter and groans echo around the circle. "Someone send a comm to Jordyn and Malachi," Isaac says. "We need proof that even their mom gets annoyed with him."

Malachi, Jordyn, and Shane are scouting out the area to confirm it's safe, and I can just imagine what Jordyn would say about her brother's antics.

"Oh, she does," Azarias says, as he and Kemena enter the circle. "I've asked her personally." He's grinning now, and whatever conversation he and Kemena were having that seemed unpleasant appears to have been resolved or forgotten.

"She's just scared of you," Retro mumbles.

More laughter cascades through the camp. I can't imagine Mrs. DeFort being afraid of anyone.

Dark thoughts invade my mind, and the peace and lightness of the moment seeps away. We're about to go to war with Talionis.

How many of these new friends am I going to lose in the process?

We rise early the next morning, and, after a quick breakfast, we're suiting up and preparing to head out. Jordyn sends an all-team comm, and the coordinates for our travel program into my helmet.

Talionis tech is another level, but Eryndale has some incredible tech of its own.

Something Ari is more than happy to discuss. Or attempt to improve.

She currently has her left blade in front of her, and she appears to be preparing to disassemble it in some way.

"Ari, no," Bryson says. "We have to go."

"But I think—"

"*No.*" Bryson emphasizes the word, and Shane and Nika say it at the same time.

I snort and turn away to make sure all my gear is stowed in my pack before securing it on my back. I want to reach for a map and look over the full route, but that's not my responsibility this time around.

As much as I haven't wanted to be the one in charge in the days since we escaped Talionis, I find I don't know what to do now that I'm *not* the one leading everyone. Azarias is trustworthy, and Jordyn is an excellent navigator, I know that. But I still want to assess the route, review potential threats, and ensure we are finding the way forward that will keep everyone safe.

Which is a little ridiculous, since our whole goal is to go *back* to Talionis and start fighting.

Not realistic to keep everyone safe while that's happening.

Still, my mind races with ways to protect this team.

"We should be able to make some good time today," Azarias addresses everyone before we skate out. "We'll be hitting some more open plains, which will allow the blades to gain decent speed." He turns to where my friends and I have gathered.

We like the Wild Dogs, but the six of us seem to automatically find each other whenever we can. I'm comforted by their presence. More than I would have ever expected. Even Shane and

I have resolved most of our differences after everything we faced together.

"You all have gotten better with the suits and blades," Azarias says. "I'm impressed. When we hit the plains, just push forward. The blades will gain significant momentum, and as long as you practice the proper technique we taught you, you'll be fine."

"Uh, how fast will they go?" Ari asks, her voice flooded with uncertainty.

"Yeah," Gabe chimes in. "Are we sure going at such speeds is the best option?" The dark circles under his eyes and his stooped shoulders leave me wondering if he got any sleep at all last night.

Azarias turns to Karyss and Isaac. "When we near the plains, we'll stop. Karyss, you tether with Ari, and Isaac, you tether with Gabe. Shouldn't slow you down too much."

They both agree, although Isaac doesn't look thrilled at the prospect.

I've never tethered with anyone, but from our training with the Skinter Suits, we learned that two suits can be tethered together to help someone when they're injured. Or, in this case, to keep Ari and Gabe from being left behind or flailing recklessly off a cliff because they can't control their blades.

Azarias slides down his shield. "Let's go!"

With that, he turns and skates away, and the rest of us follow him.

I push myself forward, weaving around some rubble. My muscles burn slightly, but I barely notice. All I can think about is the plain we're going to be heading through.

Is it the same plain where we battled Broche and Laban?

The same place Matthias almost died?

The last place I saw Storm alive? Where she screamed my name?

Before I can let my mind race too far in that direction, I set up a group comm with Nika and Matthias.

"How you guys doing?" Matthias asks once they're both connected.

"Fine," I say.

"Anyone else concerned about the plains Azarias said we're traveling through?" Nika asks.

"Yeah," I say.

I push my blades harder, gaining speed as I go down a hill and weave around trees and debris in my path.

"You think it's where we were before?" Matthias asks.

I press my lips together and don't respond.

"That's what I'm afraid of," Nika says.

"I doubt they have soldiers watching the area," Matthias says. "Tactically, they don't have the resources to leave units behind just for surveillance. Plus, our group is much bigger. Even if they saw us traveling, I doubt they'd know it was us."

His optimism is endearing. Even though I disagree with him.

If I were them and had faced my enemy in a specific territory less than a week ago, I would watch that space. Although he has a point about them not necessarily having the resources needed.

"You guys having a party without me?" Kemena's voice chirps into my helmet.

"You know it," Nika says, and I can hear the smile in her voice.

Our conversation shifts to what's coming as we near Talionis.

"I know we're looking at sabotage and covert operations," I say. "But I think we should also send in an insertion group to gain intel." And save Storm and Cai, but I keep that to myself.

"Lorenzo has a pretty specific plan about what he wants to do," Kemena hedges.

"Right." I duck under a low-hanging branch that my shield alerts me to. "But getting that intel would be beneficial."

"Sure," Kemena says. "But Lorenzo likes things done in a particular way. Especially on missions. I'd wait to hear his plans before you get too set on certain ideas."

Her warning rubs me wrong, and I go silent as the conversation shifts to other things. I want to disconnect, but I know doing so will just alert my friends to my irritation.

If I were Lorenzo, I would have a specific plan of attack. I get that.

But, despite the fact that we've told him a lot about Talionis, he's never been there. Never experienced the horrors of that city. And he doesn't understand how Demetrius Ark works. The lengths the man will go to for revenge.

I make a mental note to check in with Ari about how her and Isaac's decryption of Ark's files is going. It's been so busy lately that I haven't talked to her about it. She would say something if there was anything worth reporting, but I'd still like to know if she has any hope of understanding the files.

What could Ark have had that was so top secret he not only kept a physical version locked in his safe, but he also encoded them?

Whatever it is, I intend to find out.

TWENTY-EIGHT

Once we get to the plains, Azarias is right: our blades race over them at a speed that almost feels reckless, yet exhilarating.

I'm thankful this set of plains is not the same as the one where we battled Laban and Broche. I'm not sure I could handle that right now.

Ari does a comm with her brother, Shane, me, Matthias, and Nika, and the whole time we hear her half-panicking, half-squealing with delight as her tethered suit flies over the territory at breakneck speed behind Karyss. It's humorous but a little distracting, so I turn the volume down as low as I can, smiling at my friends' comments as they tell Ari to calm down.

The fifteen of us traveling together race over the plains like a swarm of bees.

It's one of the neatest experiences I've ever had, but it's hard to fully enjoy it. Maybe I'd be able to if I wasn't heading back into danger, wondering where my parents are, worrying about Storm, and fearing that Cai was only kept alive for that short video before Ark decided he was no longer of use. Not even worth keeping alive for the nine days left before his threat is carried out.

I shove the thoughts away as Azarias sends out an all-comm alert to signal that we're taking a break.

We come to a grove of trees with a nice patch of grass, and we settle in to give our blades time to recharge.

Azarias takes a sip from his canteen, then swipes his hand over his mouth. "Jordyn, how are things looking?"

She looks up from where she's programing our next set of directions into the system. "We're making great time. We should be to the river in the next two or three hours, depending on how fast we're able to travel."

"Good." Azarias shifts to check the solar panel charging his suit and blades.

"How exactly are we all going to fit on Catori's boat?" Bryson asks.

Azarias grins. "As much fun as it might be to cram aboard *The Fearless Lady*, I somehow doubt Catori, Davey, and Quwani would be okay with it."

I wonder for a moment who Quwani is, but don't ask as Azarias continues explaining.

"We'll be dividing the group into three different units to travel down the river. Catori has contacted two other captains who are going to join us for the travel. We'll all end up in the same place eventually, but I want to scatter our movements so that in case anyone's tracking the captains and their boats, they won't notice that they're all traveling together."

Uncertainty clogs my thoughts. This whole time, I assumed I would travel on *The Fearless Lady*. It never occurred to me that I might *not* be.

"When will we all meet up, then?" Shane asks. "Aren't we supposed to start attacking Talionis as soon as possible?"

Azarias pauses reloading his pack. "Speed is far less important than accuracy. We're going to make sure everything—and everyone—is in place before we begin our first movements. We also want to be careful not to alert the soldiers to any of your presence while on the river."

I clench my teeth until my jaw hurts. We need accuracy *and* speed. Cai and Storm only have nine days left. We can't waste a single second.

"You better be putting me with my sister-in-law," Retro

chimes in. "I'm sure she misses me." He tosses his yo-yo to the ground as though to emphasize his words.

Jordyn rolls her eyes. "Please. You know Catori misses me more. Plus, mom insisted I travel with her."

Azarias shrugs on his pack and ignores the siblings. "I've sent ahead some details to all of the captains on what we need to do. Each group will be briefed once they're aboard their ship." He glances at his watch. "But right now, we need to move. Everyone suit up."

Within a few minutes, we've all stored our solar charging panels, packed up any leftover snacks, and have our blades back on. I'm tempted to beg Azarias to let me sail with Catori, but I keep the thought to myself.

Gabe and Ari tether with Isaac and Karyss again. Both of them seem much happier traveling with assistance, but I don't think Isaac and Karyss are enjoying it as much. When someone is tethered to you, you can't fly, which is the best part, in my opinion. Plus, those you're tethered to always have an open comm link so that communication is instant, and I overheard Isaac complaining to Glacier about Gabe freaking out the whole time they were traveling over the plains.

Gabe acts like he's in control and has everything together, but clearly some things are outside of his expertise.

We take off, and I push myself to be at the front of the group, alert to any signs of danger as we exit the plains and enter the forest. Who knows where an enemy might be lurking in the trees and shadows blurring past us?

My heartbeat kicks up as my blades cut over the earth. I thrust my legs back and forth as fast as possible to gain additional momentum.

How close are the Talionis soldiers to us now?

What if Ark pulls the timeline up?

What if he hurt Storm and Cai?

Memories of the evening before we left with Essie and the others praying sweep over me as though God is gently nudging me to give it to Him. To rest in Him, trust Him.

That's what Cai would tell me to do. What Nika or Kemena would say.

Matthias would probably try to make me laugh, but his faith runs so deep. He wouldn't preach at me to do something, but his life *shows* me. His faith impacts every area.

I wish mine did too.

My faith is growing, but I still want to rely on my own understanding far more than I want to trust God.

God, I give my fears to You as much as I can, but I'm afraid. The prayer whispers from my heart.

We skate up a hill. At the top, I launch myself off, throwing my arms out to catch the wind along with others doing the same.

It's one of the first times we've been able to glide. I let the wind blowing past me wash off some of my fear and anxiety.

I can do this.

I can fight.

Even with all my questions.

TWO AND A HALF HOURS LATER, WE ARE COMING TO A STOP NEAR THE river.

The distant sound of rushing water breaks through my helmet. My blood pumps harder, partly from the exercise, but also from knowing that I'm about to be on the river again.

Mixed emotions wash over me.

Will Nalani be with Catori, or has she stationed herself somewhere else, away from the war that's coming?

She's not a soldier, not in the way I've become, or Nika, Matthias, Shane, or Bryson. Even Ari is more willing to invest herself in this war than Nalani ever was.

But Nalani's words to me after I saved her life, while she was recovering, still echo in my ear. "I've asked myself repeatedly why I left Talionis to take on this risk with all of you," she said. "But after everything I've witnessed, all you've done for me and the others, I would follow you. Even into battle."

The memory of her words still leaves me a bit uncomfortable. But they also have me wondering what decision she made once she fully recovered from nearly drowning.

Whether I see travel again on *The Fearless Lady* or not, I'm eager to see Catori and Davey.

But it won't be the same without Nate, Davey's brother.

We take off our blades and our suits and then make the quarter-mile trek to the river.

Only one boat is anchored just offshore, and it's not *The Fearless Lady*.

I stop short.

"This is the first boat going out," Azarias says. "We'll divide into three groups." He nods to the boat. "This is the smallest vessel, so four will go on this one. The rest will be divided between the other boats."

"I call Catori's boat!" Retro yells.

"Wait, I'm supposed to be with Catori too, right?" Jordyn asks. She almost sounds desperate.

"Right," Azarias says. "And so is Moses. The two of you, along with Bria, Ari, and I, will sail with Catori."

My heart lurches when Azarias says my name, and excitement and dread braid their discordant threads through me. I didn't stop to think that I might not be with my friends.

It no longer matters if I'm on *The Fearless Lady* or not. I just want to be with Matthias. Not separated as we travel back into the place of our nightmares.

We're entering a war zone, and I want every moment with him that I can get. To know I can talk to him, share my fears.

Azarias looks at Malachi. "Is that okay with you?"

Malachi inclines his head. "Whatever you need, man. As much as I'd like to see my sister-in-law, I understand why you should be the one to travel with her."

"I'd like to stay with Ari," Shane interjects before I get the chance to ask if there's a way I could stay with Matthias.

Azarias is already shaking his head no before Shane finishes. "You'll be traveling with Malachi, Karyss, Bryson, and Gabe."

"But—"

"She'll be fine," Azarias says. "We need your expertise with Malachi's group, especially since Moses and Jordyn won't be with him." He takes in the group. "The boats have already been assigned by Lorenzo. There won't be any transfers or adjustments."

Shane clamps his mouth shut, and his nostrils flare, but he doesn't argue.

Azarias takes his silence as agreement and lists out the last group: Isaac, Glacier, Nika, Kemena, and Matthias.

An unsteady rhythm beats in my chest, and I understand Shane's frustration. I want to be with Catori and Davey again, but I'd trade the opportunity if it meant I could be with Matthias, and Nika.

But that isn't an option.

"One more thing," Azarias says. "Lorenzo sent word that there's to be no use of the suit's comm units during river travel."

The words ring through my ears like they were just shouted at me by Laban. Not only will I not be able to be with Matthias and Nika, I won't even be able to communicate with them.

Malachi's group is slotted for the first ship. He tells his brother and sister to give his love to Catori, and to not annoy her too much. The second instruction is clearly for Retro.

I pull my focus away from them to watch as Shane and Bryson say goodbye to Ari. Shane waits while Bryson hugs his sister and tells her to be safe. The siblings exchange something —tech most likely—then Ari gives her brother another hug before turning to Shane.

"I'll be okay," she says.

Shane's eyes close as though he's in pain. "I can't protect you if I'm not with you."

"Bria's got my back," Ari says, cupping his cheek with her hand. She drops her tone so I can barely catch what she's saying, even though I'm only a few feet away. "Plus, we'll still be able to communicate."

She winks, and Shane gives a half-hearted smile. I wonder how she plans to communicate, but I'm not going to risk asking.

Ari stands on her tiptoes and presses a kiss to Shane's lips. He puts his arms around her and kisses her back. My cheeks warm, and I look away, suddenly aware that I was openly intruding on a private moment.

I say my goodbyes to the first group, and then they're boarding the boat and sailing away.

Ari draws in a shuddering breath, but doesn't shed a tear. She and Isaac exchange notes on Ark's encrypted files since they'll both continue trying to hack into them while traveling down river.

The rest of us have a quick bite to eat while we wait for the next boat.

Matthias grabs jerky, chips, and some dried fruit before winding his way through the group to where I'm sitting on a fallen log.

"Hungry?" He sits next to me, precariously balancing his plate of food on the tree.

I shake my head. "Not really."

Without giving myself time to think, I rest my head on his shoulder. He puts his arm around me and scoots closer.

We sit in silence for a moment, his thumb caressing my shoulder.

"Shane beat me earlier," he says. "I was going to ask to come with you. But Azarias doesn't seem to be taking requests." The words are supposed to be funny, but they fall flat.

I sit up, and his arm falls away. I miss the warmth of his touch but need to look into his eyes. "It won't be long. Just two days." I'm not sure if I'm saying the words for Matthias or myself.

"Right." His eyes flick to my lips, and I suddenly wonder if he's going to kiss me.

My heartbeat kicks up.

"Our boat's pulling in," Nika says, coming to a stop in front of us.

I stand abruptly, knocking Matthias's plate of food onto the ground. "Oh. Sorry. Um." I swallow.

Nika's eyes light up. "Am I interrupting something?"

"No!" I say, too sharply. "I mean, no. We were just saying goodbye."

Her eyebrow quirks, but she sobers quickly. "See you in two days."

I give my friend a hug. Why does it have to be like this?

Traveling back toward Talionis is dangerous, but it won't be as crazy as once the covert ops begin. And for the first time, I realize I was banking on having those days with my friends. Those last moments to talk and laugh.

Nika and I pull away from each other, and I catch a mist in her eyes before she blinks it away.

"Be safe, okay?" She nudges me with her shoulder. "I'll see you soon."

Kemena comes over, and I say goodbye to her as well. Then the sisters join Isaac and Glacier as they prepare to board the boat.

Matthias is still standing next to me. "Think they'll notice if I *accidentally* forget that's my group?"

I bite my lip, but don't respond or look at him. I just stare at the four getting ready to board the rowboat.

Matthias captures my chin in his strong hand and gently turns my gaze to meet his. "Bria, whatever happens—"

"Matthias!" Isaac calls. "We gotta go, man!"

His face compresses in frustration, but he nods to Isaac. "Be right there."

He pulls me into a hug that's fierce and tender, and I hug him back. Listen to his steady heartbeat against my ear.

"Be careful," I say.

"Always." He gives me another squeeze before we step away from each other.

I take his hand. "I'll walk you over."

The grin he gives leaves my knees feeling rubbery. He picks up his pack with his other hand, and the two of us walk to the bank of the river.

He tosses his pack into the rowboat. Then he leans forward and presses a kiss to my forehead. "Bye, Bria."

With that, he climbs into the rowboat.

I stare after them, my heart aching as I watch the guy I care about and my best friend sail away without me. I squeeze my fingers around the seaglass pendant of my necklace. Matthias and Nika both wave until the boat rounds a bend in the river and I can't see them anymore.

TWENTY-NINE

The five of us who remain settle in to wait for *The Fearless Lady*. Azarias steps away to talk into his comm to someone he doesn't identify to us. The comms work for long distances, and it's frustrating Lorenzo has decided my friends and I can't communicate through them.

I pull myself away from the bank of the river and turn to see what Ari's up to, desperate for a distraction.

Which is apparently exactly what Ari needed as well. At least, that's my best guess.

She has the yo-yo Retro gave her in pieces, and she's busy disassembling a piece of tech I don't recognize.

"What?" Retro springs to his feet and races to her. He drops to his knees in front of her. "How could you—" He reaches for one of the yo-yo halves.

Ari swats his hand away. "Don't touch that. I'm working on something."

"Working on—" He grips his head with both hands. "You *destroyed* it. A precious yo-yo. Gone too soon."

"Moses, chill." Jordyn shakes her head. "You gave it to her. She can do whatever she wants with it. It's just a toy."

Moses swivels to look at his sister. "A *toy?* Jor. Seriously?" He grabs his chest over his heart. "Do you know me? Yo-yos are—"

"I'm making it better," Ari interjects.

Moses's eyes go so wide I can see the whites surrounding his brown irises, and his mouth gapes open. "I can't even find words."

"Those were words, bro," Jordyn says.

She and I exchange a smirk, which makes me miss Nika. She would get a kick out of this.

And Matthias would probably sympathize with Retro and encourage his ridiculous display.

Too many emotions fill me, so I turn away and toss a rock into the river, scanning the bend for signs of *The Fearless Lady*.

"He's crazy about his yo-yos," Jordyn says at my side. She picks up a rock and makes it skip over the smooth portion of the river before us.

"Yeah, I noticed." I skip a rock. "Why? I mean, they're kind of neat, but it's just an old toy."

Jordyn is quiet for so long that I turn to see if she's even still there.

She's staring at a rock in her hand, turning it over. Lost in another world. I shift, wondering if I should leave.

The rocks beneath my feet crunch, and she looks up. "Micah. He's the reason Moses loves yo-yos, and all the other old stuff he can dig up." She tosses the rock into the river.

When she looks back at me, it feels like I'm looking at someone far older than her sixteen years. Someone who's seen hurt.

I should probably say something. Tell her she doesn't have to explain it to me, since it's clearly painful for her to remember.

"Whenever Micah and Catori would come visit us, Micah would bring something he found in his travels for Moses and me. Usually old toys, books. That kind of thing." She stares back out over the water. "The last time he came, he brought Retro a yo-yo."

The pain in her words steals over me.

Before I can find a way that might express my sorrow for her without sounding frail and meaningless, a boat rounds the bend.

The Fearless Lady.

The sorrow melts from Jordyn's face, transforming into a grin so wide that I can imagine her as a little kid.

"They're here!" she calls over her shoulder.

Retro and Ari join us at the edge of the river as the boat closes the distance to us.

Time to reunite with Catori and Davey, and meet Quwani.

And maybe to find out more about what actually happened to Micah.

The way Jordyn and Moses clamber up the ladder to get onboard *The Fearless Lady* reminds me of how Eli and Zeke race downstairs to find out what presents they got for their birthday. It's sort of adorable, but also strange. I know Catori and Davey, but I don't know them in the same way as they do.

I feel almost like an imposter. Another reason to wish I could have fought for a way to stay with Matthias and Nika.

Ari climbs out of the rowboat and onto the deck. The two of us barely got a word in while Moses and Jordyn chatted with Davey on the ride over in the rowboat.

He grins at me as we wait for Azarias to board the ship. "Good to see you, Bria."

His curly hair still sticks out in every direction, and his face holds the same kindness as the first day we met. But there's a sadness in his eyes now.

A sadness I feel partially responsible for.

"Good to see you too," I say. "My friends were bummed they weren't getting to sail with you and Catori again."

"Oh, we'll get them back aboard." He winks, then nods for me to climb the ladder.

I scramble up the ladder and drop onto the deck.

Azarias is in the wheelhouse, hovering over the radio system. Ari, Moses, and Jordyn are chatting a few feet away with Catori. Jordyn's on her knees, scratching Shep behind the ears. The dog's tail wags his pleasure at seeing her.

He's a well-trained dog, but I'm still unsure of what to do with the large brown-and-black animal.

A young woman I've never seen before flits about the deck, preparing the boat for departure. Must be Quwani.

She's a few inches shorter than me with a petite but sturdy build, and her skin is a warm, golden hue. Her oval face holds almond-shaped, dark brown eyes that are alight with life—and a bit of mischief—and her nose is slightly broad and compliments her full lips. Rich, dark hair cascades down her back, and there's an overall approachable air about her.

She catches me watching her and gives a flourish of her hand and a slight bow.

I wave back, unsure of what else to do.

"Nice to have you aboard again," Catori says, suddenly next to me.

My heart skips a beat. The woman moves like a cat—silent and fast. "Good to be here."

Catori gestures to the young woman prepping the boat. "This is Quwani. She's been part of our crew for several years, but she was on leave when you guys were with us before. You girls will be bunking with her. I'm sure you'll get along."

Jordyn comes up next to Catori. "I'll be taking my old bed."

Catori quirks an eyebrow at her. "Oh you will, will you?"

Jordyn nods. "Of course."

Catori attempts to look stern, but her eyes smile. "Fine."

Jordyn flings her arms around the captain, and Catori holds her close.

Moses and Ari wander over, and Catori addresses us while Davey and Quwani hoist the anchors and start the engines. Azarias is still in the wheelhouse, but Catori doesn't seem to mind.

"I'm glad to have you here," she says. "I want you all to go below deck and change. There're outfits down there that suit sailors. I don't need anyone assuming I have scouts with me, so make yourself look riverboat worthy."

She focuses on Moses, and a sadness fills her eyes a moment before she blinks it away. "You look more and more like Micah." She clears her throat, and Moses ducks his head. "I'll get you some of his clothes to wear."

Moses's head snaps up. "Really?"

"Of course. He'd be proud to know they're being put to good

use." She pushes the brim of her hat up with one finger. "As long as you don't destroy them."

The grin that splits Moses's face is wider than I've ever seen it. "Never." He throws his yo-yo to the ground, then pulls it up again.

Now that I know more of the history behind the toy, I almost want to ask him to teach me a trick. But I'm not sure I'm ready for the excessive enthusiasm that would accompany the lesson.

Jordyn, Moses, Ari, and I make our way to the lower deck as Azarias leaves the wheelhouse and moves toward the rail.

"Bria," Catori says, catching my attention. "A word, please."

"Of course."

The others give a questioning glance, but say nothing.

When my friends and I sailed with Catori, she and I talked many times. She trusted my instincts, listened to my ideas. It wasn't that long ago, but it feels like a lifetime.

We enter the wheelhouse, and she pushes buttons and prepares the ship for departure.

"How did things go in Eryndale?" she asks.

"Didn't Azarias brief you?" My tone holds more surprise than it probably should.

"He did." She gives one nod. "But I know Azarias, and I know some of those in Eryndale, which means there's more to this story than he let on."

She adjusts nobs on the control panel, then faces me. "Plus, Emmi said I should talk to you. She and Kassre contacted me as soon as it was clear Jordyn would be needed for this mission. They couldn't go into detail about *why* the C.A.E. was allowing a sixteen year old to do something this dangerous, but Emmi said you'd have more information for me."

I briefly wonder if that's why I'm on her boat rather than sailing with Nika and Matthias.

Shep trots over and sits at her feet. "It doesn't make sense to me why all of you would be heading back toward Talionis. It's not wise or safe. You should've stayed in Eryndale or gone west to gather more people to help us. Not travel *back* toward the city."

"Originally, we were supposed to go west," I say. "But then

the C.A.E. received more reports about Talionis's attacks. They insisted we join in the fight against Talionis on the front lines or be held as spies. There are several in Eryndale leadership who don't trust us." I give her a quick rundown of everything that happened and share the reason Jordyn is on this mission.

Her jaw tightens, and she releases a slow breath. "Do you still have the items you stole from Ark?"

I nod. "Yeah. The underground group in Eryndale thought it would be best if we kept everything in our possession."

She grasps the wheel, turning the boat back in the direction she just came from. "Then they're still worried about the leak." Her fingers tighten on the wheel.

I stay quiet, waiting for her to process her thoughts.

She gives one nod, as though coming to her own conclusion. "I don't like the idea of the items Ark wants being so within his reach." She flicks a look at me. "Are they dispersed between you and your friends?"

I shake my head. "No. I have them." I half-lift my pack from where it sits on the ground at my feet. "Oh, and Ari has the encrypted files."

"Good. I have a safe in my cabin. If you're okay with it, I'd like to store everything in there. They'll be protected."

I hesitate, not sure I want to part with the items. Or put Catori in so much danger. But it makes sense to have them locked away. "Okay."

"Let's keep it quiet. The less who know, the better."

"What about my friends?" Even though only Ari is here with me now, I'll want to tell Matthias and Nika as soon as I see them. And I know Ari will tell Shane and Bryson.

Catori chews on her lower lip for a moment. "If you have to tell them, then I guess it's fine."

I nod in agreement. "Where's Nalani?"

Catori pushes her hat back with her thumb. "She's found a place for herself that is proving very useful to those in Eryndale."

I raise my eyebrows. "What's she doing?"

"She's a medic."

"A medic? Really?" It probably shouldn't surprise me.

Although Nalani wasn't an elite recruit in Talionis, she's incredible with anything medical.

Catori gives a light laugh. "Yeah, the youngest we've ever had, actually. But she's a genius when it comes to all the different ways of caring for someone who's been injured. She stayed aboard our boat for several days, but then we realized she'd be best at one of the bases where we bring injured scouts and villagers."

"One of the bases?" I move deeper into the wheelhouse. "How much has changed in the days since we've seen you?"

Catori's brow furrows. "I thought they would have briefed you on all of that."

I shake my head. "We've been given some information, but not enough. Especially if we're the ones who are supposed to help determine how to take these guys down." I lean my hip against the communications board, absently wondering how long it'll take for Ari to come in and interrupt this conversation so she can get her hands on Catori's tech once again. "They still don't trust us. Lorenzo and Reginald Finnigan are the most hesitant."

"Finnigan makes sense." Catori directs the boat into the middle of the river, glancing down at the sonar panel. "The man likes to hear himself talk. But I'm surprised about Lorenzo."

Azarias's broad frame fills the doorway. "The other teams are moving on schedule."

"Good," Catori says.

Catori and I can talk more later, and I want to change and store my stuff. I slip past Azarias and make my way below deck. Plus, my unease about Lorenzo is something I haven't fully allowed myself to think about.

He's a lead scout. Part of the underground in Eryndale. But the fact that he has stonewalled us multiple times leaves me on edge. The leak in Eryndale couldn't be *that* integrated into the refuge city, that trusted. Right?

When I reach the bottom of the stairs, Quwani is standing in front of Catori's door, barring Jordyn's entrance. And talking faster than I thought was possible, her voice low and a bit raspy.

"Look. I know Catori is your sister-in-law, but she doesn't let anyone in her room." Quwani braces her hands against the doorframe.

Jordyn taps her foot. "She and I already talked about it—"

"Nope. She'd be a wreck case if she had to share that room with anyone but Micah." Her voice holds a tinge of sadness as she says Micah's name.

"Fine. Let's go talk to her together." Jordyn spins around.

Quwani watches her walk away and doesn't move to follow until Jordyn is halfway up the stairs. Then she struts after her, head thrust forward, five-foot frame held high as though she's the tallest person aboard the ship.

I shake my head as I enter the girls' bunkhouse. Quwani is unique.

Ari and I change into new clothes and stow our Skinter Suits and Blades in the trunks in the room. I sit on a lower bunk, pull my pack closer, and dig out the supplies I stole from Ark from their place at the bottom.

Files, screens, paperwork, journals. All of it bound together.

I crane my neck to look up at Ari sitting on her top bunk, screen on her lap and yo-yo back together. And . . . glowing. I'm curious, but there's no way I'm going to ask her what she did with the toy.

"Can you give me the files you're working on decoding?" I ask. "Catori wants to keep them all in her safe."

Ari cocks her head to the side. "Why?"

"Guess it's just us, ladies." Quwani struts into the room and sprawls onto her bed. "Catori said she's happy to have Jordyn join her. Who knew?"

"Bria, why does Catori want us to put stuff in her safe?"

Quwani props herself up on her elbow. "No joke, does she really? She only puts *super* important stuff in there."

"Uh." The non-word falls into the room, and I'm not sure what to say after it.

Catori wanted to keep the information in as small of a circle as possible. Sure, Quwani is on her crew. So that must mean she trusts her. But I don't want to be the one who shares information with her when I don't know her.

Ari still looks at me expectantly, waiting for an answer.

"Oh, don't worry about me." Quwani flicks her dark hair over her shoulder. "I know everything that goes on here. It's one of my special skills." She gets off her bunk. "But I'll leave so y'all can feel better about talking. I'll just ask Catori about it." She wiggles her eyebrows and prances from the room.

I shake my head as I watch her leave. She's going to be fun to get to know. But I hate that she's replacing Nate.

I blink. No, she's not replacing Nate. No person can replace another person.

Plus, Catori said she's been part of her crew for a long time.

I briefly wonder if she can make pancakes as well as Nate used to, but shove the thought away before emotions rise in me that I don't have time to address right now.

Once the door closes, I answer Ari. "Catori's worried about the leak in Eryndale," I say. "She thinks it's best if we keep the items Ark is most interested in under lock and key. With very few people knowing." I emphasize the last words.

"We can't even tell the guys?" Ari asks.

I stand from my bunk. "She said we could tell them, but it's to stay within our group."

"Right." Ari digs through her pack that's on her bed with her and withdraws the file. "I have everything entered into my screen now, but I'd like to keep the file. Is that okay? There's something about the documents that keeps bothering me, and it's helpful if I can examine them along with the scanned copies. I didn't even want to split them with Isaac, so he's working on deciphering the scanned copies."

I hesitate. It's unlikely that anyone would be able to take the file from Ari's pack—she never has it far from her. "I guess it's fine."

Everything else will be locked away.

"Thanks. I'll let Shane and Bryson know." She whips out a screen, types something, then sets it aside.

I stare at her, wondering if I should discourage her from communicating with the guys when we were told not to. But I stay silent. If I could message Matthias and Nika right now, I would.

Ari settles back in her bunk and thumbs through the file again, lips moving in a silent conversation with herself.

I grab the sack from my bed and head toward Catori's room.

I knock on the door. There's no answer. I hesitate, unsure of what to do.

Catori *did* tell me to put the items in her safe. I test the handle.

It opens easily, and I slip inside for the first time.

There are two beds, one that seems to be used more as a desk than anything, with papers and items piled on top of it. An actual desk is bolted to the floor in the corner of the room, and on it is a picture of Catori with a tall and muscular black man.

With a pang, I realize this is Micah.

This is Catori's husband.

His eyes shine with adoration as he looks down at Catori, and she grins up at him. They make a very cute couple, if I'm honest. Micah looks like an older, more mature version of Moses. Same warm brown skin, broad nose, and full lips. Even the same hairstyle. Moses doesn't have as broad of shoulders, and there's way more mischief in his eyes than—

"What are you doing in here?" Catori asks from behind me.

I spin to face her. "I'm, well, uh, I'm sorry, I thought—here!" I shove the pack of Ark's things toward her. "You said we should keep them in your room, but not let everyone know. I didn't want to find you up there." I'm rambling, so I clamp my lips shut.

Catori lifts her eyebrow at me, then takes the pack from my hands. "Fine. Makes sense."

"I let Ari know. And Quwani came in while Ari and I were talking about it, so she might know too," I say, feeling a need to confess everything to her immediately, whether I want to or not. But I manage to keep myself from outing Ari's communication with Shane and Bryson/

Catori gives a nod. "Yeah, Quwani already found me to ask me about it." She gives me a wry smile, then moves toward a bookshelf.

She slides it to the side, revealing a safe hidden behind it.

It reminds me of Ark's hidden safe in his office, which leaves me both impressed and uncomfortable with the memory of stealing everything before escaping Talionis.

"Did you guys meet Bill and Paul while you were in Eryndale?" Catori asks as she enters the code into her safe.

I avert my gaze to give her privacy. "Yeah. They're traveling to the combat zone with the scout team that took mechanical horses."

"It'll be good to see them again. They're the ones who designed this for me." Catori steps aside to reveal the open safe, takes the bag from me and shoves it inside. There are a few other items in there, including what looks to be money, but she closes it before I can get a great look.

"They seem to build a lot," I say, unsure why we're even having this conversation.

"They're the best." Catori slides the bookshelf back in place. "They even designed Hosea's wagons—the ones you all traveled in when he brought you to me."

My eyebrows raise, but I don't respond. The wagons Hosea hid us in to bring us to the river were impressive. From the outside, you would never know there were false bottoms that could hold *people.*

She faces me. "I don't appreciate you coming into my room without permission."

I duck my head. "Sorry."

She releases a low sigh. "It's hard for me to have anyone in here."

Her honesty brings my head up.

"Jor's going to stay with me for the trip, which is fine. But it brings back a lot of memories." She gives her head a subtle shake, then picks up the picture on her desk that I was studying when she walked in. "I guess you know what Micah looks like now. When I saw Moses climb on board earlier . . ." She clears her throat, but her pain is etched in her features and stooped shoulders.

"We'll find him one day," I say the words absently, almost without thought, but as I say them, a fresh conviction fills me.

She looks at me and offers the ghost of a smile. "I certainly hope so." She traces Micah's face with her finger.

I want to ask more about him. Learn how the two met. What happened that led to his disappearance. But before I can find the words, Catori nods to the door.

"Let's go. I don't want to leave Quwani behind the wheel any longer than necessary."

She waits for me to precede her from the room.

We climb the stairs topside, and I'm thankful that my new wardrobe while aboard *The Fearless Lady* doesn't include the bulky jacket I wore a couple of weeks ago.

The weather has turned warmer, and just the idea of being in the thick material makes me sweat.

Catori heads to the wheelhouse, and I make my way to the front of the boat where Ari and Jordyn are chatting.

"It's crazy being back," Jordyn is saying as I approach. "Last time I was here, I was six." She shakes her head. "And we were running from Catori's grandfather."

I remember Catori telling me that her grandfather was a founder of the Raiders, and that Micah helped her escape the compound. But I didn't realize Jordyn was involved in all of that.

"Why were you with them if you were so young?" Ari asks.

Jordyn leans against the rail. "I was a captive in the compound. Raiders killed my parents and took me as a slave. Catori and Micah smuggled me out. Gave me a new life onboard *The Fearless Lady*, and then in Eryndale with my new family." She stares out at the river as she talks. "I still can't believe he's gone."

"Micah?" I ask.

Jordyn nods. "Yeah."

The far-off look in her eyes stops me from asking any questions. Maybe one day I'll learn more about Micah and what happened to him. But for now, I need to give my new friend some space.

I gesture for Ari to come with me, and the two of us leave Jordyn to her thoughts.

THIRTY-ONE

We make our way downriver, the boat picking up speed.

Catori moves expertly through the water, and Shep trots over and sits at my side. I take a slight step away. He's a good dog, I guess, if you like dogs. But his fierce protectiveness of Catori and the way he seems alert to any possible issues is almost unnerving.

Maybe he'll be an asset in our attacks against Talionis. The idea almost makes me laugh, but then I think of Cai's dogs from the Ruins and Ajax in Eryndale.

Well-trained dogs can do impressive things.

I pick up a thick rope strewn on the deck and start coiling it.

Davey meanders over. "So, how was Eryndale? Did you enjoy your stay in the refuge city?"

With the way he says the words, I know he's already aware it wasn't the most pleasant of experiences.

"Oh, it was just thrilling." I let sarcasm drown my words. But then, I pause in moving the rope in a circle around my elbow and hand. "Essie is special."

Davey's face softens. "Yes, that she is. She's one of the most remarkable women I've ever had the privilege of knowing."

"She made it clear she wasn't happy we were being sent back

to Talionis." I move the rope around my arm again. "How have things been here?"

Davey leans against the rail. "It's been interesting. We picked Quwani up after we dropped you guys off, and it's been nothing but moving people ever since. When we got word to come pick you up two days ago, it was almost a relief. We haven't been able to sleep for more than a couple of hours at a time."

My eyebrows rise. "It's been that busy?"

Davey nods solemnly. "Yeah, Ark seems to know things he shouldn't. And Laban?" he says Laban's name like a question, and I nod, confirming he's one of Ark's people. "He's been vicious in his attacks. What happened after you guys left?"

I give him a quick rundown of how we got to Endoetin and found the mill burning, and then how Broche almost captured us.

Davey frowns and crosses his arms over his chest at the acknowledgment that Broche has been so actively hunting us as well.

"Vik radioed us about the arson at the mill," Davey says. "I should have guessed Broche had a hand in it." He grits his teeth and nods for me to continue.

I tell him about our standoff and how we were miraculously able to stop Broche and get away from Laban.

When I mention Callypso's pirates, Davey freezes.

"You met them?" The way his tone ices over causes my pulse to kick up, and an uneasiness sweeps through me.

"Yeah." Maybe I shouldn't have mentioned Callypso, but it's too late now.

"And you came out alive." He says the words as though it's a mystery to him how they could even be true.

I spread my arms wide, showing myself as the exhibit to prove that's exactly what happened. At least he believes me— unlike practically everyone in Eryndale.

"That is not how she operates," he says, almost to himself more than me. "Some people don't even believe she's real. More of a terrifying legend."

"Yeah, like everyone in the C.A.E." I settle the rope on one of the empty rods sticking out from the deck, used for rope storage.

"But she's real. Whether they want to believe it or not. Anyway, the scouts, Max and his team, found us after that. They brought us to Eryndale."

"Where they treated you like spies," Davey says.

"How did you—"

"Ari and I chatted a bit, before she got lost in the wheelhouse tech. I asked about the welcome you guys received in Eryndale. I was worried something like that would happen."

"Thanks for the warning," I say dryly.

Davey grins. "You all can handle yourselves, and you know it."

I chuckle, feeling like I've reunited with my older brother. Davey is a good man.

"How many people have you guys moved?" I ask, pushing the conversation back to them.

Davey shifts so he's facing the river and releases a low sigh. "I lost count. We've been taking them to villages that Talionis shouldn't know about. But since they're hunting so desperately for you, they're discovering them. And adding them to their places to attack, apparently."

Or the leak everyone is worried about in Eryndale is *telling* Talionis where to look. I keep the thought to myself. "Have they been destroying villages again?"

He shakes his head. "Nah, but they are entering them and devastating them in different ways. I haven't been to a village yet that hasn't lost kids and teens or at least been threatened with the loss of them. And the threats are not empty. If we don't move the marked kids and teens out within forty-eight hours, they're taken."

I pause in my coiling of a new rope. "What?"

"Yeah." He rubs his hand over his hair, messing up the curls even more. Weariness and frustration mar every line of his body and face. "We've learned the hard way. Talionis gives them forty-eight hours to produce some intel on the fugitives, as they call you. And if the villagers don't?" He clenches his hands. "They come and take their kids."

"How many do you think have been taken?"

My mind races to consider the consequences of what could

happen if Ark gets enough kids and teens to help him with his plan.

But can he even accomplish his plan if I still have his stuff?

I drag my racing mind back to focus on Davey as he answers my question.

"Hundreds," he says. "Easily hundreds. And they stopped focusing only on teens. They're taking kids too."

My stomach churns, and images of Storm and my little brothers, even Levi, flood my mind. What must it be like for these babies to face the training and torment of being in Talionis?

No love. No nurturing. No care.

Just soldiers screaming, teaching them to use guns, forcing them through dangerous scenarios. Weaponizing children for battle.

I'm ready to be as sick as Bryson is when he sails, but I swallow back the vomit rising in my throat. "I hope we can stop them."

"It's that or die trying." Davey pounds the rail with his fist.

"Maybe our fight will help distract Ark from attacking the villages," I say. "Maybe once he sees that we are coming for him, that we're doing something, he'll stop."

"Our attacks won't be that clear immediately," Azarias says.

I twirl to face him. "But maybe—"

He's shaking his head before I can get the sentence out of my mouth. "No direct engagement with enemy combatants unless absolutely necessary. You know that."

He's quoting Lorenzo, and frustration tightens my shoulders.

"What if we need to do *more?*" I insist.

Azarias's mouth forms a thin line. "Those are our orders for now. It's what the C.A.E. agreed to, so it's what we have to do. Whether we like it or not."

Davey leans his hip against the rail. "If not direct contact, then what exactly *is* the plan?"

"We're going to make ourselves a nuisance," Azarias says. "Handicap Talionis however we can. We'll be using tactics that will be irritants, frustrations, and annoyances to them that will keep them from traveling as far as they've been going. We'll do enough to draw their attention away from those they've been tormenting."

As he talks, he reminds me of Cai and what he would do in the Ruins, but the idea of annoying Talionis soldiers and doing things to keep them from moving farther into the American region doesn't feel right to me.

"But we need to go into Talionis," I say. "We need to stop Ark." And, if there's any hope for Storm and Cai, we need to do it within nine days.

"First," Azarias says, "we need to get the enemy in a position where they're not terrorizing every village they can get to. We need to give them enough reasons to stay close by to stop us. Otherwise, more and more lives will be at risk."

I clench my teeth, give a curt nod, and walk away.

I understand why they're doing what they're doing. It makes sense to distract Ark and his troops so they're entering less towns than before.

But what about Storm and Cai? What about the hundreds of kids who have been taken by Talionis?

I grab a mop and bucket from the back of the boat and start swabbing the deck. I dunk the mop into the soapy water, swirl it around, and thunk it onto the deck with more force than necessary. As I scrub it over the rough boards, I try to push my irritation aside.

Azarias isn't the one responsible for the orders we've received. He's following them, same as the rest of us.

Once we're closer to Talionis, maybe I can talk to him and Lorenzo. Give them information that will motivate them to do *more* than what we currently have planned.

Until then, I'll follow the orders, like a good soldier. The thought turns my stomach, and I dunk the mop back into the bucket. Dirt from the tool mixes with the water, turning it a murky brown color.

Talionis trained me to be a good soldier, and the last thing I really want to do right now is continue to be one for Eryndale.

At least we're going close to Talionis. At least something is happening to attempt to stop Ark.

But is it really?

I flick the mop out of the bucket and back onto the deck.

Are these kinds of tactics, these maneuvers, really going to do anything to keep Ark from training teens and kids? Keep him from hunting for us across the North American region?

I wish Nika or Matthias were here. Someone I could really talk through everything with.

Catori comes out of the wheelhouse. "If I could have everyone's attention."

I focus on the captain.

"We'll be nearing our stop in the next two to three hours," she says. "It won't be long, but I want all of you to be ready to help offload supplies."

"Are you sure we can't just make a direct line to Talionis?" Azarias asks.

Catori spears him with a look that tells me he's tried this line of questioning before, and she's not pleased to hear it again.

"As I've said before, Azarias," Catori intones in a motherly way that almost sounds like she's reprimanding Azarias, even though they're the same age. "I refuse to blow my cover, or that of my crew, just because we need to get to Talionis quickly. A quick stop to deliver supplies will not hinder us from getting into position in the time frame you gave me."

Azarias holds up his hands. "Fine, fine. Can't blame me for trying."

Catori looks less than pleased, but she goes on to tell us we'll need to bring the supplies up on deck so that they're ready to offload once we dock. "Ari and Bria, make sure you put on makeup. We don't need you being recognized by anyone in town."

We nod, but the idea of putting on makeup makes me miss Nika. She helped me with mine the last time we were onboard *The Fearless Lady* and I wish she was here to help me now.

THIRTY-TWO

We arrive in Echo Bay two and a half hours later. Right within the time zone Catori estimated.

Part of me is surprised Ari and I are involved in this venture, but according to Azarias, there haven't been signs of soldiers in the area for a long time. Talionis attacked the town before, but now they're letting them be. And there's a lot of supplies to offload, so Catori is adamant the whole crew be put to work. Even Azarias is helping.

As Quwani and I move down the dock to the town, my heart clenches in my chest. The marks of Talionis being here are evident. It almost looks like a battle took place.

Bullet casings roll past my feet as Retro kicks at them from the edge of the dock. Blackened streaks mark the harbor where some kind of bomb must have gone off. Buildings are scarred as though they've taken a beating.

But then I see there are still teens and kids in this town.

"What happened here?" I ask Quwani.

"There was enough resistance that Talionis left," she says. "Didn't expect a fight, but we showed them, huh?" She elbows me in the side. "Pretty cool when the good guys can send the bad guys running." She rubs her hands together. "My favorite thing to see. I don't like it when bullies get their way, and we certainly didn't let that happen here."

"You were part of this?"

She flicks her dark hair over her shoulder. "I'm part of all the fun stuff around here."

I stare at her. She doesn't elaborate, which leaves me with more questions, but I keep them to myself.

I drop the crate I'm carrying in the place she indicates, then she stays in the town as the rest of us make the trek back and forth on the dock, carting the supplies.

Once we have offloaded everything, Quwani and Davey send all of us in various directions with the different goods we've offloaded. We're not bringing anything on board today, and I realize that what we've brought mostly in terms of supplies isn't food, but things to help restore the town. Wood, nails, tools, equipment. Even paint.

Will it be enough to make this town look like it did before? To mask the damage?

Probably not.

But what does Talionis touch that doesn't come away permanently scarred?

"You." A man's voice catches my attention.

I let my hand rest near my hip, where my concealed gun lies.

"You're the reason my child was injured." His raw voice cracks. "She'll never be the same, all because of you." Then he's racing toward me, hands outstretched as though he's going to throttle me.

I don't pull my weapon. I just stand there, frozen in place.

Clearly, he recognizes me from Talionis's lies.

And there is truth in his words. The only reason his child would have been hurt was because Talionis arrived. And they arrived because they were looking for me.

A second before he's on top of me, Retro steps in front of me. "Whoa, whoa, whoa. She's not who you think she is."

My heart hammers in my chest.

"I'd recognize her face anywhere." He points around him. "I've studied her picture, waited for the day I might get revenge. Now get out of my way." He reaches to shove Retro aside, but Retro grabs his hand.

"No. Leave her be. Walk away." I've never seen Moses this serious before. "She isn't who you think she is," he repeats.

Blood pounds in my ears, and I hope the man believes Moses. A look of uncertainty flickers in his eyes.

Quwani jogs over. "Yo, my friend. What are you doing?"

"She's the one responsible for my baby girl not being able to walk. Her leg is shattered." His voice crackles with emotion, but doesn't hold the same amount of conviction as it did a moment ago. "She'll never be able to do anything she loved again. Running, riding horses. All of it is gone forever."

"No. It's not gone forever," Quwani says. "She can learn again."

"It won't be the same," the man shouts. "If my little girl has to live with a limp, then *her* leg should be shattered too!" He thrusts his finger at me.

I step back, but part of me wonders if he's not wrong. Maybe I do deserve to lose something because of the loss he's faced. The thought leaves me feeling a darkness inside that I don't know how to shake.

Quwani whistles, and seconds later, Davey appears.

"What's the problem here?" Davey asks.

The man is sobbing now, the anger and fight gone.

"Can you get him a little extra help?" Quwani asks. "Something happened with his daughter. He might need to be, uh, relocated." She gives a pointed look between the man and me.

Davey nods in understanding. He'll make sure the man doesn't do something rash and turn me—and all of those with me—into Talionis. He puts his arm around the man and leads him away.

The brokenness in the guy's stooped shoulders, the way he allows Davey to lead him, though a moment before he was ready to kill or at least maim me, leaves me confused.

Once the man is out of the area, Retro returns to delivering supplies.

"So this town didn't get away without injuries," I say the words out loud.

Quwani hangs her head. "No, there were injuries. And some

casualties. On both sides. We counted it as a victory because we pushed them back, and we weren't sure we'd be able to."

I nod. The scars of Talionis always run deep.

God, even if we can stop Talionis, even if Eryndale's plan works or I'm able to convince them to try something different, what damage has Talionis done that can never be undone?

My heart screams for justice. And yet I wonder if justice is even possible in this broken world.

I'm torn between wanting to sob, and wanting to slam my fist into somebody's face as hard as possible. Preferably Laban's or Ark's, but I would take anyone at the moment.

The anger and desperation and pain woven through me pulse like their own entities.

I distribute the rest of the supplies and make my way back aboard the ship, then below deck.

I close the door to the girls' bunk room, press my face into my pillow, and scream.

After dinner, Catori finds me at the back of the boat, tossing stale bread into the water. It's after 2000 hours, but the sky is still light.

Catori removes her hat and runs her hand through her short hair. "Moses told me about what happened today."

I break off another hunk of bread, hurl it into the water churning beneath us, and don't respond.

She lays a hand on my arm. "It's not your fault, Bria. Talionis hurt that little girl. Not you."

I keep my gaze fixed on the river. "But it's because they were hunting for me. For my friends."

"So it's your friends' fault?" Her question is quiet, gentle.

But it snaps my head around so fast a pain shoots up my neck. "No! Of course not."

"Then it's not yours either."

We lapse into silence, staring out over the passing landscape. The river slashes through terrain that is marked from the

Demise. And now, Talionis is destroying the new lives survivors were trying to build.

"Jordyn was telling me that you and Matthias seem close." Catori's words break over me like a bucket of ice water.

"Uh, well. Um." I clear my throat. "Yeah." Why was that so hard to say?

She leans against the railing and quirks an eyebrow at me.

My cheeks flush. "It's a terrible time to start a relationship." It's a statement, but also a question. I want her to tell me if I'm right or wrong.

Catori absently spins the wedding ring on her left hand. "That's how I felt about Micah." She bites her lip. "How could I fall in love with a guy while everything was falling apart around me? My grandfather was chasing me. People were in danger because I'd run away. It seemed not just ridiculous, but *foolish* for me to let my heart be swept away." Her eyes connect with mine. "But I did. I fell hard for that man."

I grip the railing in front of me. "I'm afraid that the more I let myself fall for Matthias, the more painful it will be if I lose him." But I'm still falling for him. More every time I'm with him. I shift to better see Catori. "Now that Micah's gone, do you regret loving him?" As soon as the question leaves my mouth, I wonder if it was inappropriate.

But the thoughtful look on Catori's face keeps me from taking it back. "Never. There are days when I feel like I can't breathe. When the pain of not having him here with me, working with him, helping people together—it hurts so bad it's like a bullet ripping through me over and over again." She pauses and stares at the ring on her finger. "But even on those days, I know loving Micah will always be worth it."

The river gurgling around us and the purr of the motor are the only sounds for a few moments as Catori's words sink in.

Part of me wishes Matthias was with me right now so I could go talk to him. Tell him once again that I care.

"What happened to Micah?" I ask the question I've wanted to know the answer to for a long time. But right now, I need the distraction more than anything.

"Three years ago, we were on a routine run in the north Midwest: transporting supplies, helping villages defend against the Raiders." Her eyes press closed for a moment. "Micah was delivering supplies to a home several miles outside of the riverside town we were in. Usually we didn't go that far inland, but the W.U.N. requested assistance getting this family what they needed. I was supposed to go with him, but I'd been sick, so he told me to stay and rest." She rubs her forehead. "He didn't get back in time, which was strange for him. Hours passed, and I started to worry that he'd gotten hurt or something happened. Davey and Vik, one of our crew members at the time, went to check on him. But they couldn't find him." She releases a weak breath. "Turns out he never made it to the family he was supposed to visit. And no one has heard from him since."

"I'm sorry." The words are feeble, and I wish I had something better I could offer.

"Me too." She steps back. "I should relieve Davey from the wheelhouse."

With that, she turns and leaves.

THIRTY-THREE

We've docked for the evening, and all of us—except for Azarias and Catori—are crammed in the galley eating dinner. We are only a short distance down the river from Talionis. Twenty miles.

I'm not exactly sure of the coordinates yet because I haven't gone over the map in the wheelhouse with Catori. That's something I wanted to do after dinner. Especially because tomorrow, we'll be going on land to connect with my friends and the rest of the Wild Dogs as well as some other teams. And the covert ops strategy will begin. It will be good to be reunited with my friends.

And Matthias.

After my conversation with Catori, I'm both excited and nervous about seeing him again. It might not be the best time for a romantic relationship, but I need him in my life. Whatever happens, I don't want to live with regrets because I pushed him away.

The terrain has changed as we've moved closer to Talionis. We passed villages that are shells, abandoned. And not from the Demise.

As we eat, Davey, and Quwani share various things that have happened along this stretch of river. Why towns have been completely evacuated. The threat of being so close to Talionis is not worth anyone remaining behind.

Although, according to Davey, some have stayed in the abandoned villages. They travel to get their supplies from other places, but refuse to leave their home.

At first, I think it sounds courageous. I can respect those who are willing to stay and not allow Talionis to push them out.

Then Davey remarks that he thinks they're on Ark's payroll. Spies he's left behind.

"Why'd he do that?" Retro asks, taking a biscuit from the basket at the center of the table.

Davey swallows his mouthful of stew before responding. "To monitor the boats going up and down the river." He takes a drink of water. "My theory is that Ark is aware we use boats for much more than supply delivery. He's too smart not to think of that. And Broche probably flat out informed him of it as well. Traitor." He spits the word, and his anger surprises me.

"Have you heard anything of Broche?" I ask. "I've wondered what happened to him after we faced him. We defeated him soundly, which won't put him in any kind of favorable position with Ark. Do you think he's still a threat?"

Davey leans forward on the table. "That man can talk his way out of anything. He's the slimiest person I've ever known. Scum."

Ari lifts her eyebrows at me. It's strange to see Davey like this.

But I find I agree with him about Broche.

What's weird to me is that Catori clearly has him working for her to help her find Micah. Something I don't think Davey appreciates. But after talking to her last night, I think I understand.

I'm not sure I'm ready to say I love Matthias, but I do care about him. And if he was missing, I would do just about anything to find him.

Even hire someone as awful as Broche.

Azarias enters the galley. "There's been a development."

I set my fork back on my plate.

"Talionis isn't just attacking and forcing teens and kids to come with them anymore. In the villages closest to the city, they're now sending soldiers in to occupy."

"Doesn't that diminish their resources within Talionis?" Retro asks. "It seems like a poor use of their time."

"It's all an intimidation tactic," Azarias says. "The more the villages fear them, the more they are able to control them." He rubs his beard. "And we don't think it's entirely their resources. Early reports show Raiders assisting the soldiers."

The words settle over our group as silence fills the galley.

"Does this change things?" I ask, certain that it must. How could Talionis and Raiders occupying towns *not* change things?

"No," Azarias says. "I just talked with Lorenzo, and the consensus is to move forward as planned."

I pick up my fork, just to have something to squeeze.

"At 0100," Azarias continues, "we'll make a three-mile hike inland to the site where everyone is slotted to meet up. We have specific maneuvers that you will be performing. Everything must go as planned. There's to be no maneuvers that are not first authorized. Everything we're doing has a purpose, and we have intel that you don't know."

"Why can't you just share the intel?" I ask, sick and tired of hearing *you don't know everything.* I stand. "When we were given clearance in Eryndale, I thought we were given more information so we could actually help you guys. How are we supposed to help if we don't know all the details?"

"Some members of leadership are still concerned that if you have all the details, Talionis will have a distinct advantage." Azarias tucks his hand into his pocket. "I'm sorry. It isn't fair to you. I'm hoping things will change once we're out in the field."

He sounds as frustrated as I am, so I bite my tongue against further arguments and sit back down. This isn't Azarias's fault.

"So, we're meeting everyone at a site?" Retro asks, bringing the conversation back around.

"Yes," Azarias says. "And tonight we'll begin our covert ops strategies. You'll be hitting a town and causing some distur-bances." There's a glint in his eye, even as I wonder what a disturbance is. "Every maneuver we make will be to handicap

Talionis in some way. We'll have our tech team working to disable and get past certain tech features Talionis has in place."

Ari's hand shoots up. "Oh, can I be part of that team?"

Azarias almost smiles at her eagerness. "That's what we expected."

"What is that going to look like? What will I get to do? Can I help with—"

"Once we get to the site," Azarias says, "I'll connect you with that team, and you'll get situated in helping them however you can."

Ari opens her mouth, but then closes it and nods.

Azarias presses forward as though afraid Ari will start talking again. "Once the tech teams are in place and doing what they can do, we will have small teams working to cause problems and diversions that will be large enough in scale to distract Talionis."

"Like what?" Retro asks.

"We'll bomb places close to the city where we're confident there won't be civilian casualties, take out guards, capture soldiers when we can, disable transports. We'll do whatever we can to show them there is a threat close to home."

"But if we're going to expose that we're that close to the city," I say, "why wouldn't we *enter* the city?"

Azarias crosses his arms and leans against the counter. "Because we aren't ready to yet," he says. "Not everything's in place for an insertion team. I know you have more questions," he rushes on before I can formulate what I want to say next, what argument I could give that would be enough to convince him. "But for now—"

"Davey!" Catori cuts off Azarias. She's standing in the doorway, hat askew and eyes flashing. "Come now. Everyone else, stay below deck."

Quwani stands, eyes wide as she stares after Davey and Catori. "I think I'll just pop out there and see if they need me." Her words come out in a rush, then she exits the room, closing the door behind her.

I stand, on edge. Catori doesn't get rattled. Not like that.

Which means something is very wrong.

Azarias strides to the door.

Before he can open it, the glasses on the table shake, clattering together. There's a whirr, a distant buzz. The hair on my arms rises.

Ari and I share a look before she whips out a screen.

We know that sound. A transport.

We've lived in Talionis. Experienced what it felt like to be aboard a transport. We know the sound of it coming for us. The fear of it hunting our every step.

We've faced them.

We've won.

But right now, there's one overhead.

And all I can do is pray they'll leave a shipping merchant alone. Because if they don't, this will be over before we even begin.

More glasses clatter, and I sense that the transport has moved closer.

I stand and make my way toward the door, then stop before anyone else can stop me. I know it's foolish to go up to see what's going on. The soldiers would recognize me. But being blind, not having any intel, this could kill me.

"What is that?" Jordyn asks, crowding close to Retro.

"A Talionis transport," Azarias and I say at the same time.

Retro's face slackens. "What if they board?"

That's a question I don't want to consider answering.

It doesn't matter if the soldiers are Laban and his unit or someone else. Any of them would be happy to receive the reward of Ark's favor if they came and grabbed us right now.

Eight days ahead of the timeline he gave us.

"They're not directly overhead," Ari says, face buried in her screen. "I can't tell how big the transport is, but it's not searching the river. I don't think." Her brow furrows as she inputs commands into her screen. "Oh, wait, wait."

The buzzing dissipates, and the glasses stop clattering together.

"Yes," Ari says with a sharp nod of her head. "They're moving out."

There's a collective sigh of relief, even though the close call is something that has left my nerves on edge.

I'm ready to go up and hear from Catori, Davey, and Quwani about what happened, but before I get the chance, Azarias is moving toward the door.

"You all stay here. I'll be back."

I know I should trust Azarias and let him lead.

I know that's the role I have at this time.

Yet every time he demands we do something, every time he tells us we can't do something, it grates against me a little more.

Especially considering the fact that for the past few weeks, I've been the one helping my friends figure out what to do next.

"I'm coming too," I say.

He shakes his head no and slashes his hand through the air to enunciate the effect. "Absolutely not. Stay below deck. We don't know how far away they are."

"Transport's moving east," Ari says. "Most likely back into Talionis. Bria should be fine."

"I said no," Azarias says again, his words sharp. "And you shouldn't be using that screen."

Ari lowers the screen, but doesn't put it away.

He might be Cai's son, and yes, he does seem to be an excellent scout. But I am sick and tired of being told what to do by any person.

It's probably not the hill I need to die on, and yet right now, with Talionis soldiers so close, the city of our nightmares looming not far in the distance, and danger lurking around every corner, I need to do something more than sit below deck and wait for orders from people who don't understand this enemy as well as my friends and I do.

"I'm coming," I say. "We're doing what you want. We're obeying your commands, but I need to know how to strategize in order to keep my friends safe."

"What do you think I'm trying to do?" Azarias asks. "Hurt you all?"

"Bria knows what she's talking about," Ari interrupts, setting her screen aside. "She's always been able to figure out ways around their traps. We had to go through trainings and strategize different things while we were in Talionis. Bria was one of the few recruits who could discover ways through scenarios and kill zones from the very beginning. If anyone can help you figure out a method to avoid detection, it's Bria. Let her come and see what's going on. The sooner she gets the intel, the sooner we'll all be able to determine out how to move forward."

At some point during Ari's speech, my mouth fell open. I've never heard Ari talk like that.

Azarias rubs the back of his neck, and I almost wonder if Ari is getting through to him.

I stare at him, trying to remove any trace of defiance from my features. "Catori trusts me, so does Davey. They would allow me to come up and speak with them."

"Fine," Azarias says in a growl. "Come with me, then."

I make my way quickly to the door before Azarias can change his mind, and then the two of us jog upstairs to see Catori and Davey.

"What happened?" Azarias and I ask at the same time.

Catori and Davey spin from where they're huddled over the control panel, radioing a contact further inland.

"Hold for more details," Catori says into the mic. After the person on the other end agrees, she presses the mute button on the radio. "It was a transport, as I'm sure you all guessed. They weren't directly over the river—about a quarter-mile inland. Now we're trying to determine if we can continue forward with the plan as it was."

Azarias shifts, but he says nothing.

"It looks like it moved back toward Talionis," Quwani calls, and I realize with a start that she's outside by the rail with a pair of binoculars staring up into the sky.

"Was she out there the whole time?" I ask.

Davey nods. "As crazy as it is, it seems to help when the soldiers see there're people moving and acting normal. If they find there's any kind of change in behavior in villages or on boats on the river, they immediately send someone to investigate. It was better for us to mill about as usual. Something other captains have learned the hard way."

My eyebrows rise at his words, but it makes sense.

"Why would we change our plans?" I ask Catori. "We're going to see soldiers. Especially this close to the city. If we let

Talionis dictate how we respond to it, we're going to have to find an entirely new plan every day." I glance at Azarias. As annoyed as I've been to not have all the details, at least there's some strategy involved in what we're about to do. And the last thing I want is to be taken *further* from Talionis now that we're this close. With so few days left to save Storm and Cai, I need to be near enough to do something as soon as I have a plan. "It's important for us to follow plans that have already been outlined, at least to start. Talionis will move in various ways, and the more I see and understand of that, the more I'll be able to give some information that might aid in changing or adjusting plans accordingly."

Azarias nods once. "Good. I agree with Bria." The man's humility, despite the fact that I've been rather annoying, is reminiscent of Cai.

I think Cai would be proud of his son.

In fact, I'm confident he would be. I only hope and pray he actually gets a chance to reunite with him.

I SHOULD BE GETTING SOME REST. BUT INSTEAD, I LIE IN BED, TOSSING and turning, wondering what the next hours will look like.

Although we're heading to land in just a few hours, Azarias told us we're not done with our time aboard *The Fearless Lady*.

It sounds as though we'll be moving up and down the river and hitting different places in our maneuvers, which I guess makes sense. I'm hoping my friends will be able to join us more for those operations.

How much danger will Catori and her crew be in if Talionis discovers she's transporting us? Jordyn's to remain behind with Catori per Kassre and Emmi DeFort's agreement with the C.A.E., but I doubt they realized how involved *The Fearless Lady* was going to be.

I kept my questions and comments to myself, but now they haunt me.

How do we defeat an enemy when we have far fewer people,

far fewer resources, and half of the group doesn't even trust me and my friends?

How can an army be defeated by only a handful of combatants?

Everything I've learned in Warfare Strategies, all the scenarios I've gone through, shows me the right training and the right trust among a group of people can make a difference in how many can be taken down with a small force.

But I still question what could happen. What *will* happen to my friends.

In different scenarios, I faced large amounts of enemy combatants with only a handful on my team. There were times where we were able to defeat them, get what was needed, extract intel or a source.

But most often, there were casualties. Sometimes, many casualties.

I don't know if I can bear for that to happen in real life. Not any more than what I've already seen. And I'm also not sure what it will be like to kill people in something that's not a scenario. Especially if. . .when. . .I'm facing recruits I trained with. Teens just like me who are being forced to fight as soldiers, whether they want to or not. Could I hurt, kill, someone like that?

The thought has been at the back of my mind, haunting me, bubbling up like too much soap in a sink full of dishes.

I don't want to think about it. I don't want to consume the thought or allow it to take root in my mind. And yet it's there, infecting everything.

Oh God, I don't know what to do. I pray the words, longing suddenly to open the Bible Cai gave me, to dive into words that could be calming, peaceful. To go back to praying with others in a way that left me settled and feeling secure.

But instead, I close my eyes, turn on my side, and try to fall asleep.

THIRTY-FOUR

The inky blackness of a moonless night suffocates the world around us as we prepare to leave. I put in my lenses, thankful for the aid in seeing clearly even on a night like this.

Brandi and Ari weren't able to replicate the tech before we left Eryndale, so Ari and I are the only ones with the advantage of the lenses. Although Retro and Azarias do have bulky headgear that apparently serves a similar purpose.

Ari, Retro, Azarias, and I will be going ashore, while Catori, Davey, Quwani, and Jordyn stay behind to move *The Fearless Lady* to a different spot on the river for a pickup point. They'll be delivering supplies to a village.

I say goodbye to them, then make my way to the rowboat. Davey sits in the middle of the boat ready to take us over, and Retro and Azarias are in the back, so Ari and I take the front.

The river churns beneath us, dark and murky and moving rather quickly. Davey navigates the skiff to the far shore, and it scrapes against the rocks. I jump, more on edge than I want to admit. The lack of sleep and the reality that we're this close to my enemies leaves me with a frustrating amount of energy that I need to release.

Maybe tonight's maneuver will help.

I need to do something.

And it will be good to be reunited with my friends.

We climb out of the rowboat, say a quiet goodbye to Davey, and hike into the trees.

"All right, let's go," Azarias says.

We follow him through the forest. We've left our Skinter Suits and Blades aboard *The Fearless Lady* since it's only a three-mile hike inland to the site where the others are meeting us.

We pass rubble and debris, and I scan the sky for any signs of transports.

My senses are alert. It's as though the days in Eryndale never happened. Like I'm on the run again, looking over my shoulder. Waiting for the next soldier to descend upon us. Waiting for someone to capture us and take us in.

But the three-mile hike to the site is uneventful.

We pass remnants of an old town, and then come to the outskirts of a village, which is closer to the site than I expected. Azarias leads us to a broken-down old barn.

"This seems like a bit of an obvious place to have a site," I say.

Azarias shrugs. "Sometimes the best place to be is in plain sight."

I want to disagree with his logic, but decide against it. There are different battles I will probably need to fight, and I'm going to save my disagreements for those instead.

When we enter the barn, there's . . . nothing. No people or weapons. No supplies.

Broken slats hang at odd angles, giving glimpses back outside, and the roof has a large hole in the center. Other than some old farm equipment and decaying hay, the barn is empty.

The four of us stare at Azarias.

"I thought you said this is where we'd be meeting up with everyone," I say.

The slight grin on his face looks so like Cai that I almost lose my breath. "Not everything is always as it appears," he says.

Ari has her screen out. Unlike other scout leaders, he doesn't seem to mind Ari using Talionis tech. "But I'm not detecting any tech footprint."

"Then Brandi's tech did its job." He waves his arm for us to follow him, leading us to a back corner.

He kicks aside some hay, then reveals a trapdoor that goes underground. He removes his headgear and tells Retro to do the same.

As soon as he opens the door, light spills out from the space. My lenses adjust to the new brightness, and we climb a rickety ladder down into a room that's as large as the barn itself. There are stations and tables set up, computers and screens people are working at. Even a wall of weapons and gear to the left.

It reminds me of Cai's first site that I ever went to. The place looked like it was a dilapidated nothing, but inside, Cai had transformed it into an intel gathering space. I'm surprised we couldn't hear any of the noise when we were in the barn. They must have soundproofing installed.

Two guards are stationed at the bottom. Azarias jumps down first, and they grin and shake his hand.

"Good to see you guys," he says.

Then he leads us through the space, past those who are working, including scouts who have a map laid out and are pointing at different regions circled on the map.

I sort of want to stop to hear what they're discussing, but I'm anxious to see Matthias and Nika and the others.

The rest of the Wild Dogs and my friends are waiting at the back of the space, and relief floods through me. Everyone is here and appears to be okay.

"Yo, yo, glad to see you all here." Retro begins giving bear hugs to each of our friends.

Ari races to Shane and Bryson, pack hanging off her shoulder and screen in her hand. She hugs Shane, then immediately starts talking to Bryson about the stealth tech being used to hide the site.

Shane watches her, as though he just wants to confirm she's there with them.

"How was your trip down?" Nika asks after giving me a quick hug.

Matthias is right next to her, and memories of my conversation with Catori about him drift through my mind. When he steps toward me, I embrace him.

"Not bad," I say, remaining near Matthias. "Close encounter last night with a transport."

They both nod.

"Us too," Nika says. Her gaze shifts to where Kemena and Azarias are talking. "Kem could have handled it better." She folds her arms over her chest. "She's not thrilled about this whole mission."

Before I can ask what happened, Azarias clears his throat, drawing our attention.

"Welcome to Site Omaha," Azarias says. "This particular site has old tunnels that lead into Ravenspire." He nods his head toward a door at the back of the room. "Soldiers are occupying that town, and we want to give them a reason to feel on edge." He smirks. "Here's what you're going to do."

He then outlines a plan where we go in sets of two through the tunnels to different points within the village. Each group will then set up an explosive in a place that shouldn't harm any of the villagers, but should impact the Talionis soldiers occupying the space—both by destroying valuable equipment, and by making it clear there's an unseen enemy nearby.

The plan reminds me, again, of Cai. This is exactly what he would do in the Ruins. Which means I have an idea of how this is will go down.

Terrorizing soldiers was something Cai did very well, and apparently Azarias inherited the knack required to continue the family tradition. Soldiers refused to enter the Ruins unless they were under direct orders. Every one of them was freaked out by the things that happened in the rugged terrain surrounding Talionis. Soldiers would go missing. Random explosions would occur. Transports would be taken down.

All through the genius of one man.

Nika leans over to me. "It feels like that time I found you in the Ruins with Cai, and he had us place explosives to scare the soldiers on the wall."

I nod, then pull my attention back to Azarias.

"So our goal is to remove their sense of control and freak them out?" I ask.

He nods. "Exactly. The more scared and jumpy they are, the easier it will be to take them down. We want them to fear something they don't see right now, and every maneuver will build on that fear. Lorenzo has other teams doing the same kinds of things in other towns. Tonight, we have one group that's going to be working at disabling a transport too."

Ari lifts her hand high into the air. "Where do you need me? You said I would be helping with the tech. Does that mean I'm working on disabling transports? Or do you have something else in mind?"

Azarias holds up his hands as though to pause her onslaught of questions. "Yes, you'll be connecting with the tech team at this site." He points to a section where a group of five are working on sorting through a pile of high-tech equipment. "Your group will be part of disabling the transports."

Ari pumps her fist. "Fantastic." She stands. "Should I go over there now?"

"I'll go with her." Shane and Bryson both pipe up before Azarias can respond.

Azarias hesitates, then nods. "It will be good to have others on the mission who understand Talionis tech." He focuses on Shane. "Your training should aid in providing any additional support if it's needed. The soldiers lock up their transports and usually leave one guard behind overnight. Malachi"—he focuses on him—"you'll go with them. You and Shane should be able to keep the soldier from being an issue for those who will be disabling the transport. You guys can go head over there and speak with Wolf. He's getting that group ready to go."

The four of them stand and leave, which leaves me, Nika, Matthias, Retro, Kemena, Glacier, Karyss, and Isaac. And Gabe, I guess, but the man doesn't seem too engaged in the plans, and I can't imagine he's going to be part of what we're doing.

"Are we setting these explosives and detonating them?" Glacier asks, rubbing her hands together. "You know I like a good fireworks show."

I don't know what she means by fireworks, but I let the comment slide as I wait to hear Azarias's response.

He shakes his head. "We want everyone cleared out before any of the explosives go off. Our spies within Ravenspire will make sure all villagers are cleared from the area before the explosives are detonated. And we'll detonate them at specific intervals throughout the day and into tomorrow night."

"So we're just setting them?" I ask. "Nothing else while we're in there?"

"Actually," Azarias says, "I'm also going to have you take what you can while you're in each of these specific spaces. Every house and building we send you to is a place Talionis soldiers are occupying. It's going to be dangerous entering, so be careful and don't go if there's a risk of being spotted. We cannot stress enough the importance of everyone remaining undercover as long as possible. They can't know we've been there. We're banking on the element of surprise causing as much damage as the explosives. But while you're there, take anything you can that could be useful. I'd like to avoid tech because of the possibility of it being traceable, but weapons and ammunition, plans —whatever you can take without it being too obvious will be beneficial."

I nod, along with everyone else.

Azarias splits us into pairs, and I end up paired with Nika, which is a relief.

As much as I like the Wild Dogs, I don't really want to be with someone I'm not used to working with. And I'm afraid I'd be too distracted if I was with Matthias.

Azarias and Kemena will remain behind to monitor all the sets going out. They give us camo to change into and hats to cover our hair, as well as paint to put on our faces. Anything to disguise us from cameras or tech that could be in position to do facial recognition. The spies Eryndale has within this village have reported every place where they know there are cameras or sensors, so we'll avoid them as much as possible. And since it's still night, we should be able to blend into the darkness. But there's always the risk of sensors and cameras being in places we don't know about.

When we're finished suiting up, Wolf gives us weapons, as well as the explosives. Then we head toward the tunnel at the back.

I glance at Ari, who is suiting up with Bryson, Shane, Malachi, and three others who will be going to disable the transport. It bothers me that our group is once again fragmenting, but there's nothing I can do about it. And for our first maneuver, it makes sense. Ari is the tech head, and she'll be far more help with that than she would be at placing explosives.

Nika and I take the tunnel to our target: the temporary barracks for the soldiers doing night patrols. Which means the building should be empty, since they're all on duty.

Retro and Matthias are close behind us. They'll be going to their target farther down this stretch of tunnel and deeper into the town.

It reminds me of the old drainage system we were in with Hosea, but this one has been cleared out and doesn't smell nearly as bad.

"It's good to be back with you guys," Nika says as we walk through the dark tunnel, aided by our lenses. "But I'm a little jealous you got to spend time with Catori and Davey. How are they doing?"

"Good," I say. I share with her and Matthias about the plan to continue working with *The Fearless Lady*.

"Maybe we can get Azarias to let us go with you guys," Matthias pipes up from behind us, which makes me smile.

"Dude. Great idea!" Retro says. "Catori would love to have all of us, obviously. We're fantastic."

Nika snorts next to me. We lapse into silence for a few moments.

"Why do you think Talionis has decided to occupy villages around the city?" Nika asks, voice low.

"Probably to instill fear," I say. "Since Ark's been sending soldiers out to find us, there's not really any reason for him to stay quiet anymore. Talionis isn't hidden."

"Good point. Unfortunately," she says.

Are there still Watchers in these villages, or has Ark removed them? Or is he using them in other places and in other ways?

If I were him, I probably would keep the Watchers in place and undercover. Use them to help gather intel. And to help aid in spreading Ark's propaganda.

Something Trill is excellent at.

The thought of the educational instructor causes me to pause. She would definitely want the villages to believe lies. She wouldn't want them fearing the soldiers, but seeking to obey them.

That's how she tried to train us.

She wanted the recruits to believe what the soldiers and Ark were doing was right. For the benefit of all. My friends and I never fell for it, but others, like Shay, believed every word. Trill would definitely carry that tactic with her into these villages that the soldiers are occupying. And some are going to believe her, which makes me wonder if we are actually safe in what we're about to do.

We stop at a ladder. The point where Nika and I are supposed to go up.

"Good luck up there," Matthias says, suddenly next to me.

I wish he was coming with me and Nika so I could know he was safe. But the strategy Azarias planned doesn't allow for that. Matthias is going with Retro.

Plus, too many people together make it easier to be spotted.

"You too," I say.

And then, Nika and I are climbing the ladder to the building Talionis soldiers have commandeered and repurposed as a bunkhouse for the night shift. The building should be empty, unless they left any guards behind to keep villagers from doing exactly what we're about to do.

But Nika and I don't have to rely on our own intuition or gut instinct. Prior to our maneuver today, other teams have entered these different spaces to place hidden cameras. There's a screen near the entrance that allows us to see what's happening on the other side of the wall.

And we see nothing.

I signal Nika with two fingers to go forward. She nods in agreement, pulls a gun from her hip, and we open the secret hatch that leads into a place where our enemy rests.

THIRTY-FIVE

Nika pushes open the trapdoor and slides out ahead of me.

I climb out after her and pass her where she's standing, gun drawn, alert to any sign of enemy combatants.

I tap her shoulder, and she moves with me, at my back, gun at the ready.

I come to a corner and pause. Carefully, I peek around the bend and see nothing. I motion for Nika to go, watching for any movement. She passes me and taps my shoulder.

Then I'm following her.

We weave our way through the old warehouse, past soldiers' bunks. Past tech and gear that causes me to cringe. There aren't any soldiers, and I see no signs of cameras or sensors in the area, which is both comforting and disconcerting. If I don't see it, it doesn't mean it's not there.

But from what Azarias said, the soldiers just started occupying towns. Maybe they haven't gotten around to setting those up yet. Or maybe they don't think they need to.

We reach the point in the warehouse near a pillar that should bring the whole thing down if it explodes the way Azarias hopes it does. We place the explosives carefully, setting up the triggering mechanism. Then we hide them with boards and gear that are around the pillar, obscuring them from view.

According to Azarias, it will be going up tomorrow evening, right after the night shift begins their watch. Or I guess later today, since it's 0300 hours. So as long as it's not discovered within the next twelve to eighteen hours, we should be okay.

I install the camera we were given so the explosives can be monitored.

Loss of life is never what Eryndale wants, which I appreciate. But loss of life is coming in this battle, and I know it deep within my gut.

And this explosion, whoever dies in it—that's going to be my responsibility. Whether they're soldiers from Talionis or kidnapped teens like me.

God, help me live with that.

I tack the camera in place and jump down from my perch on top of a large trunk. I circle around to make sure the device is hidden from view.

"Ready?" Nika asks.

I nod.

The two of us make our way from the room.

When we reach the armory, we take off our packs and strategically find items that won't be missed right away, but will cause problems once they are needed.

Extra weapons, ammunition, even food supplies and rations for units sent out on longer patrols. There aren't any plans in this building, but tech is scattered around the supply room. We leave it be. Like Azarias said, it's not safe to take stuff we aren't sure we can disable before bringing it back to a base.

That's probably one of the best things about Ari *not* being on this little escapade. If she was here, I have no doubt she'd be taking tech, whether we wanted her to or not.

After five minutes in the supply room, Nika and I make our exit. With every passing second, my shoulders tighten even more.

I can't imagine they don't send a soldier to patrol their quarters at least once every hour, and we've been here now for twenty minutes. Who knows when that patrol is coming?

We exit the supply room, guns at the ready once again, packs heavier on our backs, and move down the hall.

"Wilkins." The voice freezes us both in our tracks, and we press against the nearest wall. "What are you doing in here?"

"I forgot something, sir," Wilkins says.

"Soldiers of Talionis do *not* forget supplies," the first man says.

"Sir, I'm sorry. I left in a hurry, and I—I just . . ." The guy stutters, and his voice doesn't sound quite like a man yet.

"I know you've just graduated from being a recruit," the first man says.

My stomach churns.

They don't just have soldiers here. They have teens like us. Just as I feared.

"But we expect a great deal from you. You graduated from all our training with high ranks. You must perform the tasks given to you with excellence. Which means not forgetting supplies." He grinds out the words.

"Sir, yes, sir," Wilkins says. "My sincerest apologies, sir."

The click of boots against tiles echoes through the room, reminiscent of the soldiers walking down the streets of Talionis. And I know the officer is now facing Wilkins, even though I can't see him.

"We do what we do for the Commander, son. And being a soldier who is ready for action, has everything prepared, all supplies in order, weapons ready for combat, that is what a soldier of Talionis is. That is what we do. Understood?"

"Yes, sir." Wilkins's voice trembles. Like he's afraid of what's coming.

My hand grows slick where it holds the gun, and cold sweat trails down my neck. Memories of facing Talionis soldiers, being disciplined, pound at the door of my mind, demanding entrance.

"Don't worry." The officer sounds amused. "You've gotten through training. You're not going to be sent to the pit. Not this time, anyway."

I imagine the internal sigh of relief from Wilkins. Being sent to the pit was always one of the worst punishments anyone could receive. Especially because Laban oversaw it. I can still hear him screaming in my ear. Feel the sand grinding into every area of exposed skin.

"Now, get back to your post. We don't want any of these people thinking they can do something foolish when a post is deserted, do we?"

"No, sir," Wilkins says.

There's the sound of jogging as Wilkins leaves the space.

I want to look around the corner to see the boy who has been forced to become a man at the hands of evil people, who's been changed by situations and circumstances that are beyond what he ever contemplated facing. But I can't.

Once again, I'm reminded of the evil of the enemy we're fighting.

But as I think about the explosive, I wonder who's going to be taken out tonight when it goes off.

What will happen when some of these soldiers are back? How many of them are former recruits that I trained with? How many of them are going to be in the cross fire as Eryndale scouts work to terrorize Talionis soldiers?

I'm not sure I want to know.

The idea sickens me as Nika and I slip through the rest of the building, keeping an eye out for Wilkins or the officer now that we can't hear any more conversation.

When we're close to the supply closet where we'll be leaving, there's a click.

"Sergeant Reynolds to Talionis."

"Come in, Sergeant Reynolds," the radio chirps.

"I need extra eyes on former recruit Wilkins. His behavior has been suspicious, and I'd like his report from his trainings and his instructors. Are we sure we can trust him as one of the occupiers in Ravenspire?"

"Roger that, Sergeant. I'll get that information sent to your screen immediately," the female voice says. "Until then, proceed as you deem fit for your regiment."

"Thank you," Sergeant Reynolds says. "Over and out."

The radio clicks off.

Nika and I are once again frozen as we wait. My breathing comes in short bursts, but it's barely audible as I wait to see if the sergeant is going to round the corner and come upon us.

His books click against the floor. The door squeaks open and closed.

Nika and I move the remaining few feet to the door to our exit. Once inside, she opens the trapdoor that will lead us back to the tunnels.

The other scouts who were here before have secured supplies on top of the trapdoor so the door always stays hidden, even after we close it behind us.

But as we make our way down the ladder and back into the tunnels, more fears rise in my heart. If Sergeant Reynolds is already worried about Wilkins, what will he do to him if he survives the explosion tonight?

He's going to think it's his fault.

And does Wilkins have to be a casualty of war?

"We have to save him," I say to Nika.

"Huh?"

"The kid. Wilkins."

"I don't know what you're talking about," she says. "He's working with Talionis. He's one of the recruits who's clearly given over to everything they've been spewing at him. Otherwise, he wouldn't be able to leave the city. Come on, girl. We have to stick to the plan."

I stop in my tracks, forcing her to stop with me.

"Oh, man." She turns to face me. "I hate that look."

"What look?"

"The look that tells me I'm about to get myself in trouble because I'm listening to you. I thought that was over when we left Talionis. Clearly, I was wrong." She gives a long-suffering sigh. "All right. Let's go."

She turns to go back to the trapdoor. Despite her protests that Wilkins must be fully given to Talionis, I think part of her understands that's not entirely true.

The fear in his voice proves that.

He didn't sound like Shay. Shay has been devoted to Talionis almost from the beginning. My former neighbor, someone I wish I could have trusted when I arrived there. And yet, as soon as Elva Trill started speaking, that girl didn't do anything but believe it all. Swallowing it up like a fish swallows a worm on a hook, not realizing that it's leading to its death.

I don't even know if Shay recognizes how much of herself has died since being here.

I think of the last moment I saw her, hand severed, bleeding. Face beaten. Screaming for help as Laban dragged her to a transport.

Maybe she's changed. Maybe experiencing all of that has pushed her to a breaking point and forced her to realize what she was embracing with the soldiers from Talionis.

Then again, I don't know if it could have. I push aside thoughts of the girl who became my nemesis and never really was my friend, even when we were neighbors, and head back up to the trapdoor we just exited.

My ear-comm pings.

"What's going on?" Azarias's voice enters my ears, and I'm sure it's echoing in Nika's ear as well.

"We have to go back for a... package," I say.

"Negative," Azarias responds. *"Has the original package been left behind?"*

"Confirmed," Nika says. "But another discovery was made of a sensitive matter. We'll report when we return."

She clicks off her comm, and I hear it in my own ear as I push my button as well. Somehow, I don't think Azarias is going to appreciate his direct order being disobeyed, but he'll handle it far better than Laban would.

We get to the top of the trapdoor again, and the camera shows the room is once again empty.

"What exactly is the plan here?" Nika says to me. "How are we going to get that guy and get him out of here?"

"I don't know if we can," I admit. "At least not in a way that wouldn't jeopardize the mission. I can't guarantee he's *not* fully on board with Talionis."

"Mm-hmm," Nika says, in her classic "I know, and I'm waiting to hear what you're going to do about it" tone.

"But maybe we can leave him a message to make himself scarce tonight, or at least put himself in a position that keeps him safe so he doesn't get hurt in the attack."

"I'll follow your lead." Nika nods toward the trapdoor.

We follow the same maneuvers as before, but this time we head to the bunk space. There's no one there, and Nika keeps an eye on the door as I quickly search the bunks, looking for anything that would identify a space as Wilkins's.

A half-open pack draws me to it, and I freeze when I'm nearby. Inside the pack is normal Talionis gear: things we would be given for a scenario, everything we're given as soldiers in the city, and more. Additional weapons, ammunition, and supplies. A pack ready for battle.

But there's something glinting in it that catches my attention, something that doesn't look like Talionis. Tech that's almost too rough to be from the city. I reach inside and pull out a transponder. The exact transponder used by Eryndale scouts.

I slip it deeper into the pack, close the pack, and push it against his bunk. "Let's get out of here."

"Wait, did you leave anything?" Nika asks over her shoulder, eyes still trained on the door, gun at the ready.

"I'll explain later. Let's move."

We race from the room, then descend the stairs once again.

It seems I'm risking Azarias's wrath for nothing.

Wilkins is already working with Eryndale.

THIRTY-SIX

I explain everything to Nika as we make our way back through the tunnels and to the main base, where the rest of the scouts are waiting for us.

"You think Wilkins is working with Eryndale?" Nika asks.

"Yes. I saw a transponder that looks just like what the scouts use."

"Which means he's in even more danger," she repeats words I've already spoken.

"Correct."

"Why is that?"

"I think he's a plant," I say, everything clicking together.

"How?"

"I'm not really sure, but we'll have to ask Azarias. Either way, I think we need someone to get him out of there. Tonight. Or I suspect he won't be alive for us to help tomorrow."

When we exit the tunnel, Azarias is waiting for us, scowl on his face, arms crossed over his chest. "So, disobeying direct orders is something you enjoy doing?"

"Great question." Kemena stands beside him, eyes flashing. "Do you know what you just put us through?" Her words slap the air around us.

Nika says, "We just thought—"

"No, no. I'm talking right now." She cuts Nika off. "You were supposed to do a quick, simple insertion. Enter the space, place the compounds, and leave. Nothing else. We were finally breathing a sigh of relief. You were the last team to finish placing your explosives. You were in there so long, I thought for sure something went wrong."

I shift. "We almost—"

"No. I'm still not done." She bites out the words. "And then, once we're finally ready to believe you're on your way back, you turn around and head back into the place you were just in! What were we supposed to do? We can't send someone in after you. It's too dangerous. I'm not ready to lose you again." She steps toward Nika and points her finger in her face. "Don't you *ever* do something like that to me again."

Nika ducks her head, but there's something on her face. A bit of exasperation, maybe. "We did what we thought we needed to do." Her head comes up, and she flicks her gaze between Kemena and Azarias. "And we think one of your people is in danger."

Azarias drops his arms. "What are you talking about? How would you even know if one of our people was there?"

Nika looks at me to continue.

"Do you have a soldier named Wilkins?" I ask. "A plant?"

He shakes his head. "No, not a plant." He hesitates. "We flipped him. But how did you—"

"We think they're on to him," I say. "And Nika and I believe he needs to be removed immediately." I cast a sidelong glance at my friend, who gives an almost imperceptible nod in agreement.

Thankfully, she's okay with me adding her to my thoughts on the matter.

"Why do you think that?" Azarias asks.

We launch into a quick explanation of what happened, which has Azarias running a hand through his hair as he begins pacing.

I stand in front of him, stopping his progress. "I have an idea."

He pauses and focuses on me, then nods. "Okay, what?"

"Send in a small team and get him out during the attack tonight."

"That seems risky," he says. "The whole point of planting the explosives earlier than when they're set off is to keep the enemy from having any idea where we came from."

"I know," I say. "But if you can get word to him to be in a specific area for an extraction team to get him out, then we can protect him. Otherwise, I think they're going to assume he's the reason for the explosions."

Azarias blows out a breath. "Let me run it up the chain, see if we can make it happen."

I want to argue that he needs to make it happen no matter what the up-the-chain people might say. All I can see is Reginald's face and the others in Eryndale who don't seem to think it's worth saving one life when so many others would be at risk as a result.

But Azarias doesn't seem to be in the mood to be argued with. Which isn't too surprising, considering the fact that Nika and I did just disobey direct orders.

He strides away.

Kemena grabs Nika's shoulder in one hand and mine in the other, pulling us into a hug.

"Don't do that to me again." Her voice cracks this time, and the fierce mama bear anger she displayed moments ago leaks away.

She squeezes us tighter to herself, and I wrap my arm around her and Nika in the group hug I wasn't planning to be a part of.

"You've got to trust me, Kem," Nika says. "I'm not the same as I was before." She pulls back, allowing me to pull back with her. "'I'm still your baby sister, but I've seen things. I've gone through intense training. You have to trust my instincts." Her words are fierce and low, and she stares directly into Kemena's eyes.

Kemena puts a hand on Nika's cheek and releases a long sigh. "I know. I will."

And with that, the tension dissipates.

But my anxiety ratchets up. I might not be able to go after Storm or Cai yet, but the intel Nika and I gave could potentially save this guy's life. As long as someone acts.

The rest of the night melts into the day in a blur.

Azarias receives the go-ahead from Lorenzo to send in a team to retrieve Wilkins before his cover is completely blown. Wolf and a few of his team are going to stage it to look as though Wilkins was killed in one of the explosions, which is a solid plan. I didn't even think of the option, which tells me I'm getting too emotional and not thinking as strategically as I need to.

But it's a smart move. It allows Wilkins to get out without showing any of Eryndale's hand.

I'm impressed by Azarias's wisdom in this situation.

We are there when Ari and her team return, and some of the pressure on my chest lifts as I realize all my friends have gotten back safely.

After we're given time to rest, we head to a briefing on tonight's maneuvers.

"As soon as night falls," Azarias says, "I'll take a team back to the river. It'll be a five-mile hike because of where Catori has *The Fearless Lady* docked."

Gabe leans forward in his chair. "Who all is going on this team?"

From the look on his face, I don't think he's thrilled at the idea of a late-night hike through the forest. Or maybe it's the fact that he would have to be on a boat again. According to Shane, Gabe handled sailing about as well as Bryson. Maybe even worse.

"For the ops planned for tomorrow, I need seven people," Azarias says. "The rest will go with Malachi to a site about four miles from here, where Lorenzo is waiting."

The group is split up, and I'm relieved to be placed with the team going back to *The Fearless Lady* rather than meeting up with Lorenzo. I'm not ready to be face-to-face with someone who makes it clear he doesn't trust us.

Matthias, Nika, Retro, Ari, Shane, and Kemena will be on Azarias's team with me. It will be a tight fit, but I'm relieved I won't have to be separated from Matthias and Nika again. Bryson volunteered to stick with The Wild Dogs so Retro could return to *The Fearless Lady*. Which was both kind, and, I'm sure, a little for his own benefit.

We'll be moving farther down the river and a little closer to Talionis. The branch of the river we'll sail down curves away from the city. Another branch of it goes directly into Talionis— under the wall and into the city.

We trained on that river in ice-cold waters. It's where Ava plunged to her death. It's the place that I thought might be a way to escape.

A place where I relived nightmares.

I drag my thoughts away from the memories and focus on the upcoming mission.

The next maneuver will take place in a river village, so Catori, Davey, and Quwani will be working with us.

Those going with Malachi will work with Lorenzo and Kassre DeFort on infiltrating a town farther inland. And then we'll all join together again in two days.

The idea of being this close to Talionis and not trying to get to Storm and Cai for two more days is almost painful. By that point, we'll only have five days left. But, if we accomplish enough over these next two days, maybe by then someone will let me do something to save them.

"For now," Azarias says, "we'll remain here until the explosions go off. Then both teams will make their exits."

"Won't Talionis be looking for anyone running after the explosions?" I ask. "Maybe we should leave before they start."

"No," Gabe interjects. "If everyone did their jobs correctly, there will be enough damage to keep them occupied."

Azarias clenches his jaw at Gabe's response, but doesn't argue with him. "Leadership believes that between the transport being disabled, multiple explosions happening at scattered times, and communication lines being shut down for a bit, we should be able to move without any issues."

The way he says the words makes me think he's not thrilled with the strategy. But I guess he trusts Eryndale leadership enough to follow the orders.

But what if the leadership is as compromised as Catori and the underground in Eryndale believes?

Are we safe blindly following their orders?

Tʜᴇ ᴛɪᴍᴇ ᴄᴏᴍᴇs ғᴏʀ ᴛʜᴇ ᴇxᴘʟᴏsɪᴏɴs ᴛᴏ ɢᴏ ᴏғғ.

Getting Wilkins out is proving to further complicate keeping villagers safe, but the Wolf seems confident his team can handle it.

We watch on screens as the countdown begins.

Five, four, three, two, one.

"Now," Azarias says.

The men and women at the control panels press buttons to detonate the first round of bombs. Seconds later, the ground shakes as explosions go off less than a mile away and ripple through the village.

"All right, time to go," Azarias says.

He circles his finger above his head with the signal, and we jog away, although part of me can't help but imagine the flashes of gold and orange and yellow as buildings erupt in flames.

I want to be there when they give the report.

I want to know if the damage done was enough.

I want to know that they can stop the transport from taking off after they realize their communications are down.

But there's not time.

We need to get back to the boat and move down the river. We climb out of the site and into the crumbling old barn.

THIRTY-SEVEN

Our hike back to the boat passes quickly and with little conversation. Although we're moving at close to a jog, Ari keeps up with the rest of us. Maybe the time running from Talionis and the training with scouts in Eryndale has helped her get stronger and faster.

Tonight, she's not breathing as hard from moving so fast, and, with Shane's help, she stays close to the rest of us.

We come to the river, the rushing water almost a soothing melody.

We've made it, and there have been no incidents.

A thunderous *boom* shatters the stillness. Another explosion has been detonated. We're too far away to see the flames or smell the smoke. But I can envision every detail.

Azarias instructs us to wait in the trees as he goes to the rocky shore to signal over to Davey that we're ready and waiting. Several moments pass, almost interminable in the quiet of the forest after the explosion.

An owl hoots in a nearby tree. The leaves of the trees stir as the wind courses by.

It smells like it's going to rain soon. Hopefully we can be on board the boat and stay dry for the duration of whatever weather is about to hit.

"What's taking him so long?" Shane asks the question that's beginning to echo in my mind.

"Maybe one of us should go check," I say. "See if everything's okay."

"Right. Because just doing what we want despite what Azarias says seems like a great idea," Nika mumbles with her sarcastic tone.

"I'm just saying, it might be worth knowing," I say.

"Let's get moving." Azarias's voice right behind me almost makes me leap out of my skin.

He is so quiet that I missed him being nearby. I wonder how much he heard of our conversation.

"There have been some developments," he says.

The words are enough to bring on a flurry of questions.

"What do you mean?" I ask.

"What's going on?" Shane asks his question a mere second after mine.

"I'll tell you on the boat."

We follow him the short distance to the rowboat Davey has brought for us. Shane, Retro, Kemena, and Ari are the first group to board. The rest of us wait at the shore for the rowboat to return.

A few minutes later, the rowboat is scraping the edge of the bank. Azarias, Nika, Matthias, and I quickly pile in.

"Did you tell them anything?" Davey asks as the rowboat makes its way back to *The Fearless Lady*.

"No," Azarias says. "Best to wait until we're all gathered together."

Davey nods.

The rowboat goes silent as questions fumble their way through my mind.

He said there were developments. That doesn't mean it's bad news.

Still, as soon as my feet are planted on *The Fearless Lady*, I'm ready to go below deck and have the conversation.

A raindrop plops on my shoulder, and the wind cools as a storm blows in.

Catori pokes her head out of the wheelhouse. "Should I move

the boat, or do you want to stay here for the night? Storm coming in doesn't look like it'll be too bad, but it always makes travel a little more difficult."

Azarias tilts his head, and I can see his mind churning. "We'll move later. For now, let's all go below deck. I want to have you share what you've learned, and I'll share what I heard from my contacts back at the base."

Matthias, Nika, and I go below deck. As soon as we enter the galley, I stop short.

My team and the crew of *The Fearless Lady* aren't the only ones present. Several people are crammed into the space with my friends.

I don't know how all of us will fit inside, let alone have a seat.

I've never seen *The Fearless Lady* this full of people. Those gathered here that I don't know look almost terrified as they huddle together in the corner. Most seem to be around my age, but a few are several years younger.

Jordyn hovers near them, like she's trying to reassure them they're safe.

My mind whirls as I attempt to understand what's happening, but Azarias and Catori shoulder past me. I focus my attention on them. They press through the room until they are both in the middle, near the kitchen counter.

"As you can see, we're a bit full tonight," Azarias says. "Before Catori explains what's going on with our guests, I wanted to give an update. I heard from the base, and the attack went according to plan. Wilkins has been removed."

I breathe a sigh of relief at the words.

"And the transport was successfully disabled," Azarias adds.

"Of course it was," Ari mumbles behind me. "I was part of the crew. Disabling a simple transport is not a problem."

Azarias raises an eyebrow but otherwise doesn't respond to Ari's mutterings.

"We believe they will be shorthanded, at least in this area, for a few days since we've been able to damage their communication systems." He shifts. "We're pleased with the efforts that have been done so far, and we thank all of you for what you did in aiding us in the town."

He turns to Catori.

She speaks without him saying a word. "We have brought some new guests aboard." She gestures to the group huddled in the corner.

Now that I've edged further into the crowded room, I catch sight of a little boy who can't be older than nine.

Same as Storm.

My heart seizes at the thought of the little girl, and I have to force my attention back on Catori so I don't get lost in my own imagining of what Ark will put Storm through if I can't get to her in time.

"They were all marked by Talionis soldiers."

"Marked?" Matthias interrupts. "What do you mean?"

"It's a tactic they've been using," Catori says. "Instead of just grabbing teens and kids, they mark them when they enter a village or town. They give their parents opportunities to . . ." She hesitates. ". . . release their children into Talionis's custody. If they do, they're given food, money, and opportunities from Demetrius Ark. Most families don't take him up on the offer. But if they end up with their children being marked, it's mere days before they're taken. If a family can get word to us or to one of the other boats in the area to get their kids smuggled out and to safety, they do. Not everyone takes us up on that either. Families believe they can protect their kids. Hide them themselves."

Her nostrils flare. "But we've seen the lengths Talionis will go to in order to gather every marked kid, and it's not pretty."

I imagine Laban entering a town looking for those he's supposed to take into custody and destroying anyone who would get in his way.

Trill might not even be able to stop him at that point.

"When we were in Plainton," Catori continues, "I had a dad come up to me." She nods to the back of the room, to a boy of about eleven who ducks his head at the attention. "Barry's dad begged me to help him. I will never say no to helping a child. As soon as he received my confirmation that I would assist him, I was put into contact with other families who were desperate for help as well. We need to get them to safety."

Azarias nods. "We'll bring them to a safe house and get them connected with the underground."

I know we're going to be helping these kids and teens, but this must be terrifying for them.

It was horrific to wake up in a forest alone, unsure where I was, away from everything I knew. Then to face Laban and the soldiers with him, to be brought to Talionis and forced to train to become soldiers ourselves. Pushed to the limit physically, mentally, and psychologically. It was more than I ever expected —ever *wanted*—to experience in my life.

But this has to be hard in its own way. Talionis is still forcing kids to be removed from their parents. Under Ark's commands, soldiers are introducing horrors into villages. Although Azarias and Catori are going to bring these kids to safety, all I can think about are the ones who are left behind. Who are still with their parents, and yet in great danger.

And what will happen to these kids?

Will they ever see their moms and dads again?

Will they ever feel like somewhere is *home* again?

The questions pound me, and once again, I realize the power of Talionis's reach, the power of the horror Ark is raining in this region.

"We'll still continue forward with the plans we have for our next set of maneuvers," Azarias says, drawing my attention. He turns to Catori. "But I might have a few of them go with you to get everyone settled."

She nods. "I'd appreciate the assistance."

It registers with me that, unlike my friends and me, these teens aren't trained for hand-to-hand combat. They don't know how to use weapons. They don't know how to avoid detection or make a site and disappear from plain view.

We know how to do that, and helping them makes sense.

It's something I'd rather do than whatever maneuver Azarias has planned for us next. But if participating in the maneuvers means I might be able to make Eryndale's leadership happy enough with me to let me attempt to rescue Storm and Cai, then I'll do it.

THIRTY-EIGHT

My friends and I give up our bunk spaces so the rescued teens and kids can rest for the evening.

We've camped in worse conditions than the galley floor of *The Fearless Lady*.

It's spotless, which would have pleased Nate. And I'm sure that's Davey's doing. I've watched him in here, fastidiously doing everything Nate used to do. Washing dishes the way Nate insisted they be washed. Putting them away in the same order Nate would.

Quwani might handle the cooking now, but Davey is keeping his brother's memory alive even in the midst of the insanity. I appreciate that.

He's doing something I never knew how to do with Ezri.

Maybe it's because I lost my brother when I was so young. Or maybe it's because I was partially responsible for his death. Either way, I appreciate seeing someone who will keep a memory alive and yet continue to move forward with his life as well.

Once the other teens have left the room, Azarias gestures for my friends and me to take our seats. "I wanted to give part of the briefing when they were here. Let them see that things are being done. That they won't have to live in fear forever."

I hope he's right and nod in agreement along with everyone else.

"Our next set of maneuvers will include distractions as we attempt to remove kids who have been marked from other villages, but we're also going to be moving closer to Talionis."

"Closer?" Shane asks. "I thought we were already within fifteen miles of the city. How close do you want us to go?"

Azarias focuses on Ari. "Close enough for us to see if we can do anything to that wall they have."

"I'm not sure if even I can get into that," Ari says. "I mean, I'm good, and I probably could, with the right equipment and time." Her eyes move back and forth. "But I don't know."

"It doesn't have to be a major tech destruction," Azarias says. "But we want to give them reasons to pull away from the villages. So, if there are things we can do that would alert them to something happening by the wall, that would be beneficial."

"Oh yeah, that I can help with," Ari says. "You don't even really need tech for it. The wall is so sensitive that—"

He holds up a hand to stop her. "Excellent. I'm going to have you brief the team tomorrow on what to do. Until then, I also wanted to let you know that we've heard word from the other sixteen teams in the area. Maneuvers are going well and as planned. The coordinated attacks tonight have done damage to Talionis's forces outside of the city. We have word coming in from all over that transports have been destroyed or dismantled. Communication centers within towns that Talionis has occupied are now not working, or at least temporarily crippled. And there have been Talionis casualties throughout each of the villages. We don't aim for death here, but destroying an enemy is important, especially one as powerful as Talionis. And so far, we have not lost any of our people, which is a miracle in and of itself."

A tendril of relief courses through me, but then is almost immediately squashed.

I know Demetrius Ark. Laban. Colonel Valarius. I know the lengths they go to when they want something.

And I know how they react when things aren't going their way.

There may have been victories tonight, but what will happen

once Talionis realizes these attacks are going to continue? That every day new things will happen, new targets will be taken out?

Will they take it lying down? Will we still have these kinds of victories?

No.

What will happen then?

I wake early, and my friends are all still asleep. Except for Matthias.

I catch his eye as he looks over at me. A smile warms his face that sends flutters swirling through my chest.

"Good morning," he mouths to me and props his head up on his elbow. He's only a few feet away, and his hair is mussed from sleep. But he still looks amazing.

"Good morning," I mouth back, then I get to my feet.

He rises with me, and as though we agreed to do it, we both leave the galley, stepping carefully over our friends.

"How'd you sleep?" he asks as soon as the doors close behind us.

"Not bad." I stretch my neck to the side to loosen the kinks from sleeping on the hard floor. "Better than having a tree root in my back." I grimace with a flourish.

He grins at me. "I've missed you," he says, suddenly serious.

"Matthias, it was only a couple of days."

He shrugs. "I know. But"—he tucks a curl behind my ear, his fingers calloused and yet tender—"I haven't really gotten any time with you. It'll be nice when things slow down."

My throat thickens at the thought, so I just nod.

He stares into my eyes with a depth of emotion that stops my heart for an instant.

"Should we go see what's going on upstairs?" I ask, desperate for a reason to look away.

I care about Matthias a lot more than I know how to admit to myself. But it's still strange trying to deal with all the emotions and figure out how to function in life-or-death situations while caring about someone in a way I've never cared about anyone before.

I can tell by the look in his eyes that he's disappointed, but he's quick to agree to go topside with me.

We jog up the stairs. With each step, I feel more annoyed with myself. Matthias deserves better than me acting according to my fears. I need to give him—give our relationship—a real chance.

Catori is in the wheelhouse with Azarias, and Davey and Quwani are managing things on the deck. We approach Davey first.

"Any news?" I ask.

It seems like a poor greeting for this early in the morning, when the sun is just edging its way over the horizon and darkness clings to the trees lining the edge of the river. Yet, it's the question pounding in my mind.

Davey hesitates. "Yeah, and it ain't good." He sets aside the mop he was using to wash last night's rain off the deck and gestures to the wheelhouse with his head. "Come on, let's go talk to Azarias."

A sickening feeling twists my gut, and Matthias and I follow Davey to the wheelhouse.

When we enter, Azarias and Catori stop talking.

"What happened?" I ask.

Even if Davey hadn't just said there was news and it wasn't good, I would know from the look on Azarias's and Catori's faces that something had just gone down.

Azarias frowns. "I was gonna wait and share everything with all of you when everyone woke up, but I guess there's no harm in talking a little now. You'll know soon enough, anyway. The attacks last night were a success, as I said." He pauses. "But the retaliation is far worse than we expected."

I absently reach for Matthias's hand, needing someone who understands the depth of Talionis the same as I do. Maybe even more, considering who his father is.

Dread slithers through me like a snake.

"What happened?" I ask again.

"Ravenspire is gone," Azarias says. His words are leaden, and they sink into my soul like a serpent's toxic poison.

"What do you mean, it's gone?" Matthias asks.

"Somehow, word got to Talionis. The few soldiers left evacuated in the middle of the night—at least as far as we can tell. And then, it was bombed."

My chest tightens. "I thought they'd changed their tactics."

"They did," Azarias agrees. "They stopped destroying villages weeks ago. But I believe it was a message." He rubs the back of his neck. "In the other towns where we attacked, the results weren't as fierce, but they were still bad. Raiders worked with soldiers from Talionis. They took teens, kids, even some adults in their early twenties. They were removed from their homes in the middle of the night. Parents were murdered if they tried to stop it from happening. It was a bloodbath. We expected there to be retaliation, but not for it to happen this quickly or so brutally."

"Because you don't fully understand who you're facing," I say. "We've tried to tell everyone, tried to tell Eryndale."

Matthias squeezes my hand in silent support.

I press on, my voice rising. "Talionis will stop at nothing. Ark will stop at nothing to do and get what he wants."

Catori places her hand on my shoulder. "We know, Bria. We get it. We understand that this enemy is evil. That's why we're fighting."

"We need to do more." I let go of Matthias's hand and pace the small distance in the wheelhouse. "We can't just keep doing these small maneuvers. We have to attack, do something bigger."

Azarias crosses his arms over his chest. "We can't. We don't have the forces yet. Scouts are going through villages out west, training people in Eryndale even now, to help us in this fight. But at the moment, all we have manpower for are small maneuvers. Yes, their retaliation last night was brutal, but they can't afford to keep that up. They're going to have too many kids and teens to deal with if they bring them in at this rate. You said before that they only had a specific number planned for every extraction, right?"

"Yes, but—"

"Then that's good. That means they know they can handle a certain amount, but having more than that will cause damage. Not to mention, these teens, these kids, have seen worse things than any of you did before you were brought to the city. They're less likely to believe the lies told by—what's her name?"

His words make me pause. He might be right.

"Elva Trill," Matthias supplies when I stay silent. His face is impassive. Hard. He doesn't look like *Matthias*.

Then it hits me.

His father is probably partially responsible for the attacks being ordered. After all, he's one of Ark's right-hand men. Besides Laban, Colonel Keenan Valarius is one of the most ruthless men I know.

"It gets worse," Catori says. "Even the town Davey and I were in yesterday was hit. We suspect there are Watchers within the towns everywhere near Talionis now, even ones who before this may not have had anyone spying for the city. Otherwise, there's no way they could have moved as quickly as they did." She digs her fingers into Shep's fur, and the dog leans against her. "Most of the kids below deck no longer have parents." Her voice drops to a broken whisper at those words, and my heart drops with her.

"Will you tell them?" I ask.

She releases a long, low sigh. "We'll have to, but I want to get them to safety first."

The influx of information almost leaves me breathless. I don't know how to process it, and part of me just wants to scream or fight someone in hand-to-hand combat, release some of the anxiety spreading through me like a virus.

But I have to stay cool. Level-headed.

My friends are still safe, still alive, and we can still do something to stop Talionis. My mind whirls as I allow the information Azarias just shared to seep in.

"So you have reinforcements coming?" I ask.

"Yes," he says. "We're hoping within the next few weeks our numbers will double, if not triple."

I nod and begin pacing again. "That's good."

As much as I hate the fact that these small maneuvers are the only option, it makes sense if it's to prepare for something bigger.

But a few weeks is too long for Storm and Cai.

"We need to draw the Talionis forces further apart," I say. "Spread out their resources. Don't just attack in the places closest to Talionis, but find out where the soldiers will be deploying in order to search for us so that we can hit those soldiers as well. We want the attacks spread out enough that Ark and Laban can't just destroy villages whenever they want. They still need villages. They still need teens and kids. And like you said"—I nod to Azarias—"they won't be able to continue capturing them in such a frenzied way. Ark has a plan, and accomplishing that is his biggest goal right now. He needs to be stopped."

I pause in my pacing. "But he also gave us a time limit, and if we don't return his items within six days, what's he going to do to Storm? To your dad?" I clutch my necklace and wait. Azarias knows I want to do something to save them, but he can't give the okay for such a dangerous mission.

His eyes seem pinched in pain for a moment, but that's the only indication he gives that he's concerned for his father. He's a soldier through and through. "Our hope is that with everything happening, with all the attacks we're planning and continuing to follow through with, we'll distract Ark from that timeline."

Matthias speaks up. "Ark is a very difficult man to distract. And he'll do anything to accomplish his plans."

"Nevertheless," Azarias says, "I think we might be able to cause enough of a hindrance that the timeline will be the least of his worries."

Matthias and I share a look, and I know he can feel my increasing anxiety. I step closer to him, needing his stability.

Azarias shifts his gaze to Catori. "Bill, Paul, and Wade will be here soon. They'll refit the supply room as you requested. With all that's happened, Lorenzo agreed it was a good idea to have you prepared for whatever may come."

"Good," Catori says.

Although I'm curious about what Bill, Paul, and Wade will be doing, I don't ask. There's stirring on the deck. My friends are awake and coming topside.

Kemena enters the wheelhouse and looks around the room at all of us, then zeroes in on Azarias. "What's going on?"

He begins telling her the same things he's told us, and I slip out of the wheelhouse.

The rest of my friends will know what's going on within the next few minutes.

I need a moment to think. To wrap my head around what will happen next. Matthias trails after me, but he remains silent, and I'm happy for his company.

God, what do we do?

There's too much happening. And our enemy has too many advantages.

Fear not. The words whisper through my heart, memories pulsing through me of verses I've read from Cai's Bible. But I don't know how to stop being afraid.

Matthias and I stand at the back of the boat and stare out at the river passing behind us as the boat continues forward to a destination that is unknown to me at the moment. I didn't even ask Azarias where we were going, the name of the towns we would be near, or exactly which maneuvers we'd be doing. None of it seems to matter.

"Hey, didn't expect to see you back here," Quwani says as she brings a bucket full of dirty water to the edge of the rail and tosses it into the river. She faces us. "Guess you heard the news. You both look like wreck cases."

My eyebrows rise at her strange use of words, but the meaning is clear enough.

"Yeah." I clear my throat. "How did you end up part of Catori's crew?" I ask, desperate for a new conversation topic, anything to pull me away from the reality of what we're about to face.

"Oh, that." Quwani sets the bucket on the ground. "Well, my family, they act like I'm really—what do you call it?—the black pigeon of the family."

Matthias covers a laugh, but Quwani doesn't seem to notice.

"And they didn't really want me around much because, you

know, I like to say things like it is. They don't really go down for that kind of stuff."

Quwani's quick words and strange vocabulary make it clear why she and Retro get along.

"Anyway, I was looking for something that would give me a little purpose, you know. And, one day I was in a town, and I found out Catori's crew was looking for some more people. This was about three years ago now. I'd heard great things about them and all the work they do, so"—she shrugs—"I volunteered to jump in. Well, I guess volunteer is a strong word, since they pay me and everything. And, you know, there was also a very difficult onboarding process."

She shudders. "They are picky about who they let in, I will say that much. But when they heard more about me and realized I wasn't idiotical, they were happy to have me on board. Don't get me wrong." She holds up her hands. "I made sure to prove myself before I told my sob story. Wanted them to know that they were getting someone who was gonna work hard and be a great asset to the team." She pounds her fist into her hand. "Not just someone who wanted to share things that could be cried about, you know?"

I'm nodding, even as my mind swirls with the person who is Quwani.

"So, yeah." She flips her hair behind her. "They've been family ever since. Best family I ever had, really. Not that my first family was much to talk about. But this family, they like black pigeons."

Matthias full-on laughs now. "I have never heard that saying before."

Quwani grins at him and shrugs. "Well, maybe I'm getting it wrong, but you understand what I mean, right?"

He nods, then sobers quickly. "How do you handle it? Having a difficult family."

Quwani's face goes serious. "I was real bitter for a while, but didn't want to stay a bitter face. So, I just asked God to help me forgive them. And He's been good to do that. Now I try to be sweet as a sheep and spicy as a serpent, you know?"

"Do you mean wise as a serpent and harmless as a dove?" Matthias asks.

"Oh, is that how that verse goes?"

At Matthias's yes, Quwani nods vigorously. "Then yeah, exactly that."

I grin at the young woman before me.

She is special.

I've thought that from the beginning, but hearing just a small amount of her story, seeing how she is in her life and actions, just proves to me that you can overcome your past. I've seen it over and over again with Nika, with Matthias.

Family can play an important role, but it also can break you in ways you never expected. I've seen that with both of my friends, felt it in my own life with my aunt. But that doesn't have to be what defines us.

And God can give us new family. Family that will stay with us through the good and the hard. Fight with us when everything is falling apart, and stand strong against enemies who would seek to destroy.

The thought gives me some courage to step into whatever we're about to face today.

"Oh hey," she says, "sounds like I'm going with you to this next smackdown of Talionis. Retro taught me that word. Great word."

"You are?" Matthias asks.

She nods. "Yes, sir. Azarias wants a few of you guys to go with Catori and Davey to bring the kids to the safe house. And since I've done some training"—she stretches her hands out in front of her, revealing slender arms with toned muscles—"I think I can be a bit of help. At least I know how to shoot a bow and arrow. That's something, right?"

"We rarely use bows and arrows," Matthias says, "but if you know how to point a weapon and shoot it with some accuracy, we can probably help you handle a rifle."

She grins. "Excellent."

THIRTY-NINE

Bill, Paul, and Wade arrive at *The Fearless Lady* right before we leave. The three men were more somber than I've ever seen them, but before we get off the boat, sounds of them working ring through the air.

Our group ends up more split apart than I realized it would be. Shane and Matthias are traveling with Catori and Davey to get the group of teens and kids to a safe house. I'm disappointed to be separated from Matthias again, but I know he's an excellent choice to help those kids. Before we left, he was showing Barry how to break free from a hold—but he was doing it in such a comical way most of the kids were smiling or laughing.

I can't imagine a better guy than Matthias.

Azarias and Kemena are meeting up with the local site and connecting Ari with a tech team from Eryndale to discuss how the wall works. Ari's also planning to share how they can use teams to manually cause issues on the wall that will provide a distraction to the soldiers patrolling the outer perimeter and those on the wall towers.

Which leaves Retro, Jordyn, Nika, me, and Quwani.

Because of the attacks last night, things changed. Our maneuvers were supposed to be more direct, but Lorenzo sent word that the mission objective shifted. Now the five of us are on an intel-gathering op. Which I think is the only reason Jordyn was able to accompany us.

Within a few hours, I'm in a very cramped site, camouflaged as I point a rifle at a group of soldiers patrolling a town.

Nika is camouflaged to my left as my spotter, and Quwani is stationed with Retro and Jordyn a quarter of a mile away. We're connected through comm units, but nobody's using them since we're not far from Talionis and don't want any of our communication intercepted.

The comms are for emergency purposes only.

Our mission today is to watch the patrol through Shadowvale to see exactly what they're doing. Gather intel. Apparently, the informant Eryndale had in Shadowvale was discovered a week ago and executed. They haven't been able to get anyone in since. Not that I think they would want to get anyone back in there, considering how dangerous it is.

I blink and shift ever so slightly to adjust my view through the scope of the rifle. Still nothing interesting to report.

We're only ten miles from Talionis, and it's like I can feel the tech and the power of that city breathing down my neck like a monster eager to pull me back into its trap. It reminds me of the monster I face when I swim, when I try to defeat the memories of what happened the day Ezri drowned.

The monster of Talionis is far worse, because the monster in the rivers and the ocean—that monster just wants to destroy me like it destroyed Ezri.

But this monster . . . the monster of Talionis will destroy everything and every person I love. It'll ruin everything that's good.

I glance out of the side of my eye at where Nika lays next to me, watching the town through the spotter lens.

My life before Talionis wasn't easy, but it was good.

Unlike all of my friends who I met there.

It's almost like Talionis has specifically chosen kids who went through something traumatic or have families whose home lives are awful. I pause as the thought filters through my mind. That makes sense, actually. From a strategic standpoint, it'd be easier to manipulate someone who has trauma in their past, especially someone who is young.

The propaganda of Elva Trill would sink in much better if teens had already dealt with things in their homes that were difficult or horrifying.

From what I know of Ari's and Bryson's upbringing, their dad physically abused them.

Nika went through more trauma than I could ever imagine.

Shane was abandoned, looking for family and home.

Even Shay. Shay's mom treated her like garbage after her dad left. No wonder she was so ready to believe the lies of Elva Trill. She's longed for a mother figure for as long as I could remember.

And Ark knew about Ezri's death. Knew how deeply it impacted me. It was the reason he chose to give my necklace back to me—another way to control me. The seaglass pendant Ezri gave me is now interwoven with a chain from Ark. It rests on my neck, the new chain far more familiar to me than I wish it was.

My fingers tighten around the rifle and I release a slow, steadying breath as I watch the town. It's still quiet.

But my thoughts scream at me.

Talionis chose every single one of us on purpose.

I mean, I've known that for a long time. But at first, I thought it was mainly because of the physical conditioning ability, the strength they could gain from us that way. Or through recruits skilled in tech like Ari and Bryson. But they also wanted broken minds they could mold.

Broken kids they could change.

What will they do now that they're just taking in every teen they can get their hands on?

Not all of them will come from the broken homes and lives that my friends experienced. Or even the trauma of losing a brother like I experienced.

Will there be more resistance in Talionis? More teens and kids ready to stand up and fight against what they're being taught? Not ready to believe every lie and succumb to every privilege they gain from doing what Talionis says?

Maybe.

The thought is almost encouraging.

If there are those in the city who are being trained and conditioned to fight, but who are also ready to turn against their captors, maybe we can actually bring Talionis down. . .with help from the inside. I tuck the thought away, making a mental note to bring the idea to Azarias later, and focus through the rifle at the new group of soldiers coming down the street.

I look through the scope to get eyes on each of their faces. They're different from the last patrol that went through. I click the counter in my hand seven times to account for the seven soldiers, seven new faces, bringing the total to thirteen soldiers occupying the city. At least that we know of so far.

My guess would be that number would include an additional five to seven people for whoever they have in leadership. And that's not counting whoever Quwani, Retro, and Tracker are spotting on the western edges of the town.

My body goes numb as I stay in position for the next four hours. Nika is as still as a statue next to me. Sometimes I wonder if she's even breathing, but her eyes flick my direction every once in a while, and I know that she's as alert to everything as I am. I've counted an additional ten soldiers, which makes me assume there's at least thirty in the city.

Thirty Talionis soldiers in a town that's ten miles from the limits of Talionis.

Why is this one so important? Why would they have so many stationed here?

Are they guarding something, or is this just somewhere Major Vasco believes would be vulnerable to attacks that could actually harm Talionis?

The thought makes me want to explore further.

When there's no sign of soldiers, I shift. Nika's breath hitches as she realizes I'm moving. Getting to my feet.

"What are you doing?" she hisses. "We're just here for intel gathering."

"I know," I say, "but I think we could discover more if we actually get into the town."

She grunts. "Girl, you got mud caked to every inch of you,

green paint on your face, and your hair is a mess of twigs and leaves. You gonna stand out like a sore thumb!"

Her words are true, but I step forward, adjusting my rifle strap so the gun is easier to carry. "No one's going to see me. I just want to slip in and see what I can find out."

It's late enough now that the sun is setting, which means it's probably close to 2000 hours. People should be settling in for the night, especially in an occupied town. From what we've heard from the other scouts who have been gathering intel for the past week, towns that are occupied by soldiers have a strict curfew of 2000 hours.

Which I guess means I'm a little more conspicuous if I'm moving about, but I stick to the shadows as I enter the town.

A tap on my shoulder causes me to twirl and lift my rifle.

Nika presses it down. "Girl, calm your little feathers. I'm coming with you. Can't let you go drag your sorry butt through town and get yourself captured without any backup," she grumbles. "My sister is going to lay into me so bad when she finds out I'm doing this."

I smirk, knowing Nika is not wrong.

Hopefully Kemena doesn't find out, because I'll likely be getting that tongue-lashing as well.

We creep into the town, and as I suspected, there's nobody in sight, not even soldiers. I pull out the small device Ari gave me that helps detect if there are any cameras or sensors nearby. Nothing pops up on the screen.

"Why do they have so many soldiers here?" I ask.

"Probably because it's so close to Talionis," Nika says. "They want control, girl. You know that. And people who want control, they do everything they can to intimidate and show their power. Of course Ark would want to jurisdiction in villages this close to the city."

"I know, but my guess is there're between thirty and fifty soldiers here. Talionis has a lot of soldiers, but how could Ark spare that many to come to this town? Why here? Why this place?"

Nika shrugs. "Not the worst point you've ever made. And I will admit you're a little better at strategy than I am."

I pause in my movement to look back at her. With the mud on my face, I'm not even sure she can tell my eyebrows are raised, and my skin pulls at the effort.

We go silent as we creep through the town's back alleys. We make a sweep of the village as I follow a map in my head from what Azarias showed us before we were sent on this mission. Another team was supposed to plant diversions, as Azarias called them, throughout the town tonight, but not until much later. Which is probably a good thing, since we'd definitely get in trouble if they spotted us.

I suddenly wonder if we might need to leave this town be, just to see what Major Vasco and Demetrius Ark are planning. The amount of troop movements here has Major Vasco's fingerprints all over it.

It feels like I'm entering a scenario, and the original purpose of the mission needs to change because of what I'm discovering. Instead of gathering intel, I need to bring down the enemy's intel source.

I'm guessing this town is becoming a hub for sending out soldiers. I drop to my knees and risk a glance around a corner of the building that Nika and I are pressed against.

No one in sight.

I pull back around the corner, stay where I am, and think. My mind races over the map of the area, the map I think my mom made.

Now I know that it doesn't include every village in all the spheres of Eryndale. Which was intentional and done through working with an inside source—a source still in Talionis who no one will name.

But I've also seen maps that Thaddeus had in Eryndale and the maps that are being used in the different stations of scouts throughout the area.

This village is equidistant to five other villages. So maybe all thirty to fifty troops aren't stationed here, but they're being sent out at various times to those other villages. And maybe it's to villages that haven't given any sign of being occupied. What if those villages are being observed through the large force of soldiers here?

"That might be it," I whisper to myself.

There's the clip of boots on the street, and Nika grabs my arm and pulls me to a standing position. Her thumb points almost violently back in the direction we came, and I nod. We jog as silently as possible back through the town and to our position, dropping to the ground as soon as we can.

No one followed us or even seemed to hear us. But a minute or two after we're in position, another group of soldiers passes by.

Their faces are, again, different from the ones we saw earlier. Could Major Vasco suspect that they're being watched? Does he want the maneuvers we're doing to be aimed at a town that is far more fortified than we realize?

If I were him, I'd replace the villagers, even relocate them to other villages that are being monitored, and have soldiers disguised as villagers here. Maybe even throw some Raiders into the mix.

After all, Lorenzo sent us here because they have seen more and more movement from Talionis troops to this town. They know it's important, but they don't know why.

Maybe the S.O.C. doesn't even *realize* it's a hub. But it is. And it's also a trap.

I know it deep within myself. We remain in position for another hour until darkness has fully consumed the area. Nika and I use sanitation wipes to clean our hands before we put our lenses in and hike back to the site three miles away.

I quickly share with Nika what I believe is going on in the town.

"That sounds ridiculous. But," she says before I can argue my point, "I believe you. I mean, I saw the scenarios we went through same as you did. Didn't always understand them the way you did, but went through them just the same. And you're right. This would fit with something Major Vasco would do. Distract and divert from the real reason, the real target."

"Which means," I say, "if a group went in to set traps in that town tonight . . ."

"Then they're in danger." Nika finishes for me.

FORTY

Nika and I follow the map Thaddeus gave us back to the site. This site is different from the one we were at yesterday. It's settled in a broken-down building in the midst of a pre-Demise town. There's nothing as we travel through the rubble of the old city that would indicate there's any kind of movement in the area, which is impressive but barely registers in my mind.

I'm too busy trying to race through the possibilities of what could happen later tonight.

From what we were briefed on earlier, the team going into the town Nika and I were just observing shouldn't be heading in until midnight, when things are at their quietest.

But I'm desperate to keep Lorenzo from sending them in at all.

We duck under old boards that have fallen over the doorway to the building, then weave through the debris before coming to the door that leads to the entrance of the site. We knock. A moment later, the door opens, and light spills into the darkness of the night. My contacts adjust, and Nika and I enter.

The door shuts behind us immediately. Different groups are spread around. Some are working on maps, and I catch sight of Thaddeus directing everyone on how to handle the new information that's coming in steadily from different teams out in the field.

There's a group suiting up and preparing to go out, but it's too early for them to be heading to the town Nika and I just left.

Retro, Jordyn, and Quwani are off to the side cleaning off their camouflage. Nika and I make our way toward them. We need to head to a briefing, but no one wants us tracking the mud caked to our skin farther into the site than we already have.

My body itches, not just from the debris clinging to me, but even more from the need to share the information that is becoming more and more of a reality in my mind.

I only hope they believe us.

Being distrusted by Eryndale has left a mark on me.

It's a little strange when I consider that my fellow recruits trusted anything I said in a Warfare Scenario without question. Or if I had a group of recruits trying to get through a kill zone, no one would second-guess my instincts on how the whole thing was set up.

But here, I feel on edge.

It's not right. The place where I should feel the most comfortable and at home is uncomfortable. Like an old pair of pants that just don't fit right.

While Retro, Jordyn, Quwani, and Nika talk, I step fully clothed into the makeshift shower that's been set up, rinsing dirt from my body and clothes. Once most of the mud is washed away, I walk as quickly as possible to the changing room. I change into a new pair of camouflage pants and a black T-shirt.

Nika, Quwani, and Jordyn aren't far behind me.

"You took off faster than a jackrabbit in spring," Quwani says to me. "You okay?"

Nika glances at me, waiting for me to answer the question. But my mind is still revving like a transport about to take off, trying to figure out how I'm going to broach this topic with groups of people who don't know me well enough to believe everything I say.

When I don't respond, Nika speaks for me. "Bria—oh, and me—have a suspicion about the town we just observed."

"Old Milford?" Quwani asks. "From what we saw, there's a

lot of activity there. Seems like a great idea to do something tonight to slow them down. They're preparing for something."

Nika looks at me again.

If they saw as much movement on their end of the sprawling town, it confirms my suspicions.

I scrape my hand over my face. "Let's just get to the briefing. We'll explain more there."

The three girls follow me from the room, but we don't make it more than a few yards out of the door before Kemena rounds on us.

"Girl, you can't keep doing this to me." She puts both hands on Nika's shoulders, staring her in the eye. "You go off script every time we send you out. That's not how scouts work. That's not what we do here."

Nika says, "But Bria—"

"No, no. I'm sure there was a reason you two thought was good enough to leave your cover and enter a town crawling with Talionis soldiers and Raiders." She pinches the bridge of her nose. "Do you want to be captured again? Do you want to face what you told me was the worst time of your life, even with everything else you've gone through?"

Nika reaches up to grab Kemena's hands. She stares her in the eye. "I know it's scary, but Kem, you have to trust me. I know what I'm doing, and I trust Bria. If she has an instinct about something, we need to listen."

"This has nothing to do with Bria," Kemena says.

Nika squeezes her sister's shoulders, then steps back. "Yes, it does. Bria is someone I will follow anywhere. I trust her instincts. I trust her leadership. She believes there's something going on in that town, and we need to get to the briefing so we can share about it."

Kemena's jaw quivers for a moment, giving way to the real-ization that she's less angry and more terrified of losing her sister again.

Which I understand.

I can't imagine how I'd feel if my brothers were putting themselves in harm's way. Especially if it meant they might be taken by Talionis soldiers. It's weird being around people who care about us again. I'm sure if my parents were here, they would be furious with me for going "off script," as Kemena put it. For putting myself in that danger.

But our loved ones don't fully understand who we are now.

They don't know everything we've gone through. They don't know how we've had to step up and make decisions. It's oddly difficult to navigate.

How do I become the woman God is calling me to be while also considering those who are watching? Those who are afraid of losing me or one of my friends again?

I push the thought aside as I remember the village we were just in.

I nod toward the briefing. "We should go."

Kemena grunts, then pulls Nika into a hug once again. There's a fierceness this time. It's almost as though she's decided every hug with her sister could be her last.

And I guess that's the experience she's had.

When I think about it like that, more compassion fills me.

God, show me how to handle this. It's all beyond me. How to fight an enemy and care for those that you love.

But right now, there's a more pressing matter to deal with.

Keeping a team of scouts safe.

THE BRIEFING IS ALREADY IN PROGRESS WHEN WE ENTER.

Matthias and Shane are there, along with Catori and Davey. I make my way through the room toward them with Nika, Quwani and Jordyn.

Ari is at a back table with two other tech people, muttering quietly. Nika and I never understand her tech mutterings, and she *knows* we don't get tech like she does. I can only imagine what she sounds like when she's talking to other tech heads.

A team is sharing about how they have sabotaged four transports within the past twenty-four hours, hitting different towns on their route. They look exhausted but pleased with their efforts. Grease stains their hands, and sweat and black paint drip down their faces.

There are six of them, four girls and two guys.

They aren't scouts I recognize, but I'm impressed as they detail hitting the towns they were directed to go to, as well as an additional one they discovered soldiers in while traveling back, and what they did to disable the transports.

It may not keep the Talionis soldiers grounded for long. But it will hinder their efforts, and it's all supposed to build into the attack tonight on Milford.

The attack that can't happen.

Another team talks as soon as the first team finishes, and I realize I missed my tiny window of opportunity to share my intel.

This team includes Wolf, who is speaking on behalf of his team. Even though I don't know him well, it's nice to see a familiar face.

Azarias listens, but he's acting strange. He keeps glancing at the door, and at first, I wonder if he's even hearing what Wolf is saying. But he nods and asks the right questions.

Wolf tells him what they have done in terms of setting up booby traps and stopping the soldiers from their normal rotations. He also shares what they've seen of Raider involvement, which seems to increase by the day.

I listen, itching to dive in with what I need to say.

I'm not entirely sure how any of this will make a long-term difference. Then again, the Talionis soldiers can be a bit superstitious. What Cai did in the Ruins freaked them out and kept them from venturing out there unless they were under direct orders.

When Wolf's team finishes, Azarias focuses on a female scout I don't recognize. Before he can ask her how things went with her team, I jump in.

"We have something we have to share," I say.

Everyone's attention zeros in on me, and the focus is almost suffocating. They all look shocked that I interrupted Azarias.

Eryndale has an order and hierarchy, similar to Talionis.

I guess that's how it works in any group of people that need to enter battle together, but there's too much I need to share right now for me to care if I'm upsetting a chain of command.

Azarias almost seems to smile, and he nods at me. "Go ahead."

I quickly lay out what Nika and I found in the village.

His frowns briefly when I mention that Nika and I took a moment to check the town. Since Kemena knew we went in, I assumed he did too. I can already feel the rebuke that'll come when he gets a chance to talk with us later. But as I outline what I think is going to happen, his face turns thoughtful.

"I'm not sure it's worth us completely shutting down the attack we were building up to tonight," he says.

"You have to," I insist. "If they go in, they're going to get hurt. Or worse." The intensity of my conviction would have surprised me months ago. But I've learned to trust my ability to see through situations. To embrace it and use it to help others fight better, and fight to win.

Cade always encouraged me and listened to my theories. Pushed me to tell others so I could help them. Even though Cade's not here, I can honor his memory in that way.

Thaddeus and Kemena enter the room.

Azarias nods to them. "Bria, can you share with Thaddeus what you just told me?"

I give a faster outline of what's about to happen.

"Alpha Team's ready to move in," Thaddeus says. "It'll ruffle some feathers, but if she's right, we need to adjust our plans. You make the call, Azarias. But if you want to call it off, you need to call it off now."

I clamp my hands into fists at my sides until my nails dig into my palms, but I keep my mouth shut. I've relayed the information. They need to make this decision.

Azarias stares at me. Then, for an instant, his eyes close. Maybe he's praying about the decision he's about to make.

Do leaders who follow God do that? Do they pray every time before they're about to do something that could impact the lives of others?

It's what I would want to do.

People look to you for leadership, and it's not something you expect in a moment. Or maybe some people do. Maybe they grow up wanting to lead. But that wasn't me. It's not something

I anticipated when I was taken to Talionis. When my life was shattered and changed. And it's not something I expected when I escaped.

But now, it's something I feel like I have to walk in. To lead in a way that will save lives. In a way that will help people find an escape and hope and truth. That will break the lies that are being woven over the hearts and minds of the youth in this region.

I'm not able to make a decision that will change anything. Not in this moment. But even speaking up in the way I have is putting myself at risk of being turned over to Talionis if anyone in the C.A.E. believes I'm trying to disrupt their attacks.

It's worth the risk.

"Radio Alpha Team," Azarias says. "Tell them to change their mission from insertion to intel gathering. Spread around Milford, and maintain as low a profile as possible."

Thaddeus nods. He turns and exits the room faster than I've ever seen him move.

With a start, I realize the attack on that town was supposed to happen much earlier in the day than I expected. I release my hands from the fists at my side and look at Azarias with all the gratitude I can muster.

He focuses on me. "There was a lot riding on that tonight, but we'll let it play out to see if your instincts are correct. It's a gamble."

His words are cautionary, and I feel the weight of what could happen if I'm wrong. But I am thankful that for now, Alpha Team is safe.

FORTY-ONE

The briefing ends, and my friends and I are dismissed to go to bunk houses that are additional sites in the pre-Demise town. They've been set up to house scouts who are waiting to go on mission or in between missions. We make our way to one of the buildings and settle in for the night.

I breathe a sigh of relief that this day has ended. But as I lie on my cot, dark thoughts assault me.

What if Eryndale's tactics fail before reinforcements can arrive?

Ark is relentless, and Talionis's resources run deep. Especially now that Ark is working with Raiders as well.

Plus, he has connections in Sitreea. The chancellor there, and all those who are part of that country across the ocean, don't realize Ark is planning to attack and destroy it.

They think Talionis is an intel-gathering base of its own. I'm sure Ark could spin everything that's happening for his own gain. Make it like somehow Talionis was discovered by a militant group in the wasteland that was once America. Which means he could have more soldiers sent in. But then he'd also have to hide the now hundreds of teens he's got training as recruits.

I turn to my side, the thoughts whiplashing me worse than a right hook in the jaw from Laban.

Ark could spin that as well, say that he was able to gather

those who could help him push off the attacks happening around the city.

If Sitreea got involved, it could make everything a thousand times worse.

My stomach churns, and I feel sick.

This isn't going to work.

We're never going to stop Demetrius Ark. Even though I saw through one of the plans Major Vasco has in place, somehow I know I'm not going to like whatever news I hear tomorrow about the change in the mission.

Drastic measures need to be taken. First, we need to get Storm and Cai out of that city. And we only have five more days

---

THE NEXT MORNING, MY FRIENDS AND I MAKE OUR WAY THROUGH THE pre-Demise town and to the main site to find out what our orders are for today.

The air is still, and thick fog lies over the earth. The sky lightens as the sun attempts to break through the fog, but it hasn't found the strength to do so yet.

A sense of foreboding wraps itself around my mind and heart.

I don't even want to know what the next plan is. Or hear the results of last night's change in mission.

But I enter the room ahead of my friends.

We're pointed to the back briefing area by a scout who's working near the door. "Azarias said to send you guys back as soon as you got in." He hesitates. "Don't think it's going to be a fun meeting."

The way he says the words almost apologetically leaves me feeling anxious, but I square my shoulders and practically march my way to the back of the room.

I open the door to the briefing station to find Gabe pacing the room.

His arms fly through the air as he gestures and enunciates every word he's practically screaming at Azarias. "You can't call off an attack like that without prior authorization. Other higher-level scouts in the S.O.C. authorized this attack. It was part of a larger strategy." He points an accusing finger at Azarias. "And you knew that."

Shane is the last one to enter the briefing room, and when the door clicks shut behind him, Gabe rounds on us.

"And you two." He focuses on me and Nika. "You can't defy orders like that. That's not how Eryndale works. We *follow* orders here. We obey our leaders because we trust them." His words are emphatic, and his eyes flash.

If this was Talionis, I'd be sent to the sandpit for disregarding a direct command. Or maybe even to the Ruins if I went against someone with enough power to enact that punishment.

But I don't know what types of punishments Eryndale gives out. I only hope the line I've crossed isn't bad enough to get my friends and me turned over to Talionis.

Azarias doesn't appear fazed. "We reacted based on intel we received in the field. I understand that orders were disregarded, but it is what needed to happen."

Gabe pounds his fist into his hand. "No, it wasn't. The team came back this morning with no additional intel to corroborate what Bria and Nika said was supposed to be there." He focuses on my friends and me. "And if you keep providing intel that's so shoddy, then how are we supposed to believe you're anything but spies working with Talionis?"

The words slice through me, but before any of us can argue, he presses forward. "That maneuver last night was going to be crippling. The base in Milford is one we've been preparing to hit for days. You come in, and in less than eight hours, you decide it's a plan that can be scrapped and changed? Do you know what *details* went into this strategy? The resources we've expended? Every maneuver for the past four days has been used to push soldiers into Milford so that when the attack happened, it would provide the greatest amount of damage to Talionis and its troops. How could you just change it without knowing any of that?"

I blink. That is information I didn't have before.

And, with the way Azarias's eyebrows rise, I wonder if even he knew.

"As one of the leaders in the field," Azarias says, "I need to be briefed on all the intel as well."

Gabe flicks a glance at him. "Everyone is given what their clearance allows."

"What their clearance allows?" Azarias asks, incredulous. "What a bunch of bull. You've never even been in the field. You just dictated things from your high tower in Eryndale. But that's not how things work when you're on active duty. Which is something we've tried to tell you over and over again."

Their voices rise in volume, and part of me is relieved that Azarias seems as ticked as I am. Which means Gabe's focus and anger are away from us, at least for now.

Thaddeus pokes his head into the room. "Wow, there's a lot of commotion in here today."

Lorenzo is a few feet behind him. "What's going on?" He inches around Thaddeus.

I shift, uncomfortable at the thought of having Lorenzo here too.

"We're just having a discussion about how intel is not shared in a way it should be," Azarias says.

Lorenzo closes the door behind him. "Well, you're disrupting everything else happening out there, and it's not very good for morale."

His scrappy build and wiry frame remind me of some of the best hand-to-hand combat fighters in Talionis. Although the man isn't as young as some of the other scouts, I'm sure he could hold his own in a fight.

"There was a breakdown of information sharing," Lorenzo says, "and it impacted what happened last night. But we're moving forward now."

His words surprise me. I expected him to blame me for this— yell at me as much as Gabe. Maybe more so. I'm not sure if I should be relieved or concerned at how well he's taking the news.

"Milford will be attacked later today," Lorenzo says. "Before that happens, there are other things we need to discuss."

The idea of the attack continuing leaves me on edge. Even though I didn't have all the details about Eryndale's plans, I still believe something is off. Major Vasco is too skilled a strategist to allow himself to be manipulated in the way Gabe suggested.

Gabe opens his mouth.

"Gabe, we have you here as a courtesy to the leaders of Eryndale." Lorenzo pushes up the sleeves of his shirt. "The S.O.C. is allowing you to be present, but that does not mean you get to order my people around. Understood?"

Gabe's gray eyes flash hot and then cold, but he nods. Ever the diplomat.

I'm sure his report to his superiors is going to cast all of us in a terrible light. Including Lorenzo and Azarias. But neither of the men seem to care, which I assume means my friends and I are safe from being handed over to our enemies.

For now, Gabe steps back, acquiescing to the fact that Lorenzo needs to share something.

"I just arrived in," Lorenzo says, "and the reports aren't great. Yes, the Milford attack should have gone down last night, but I fear that's not our only problem."

My blood turns to ice in my veins as I wait for him to continue.

He glances at us, then focuses back on Azarias. "Talionis is retaliating in a way that is beyond what we anticipated. For every person we save, someone else is taken within hours. And for every attack we pull off—every transport that's disabled or explosion that happens in a town—Talionis is responding with brutality. We need to readjust. Move locations and shift everyone around. We're clearing this site tonight, and everything needs to be scrubbed and put in order today."

He nods to me and my friends, but speaks to Azarias. "Get them back aboard *The Fearless Lady*, move a few miles down the river, and set up a new site for us there. Thaddeus"—he turns to the man—"determine the best location, and give them the coordinates. Catori will be able to get them wherever you think is best without a problem."

Thaddeus nods. Before he leaves the room, he looks at me. "You want to come with me? Go over the maps and help me figure out the best locations for each of the next sites we're setting up?"

The offer leaves me speechless. Gabe sputters, clearly ready to tell Thaddeus that is not an option. Before Gabe can get out his arguments, I say yes and rush out of the room.

Thaddeus exits behind me as Gabe finds his voice to protest what's happening.

Lorenzo shuts him down, and then I can't hear anything else going on in the room as I follow Thaddeus to the cartography section of the site.

It's an area with three walls and one side that opens to the rest of the site. Maps are spread everywhere, some hanging on walls, others open on tables. I think of the map in my pack. The map I'm confident my mom made, even though no one will confirm that.

Part of me wants to pull it out and use it now. But it doesn't have all the intel we need. The maps Thaddeus has out are meticulous, and I'm sure they're accurate. But they're not nearly as beautiful as my mom's.

Thaddeus has an eye to catch the smallest of details and make sure they get added to a map. Which reminds me of how my mom works.

I step up next to Thaddeus, ready for a distraction from thoughts about my mom. The map laid out on the table displays the terrain for this region and everything within a twenty-mile radius of Talionis.

"Something I tell every one of my cartographers," Thaddeus says, brushing dust from the map, "is that the greatest mistakes and the most profound discoveries—"

"Are in the details," I finish with him, my voice shaking slightly.

He spins to look at me. "You've heard that before."

"My mom." My throat thickens as I say the words. "You worked with her, didn't you? Do you know where she is now? Have you heard anything? Do you know if she's safe?"

Questions I wanted to ask days ago spew from my mouth at Thaddeus. He looks as surprised as if I just shot him with a dozen bullets.

He inhales and releases a breath slowly through his mouth. "Yeah, I know her." He gives a huff that's somewhere between a sigh and a laugh. "The saying came from her, actually." His eyes take on a faraway look. "When your pupil starts to surpass you, when they discover more than you ever thought you could know about something that was your trade for years, you listen to what they have to say."

He shakes his head as though lost in a memory. "Your mom was one of those people. I taught her everything I knew, but before she was eighteen, Lily knew more than me. She thought of questions that shocked me. Had ways of looking at cartography like an art. In a way that was beautiful. There's something special when you're young and passionate and eager to learn. And that was your mom." He clears his voice as though overcome by emotion.

"Your other questions are above your clearance level." He points at something on the map and nods his head to it as though I need to focus there as well. "Just look at it and act like you are thoroughly engaged in what I'm saying about it, okay?" His voice is so low I'm confident no one else is hearing our conversation.

Especially since the different sections are now preparing to clean up, and the murmuring in the building fills the air with a dull hum that masks any whisper.

"You aren't cleared for this information," Thaddeus repeats, "but I'll tell you this much. Your mom was sent in undercover." He shifts the map. "After you were taken, your parents came to Eryndale. Both your mother and father worked as scouts when they were younger, before you were born. Your mom was the best cartographer I ever had the pleasure of training. Cai brought her back in to create the map for his mole in Talionis. Once she was done, she and your dad moved to Derbe. It was a new village, and one she purposefully kept off the map along with the Center Villages of each sphere."

My mind feels unable to process as Thaddeus speaks words I can't comprehend. My mom and dad were scouts? I knew my mom made the map—at least, I suspected she did—but the fact she was a scout . . . I force myself to focus.

"When you were taken, she knew right away it was because of Talionis. She and your dad arrived here a month after your capture, coming as soon as they were able. It was then that we realized how compromised things were. There were spies for Talionis everywhere. In almost every town and village in the east, at least as far as we could tell."

I stare unseeing at the map Thaddeus is, once again, adjusting.

He continues, "Your mother insisted on going undercover in Talionis to get us the details we needed. And to find you."

"What?" The word is somewhere between a gasp and a sob. My mom can't be in Talionis too. "Is she there now?" The answer to my pathetic question should be obvious, but I still ask it. Desperately hoping the answer isn't the one I fear it is.

Thaddeus removes a small pin from the map. "Our contact in Talionis got her past the wall not long after you escaped. Actually, based on what you've shared with us and the intel I have, it looks like it all happened the same day."

My hands shake, and I clasp them together. My mom entered Talionis the day I left?

"But why?" I ask, as my mind fights to understand.

"She was right. We needed someone to go in. Your dad wasn't thrilled with the option, but he also understood it. Your mom's skills are unique. I'm not lying when I say she's the best I've ever worked with. Plus, she's trained as a scout."

The words are almost like a slap in my face. I know my mom, but I don't know my mom. She hasn't shared this part of herself with me, and it hurts a bit.

Or maybe it's just because I miss her so much, and I wish she was the one telling me everything.

"We knew your mom would be able to leak out the intel necessary to hurt Talionis. So, we sent her in with the ability to communicate with us. Our contact in the city is a little more hesitant to work as freely as they did before."

It doesn't escape me that Thaddeus refuses to give me the gender of their contact in the city. Once again, I wonder who within Talionis would go to such lengths to attempt to sabotage Ark's plan. But I ignore it for now, desperate to hear more about my mom and dad.

"She's given us great intel. Up until now." Thaddeus's shoulders slump. "A week ago, she went dark."

A gaping ache explodes through me, more painful than being shot by Colonel Valarius's training bullets.

"They caught her," I say, the words cracking as they escape my mouth.

Thaddeus shakes his head. He shifts the position he's pointing to on the map to a new place as someone walks by. "And here is where I think the next site—"

Once the person's out of earshot, he continues, "I don't think so, but I don't know. I want to think the best. I can't imagine Lily being gone or taken by those people. My hope is her communication gear shorted out or had some damage. Or that she's in a position that would be compromised if she attempted to get information out." He licks his lips. "We have others who are feeding us intel, but they don't know about your mom."

I blink. "But why?"

"It's been important that each group function on their own until we could coordinate efforts to bring them together. There's too much at stake if Talionis carries out their plans. Which is a far greater scheme than we first expected. We can thank you for that knowledge." He nods his head at me. "Not everyone's ready to trust anyone who was in there, because we know enough to know that it's a dangerous place." He shifts to better face me. "It might not feel like it, but what we're doing *will* have an impact. You gotta trust that the plan is more far-reaching than what you can see."

I want to argue that it'd be easier to trust them if they shared this "far-reaching" plan with me and my friends. But I incline my head in agreement. Thaddeus has shared way more with me than he should have, and I'm thankful for his trust.

"What about my dad?" I ask, almost afraid to hear his answer.

Thaddeus hesitates. "Josiah's back in Eryndale now. I heard word that he arrived late last night. He, Kassre, and Hosea are working on something so top secret, even I don't know the details."

Air rushes out of my lungs. My dad's alive. *Thank you, God.* As much as I long to see him, I'm thankful he's with my brothers. Safe.

Although I wonder how long he'll remain safe if he's actively planning something with Kassre and Hosea.

"Now, I really do need you to help me figure out those sites." Thaddeus nods to the map. "I have some ideas, but since you know Talionis and the area fairly well, I figured you might be able to lend some help. Especially if you're anything like your mom." His face softens, but sadness tinges his eyes.

I shift my focus to the map that's in front of us. As much as I wanted to know what is going on with my mom and dad, it's almost too much to take in. I'm ready for a distraction.

FORTY-TWO

Over the next hour, Thaddeus and I determine the placements for three dozen Eryndale sites. Which is way more than I anticipated there being. They're spread around the area in a shotgun scatter approach, and yet there's an order to it that I see as I put it together with Thaddeus.

We adjust each location based on how Talionis has currently been moving. We even end up working with Lorenzo to establish a plan of action for the attacks that are going to come.

I listen as they talk, but I don't enjoy hearing the options that are available to us.

It's more of the same. The same things that don't seem to be working.

I know they thought covert ops were the answer. That maneuvers like this and fighting from the shadows would stop our mutual enemy. But I don't think it will.

Especially now that I know my mom's inside Talionis and no one's been able to communicate with her.

The knowledge leaves me feeling raw, afraid, and unsure of what to do.

After I've listened to them go back and forth about prepping teams for disabling transports, setting up teams who will go in to take down soldiers, and working with other teams to smuggle out those who have been marked for extraction by Talionis, I interrupt the two men, who almost appear to have forgotten I'm here.

"Send me in with a team into Talionis," I say with as much conviction as I can muster.

"Impossible," Lorenzo says. "No one in the S.O.C. would agree to that right now. There's too much that needs to be done. Not to mention, if we sent in an insertion team, we'd need to make sure we had a strong attack plan in place to draw their attention."

"But you've sent people in before, right?" I argue.

Thaddeus's eyebrows rise, and I realize I've just shared that I know more than I should.

Whoops.

Lorenzo's head snaps up, and his eyes narrow as he looks at me. "Why would you think that?"

"Uh, I . . ." I'm stumbling through words and desperately trying to find an answer when Ari pops over to the cartography area.

"I think I have a plan," she says. "I know we've been doing these different *maneuvers*"—she does air quotes at the word—"but I was thinking. If I can use some of my tech and set up a cyberattack, we could disable more than we currently are. Way more."

Lorenzo and Thaddeus are both shaking their heads before Ari finishes her statement.

"But it would work great," she argues.

"No," Lorenzo says with finality. "We appreciate what you've done in helping our tech teams determine ways to disable things that are connected to Talionis, but we don't want to engage with them directly in cyber warfare."

"It's a good way to engage," Ari mumbles. "Talionis runs on tech. The wall runs on tech. If I can get in and start hacking some of the code, we might be able to—"

Lorenzo drops his fist on the table, and the bang is loud enough to stop Ari's mumblings. "We can't risk that kind of attack. Not right now. Too much is on the line as it is, and we're scrambling to readjust. Talionis is too advanced in technology for us to hope to defeat them through cyber warfare."

"Which means it's a good time to go into the city and figure out more of what's going on," I say, risking Lorenzo's censure. "We at least need to save Cai and Storm."

And my mom. I keep thoughts of her to myself. If I say her name out loud, I'll be exposing that Thaddeus shared more with me than he was authorized to. I don't want to do that to my friend.

Lorenzo's face echoes sadness for a moment, but he still shakes his head. "I understand wanting to get them out."

"*Needing* to get them out," I emphasize. "Ark is threatening their lives if we don't return what he wants within five days' time. We're literally adjusting every plan we've had to fight against them because our efforts aren't working. We can't assume we'll figure out something that will work. But we *can* do something to save two people whose lives are on the line."

My cheeks are wet. I swipe the tears away. I'm crying in front of important men when I need to appear strong. But the reality is, I'm tired.

And I'm tired of fighting in a way that's not going to work.

Sure, Thaddeus and I have found new sites. And I do think some of their strategies could prove useful over time. But not now.

Now, there is an urgent matter at hand. Lives at stake. Ark is willing to go to any lengths to get what he wants. And what he wants right now are the items I have.

My mind flicks to Catori's safe on her boat. As much as I wish all the items were with me, it's probably better to have them locked away.

"It doesn't even have to be me." I try for a new tactic. "Somebody needs to go in and save that little girl and a man who's been important to Eryndale for as long as it's been in existence. He's Essie's son. Can't you at least use one of your contacts within the city to get Storm and Cai to safety? Tell them to get them to the Ruins. Cai knows that place better than anyone."

"No, it's impossible," Azarias says, entering the now cramped cartography space. "I want my dad safe, so I understand what you're saying." He presses his lips together, brow furrowed. "But we can't risk it."

"He's right," Lorenzo says. "We believe Talionis suspects we have someone in the city. If we do anything out of the ordinary, if our contacts don't lie low right now, we're putting every life at risk. Everything we're doing will be jeopardized if we attempt to warn or save Cai and that little girl."

"But she is a *little* girl," I say. "Why is nobody okay with doing something to save her? I thought that's what Eryndale did. We're saving kids from towns, stopping them from being taken just because they're marked. This kid has already been through so much that you can't even understand."

"I get it," Azarias says. "When a kid has seen evil, looked it in the face, it changes them. And all you want to do is protect them from ever having to witness it again." The passion in his voice is so deep that it silences me. "Levi still has nightmares. My son can't sleep sometimes because of what he went through before he was even four years old. So, I get it. I'd do anything for him, just like you would do anything for Storm." He pauses. "But right now, Storm is safer if we leave her be. Based on Ark's timeline, we still have five more days, and we need those five days, Bria. We need them. End of discussion."

"So if Levi was in Talionis, you would just leave him be?" I ask.

Azarias steps back, then breaks eye contact.

Which is enough to answer my question.

I turn, and walk away, out of the site and into the ruined town.

I meander through the streets, not caring that it's daylight or that a transport could go overhead at any moment and spot me. At this point, who cares?

At least then I'd be in the city. I'd be able to see Storm.

God, help me know what to do. Protect her, because I can't do anything.

FORTY-THREE

The site is scrubbed within six hours. Everything is packed, put in order—or rather, made to look like everything is disorderly—and broken down, like it was before any scouts arrived.

Matthias, Nika, Retro, Ari, Shane, Jordyn, Kemena, Bryson, and I hike with Catori and her crew back to *The Fearless Lady*. We move in small groups of three spread out over the area so we're not as obvious. But traveling this close to Talionis in broad daylight is unnerving. Azarias will meet up with us tomorrow, but he had more work to do with the site cleanup.

I hike, weapon in hand, next to Matthias and Nika.

I'm a bit surprised Kemena and Nika aren't hiking together, but despite the hug, something still felt strained between the sisters.

"You were in a heated discussion earlier," Nika says.

I step over a log before replying. "We need to do something. Go in. Get Storm."

Matthias squeezes my shoulder. "We still have five days. Maybe we can convince them to send in a group before Ark's timeline is up."

"Maybe," I say. "But they are dead set against it happening soon. What if we're too late?"

For some reason, saying the words to two of my closest friends makes me want to sob. It's like they both sense it and move closer to me, which thickens my throat even more.

"How are things with you and Kem?" I ask, desperate to change the subject.

"She'll be fine after she cools off a bit. She's just worried about me." Nika pauses as we duck under an old bridge. "I'm worried about her, too, honestly. She's been trained by the scouts, but she's not as strong as we are. She doesn't know what it's like to face the soldiers of Talionis. Not to mention, all of her maneuvers so far have been, well, not maneuvers. She's staying in the sites, which I think is good. But before we left this morning, she was talking to Azarias about actually taking on some tactical ops with us tomorrow."

My eyes widen. "What'd he say?"

"I don't think he had a choice in the matter," Nika says. "Kem's just upset that you and I keep going 'off script,' as she says, and she doesn't want to see us do it again. She thinks if she's with us, she can stop us." Nika lifts her eyebrows at me and makes a face so comical I almost want to smile.

Matthias chuckles. "But we all know that whether she's with you or not, it doesn't matter. You two are gonna do what you want." He scrambles up a steep hill. "Man, I should make sure I'm part of whatever group you guys are in tomorrow. Be much more fun than just gathering intel. Need to spice things up a bit, right?"

He jostles me with his shoulder, and I lean against him for a moment before he pulls away to step around a tree. I want Matthias to join us, but it is a little disconcerting to think about having Kemena there as well.

"These maneuvers won't work." I keep my voice low. "Major Vasco will see right through everything we're doing. I think he already has. That's why every attack from Talionis is more damaging to us than whatever it is we just did to them. They're too strong of an enemy for us to face with minimal troops. We just need to save who we can and get out of here."

I wish I felt more conviction behind the words. But I know

they're hollow, based on my fears about what's going to happen to those I care about.

"You don't believe that," Nika says, calling me out.

Which is exactly what I expected her to do.

"You know God's put us here, Bria." She ducks under a branch Matthias is holding out of the way for us. "We have to fight against evil. We have to stand against them, because God's given us this opportunity to do just that. Eryndale, the scouts, they have a plan, and there's only six of us that have actually been in Talionis. So yeah, we give the information we can. But at the end of the day, they've got the resources to stop them, not us. We have to listen."

"But what if they're wrong?" I argue. "What if we need to do something different from what they think?"

She hesitates. "I don't know. But right now, the best option is to keep doing what they tell us to do. Follow their orders."

"Every time I've followed someone else's orders, it's burned me," I say.

"Then you just gotta trust God, girl. At least these people are good. We can listen to them in a different way than we could those in Talionis."

"I know, but"—I leap over a rock instead of going around it just to burn off a little extra energy—"even though I actually like Essie, the DeForts, the Wild Dogs, I still can't stop thinking about that leak Catori talked about. I mean, even Gabe, why is he here?" I don't give either of them time to respond. "He's here because they don't trust us. They think we're spies. They don't want to hear what we have to say, which to me says somebody is high enough up in Eryndale to poison them against us, right?"

"Or they're just afraid," Matthias says, his voice soft and reasonable. "People do weird things out of fear."

I tilt my head in acknowledgment of his words, even though I kind of want to argue with him. "But this is more than fear. This is ridiculous. We have information. People whose lives are at stake. We barely got to brief Eryndale on all the things Ark is planning, because they said they wanted to stop him before any of that mattered." I grip my gun tighter. "But you have to know your enemy. I mean, if anything got drilled into us while we were in Warfare Strategies, it was that, right? We need to take what Talionis trained us with and use it against them."

"I don't disagree with you," Nika says. "But we need to bide our time."

"We don't have time," I say. "We've gotta do something. Eryndale is more compromised than we want to believe. It's not perfect there. It's not how I thought it would be." The anger in my words tapers off until only sadness remains.

"Sure, they're not perfect," Nika says, "but they do it better than Talionis, girl. Like, they have *teams* of scout, not units. They're brothers and sisters. You've seen it. We've been embraced by people there."

"But there's still evil in Eryndale," I say, wishing the words weren't true. "I can feel it. Still somebody looking to bring destruction and stop the good we're trying to do."

Nika stops, and Matthias and I stop with her. "It *is* concerning that there's a leak in Eryndale. But there's evil every-where, Bri," she says. "You know that. We've talked about it."

I look at Matthias. He stares back at me, his blue eyes glis-tening against his dark skin.

"We overcome by doing what's right," he says, his words passionate. "And right now, we *are* doing something. We're fighting. It's good, Bria. We keep doing that." His eyes flick back and forth as he studies me intently, trying to encourage me.

But my fears, my desperation to do something for Storm and Cai and my mom, scream louder than my friends' words.

"We should keep going," I say.

THE SOUND OF THE RIVER RUSHES TO MY EARS THIRTY MINUTES LATER. The three of us position ourselves with the best vantage point of the water as we wait for *The Fearless Lady* to come to the pickup spot.

There's no movement in the air around us, no sign of other people. Which hopefully means the other teams are where they should be waiting to be picked up.

It's not long before we catch sight of the rowboat coming

toward shore. Davey whistles, and Matthias, Nika, and I jog onto the rocky shore as he guides the rowboat over.

We climb aboard, and Davey looks at me. "Rough day, huh?"

I lift my eyebrows. "Yeah."

"I think I should make pancakes for dinner." His smile doesn't reach his eyes as he says the words. "It's what Nate would do if he were here. Make a ridiculously unhelpful meal to try to make everyone feel better. I mean, pancakes have no protein. I always thought it was dumb that he thought that was the best option after a really hard day and when we knew the next day would be filled with a lot of physical activity." He shrugs. "But something about his fluffy pancakes with their gobs of maple syrup and butter, well, it did make things better for the moment. At least gave us something to tease him about."

Nika, Matthias, and I stay quiet as Davey relives the memory of his brother.

I stare at the river as we make our way to *The Fearless Lady*. It's calm here, tranquil, but it could just as easily become a raging torrent a little farther down or during a storm.

And Nate's body rests at the bottom of it, miles away from here, because he could look Talionis in the eye with defiance. Because he could say what needed to be said in the face of evil.

And when he stood for his last time, he died a hero.

But we're all still mourning his loss, and no one more than Davey.

"Pancakes sound great," I say, needing to fill the silence.

I grin at him, knowing my smile doesn't reach my eyes either. But I want him to know I get it. I understand. We can keep his brother's memory alive with him.

"I just hope your pancakes are even half as delicious as your brother's," Nika chimes in. "Those were some *good* pancakes."

Matthias shakes his head. "I'm feeling a bit skeptical. But don't worry, man. I'm gonna be a real difficult judge to please. If you can manage to do it"—he wiggles his eyebrows—"then I will be thoroughly impressed."

"That does not sound like much of a prize," Nika says from her seat at the back of the boat.

"What? Not much of a prize?" Matthias puts his hands over his heart. "My approval is everything, right, Davey?"

At that, Davey laughs. A full-on, wholehearted laugh.

My heart squeezes. As I watch Matthias laugh with him, I fall for him a little more.

FORTY-FOUR

"Well, that seals it," Matthias says. "Cooking is *not* an inheritable skill." He rubs his jaw from where he just chomped down on one of Davey's very hard pancakes.

"Seriously," Shane chimes in. "How do you even *make* hard pancakes?"

Another course of laughter ensues, and Davey grumbles about nobody being grateful for somebody who goes through hard work to put together a meal and cheer everyone up. But the laughter and tears coursing down everyone's face at Davey's expense, and the small grin that he keeps trying to hide, proves to me that the pancakes are doing their job.

Although there's a weight to every laugh that I can't shake.

I'm still desperate to find a way to convince Eryndale leadership to let me act. My frantic thoughts won't allow me to relax for more than a few seconds at a time.

As night falls, we take turns being on watch on the deck. I take the first watch since I know I won't be able to fall asleep yet.

Talionis's troops are becoming increasingly active, but they don't engage in any direct attacks against Eryndale scouts. Part of me wonders if that's because they can't exactly figure out where the bases are, but I'm not so sure that's the reason.

It seems like they just want to prove that they're the stronger force. Like a big brother who pushes his little brother down after he smacks him on the head, then doesn't do anything else because he's made a point that he's more powerful.

I walk around the deck, contacts in as I scan the shoreline. Everything is quiet. Almost peaceful.

This area was once very populated.

If the amount of broken-down houses, discarded cars, and empty truck containers strewn all about are any indication, everywhere near Talionis appears to have once been a metropolis of some sort.

There's no movement. But that doesn't mean no one's there.

I pick out the places I would choose to hide if I were looking for intel-gathering sites. I'm not sure if Talionis is doing the same thing as Eryndale in that way. But if I know Major Vasco, he wouldn't allow there to be spaces where he wasn't sure what was going on.

And now that Talionis is well-known in this area, why wouldn't they have set up stations to gather intel?

So many potential options.

So much room for failure.

But maybe this next maneuver will prove as successful as Lorenzo and Gabe believe it will be.

As I circle back around toward the front of the boat, the door to the lower deck opens and Matthias comes out.

His hair is rumpled from sleep, but it somehow makes him look even cuter. My stomach flips when his eyes connect with mine.

"Hey." His voice has a gravelly, exhausted rumble to it.

"Hey." Once he's next to me I start walking again. "You're shift doesn't start for another hour."

"Davey's rock pancakes don't lead to a great night sleep." He smirks, and I know he's teasing.

I chuckle.

He takes my hand in his. "I wanted a chance to talk to you alone."

"About what?" I glance over at him, but he's watching the shoreline.

He gives my hand a light squeeze. "Anything. Everything."

We stop at the front of the boat and lapse into a comfortable silence. Being back on the ship, it's hard to not think about Catori's and my conversation about her and Micah.

Without giving myself time to overthink, I lean against Matthias and rest my head on his shoulder. His arm comes around me. Solid. Secure. I wish I could close my eyes and let him hold me until I forgot everything going on.

"Are you ready to be so close to Talionis?"

His question brings my head up and his arm falls away.

Tomorrow, we will enter a town about seven miles from Talionis.

It feels *so* close. Like I could almost reach out and punch the city. But we're not to engage with Talionis at all.

"I'd feel better if we could do more than just deliver supplies." We start walking again.

"We're also smuggling out the kids who've been marked," he says. "That's a bigger deal than just delivering supplies."

"True." I can't help but acknowledge the truth that saving the lives of teens and kids is vital.

We pass the wheelhouse and move to the back of the boat. "And the way Bill, Paul, and Wade transformed the supply room is ingenious."

"It really is," I say.

Bill, Paul, and Wade finished construction on the lower deck. The supply room isn't as big as it once was, but now there's a false wall with a hidden compartment that can hold almost a dozen people if they're packed in. What those guys can do together is impressive.

We'll smuggle out as many kids as we can fit into the new space. They'll be free to move around on the lower deck, but this way, they have a place to hide if needed.

Matthias and I pause at the back of the boat to scan the terrain we've already passed.

"I can't believe Wilkins wanted to go back into the field so soon," Matthias says.

The guy we saved the other night by faking his death has taken on the role of a trader who is going through the area. Since this town has seen many strangers recently, the S.O.C. is hoping his cover goes undetected.

I shake my head. "I think it's a terrible idea. I get that Talionis doesn't appear to have troops occupying Cinderforge, but there must be Watchers. What if someone recognizes him?"

Matthias shrugs. "I asked Catori about it after the meeting wrapped up. She said he was insistent. And annoyed that he was pulled from his role as a leak within the Talionis troops."

We adjust our position to the port side of the boat.

Wilkins isn't more than a year older than me, so that makes him about eighteen, maybe nineteen. And very strong-willed, apparently. Something I can respect, even though it would annoy me to work with him, since he seems to be of the opinionated sort.

I move to the railing and squint out into the murky blackness on the bank of the river. I blink twice to zoom my lenses in, scanning the terrain. Matthias's solid presence at my side is soothing, despite everything going on. All we're preparing for.

The time for my shift to end comes and goes, but I stay with Matthias. The way he keeps taking my hand while we watch for any threats almost makes me wonder if he's making sure I'm still here.

Over the next hour, we spend long moments in silence, but we also talk. I share with him about what Thaddeus told me about my mom. He shares his uncertainty about being so close to Talionis. And his dad.

When Bryson comes to relieve Matthias of duty around 0200 hours, I'm disappointed.

I'm not ready to be alone with my thoughts, but the grittiness in my eyes and the yawns I keep suppressing tell me I need to sleep.

Matthias and I go below deck. He walks me to the door of the girls bunk room and I turn and face him before going in.

"Thank you for starting your shift early," I whisper.

"For time with you? Always." He brushes his finger along my cheek, sending a shiver through me. "And thank you for staying up after your shift ended."

I smile. "You're worth losing a little sleep over."

The look he gives me—like I just gave him the greatest gift he's ever received—melts my heart. And I understand more of what Catori meant. No matter what happens in this battle, I'll never regret caring about Matthias.

I want him to know that.

"You matter to me. A lot." I remove my necklace. "Whatever happens, I want you to have this." I hand it to him.

He hesitates. "Are you sure?"

My neck feels empty not having Ezri's seaglass pendant on it, but my heart is full. I nod.

He takes it from my hand and immediately puts it on, tucking it under his shirt. Then he steps closer and cups my face with his hands. I suddenly wonder if he's going to kiss me, which leaves me with a sense of anticipation and a rush of nerves.

"You mean more to me than anyone ever has." His thumb strokes my cheek. "I know it's been hard." His voice is tender. "But Bria, don't forget: you're not alone."

The words steal my breath and all the emotions of the past weeks crowd behind my eyes, ready to spill out.

Then he pulls me into himself and gives me a hug.

His chest is solid beneath my face, and I squeeze my arms around him and let him hold me for a moment. One tear leaks out. Then another. I swallow hard, pulling myself together before I break down completely. The tears come closer this time, so I push away before they get the better of me.

I stand on my tiptoes and kiss his cheek. "Goodnight, Matthias."

WE'RE A HALF MILE FROM CINDERFORGE. ALL OF US ARE ON DECK preparing to offload supplies—which are really a series of empty boxes with false lids that will allow us to smuggle people back aboard the boat. Another of Bill and Paul's creations. We plan to trade in various spots within the town that are hiding kids and teens who have been tagged by Talionis.

"Davey, prepare to anchor close to shore," Catori shouts out from the wheelhouse. "Now!"

I whip around to face her. She's frantically speaking into the radio mic. I'm too far away to catch what she's saying, but the look on her face adds a weight to my chest.

She moves back to the wheel and focuses intently on the sonar radar as she navigates toward shore, getting as close as possible before yelling, "Drop anchor."

Davey and Quwani obey her orders without question, even as I remain frozen in place, mind racing as I try to envision the news we are about to hear.

Based on the almost panicked look in Catori's eyes, it's not going to be good.

Seconds later, she races from the wheelhouse and points directly at me. "Get your friends and Moses and Jordyn below deck."

I rush around topside to tell my friends to get below deck.

"What's going on?" Shane asks as he sets aside the box he was maneuvering into place with the other supplies on deck.

"I don't know," I say.

The eight of us dash toward the stairwell.

As I follow my friends down the steps, I hear Catori yelling at Davey and Quwani to get us into the new compartment.

My heart races. Why would they need to hide us?

Davey leaps down the steps. "In here." He opens the door to the supply room, shifts a box, and the false wall cracks open. He pulls it open farther. "Get in. All of you."

Quwani shoves my friends into the opening.

I stay off to the side, waiting to make sure everyone is hidden. Ari, Shane, Jordyn, Retro, and Nika go in. Then it's just Matthias and me.

"Get in," he says.

"But—"

"No, Bria. I'm not getting in until you do."

I cram myself in next to Nika. With all of us in here, we're pressed together. Matthias enters after me.

Quwani shuts the false wall. Blackness encases us.

And then I hear it. The low buzz of a transport.

They're coming.

I listen intently, wishing I could see what is going on. The air becomes suffocating.

The transport is right overhead. I feel as though a thousand eyes are searching for me. The hair on my arms stands up straight, my heart pounding in my ears.

What if they board?

What will they do to Catori, Kemena, Davey, and Quwani?

Especially if they find Catori's safe is holding everything Ark wants back.

But then it passes. The buzzing goes away.

Too fast.

The low glow of Ari's screen lights up the cramped quarters. "They're moving east."

I fumble near the door for the switch that will let us out. After a moment, I find it. The wall clicks open an inch.

"Where are you going?" Matthias asks.

"They left too soon," I say, moving through the opening. "And they're heading east."

My words make no sense, but I don't take time to explain.

I'm halfway up the stairs when I hear Davey confirm my fear.

"They're heading right toward Cinderforge."

Catori murmurs, "I know," and a sinking feeling twists in my gut.

They've moved their extraction to today. I know it deep within myself. Within the hour, the transport will be filled with teens and kids from Cinderforge—which means it's unlikely they'll be coming back to check out a riverboat anchored near shore.

But that doesn't even matter. We were supposed to save these kids.

How did this happen?

I scramble up the last two stairs.

Quwani gives a little yelp when I appear.

"That extraction isn't supposed to happen for another two days," I say.

Catori nods. "I know, which means we have a leak."

The words cut through me like a sledge of anxiety and frustration.

A leak.

We have a leak.

Is it another leak or the same one?

Who isn't who they seem to be? And how many are there?

FORTY-FIVE

"How far are we from Cinderforge?" I ask, even as I search my mental map of the area to figure out the answer.

"One mile," Catori says.

I nod sharply. "We need to go see what's happening. Watch how they're moving, and see if there's any sign of who the Watchers are in that town." My words rush from my mouth, and my friends emerge from the lower deck.

"I'll go with you," Matthias says.

Catori hesitates. "Leadership won't like it if I send any of you close to this town while there are soldiers actively pulling teens from it."

"We need the intel." I force myself to stop and not argue further.

Catori gives a quick nod. "All right. Davey will go with you."

In a few moments, I'm in the rowboat heading to shore with Davey, Matthias, Nika, and Shane.

Davey doesn't have the same training as the rest of us, but over the past few weeks, we've spent enough time with him that the five of us move in a synchronized rhythm that reminds me of training in Talionis. Which feels comfortable, even though I know it should feel wrong.

We race through the forest as quickly as possible, avoiding

old roads and open spaces, and staying close to debris-filled areas for additional cover. If the soldiers are actively grabbing teens, they're less likely to be patrolling the forest around the town.

At least that's what I hope.

There are shouts and cries as we near the outer edge of the town limits. I put my fist into the air, drawing my friends to a stop.

I point to myself, Nika, and Matthias, and then with three fingers signal that we'll go to the left. Then I point to Davey and Shane and gesture for them to head to the right.

There aren't any arguments. No one says a word.

Everyone just moves and does as I instruct.

We're not here to save anyone. We're here to watch.

But as the cries of villagers reach my ears, and the shouts of the soldiers of Talionis pierce the air, my blood pressure elevates. My temples throb. A pulse flutters in my neck.

They're doing it again. Taking kids, taking teens.

What are any of these covert ops accomplishing?

They're not stopping them from their actions. It's making everything worse.

Ark is moving more ferociously, sweeping up his targets as easily as picking pawns off a chess board.

Nika, Matthias, and I weave our way through the village streets, ears alert, weapons ready for any movement.

Although I have a pistol strapped to my shoulder, I hold two knives in my hands, Cai's words ringing in my ears. *No need to alert an enemy of your presence. Not until it's absolutely necessary.*

We creep to the edge of an alley.

Nika tries a door as Matthias and I watch the road to see what's happening. It opens easily for her, and we slip inside the building. It's someone's home, but after a quick sweep, we realize it's empty.

We make our way to the top floor and position ourselves near a set of windows overlooking the town square.

Soldiers fill the square as they drag teens and kids into the town center.

Parents cry, some lie unconscious or dead. This extraction hasn't happened without a fight.

"You said we had a few more days," one woman cries on her knees as she reaches for the little girl being carried by a soldier.

He whips back around. "Don't you dare question us." He points a gun in the woman's face.

The girl shrieks in his arms. She flails, kicking and screaming.

He holds her tighter and shakes her ferociously. "Shut up, you brat."

I don't recognize this soldier, but I recognize how he acts, how he treats a little kid. Same as every other soldier in Talionis.

My stomach churns as memories of the day Laban had Storm removed from the recruit living quarters ripples through my mind. She screamed the same way as the little girl on the street below. Kicked. Yelled. Cried out my name. All in a desperate attempt for me to stop her from being taken by those she feared most.

But I couldn't.

I couldn't then, and I can't save this little girl now.

Anger pushes aside my panic and pain from my memories.

I grip my knife tighter, wishing I could rush out there, wishing I could remove that child from that evil man's arms.

Nika puts her hand on my shoulder as though she can sense my thoughts. "We can't do anything right now." Her words are a whisper.

I nod, teeth clenched so hard my head aches. "I know. But we have to do something soon."

A familiar face strides toward the soldier carrying the girl.

Matthias frowns. "Isn't that . . ."

"Wilkins," I finish.

Wilkins helps the soldier bind the hands of the little girl. Then he shakes the soldier's hand, before moving on to help gather more kids.

My nostrils flare. The man we thought was helping us by leaking information from Talionis is actually a double agent.

He's not helping Eryndale at all.

No.

He's the reason the soldiers are here right now.

But he didn't know how we were going to extract the teens and kids. That intel is only for the team who is entering and gathering the kids. It's so the information can't get to Talionis, either intentionally or unintentionally.

And at the moment, as angry as I am at what I'm witnessing, I whisper a prayer of thanks that Wilkins didn't know. He's not aware of Catori, not aware of how those kids should have been removed from this town before the soldiers ever had a chance to take them.

Which means at least some are kept safe. Like my friends back aboard *The Fearless Lady*.

The limited information sharing among the scouts has been frustrating. But in this case, I'm thankful about how careful they are.

My mind spins. Azarias was supposed to meet us after this mission. He was supposed to meet us in this town.

I briefly wonder if he's nearby, then realize he must be. We were supposed to arrive in an hour.

Is he witnessing this?

Is he seeing Wilkins as the traitor that he is?

I should never have advocated to save the man. Will I be blamed?

Because the reality is, since Wilkins couldn't have known what we were planning, someone who was given clearance for the intel must have leaked it. That's the only way the extraction could have been moved to today.

In less than an hour, the soldiers have cleared the town, taking Wilkins with them.

Bodies litter the streets, and townspeople help whoever they can. But sheets are laid over those who will never open their eyes again in this life.

I've witnessed more death in the past year than I ever thought possible.

I want to stay and see if there's a way I can help bring comfort to these people, but most likely, they've seen screens depicting me as the worst enemy they could ever know. Claiming I'm the reason for what's happened.

"We'd better get out of here before whoever owns this place comes home," Matthias says.

I nod in agreement, and the three of us make a silent exit from the house.

Matthias communicates with Davey through a comm unit, and we meet up again with Davey and Shane. The frowns on their faces show me they're just as distressed as I am about what we've witnessed. We silently jog the distance back to *The Fearless Lady* and board the rowboat.

Everyone is lost in their own thoughts, and my thoughts are solidifying.

Something must be done. And I am going to do it soon, whether Lorenzo and the leaders like it or not.

Assuming they don't link me with Wilkins and deliver me to Talionis troops by the end of the day.

As soon as I jump aboard *The Fearless Lady*'s deck, Lorenzo's stern scowl meets me.

"Who authorized you to go on that mission?" His gaze flicks from me to Nika, Matthias, Shane, and Davey.

"No one." He answers the question before any of us have a chance to explain ourselves.

Catori steps forward. "They were under my command."

He turns to face her. "I know, but I didn't say they could go. It was dangerous. Foolish." His words are sputtered breaths, and I think for a moment that they're more out of concern than anything.

Catori raises her eyebrows as she looks at Lorenzo. It doesn't matter that she's a few inches shorter than him and twenty years his junior. Somehow, her look and posture are enough to silence the leader.

"I handle my crew, Lorenzo. That was Micah's agreement with Eryndale, and it's mine as well. I make my decisions for the best of my crew *and* for those we are looking to protect. You know that. So trust me."

Lorenzo looks like he's about to say something, but then he stops himself.

"We need to move," I interject. "There's a leak, and it's Wilkins." Hopefully sharing the intel right away will put me in good standing.

That brings Lorenzo around. "What?"

Shane and Davey look at me quizzically, but Nika and Matthias jump in to agree.

"We saw him working with the soldiers. He left with them," Matthias says.

"Which means there are leaks that go deeper than we understood," I say. "We need to do something."

The little girl that was taken flashes through my mind, along with an image of Storm. I want an extraction of the people I know and care about, but I'm beginning to think I'm going to want to take far more than just two people from Talionis if I enter.

"Send me in. Send a team in," I say. "A few teams. Let's at least try to get some of these kids out."

"No." Lorenzo frowns and crosses his arms over his chest.

There's no way he's going to agree to this. I see it in every fiber of his stance, the way his shoulders are stiff, his back straight. He's fine with a fight because he knows I won't win.

Thaddeus exits the wheelhouse, and then Gabe strides from the shadows of the back of the boat.

There are more leaders here than I realized.

"Lorenzo is right," Gabe says. "There's no way we can send in a team. It's too dangerous."

"Nothing is safe," I say. "Danger is what we've all signed up for here. At least let the danger be used to save people from the clutches of Talionis. Or send in someone to get better intel, someone we know we can trust."

All three of the men are shaking their heads.

"There's no way we could get that clearance," Thaddeus says, his voice gentle. "And we would need clearance from *everyone* if we were to put a team in that much danger."

"What are your contacts in Talionis saying?" I ask.

Lorenzo and Gabe both swivel to focus on me, and Thaddeus ducks his head almost sheepishly.

"How do you know about that?" Lorenzo asks. "It's the second time you've mentioned it."

"It doesn't matter how I know," I say. "If you refuse to send anyone in, we at least need intel. Find out if these kids are okay. If Storm and Cai are okay."

"Our contacts have been quiet for several days now," Lorenzo admits. "We think things got too heated in the city for them to relay the intel we needed from them."

"Then send someone in," I press my argument, even as the logical side of my brain tells me I'm never going to win.

"It's out of the question," Gabe interrupts. "So stop asking, and do what you're commanded to do. Unless you want us to assume your fondness for Wilkins is because you're working with him." His words are harsh and remind me too much of how I was treated in Talionis.

So much for him being on our side. Being out on the field has brought out a harsher version of the man than I wanted to see.

I lock my jaw in place, give a curt nod, and stride down the stairs of the boat, away from these leaders who refuse to listen to reason.

LORENZO REDIRECTS CATORI TO GO TO A NEW LOCATION A FEW MILES away. There's a site close to the river. One of the hubs where teams are sent from. Others will be gathering there as well so everyone can regroup.

I don't know if my friends and I were ever supposed to go to this site, but I don't care.

I make my way below deck to gather my things.

"But I know this would work," Ari says. Her voice is low and coming from the galley.

The door is partially closed, and I pause, curious.

"I could get in, hack into their servers. Find so much intel that we could use."

I creep closer to the door.

"Ari, no," Shane says, his voice fierce and desperate. "They've told you no, and we have to respect their decisions. They don't trust us as it is. I know you want to help Bria, but—"

"And I want to do something that will make a difference in this fight," she says. "And stop Demetrius Ark. Isn't that what we left for? Isn't that why we're here, putting ourselves in danger?" She sounds more determined and frustrated than I've ever heard her. "Why can't I use my skills? It doesn't make any sense."

She releases a huff that sounds almost like a little kid.

I remain in the shadows as I listen to Shane comfort her and then attempt to distract her with new conversation topics.

"I'm not letting this go," she says.

"I know, but you do look cute when you're mad," Shane flirts.

Ari giggles.

That's enough for me. I make my way to the bunk room I share with Nika, Quwani, Ari, and Kemena, but an idea stirs.

Ari understands tech, and I understand intel and strategy. Together, we could do something that would make a difference in this fight. And I could at least get *some* information about Storm and Cai.

Maybe even about my mom.

When we get to the site, I'll talk to Ari.

For the first time in days, I feel a sense of anticipation. It's time to act. No matter who is against us.

THE SITE WE ENTER A FEW HOURS LATER IS REMINISCENT OF THE OTHER sites we've been in, but significantly bigger. We're close enough to the river that I can still make out the glint of the water through the trees as we enter a warehouse that sprawls the length of several houses.

It's probably as big as some town centers in the area. It's old, pre-Demise, but the structure was made of steel and is still standing.

And they've worked on setting it up in such a way that it looks like there's nothing within this place. When we enter, it appears deserted. But once we move past the first rim, we can see that it's full of four stories of scouts and intel stations, weaponries, and even an entire cartography section with more maps than I've seen anywhere other than Eryndale itself.

Azarias brings my friends and me to the bunk area. "You'll be sleeping here. Get yourselves settled, and then you'll need to be at the next briefing in thirty minutes."

With that, he beckons to Kemena to walk with him, and the two leave the bunk area.

I make a point of settling myself close to Ari's pack.

When she turns from fixing her bed so that its sheets are perfect, I catch her eye.

"We need to talk," I whisper.

Her eyes narrow ever so slightly, but she nods.

"Bring your screen," I say.

This brings a light to her face that only tech can do. It would be comical if not for the fact that I know what I'm about to ask of her is dangerous. And goes against every order we've received since working with Eryndale.

But I can't wait anymore.

I need intelligence.

They're taking kids, so what are they doing with the one kid they've been training for months now?

She looked so afraid in the video from Ark.

Is she even still alive?

She's supposed to be, at least until the end of the week. Four more days until my time is up for meeting Ark's timeline and demands.

Four more days to return what he wants and save the life of a child.

But there were supposed to be a couple more days before those kids in the last town were taken.

Ark is not a man of his word. He wants to pretend he is, but when it comes down to it, Ark will always do what's best for himself and what furthers his own plans.

Ari and I slip from the room, relatively unnoticed. A few scouts wave at us. Some say hi, but we don't stop. I weave our way through the building, sneak past the guards, and outside. Ari follows me without question.

I'm not sure if putting her in this kind of position is wise, but desperation fuels me. And I comfort myself with the knowledge that she wants to do this too.

We move a little away from the warehouse. I duck into an old house that no longer has doors or windows. There's a table and five rickety old chairs that look like they've been gnawed on by animals, but when I test one out, it holds my weight.

I settle more into the chair. "I overheard you talking to Shane."

Ari does the same with the chair across from me. "What do you mean?"

"You think you can hack into Talionis." My heart races as I say the words.

The thought that I shouldn't be doing this tries to silence me, but I push it away.

Ari's chin tilts up. "I know I can."

Her confidence when talking about tech, as always, borders on conceit. But if anyone deserves a little arrogance, it's Ari. She can do everything she claims she can do.

"Do you think you could get in, figure out where they're keeping Storm and Cai? Maybe even some of the other younger kids they're bringing in?"

She nods. "Definitely. We're close to Talionis, and this site is high-tech enough that I can piggyback off of Eryndale's servers and backdoor my way in through tech Talionis has in place in the towns they're occupying. Since it will be less secure."

"Do it."

She whips out the screen and immediately begins typing. No hesitation. Her loyalty and friendship are rare gifts.

This site is about twelve miles from Talionis.

While Ari works, I let my mind walk through a mental map of the area: the towns and villages, the ones we know are occupied by soldiers and Raiders, and the ones that we suspect have Watchers entrenched deeply enough to relay all the information Talionis wants.

I clench my jaw.

Talionis's arm reaches too far, and I'm sick and tired of being one step behind them.

"I'm in," Ari says with a grin.

Her fingers continue to fly over her keys, and the screen is a bundle of code that I can't read, let alone understand.

Her brow wrinkles. "That's not good."

"What?"

"Nothing." The uncertainty in her tone slices through me.

"What's wrong, Ari?"

"I don't think—" Sweat beads her forehead. "I gotta get out."

She types for a few seconds more, then practically slams her finger down to exit the screen she's on.

The whole thing goes black.

I stare at her. "What just happened?" Even as I ask, I know I don't want the answer.

She swallows. "I think someone in Talionis might have been able to track me."

FORTY-SEVEN

The words send a chill through me.

How could I be stupid enough not to assume that Ark and Mandeville would expect a cyberattack—especially knowing Ari and her skills?

It was a trap, and attacking them this way, with Talionis gear, is sure to bring about severe consequences.

Ari and I race back to the site. We're just a few steps inside the main section of the warehouse when Azarias's voice comes through the wall comms set up throughout the site.

"Everyone, prepare. We have an imminent threat inbound. A small transport is heading this way. Everything indicates we are the target. Teams, get together, gather your weapons, and spread out to prepare for whatever attack is about to come."

My chest squeezes. This is my fault.

I sprint to the weaponry station.

Swarms of scouts grab weapons and pass them around, and teams jog out.

The Wild Dogs are here, and Retro tosses me a rifle.

I catch it with one hand, then grab a belt of knives near the door and join the Wild Dogs as my friends spot us and come our way.

Azarias's voice comes over the comms again. "Enemy incoming in T-minus twenty minutes. Get to your stations."

Everyone sprints out into the old, pre-Demise town, like ants scurrying from a anthill that was smacked with a stick. The Wild Dogs make their way to a dilapidated high-rise building near the center of the old city, so I follow them. I'd rather be running into the woods, but the lines of sight the building provides to the rest of the town will be valuable.

Ari's face is pinched, and I drop back to run with her.

"It's not your fault," I say.

"But it is," she says. "This *is* my fault, Bria."

"No." I guide us around a broken down wall. "It's mine. I asked you to do it."

She gives me a small smile that doesn't reach her eyes. "I'm good. I don't know how—"

"Mandeville."

She stumbles at the mention of the head tech instructor in Talionis. The man who taught Ari most of what she knows. "Oh. If it was him . . ."

I see her mind spinning as she gets lost in that tech brain of hers and her steps slow. The next thing she'll say won't make any sense to me.

So I focus my attention on the Wild Dogs who are now entering the high-rise, tugging on Ari's arm until she's jogging toward them with me.

We gather inside the building.

"Up to the roof," Malachi says, leading the way to a set of concrete stairs several feet away.

As we race up the flights of stairs, he gives us our instructions. "Once we're on the roof, we'll spread out in groups of three or four and take different vantage points. Stay hidden. Our goal is to not give the inbound transport any reason to stop here. And if they do, then we want as clear of a view of the enemy as possible."

There are nods of agreement.

We burst onto the roof, and Malachi separates everyone, instructing us where to go. He sends Nika, Retro, and me to the eastern part of the building.

We camouflage ourselves as best as we can with old boards and debris on the roof, preparing to wait and watch.

The hum of the transport, the electrical buzz that fills the air, comes in less time than what Azarias expected.

At least I think it's less. Or those twenty minutes went much faster than any other twenty minutes in my life.

The small transport can't hold more than two people, so there are probably more inbound. Seconds later, the transport descends into the belly of the pre-Demise city.

The door shifts and opens. I gasp as I stare through the scope of my rifle at the person who's there.

It's Shay, and she looks nothing like she did before.

"Bria, I know you're here." Shay's voice is almost singsongy, and it echoes like it's being projected through a dozen speakers.

Broche had a mechanical eye, but Shay has a mechanical just-about-everything else.

Her face is still the same and her red hair billows behind her, unhindered by a helmet. But that's where the similarities to the girl I knew stop. Metal plates snake up her neck and her body looks like a Talionis tech experiment gone wrong. The hand she lost in our battle with her is now robotic, and it appears as though they replaced her entire arm to her shoulder. A gun is mounted on her forearm, and her other arm has had work as well, although it's not as extensive. Drones swirl around her, their laser eyes focusing in every direction, scanning for any sign of movement.

"Come out, come out, wherever you are," she says. "Your friend Ari did such a nice job providing a beacon to your location."

I want to leap up and come to Ari's defense, claim that it was my fault, but I remain still.

There's movement in a different section of the town, and a drone focuses its laser there. A bullet zings from the small mechanical device.

The team of scouts in that area return fire, attempting to hit Shay, but the drones cut the bullets from the air before they can get close enough.

A drone drops.

Someone found their mark.

The rest of the teams wait, not giving any hint of our locations.

Just because someone else has drawn the focus of the enemy doesn't mean we should engage. At least not immediately. We need to let them focus there long enough so they think that's all there is, and then we'll attack from behind.

Unless more soldiers arrive before we get the chance.

Shay lifts her robotic hand. "Send in the troops," she says into a comm unit. "They're not far. The Commander will have what he needs soon enough."

Moments later, the air fills with a cacophony of noises. A transport is inbound. Aimed right for the roof that my friends and I are on.

"Get ready!" Malachi's voice rings through our ears in our comms.

The transport door slides open, and ropes drop out.

"Aim!" Malachi says.

I raise my rifle, focus on the ropes.

Soldiers repel from the transport.

"Fire!" Malachi shouts so loud that I hear him in my comm and his voice echoes from my left.

I squeeze my trigger. The rifle kicks back into my shoulder. The sulfuric scent of gunpowder fills my nose. My bullet hits the soldier I aimed at. She falls from the rope.

Bile rises in my throat each time I pull the trigger.

I hate that I have to do this.

Other soldiers drop. Return fire comes from soldiers still in the transport.

Other transports are arriving. Soldiers descend upon the old city.

For the first time, Talionis soldiers are fighting Eryndale scouts head-on. And it's because they know the six of us are here. Because of me.

In minutes, the old city is a battlefield.

Raiders ride in from the forest on mechanical horses, their fierce battle cries barbaric. But I don't have time to watch.

The influx of soldiers descending from the transport to the roof is too much.

I shoot at the advancing soldiers as we try to hold them off from moving through the building and down to the streets below. I don't give myself time to see if bullets hit their marks before turning to attack another enemy combatant.

"Retreat to position two!" Malachi yells.

Our team rushes from the roof, locking the door behind us as we make our way into the old city.

Even though this is a hub for other sites in the area, there are more soldiers and Raiders here than scouts. And as I take into account the numbers, a sickening sensation sweeps over me.

There's no way we can do this.

There's no way we can defeat them.

We spill out into the streets of the old city, taking up positions near the tower's entrance.

Another transport arrives. More soldiers repel down. Scouts shoot at them, but there are too many to hold off. Soldiers are streaming out of the tower.

Shay is in the center of the fray, guns blazing from her arms and lasers shooting from the half dozen drones circling her. No matter how many scouts attempt to shoot her, no one can hit their mark. She literally has eyes all around her.

A flash grenade explodes deeper in the city. The metallic scent of gunfire thickens the air. My ears ring.

But I stand firm.

I will not back down.

I'm back-to-back with Nika, shooting a gun that is perilously close to going empty.

"On your right," Nika shouts as she shoves a new clip into her rifle.

I spin and take a shot at the soldier. Then I catch a glimpse of a Raider moving in Nika's direction and shoot.

"Ugh!" There's a grunt to my left. Isaac goes down. Blood pools from a wound in his side.

"No!" I drag my gaze away from Isaac as Glacier pulls him behind a broken-down wall.

A low growl grabs my attention, and then Shep attacks a soldier who's aiming his gun at Catori. The man tries to fight off the dog, but Shep drives him to the ground. He screams, then goes silent. Catori kicks the weapon away.

A noise above me draws my attention.

Laban.

He's standing on top of the tower we vacated, looking like a ruler.

Even from here, I can see the maniacal gleam in his golden eyes.

Or maybe I'm imagining it.

But that grin on his face as he watches the battle, as he sees the bloodshed, is enough to make me want to scream.

Thick hands grab me from behind, and I'm dragged away. I fight, shift, reach for a knife. But my hands are held, locked tight in a death grip by two assailants.

Despite all my training, being held by two trained warriors is more than I can handle.

I cry out, but it's cut short as someone's hand clamps over my mouth in a painful grasp.

And then, I'm dragged into the forest.

My heels dig troughs in the soft loam of the earth. A rock kicks up into my thigh, but I barely register the pain.

I twist, turn, and yell against the hand on my face. But it only serves to make my throat raw. No sound pushes past the thick palm of the person holding me.

My lungs burn as I become more desperate for air.

I'm brought to a halt. But not near any transports or even mechanical horses.

Those who grabbed me spin me around, and I'm facing a woman I never thought I'd see again.

FORTY-EIGHT

Callypso stands before me, her blond dreadlocks clinking together in a discordant melody as the metal studs throughout hit against each other. At least a half dozen of her pirates surround her.

"Good to see you again, Bria." She flicks a dreadlock back over her shoulder. "I'm here to collect."

The men who dragged me into the forest shove me to the ground.

I catch myself before I hit my face, pebbles and small sticks digging into my palms.

I stare up at her. "What? Right now?" I sputter. "In case you didn't notice, I'm not really in a position to do anything."

I gesture back to the battle that's still echoing behind us. "There are Talionis soldiers and Raiders here. Which means there's nothing my friends and I can do for you at the moment."

She taps a finger against her lip. "And yet, here I am." Her eyes are hard, icy.

She crouches, resting her forearms on her knees so she can look me in the eye. "You do me this favor, and I'll help you with the little scuffle." She flicks her fingers in the direction of the battle behind us. "I have enough people in the area to do what needs to be done, to get them to move away from you and your little friends. You just have to do something for me in return."

She stands and brushes her hands against her thighs. "Really, I'd be doing you a third favor, so you'd be even more in my debt. But hey, let's just call it even, okay?" She winks at me, and my body feels leaden.

"How can you help us?" I'm uneasy at the thought of accepting help from someone like Callypso, but I can't stop myself from asking.

"I have my ways." She lifts her shoulder in a lazy shrug. "I mean, I helped you before, right?"

I get to my feet and swipe the dirt from my hands and knees. "What do you need?"

"Oh, good. I do love it when people are cooperative." She says that last word with a sickening lilt.

I know I shouldn't help this woman. I know she's evil. But if there's a way to save my friends from being taken, to stop more people from falling dead in the streets of an old city, I'm willing to help her. I'm willing to do something. Especially since I don't exactly have a choice in the matter.

"Clearly, you're able to hack into Talionis," she says. "I need you to do so again."

I blink, unsure of how she knows that information and how she knew it so fast. But I push those questions aside and focus on the more important issue.

"Hacking in there is what got us into this mess." I gesture behind me. "Not sure it's the best idea."

"I know you fancy yourself a nice little *leader*"—she puts quotes in the air as she says the word—"but really, I like to give the commands around here. 'Kay?" Her words are sharp.

"I don't know how to hack Talionis," I say, settling for truth. Even though I know she won't like it.

And it's not necessarily *all* the truth.

Her hand whips out, slapping me across the face so fast that I don't see it in time to blink.

Pain radiates through my cheek as something pierces it, and I feel the warm blood before my fingers find the new wound on my face.

"But you know who can," she says. "Don't have the audacity to think you can play me, Bria. I know more than you think, and I want my rule back in this area, so you're gonna help me, understood?"

The words are a confusing blur.

She lets out an almost crazed laugh. "Actually, let me throw in a little bonus."

She snaps her fingers in the air, and a few more of her pirates appear. They come from the shadows of the forest, and they're dragging someone behind them. A man.

He stumbles. He's thin, almost emaciated, and a patchy beard covers his face. But when his eyes meet mine, I recognize him.

He's Catori's husband.

Micah is alive.

"Now," Callypso says, "focus here, Bria. I don't need you staring at the little man who is becoming more of a nuisance than I'd like to admit."

I drag my attention to Callypso, not wanting to risk another slap across the face. Although her use of the world *little* to describe Micah is strange. Even in his frail state, he's still taller than her by several inches.

"You help me, I help you. And I throw in this fun little extra care package." Callypso pulls a short sword from her side. "You don't help me, then we'll kill him now."

She tosses the knife to one of her pirates. He snatches it from the air and puts it immediately to Micah's throat.

A gasp catches in my airway, choking me, but Micah doesn't even flinch. His eyes stay calm. Steady. As though this is a normal occurrence for him.

"And I take out all of your little friends," Callypso continues. "Do Talionis a favor. What do you think of that?" Her eyes narrow as she spews the words.

"What do you need?" I ask.

"Tell your friend who can do the hacking that I need some intel placed on Talionis's servers."

There's another click of her fingers. It's as though she choreographed an entire blackmailing effort against me.

Broche emerges this time. "Hey, princess. How's it going?"

In an instant, I'm getting a living display of the people I most did *not* want to see again parading before me.

Now all I need is Elena to walk from the shadows as someone who's helping Callypso. Or maybe she'll stand next to Laban, whispering helpful hints about how to capture us and bring us in.

"You working for her now?" I direct the question to Broche, biting out each word.

"She gives a very persuasive argument. And this"—he gestures to Micah—"is my way of finalizing some things with a past client." He tosses his ball into the air, and his mechanical eye swivels. "Here."

He passes me a microchip. "Get Ari. That is her name, right?"

I don't nod. I just stare at him, wishing for a way to stop this whole thing from happening.

This whole mess that's my fault.

"Get her to plant this information on the server in Talionis. That'll give my lovely employer what she needs."

I hesitate. One of the pirates who brought me out here shoves a gun into my neck. I reach for the chip Broche is offering me.

It's so small that I could drop it, lose it completely.

"Don't you dare." It's like Callypso can hear my thoughts. "Or I'll find you and kill you." Her eyes narrow as she looks up into the sky for a moment, as though lost in thought. "Or I'll kill everyone you love." Her eyes, cold and hard, connect with mine. A stark contrast to her overly sweet tone.

But really, there's malice woven into each syllable that takes me by the throat.

I clasp the chip in my hand, fisting it tight. The tiny electronic unit imprints itself into my palm.

"I won't," I say. "I'll do what you want, but I need Micah to come with me."

"Oh, I'm a woman of my word, Bria. Of course he's coming with you." She nods to the two pirates holding him, and they shove him in my direction.

I clench my fist even tighter. I can't believe she's releasing him that easily. What is her endgame? There's something in all of this I'm missing.

Micah takes a staggering step and then walks the rest of the way to me. He glances between me and Callypso, a line forming between his eyebrows. Like he's as unsure as I am about why she would let him go.

I feel like I know this man at least a little, but he has no reason to know me. Or trust me.

"Do it now, and I'll give the all clear for my people to help push away your not-so-savory friends, 'kay?"

"Fine," I say.

"Take them back," Callypso says.

A pirate grasps my arm in a firm handhold.

I try to pull away. "I can walk myself back."

"Oh, no," Callypso says. "I want to be hospitable, of course."

She tosses me a clip of ammo, and I catch it with my other hand. "From my earlier observation, you're in need of some more bullets."

The way the woman knows things is creepy. But I tuck the ammo into my cargo pants pocket.

The pirates drag Micah and me back to the edge of the forest.

The battle rages.

There are bodies strewn throughout the town, soldiers and scouts alike. Lorenzo is in the thick of everything, shouting orders and fighting like a man half his age. He shoots two pistols, then throws a kick in the face of a soldier who's getting up on his feet.

The fierce determination on his face erases every doubt I had about the man. As I watch him fight, I know he would never do anything to betray Eryndale.

I catch a glimpse of Ari, not far away, crouched behind a crumbling wall.

"Find her now." The pirate releases my arm and shoves me in the back.

I don't reply. The pirates melt back into the forest, leaving me and Micah alone.

"Wait here," I say. "There's so much I need to tell you."

Micah raises his eyebrows. "Maybe we'll start with how you knew who I was."

The comment almost makes me smile, but my mind is too full. So I nod, then jog over to Ari and pull her away from her hiding spot at the edge of the battlefield.

"Do you have a screen?" I ask.

She nods.

"Good," I say. "Come with me."

I bring her back to where Micah is waiting.

He's crouched, watching the battle. He steps forward as though he's about to join them.

I put my hand on his arm. "You don't have any weapons."

"I fight for what's right," he says.

"Okay." I pass him my gun and the new clip of ammunition. "Then guard us while we do what we need to do."

His dark eyes find mine, and I see the ghost of the man who is in Catori's frame on her desk. He's still handsome, even with his cheeks hollowed out from lack of nutrition, and his dark brown eyes hold the same depth I could see in the image on Catori's desk.

Micah doesn't even know Catori's here. My heart leaps at the thought of the two of them being reunited.

"Callypso is up to something," Micah's gravelly voice brings me back to the harsh reality before us. "Handing me over to you was a calculated move." He loads the gun.

"I know. But we need her help," I say, wishing it wasn't true. Even if I didn't need Callypso's help, I can't imagine a scenario where I would walk away if it meant the chance to save Micah.

Micah lifts my gun, aims at a soldier who's coming toward us, and takes him out.

He's a good shot, at least.

The three of us back deeper into the forest and away from the battle. I turn my attention to Ari and quickly tell her what happened with Callypso.

She powers on her screen. "Where's the chip?"

I open my fist to show her. Micah crouches beside us, eyes fixed on the battle, gun at the ready. Thankfully, none of the soldiers or Raiders have spotted us. Yet.

Ari bites her lip as she punches numbers into the screen. "I need an adaptor for that kind of chip." She types for another few moments. "Here." She shoves the screen at me. "Punch in this sequence"—she demonstrates a sequence of letters, numbers, and characters—"over and over until I get back."

"Wait, what?" I shove the screen back, but she doesn't take it. "Where are you going?"

"Back to the site to get the adapter." She moves to stand, but I tug her back down.

"No. You can't expose yourself right now. I need you to hack into the server."

"Do you know what the adapter looks like?"

I blink. "Uh . . . no."

She pulls her arm out of my grasp. "Then punch in the sequence I just showed you while I go get it. By the time I'm back, you'll be in the servers. And I'll be able to upload the information. Got it?"

I wish I had an excuse, a reason to stop her, but nothing comes to mind. Enemies surround us, and Callypso is our best shot at surviving this battle. "Sure. But Micah will go with you."

"Of course," Micah agrees.

Ari gapes at him as though really seeing him for the first time. "You're Micah DeFort?"

Micah gives a hesitant nod. "Yes."

"Wow." Ari shakes her head. "We should go!"

Before Ari and Micah can move to stand, rockets are fired from the forest. One of the five transports explodes in flames. The Talionis soldiers and Raiders become frenzied as they move to figure out where to focus their attention: on the scouts attacking from every angle of the old city, or on the fire now coming from the forest.

At least Callypso's doing what she promised. But Micah's right. She is up to something, and I dread the moment I discover exactly what it is.

Ari and Micah rush from where we're hiding in the forest, with Micah in the lead and Ari crouched behind him. They move toward the warehouse.

I glance up from what I'm typing on the screen every so often to watch their progress. They jog forward, ducking behind covering as much as possible, with Micah only firing his weapon when needed to avoid drawing attention.

"There!" a soldier yells. "I see one of the fugitives."

He lifts his gun, points, and shoots.

Ari's body crumples to the ground.

"No!" I scream, dropping the screen and sprinting toward my friend.

Micah fires at the soldier who shot Ari, and the soldier falls.

More explosions come from the forest around us.

Bullets burst from guns. Fire erupts from buildings.

The battle sounds become deafening.

Two more transports go down.

I leap over bodies, duck under debris, and barely register those around me as I focus on Ari.

A Raider steps in my path. I pull a knife from my belt and fling it at her. It sticks in her arm. She screams, losing her grip on the rifle in her hand.

I grab the gun and wrestle it from her grasp. Her breath bursts in and out as we stare at each other, me aiming her gun at her chest.

A signal sounds for the soldiers to fall back, with a call for the Raiders to retreat echoing seconds later.

The woman takes a hesitant step back, her foot skidding on loose gravel. My finger hovers over the trigger, but I let her run. She retreats to the forest with the other Raiders.

Once she's far enough away, I drop to the ground next to my friend. Micah's putting pressure on her wound, the gun discarded at his side.

The shriek of transports taking off fills the air, but I can't even look up.

Ari's eyes are closed.

Her chest still rises and falls, but so lightly I almost can't see it.

I pull her head into my lap. "No, no, no, no, no. God save her. Please, please, she can't die. Not like this. It can't be my fault. I can't lose my friend."

The prayer, the words, they're desperate as they careen through my mind and out of my lips.

"We need someone with medical expertise," Micah says, the desperate tone of his words piercing me deeper than a bullet.

I grip Ari tighter, and a scream erupts from me. "Help! We need help over here right now." The desperation in my voice is enough to draw the attention of a nearby scout, who runs over.

Wolf drops next to me. "We need a medic!" he calls over his shoulder. He looks at Micah. "Keep putting pressure on her wound."

Micah's focus remains on Ari, but he tilts his head in acknowledgement.

A team of medics arrives, and I'm not sure if it's seconds or minutes later.

They have to pry me off Ari, and then they're carrying her into the site. Micah and I follow.

"We need to get her cleaned up and make sure there are no bullet casings still in the wound."

With a start, I realize the lead medic is Nalani.

"I'll take care of her, Bria," she says. "But you need to stay out here." She puts a hand on my chest, keeping me from moving forward into the infirmary.

"But—"

"No, we can't have more people in there than the injured and those with the medical skills to help them."

With that, she spins away, shouting orders to those in the room. The door closes with a thud, leaving me staring at it.

"Bria, are you okay?" Matthias is next to me, hands on my arms, then on my face, looking me over. "Is this your blood? You need to get treated."

Micah steps back as Matthias crowds closer.

"It's not mine." The words break from my throat, taking a piece of me with them. "It's Ari's."

"What happened to Ari?" Shane is here now.

I note with some relief that they're all here: Bryson, Shane, Nika, Matthias.

But Ari's not here. She's in the medic station. Being treated.

"She was shot," I say.

Bryson's face drains of color.

"Shot? How?" Shane's voice is desperate. "She was hiding. She was safe."

The door opens behind me, and a medic rushes out.

Shane moves as though to go in.

"No." The medic thrusts his arm out. He's a big guy, enough to withstand Shane, at least temporarily. "You can't go in there right now. She's in surgery."

"Where are you going, then?" Shane asks.

"We need more antiseptic. It's not looking good. If you guys have any religious bones in your body, you need to pray for your friend." With that, he jogs away.

I drop to my knees, my breath coming in shallow bursts. I'm hyperventilating, but I can't stop.

This is my fault.

"You gotta breathe deeper, okay?" Micah's voice next to me pulls my head up. "Don't let the panic take over. In, out. Slowly."

He demonstrates how to breathe, and I do as he says. In and out. In and out.

My breathing stabilizes.

A medic ushers our group away from the door as more wounded are brought into the infirmary. The medics scan key cards over a pad by the door, and it opens for them. Then they disappear inside.

"Micah?" Catori calls from several yards away. She looks as though she's in a daze.

"Catori?" Micah's voice breaks.

And then the two are moving toward each other, embracing, kissing, hands caressing one another's faces as though memorizing them.

They hold each other and cry.

"You're alive," Catori says. "Wolf said he thought he saw—" her voice breaks. "I thought, I hoped." Sobs burst from her, and she buries her face in Micah's chest.

A moment later, Davey joins them, and the two men embrace like long-lost brothers. Tears flow from Davey now as well.

Wolf brings the DeForts over, and then Malachi, Moses, and Jordyn are there, sobbing, hugging Micah. Clinging to him.

The emotional reunion is powerful enough to distract me from what's happening in the infirmary behind me.

But then Shane is pounding on the door. "Let me see her!"

He shakes the doorknob, but it's locked. He can't get in without a medic opening it for him.

"I don't even know how this happened," Shane says again.

As much as I'd rather focus on the reunion between Catori and Micah and their family, I can't allow myself the luxury of hiding from what I've done.

"It's my fault," I say. "I needed her help with something."

Micah and Catori and the DeForts join our conversation.

"It was Callypso," Micah says. "Not you, Bria. She forced your hand."

"But I shouldn't have . . ." I want to say more, but Shane's face is bright red.

"I can't believe . . . I can't believe . . ." He can't find words to finish his sentence. He rubs a hand down his face. "How bad is she?"

Micah answers. "She lost a lot of blood. It was one of the worst wounds I've seen in a long time." He hesitates. "From what I saw, it would be a miracle if she makes it through the day."

Shane's body jerks as though Micah punched him in the gut. Bryson inhales sharply and backs against the wall and then sinks to the ground.

Shane turns on his heel and storms away.

I take a step as though to go after him, but Matthias stops me.

"Let him go," he says. "He needs to cool off. We can't do anything for Ari right now, but we can pray."

FORTY-NINE

Lorenzo calls for a meeting, and it takes everything in me to pull away from pacing outside of the medic station. Since Ari was taken in, all we've been able to hear are the muffled noises from inside as medics call to one another. Nothing they say is clear.

But maybe that's not the worst thing. I'm not sure I want to know the blow-by-blow of what's happening in there. Plus, I'm not sure if we're hearing the medics working on Ari or on other injured scouts.

Nalani is different when she's in this kind of circumstance. She forgoes her normally quiet, almost mousy personality and takes charge.

Catori's words about her being one of the youngest medics the scouts have ever had aren't surprising to me. What is a little shocking is the fact that she's the one giving the orders. Her training in Talionis must have been more advanced than I realized.

I make my way toward the site with my friends, the DeForts, and Catori and Micah.

The two haven't stopped staring at each other or touching one another's arms and hands as though just to confirm they're actually there. It's kind of adorable. Maybe one good thing happened today.

But I'm responsible for so many bad things that I almost don't know what to do with myself. A sickening sensation twists my gut, pulling me down and slowing my steps as I make my way to the warehouse where the meeting will take place. Nika is on my left and Matthias is on my right, both silently supporting me. But they don't know what happened.

So much is my fault.

I need to give a report on what's taken place, and everything in that report is going to prove that me being here was not helpful. In fact, it was a hindrance.

People like Reginald Finnigan, who were just waiting for us to mess up, will surely claim we're spies. At least call *me* a spy.

Then again, striking that deal with Callypso meant the soldiers were pushed back. Not that Reginald and most of Eryndale even believe Callypso is real.

What will she do now that we haven't accomplished what she demanded?

She let Micah go, which seems strange to me from a negotiation standpoint. It tells me she no longer had a use for him. Or that there's a deeper purpose and plan in everything she's doing that hasn't become clear yet.

She's someone I can't get a read on, and I hate that we have an enemy who is actively using different players to accomplish her purposes at the same time as Talionis.

Why does evil have to take on so many forms?

Why can't we just have one enemy at a time?

Why does it feel like a million things are happening at once?

Broche's face with his odd mechanical eye flashes through my mind. Guess he's not working for Ark anymore. Then again, it's clear he'll work for anyone. But from what he said when Catori and I met with him in the old bar, he only actively works with one client at a time.

Maybe Talionis fired him.

After all, we thoroughly defeated him before Laban showed up a couple of weeks ago.

I enter the warehouse and join the crowd gathered off to the side of the door.

"We need to strip everything down and relocate," Lorenzo is saying.

So similar to what he told us when we attacked Milford and the soldiers brutally retaliated. Everything is unraveling, and my part in the unraveling leaves me feeling uneasy and sickened.

When do I tell everyone what I've done and tell them the information I have about Callypso?

I'm not even sure if everyone here *should* be read into that information, though part of me wants to confess my failures in front of them all. Let them see me as responsible for what's going on. And I don't want to be viewed as a spy because I kept the intel quiet for too long.

"We need to retreat from Talionis and regroup," Lorenzo continues. "I've gotten word from Eryndale that we will receive an influx of newly trained scouts within the next week. That should help us establish additional bases that will allow for new ways of attacking the enemy. But for now, we need to tend to our wounded." The lines of his face grow even more pronounced. "We've lost twelve scouts."

He reads off a list of names. People I don't know. Names I don't recognize. But with each one he says, thick emotion fills his tone, as though every one of them was important to him, special to him, mattered to him.

Lorenzo is a leader of the scouts. Even Azarias has looked to him for help and information. Now I can see why.

The man cares deeply, and I watched him fight during that battle. He is quick, and able to read what's happening before it even happens. He reminds me of Cai in that way.

Cai.

What would he say or think if he heard everything I did? All the ways I failed?

Will he even be alive by the time we can reach him? There are only four days left on Ark's deadline, and the new scouts won't be arriving until next week.

The thoughts make me want to vomit, and I drag my concentration back to the meeting.

"We have dozens more who are injured, and—" Lorenzo stops speaking.

His eyes zero in on my group and me. But he's not looking at me.

His face drains of color, his mouth unhinging as he stares. "Micah? Is that you?"

Micah offers a grin. He's leaning heavily on Catori, as though his body doesn't want to cooperate and keep him standing. I briefly wonder what he's gone through over these past few years in captivity, held by Callypso.

He lifts a hand in greeting. "Hey, brother. It's been a while."

Lorenzo lets out a shallow huff of a laugh that's coated in far more surprise than humor. "That's one way to put it. Never really thought I'd see you again."

The hundred and twenty or so people in the room shift as everyone focuses on Micah. Tears form in some of their eyes at the reunion. Moses, Jordan, and Malachi are all near the couple. And for a moment, peace fills me.

Reunions *can* happen. People can find each other again.

An instant later, that thought is cut in two as I wonder what their life will be like now.

Will they ever get back what was stolen?

No.

They've lost years together. Years. And who knows the horrors Micah experienced that will haunt him night and day?

Is he the same man Catori remembers?

Does he have that same strength and character?

The question arises, and almost instantly, so does an answer.

I suspect he is.

Yes, there will be nightmares and fears, but he's still a good man. An honorable man. He recognized who Callypso was, the danger in doing what she said. I think he would have remained in captivity if it meant her not getting her way.

But he cared enough for my life—the life of a stranger—to not do anything rash.

The briefing is interrupted for a few minutes as everyone reconnects with Micah. An air of excitement steals over the room as they embrace one they thought was dead, but who has been returned to them.

When the hugs and greetings have died down, questions bubble to the surface.

"Who held you?"

"Where have you been?"

"What happened?"

He takes Catori's hand in his and stares around the room for a long moment before responding with one word. "Callypso."

The name sets the room into frenzy as everyone starts talking at once.

Questions, gasps of disbelief, uncertainty if Micah has experienced a blow to the head that would cause him to believe a legend that has circulated the region for many years.

But Micah tells them she's very real, and I join in to corroborate his story.

"She helped us push back the soldiers," I say.

Azarias and Lorenzo don't seem surprised at the words.

In fact, they exchange a long look of understanding. Then they are busy telling everyone to prepare to leave.

"If this location is known by not just one enemy, but two, we could be facing another attack at any moment," Lorenzo says.

Azarias nods and jumps in. "We're going to move further down the river, away from Talionis. We'll scatter everything and discuss with the S.O.C. ways to reestablish some firm bases. But for now, we need to take all the information we've just received and pull it together. Prepare to leave within the hour."

The crowd breaks apart as everyone moves to different stations to pack up gear.

They still don't know that I'm the reason for the attack, the reason Shay found us.

Then again, maybe they do know.

They all seem to know far more than I ever think they should. And maybe I needed to rely on that sooner. Trust the leaders.

Just because I haven't known how to trust leadership in the past because of Talionis doesn't mean I can't trust the Eryndale leaders now.

Nalani comes into the site, and I see her before she spots us. I know she's looking for me and my friends. And the look on her face, the blood staining her scrubs, makes me wish I was the one she was coming to inform my friends about.

I'm not ready to hear her report on Ari.

She weaves her way through people until she can get to us.

My friends and I haven't moved to do anything yet, which is probably not the best thing. I'm sure Azarias and Lorenzo have new plans for us. And the Wild Dogs, aside from Jordyn and Moses who are still with Micah, are busy packing gear and cleaning themselves up so that they can get ready to move to whatever their next location and assignment will be. Isaac's wounds have already been bandaged, and he's working with them.

Will we be placed with them again?

What's going to happen now?

Talionis showed their hand, but it was only because they knew where my friends and I were located.

And in a full-out battle, the scouts didn't stand a chance against Talionis.

I briefly wonder if Azarias or Lorenzo or Thaddeus—or anyone in the S.O.C.—would make a deal with Callypso. Get her help in defeating the city that has sunk its claws into the region in a way that seems like a death grip that could never be released without severe loss and casualties.

But I immediately dismiss the idea.

They would never make a deal with one devil in order to defeat another. Not like I did.

Nalani is in front of us now. "You need to come with me."

The five of us freeze, and I know we are all aware of what her grave expression indicates.

"Where's Shane?" she asks as we follow her to the door.

"No one has seen him for a bit," Nika offers, her voice strained.

"We're going to need to find him."

We follow her from the noisy room.

She stops once we're outside, pulls off her glasses, and wearily rubs her face. When she pulls her hand away, I see the tears in her eyes.

"We did everything we could, but I've never seen a person

survive injuries this bad." She swallows hard. "She's not going to make it through the day. It's best if you go in and say your good-byes now." A sob chokes out her last word, and she shoves her glasses back on her face before scurrying away.

A part of me almost wants to go after her and comfort her, but how could I?

I'm the reason Ari is going to die. A numbness steals over me as my body and mind go into survival mode.

The five of us walk the short distance to the infirmary in silence.

With each step, a memory of Ari surfaces in my mind.

Her exuberance. Her questions. The way she assumed she always knew tech better than everyone else, and how so often, she was right. The times she covered for me in Talionis and kept them from tracking my movements by inputting false information into my band. How she smuggled so much out of Talionis and used it to keep us from Laban and Ark's ferocious hunt for us.

Her grin and smile. Her tears and sensitivity. The way she loved Shane and brought out something different in him.

I wonder where Shane is. Will he make it in time to say goodbye?

Although if I was as angry as he is, I don't know if I could say goodbye. But I know from losing so many people that every minute you have with them is something you should cherish.

I squeeze my eyes shut as we round the bend to the infir-mary. But now, I don't see the memories of Ari in the past. Not her vibrant smile and blond hair bouncing about. Or even her meticulous way of keeping things clean and making her bed to perfection. Not her tech ability, sense of humor, or confidence.

What I see is an image of my friend shot. Bleeding out. Going as pale as others who I've watched die.

I'm steps away from going in to say goodbye forever.

God, how do I say goodbye to her?

With the prayer comes another sickening thought. Does she even know God?

My eternity was damned before Cade died for me. But did I

ever take a moment to tell Ari about my faith, to give her a chance to make a decision that led her to Jesus?

I'm not sure I did. Maybe Nika or Matthias did.

But if not, now . . . there's not time.

What does it mean for her to die if she didn't know Jesus?

My baby understanding of my new faith tells me that without Jesus and His salvation, hell is our eternal destination. So what does that mean for my friend?

She wasn't bad.

She did great things.

She saved my life.

Will my act of impatience cause her to lose her life and her eternal destination?

We arrive at the door and Nika steps forward and opens it. We press into the medical site behind her.

The lobby area is empty. Medical personnel rush in and out of other rooms. Machines beep. Other wounded are treated.

A medic points us to a door off to the side.

Bryson is shaking, tears streaming down his face. A face that's red and blotchy and pale. He's about to lose his sister. Will he ever forgive me?

Will I ever forgive myself?

Oh God, I don't know what to do.

This time, it's Matthias who opens the door. It creaks as though it has its own weight of regret. Like it wishes it didn't have to reveal our friend dying before us.

Matthias barely steps through the door before he stops short. The rest of us crowd behind him, and I crane my neck to see into the room.

The bed is empty.

Ari's gone.

CHAPTER

FIFTY

"Where is she?" Nika asks.

We all stare in shock at the empty bed. Nalani *just* got us. How can Ari be gone already?

"I didn't even get to say goodbye." The heartbreaking words sputter from Bryson's lips.

Without thinking, I put my arm around him.

He clings to me, sobbing on my shoulder.

Someone else should be the one to comfort him. I'm contaminated. The *reason* for all of this. But his tears allow some of mine to leak out as well.

A door on the far side of the room opens, drawing all of our attention.

Ari walks in. "Hey."

Bryson's head shoots off my shoulder. Then he's flying across the room and pulling his sister into his arms, crying on her shoulder instead of mine.

She almost buckles under his weight but stays standing. There are circles under her eyes, and she's still scary pale. But she's alive. Standing. Conscious.

This isn't possible. Right?

"How?" The word croaks out of my mouth.

She shrugs, and Bryson pulls back, looking for the answer himself.

A medic comes in before Ari can respond.

"She's a miracle," he says. "I've never seen anyone recover from what she faced. We weren't even sure you'd make it in time to say goodbye when Nalani went for you." The man is older, and the depth in his eyes suggests he's seen a great deal.

He shakes his head in wonder. "Then she stopped bleeding. Woke up. I've heard of miracles like this, but I've never witnessed one myself." He pats a fatherly hand on Ari's shoulder. "But you still need to rest, okay, kiddo?"

"I know, I know." She makes her way back to the bed and sits with a relieved sigh. "I'll be a model patient." She gives a cheeky grin.

The medic leaves, chuckling.

Once he's gone, Ari's face turns serious. "Can someone get me a screen? I thought of something when I woke up, and I think I might actually be able to hack into Ark's encrypted files. Find something."

"Seriously?" Matthias asks. "How?"

Access to Ark's encrypted files could give us information that changes the tactics Eryndale is using. Might even allow us to discover the key to stop him. But I'm still processing the fact that Ari's alive. Plus, she *just* woke up. She might not be thinking clearly yet.

Her brow furrows, and then her eyes scan the room. "Wait, where's Shane?"

I shake my head in bewilderment. "I'll go find him." After all, I was the reason he stormed off earlier.

I leave the room feeling lighter than ever before.

God, if you can work a miracle like that, if you can take someone who was at death's door and bring her back to life, then nothing's impossible for you, is it?

I've read those words before: *with God, nothing is impossible.* And I think I believed them, at least in part. I mean, I've seen miracles, watched God work and do things that seemed impossible.

But my friend being alive, who I thought was dead—that's a miracle.

I scour the warehouse, looking amidst the buzz of activity for Shane, but don't find him anywhere.

Scouts are clearing things out, and Wolf and Azarias are distributing weapons to the different teams. Thaddeus is going over an area map with team leaders, instructing them on where to head next. I glance at a clock and realize there are only twenty-five minutes left on Lorenzo's timeline of when we all need to be clear of the site. I need to find Shane immediately.

Quwani pulls an armload of supplies together and heads to the door.

I jog to catch up to her. "Quwani!"

She pauses. "Hey, I heard about Ari."

I blink, wondering how she heard so fast.

Before I can ask, she continues. "Wow, that's crazy. Love seeing miracles. And then there's Micah. How much can happen in one day that's straight up good? I mean, there's been hard things today too. Don't get me wrong, but I'm just on top of the moon, you know?"

She grins at me, and it's so contagious that I smile back.

"Yeah, it's wild. Speaking of Ari, she's wanting to see Shane. Have you seen him?"

She nods toward the river. "I think he headed to the boat, least last I saw."

"*The Fearless Lady*?"

"Yeah. He made a comment about needing something on board."

All the relief and joy I felt dissipates like early morning fog under a hot sun.

Before Quwani can continue, I turn and sprint toward the river. It's close, but not close enough.

I dash past people, jump over debris and logs, make my way past fallen soldiers and Raiders.

The bodies are disconcerting. More death and pain and heartache in the midst of good things. But my brain can't register what's going on right now.

It's too much. Something to process later.

Getting to Shane is of utmost priority.

A sinking premonition settles in my gut like it's a certainty, and desperation to prove myself wrong courses through me.

I make it to the river, skidding on the pebbles of the shore.

The short dock to Catori's boat is old and rickety, and I barely felt confident walking cautiously over it when we came ashore earlier. But now, I leap onto it and race across without care.

The boards creak beneath me, one of them splintering slightly.

I vault onto the boat.

No one's topside on *The Fearless Lady*, and there are some new bullet marks and scuffs. Even this ship didn't make it out of the battle unscathed.

I run below deck, taking the steps as fast as I dare.

But no one's there.

No sounds of movement or anyone being close by.

But the sounds matter a lot less than the sight in front of me.

Catori's door is wide open, hanging on a hinge. Splintered fragments coat the floor in front of it. It was busted down.

I surge through.

"Please, please, please." The word cascades from my lips like a torrent of rain.

But as I turn to where the safe was hidden in the wall, hope vanishes from me.

It's open, and everything in it, the intel we had from Ark, every single thing he's been looking for, the letters, the key, the battle plans—they're gone.

Someone stole them.

I turn and rush into the boys' cabin. My fears can't be true.

I want to find proof that everything of Shane's is still there. That there's no way he was the one to break through Catori's door, crack open her safe, and steal the items. I want to think that maybe someone from Talionis, Laban himself, got aboard *The Fearless Lady* and somehow knew exactly where to look for every item Ark wanted.

I want to believe all of that is possible.

True.

What happened.

But as I face Shane's bunk, see it cleared of everything, and find only two Skinter Suits remaining in the trunk at the foot of the bed, I know with every ounce of my being that Shane betrayed us.

I want to sink to my knees, to sob over the loss, over *another* betrayal.

Yet this betrayal is different from my aunt's. I almost understand why Shane did what he did.

What if it was Matthias lying dead in the room?

What if I had gone through everything Shane did in his life, and Talionis was one of the few places that felt like home?

Shane has been angry at Eryndale since we undertook this mission to fight Talionis. He fought with anyone he could talk to, saying that Ari and Bryson weren't trained for the battle that was coming.

Bryson heard him and got instantly annoyed, so Shane left him out after the first or second time he told someone they shouldn't travel with us. And Ari did not appreciate her boyfriend interfering and talking about her in that way. She wanted to come and fight as well, but Shane didn't want her to.

He believed she wasn't safe. And he was right.

But he doesn't know she's not dead, doesn't know that she's actually a miracle.

All he knew was that she wasn't going to make it through the day.

Right now, the things Ark wants are racing toward Talionis. Which means my small amount of leverage against the man— the hope I had that by keeping his items, he would not harm Storm and Cai—is gone.

Unless I can get to Shane first.

I jump up and sprint to my cabin, grabbing my Skinter Suit and an extra pack. As fast as possible, I throw in some weapons and food. Most of the supplies were cleared from the boat and brought to the site, but I find what I can.

I'm pulling on the Skinter Suit when there's noise above deck.

Oh man. I don't need anyone to stop me right now.

I'm not sure they *can* stop me.

My actions lately have cost people more than I ever will be able to repay. I've acted rashly, and I regret it.

But this is not me being rash.

My actions put Ari's life on the line.

My actions resulted in the conditions that pushed Shane over the edge, that left him feeling like he had no choice but to do what Ark wanted and earn back his favor.

I don't fully understand Shane's motivation, but I understand it partially, and it's enough. I don't want someone else finding him and taking him as a spy to Eryndale.

I need to find him. Convince him to come back and see that Ari's okay.

I tuck the blades under my arm, inhale deeply, and go topside. I half-expect to see the crew of *The Fearless Lady*, but instead, Nika, Matthias, and Kemena greet me.

"What are you doing here?" I ask.

"What are you doing wearing your suit and carrying your blades?" Nika retorts, folding her arms over her chest and giving me one of her Nika looks.

"I need to do something," I hedge.

"Nuh-uh, none of that," she says.

Kemena steps forward. "Quwani told us you took off like a scared rabbit. She used different terms that are classic Quwani, but we knew something was wrong, so we came to check on you, to see if we could help."

Matthias moves to go below deck.

"Where are you going?" I ask him. "Don't you want to hear?"

"Well, yeah, I want to know what's going on." He nods downstairs. "But I figure if you've got your stuff on, I better get mine on. Looks like we need to move quickly."

I raise my eyebrows. "You don't have to do—"

He turns, comes to me, and plants a kiss on my lips, cutting off my words completely. He pulls back, but keeps his hands on my face.

"No, Bria." His voice is husky with emotion. "You're not in this alone."

I stare at him, wide-eyed. I didn't expect my first kiss to be used more to shut me up than anything. But it leaves me speech-less as he sprints below deck and then is back up moments later.

He passes out suits and blades to Nika and Kemena. "Where are we going?"

I shake off my stupor and focus on my friends. Part of me is ready to repeat that it's nothing, but I doubt that will go over well. Although I don't really mind the idea of Matthias kissing me again.

The thought makes my cheeks warm, and so I hurriedly push it aside and tell them my suspicions about Shane and the evidence that suggests I'm right.

As I'm talking, they each put on their Skinter Suits and grab their blades.

"Let's get moving," Nika says. "Sounds like you're right to me."

"One second." Kemena rushes into the wheelhouse. She returns a minute later. "I left a note. I want Catori and Azarias to know where we are and what's going on. We can trust them."

I nod in agreement, then the four of us scramble back over the rickety dock, pulling on our blades and racing toward Talionis.

None of the other scouts have come back to the river yet, which is a relief.

I need to get to my friend before he turns us in.

Yes, I want to save Storm and Cai. But I also want to convince Shane this is not the action he needs to take, to tell him Ari's alive and safe and well.

"Since he has a suit, we might be able to track him," Kemena says through the comm system. She's silent for a moment. "There. I found him."

She knows far more about Eryndale tech than I do, so we follow her lead and race along the river and turn inland.

Right toward Talionis.

FIFTY-ONE

Our blades cut over the ground at rapid speed. Nika, Kemena, Matthias, and I push ourselves to a level I don't think we would have if the intensity of the moment didn't call for it.

I'm tired and battle weary, but none of that matters as adrenaline courses through me.

We leap over logs, swerve around old homes, and let the blades take us as fast as they're able. My thighs burn with the exertion.

Once we hit stretches of old pavement, we're able to move even faster, going down one hill at breakneck speed by staying on the blades and keeping our arms tight against ourselves. I'm not sure if a fall at this rate would be something the protective layers of the suits could save us from.

More than likely, we'd injure ourselves or break something. At the very least, we'd end up with bruises and scrapes. But the four of us stay standing as we crest another hill and move toward the clearing that's only a half mile from Talionis.

I can't allow myself to consider what will happen to Storm and Cai if we don't get to Shane in time. If Shane returns the items Ark stole, Ark won't need to hold them as leverage over me anymore.

My heart races in my chest, faster than my blades across the earth.

I don't know what to think, how to pray, how to process a single thing that's going on, but I push my body and allow my instincts to take over.

Kemena sent us the map through our comm unit, and I see it on my shield over my face.

We're close, and the target of Shane blinks.

He's stopped in the clearing, which could only mean one thing: he's waiting for a transport to pick him up.

Oh God, let us get to him in time.

We cut through more trees, crest a hill, and then I see him waiting below, blades off, pacing like a caged animal.

We descend on him, and he faces us, pistol trained on us. I sense more than see Matthias and Kemena moving out to flank Shane.

I flick up my face shield and close the distance. "Shane. Don't do this. Please, come back with us."

"Don't do this?" He trains the gun on me as though ready to shoot me at the very words. "Because of you, my girlfriend's going to . . ." He releases a shuddering breath and clears his throat.

"She's okay, Shane," Nika injects before he can continue.

He winces like he's been slapped. "Yeah, right. You'd say anything to get me to go back. "To get this." He lifts the satchel carrying the items I stole from Ark.

"No, really." Nika skates closer. "It's a miracle."

He snarls. "I don't believe in miracles."

I skate toward him. "Talionis is evil, Shane. You can't go back there."

He eyes me up and down, pistol trained on me, lip curling into a sneer. "You gonna stop me?"

"Yeah," Matthias says. He's on Shane's left and outside of his field of vision.

Shane spins to face him, putting his back to Kemena who was flanking him on the right.

Matthias doesn't appear at all unsettled by the pistol aimed at his chest, but my heart is beating so fast it hurts.

"We will if we have to," Matthias continues. "But we don't want to. Just come back with us, man. Ari wants to see you."

Something flashes in Shane's eyes that I can't identify, but then it disappears. "You're lying. Ari isn't gonna make it through the day."

At some point, Matthias kicked off his blades. He edges toward Shane. "Give us the items back. Whether you believe us or not, we won't stand by and watch you give Ark what he needs." He shifts into a fighting stance.

Shane moves to secure the satchel to his pack, and the pistol dips from where it was trained on Matthias's chest.

Matthias takes the opportunity and rushes Shane. He wrestles the pistol from his hand, but it falls to the ground before he can get ahold of it. Matthias throws a punch at Shane's jaw, but Shane ducks out of the way.

My pulse ratchets up. This wasn't how it was supposed to go. Shane was supposed to believe us, ditch his plan of returning to Talionis. Not *fight* us.

I take off my blades, and Nika does the same. We crouch into fighting stances and move toward them.

This feels so wrong.

Shane jabs Matthias in the side. Matthias absorbs the hit and delivers a right hook to Shane's face.

The force of the blow whips Shane's head to the side, giving me a clear view of his face. He looks menacing, brooding. I don't even recognize him. I've had my disagreements with Shane. Didn't like him for a time. But he's become my friend.

He's had my back in battles. Saved my life. And I've saved his.

Bonds have been forged over these past few weeks that I didn't anticipate. But my heart cracks as I watch those bonds shatter before my eyes.

"Bria and Nika, hold your position," Kemena's voice comes through the comms.

I want to ignore her and join Matthias in the fight, but something about her tone keeps me in place.

Kemena skates full speed at the guys from behind. "Matthias *move!*" She screams the word, and Matthias leaps backward.

Kemena careens forward, ripping the satchel from Shane's pack. He falls to the ground as she skates into the trees.

"Fall back," her voice comes over the comms. "We got what we need, and he's not going to listen."

Matthias nods although Kemena isn't there to see it. The three of us back away as Shane leaps to his feet, the pistol in his grasp.

His eyes lock on me, and he aims the gun at my head. "You get those items back for me, Valarius, or your girl is as dead as mine." The venom in his words dissolves any shred of hope I was desperate to hold onto.

He'll kill me.

"No." Matthias shifts to move toward Shane, but the click of a bullet loading into place stops him.

"Don't even think of trying anything. I'll shoot her before you take two steps." Shane's eyes never leave mine as he says the words. "Get me the items. Now."

"I'm coming back." Kemena's voice comes over the comm unit.

Pain squeezes my chest. "No. Don't give him what he wants."

"Bria." Matthias says my name as though he's in pain.

"I won't let you save my life just so I can see Storm and Cai die," I say, my eyes never leaving Shane's.

His eyes narrow.

Before any of my friends respond, the sky darkens, and a sickening rumble fills my ears. My stomach knots.

I glance up as the transport descends. I want to retreat, run away. Escape the nightmare I know is coming.

But if I move, Shane will shoot me.

At least Kemena got away with the items.

"Run!" I yell to Matthias and Nika, desperately hoping they listen.

"Never," Matthias says.

I look over to find he's closer to me than I realized. But I don't see Nika.

God, help her to get away.

The door to the transport opens, and soldiers rappel into the clearing before the transport lands. They surround us, guns at the ready. And I know there's no way we can stop them.

A glimmer of uncertainty sparks in Shane's eyes before he snaps to attention, like a perfect recruit of Talionis. Laban stands at the door, hands braced behind his back, golden eyes flashing in victory. Shane salutes him, and Laban salutes back.

Dread drips over me, coating me from the top of my head and down to my toes, as Laban jumps to the ground. His sick, twisted smile sends a tremor through my body. This can't be happening.

More soldiers pour out of the transport, joining those already surrounding us.

Laban's lip curls into a wicked grin as he glances at me, then walks toward Shane. "At ease, recruit. At ease." He claps Shane on the shoulder. "Well done, Malton. The Commander will be very pleased with you."

Shane stiffens. "One of them got away with the Commander's items, sir."

Laban's eyes narrow. "I know. Your honesty will do you credit."

How does Laban know Kemena got away?

Laban snaps his fingers, and four soldiers drag Kemena and Nika into the clearing.

No. Matthias grabs my hand, as though he can sense my dread. Feels it himself.

One of the soldiers surrounding us jogs to the soldiers with Kemena. She retrieves the satchel and brings it to Laban.

He opens it and sifts through it before giving an approving nod.

"Good." He tilts his head to the side. "How did you stay hidden for so long?"

Shane gives an almost imperceptible glance in our direction. Fear grips me, but there is nothing I can do. If he tells them about Eryndale, about the scouts we've been working with, every chance of stopping Ark may end before it can be attempted.

"We were a small group, sir, and well trained. We secured hiding in a variety of ways."

I blink. No word about Eryndale. At least not yet. But why? He's clearly made his alliance with Talionis, so why not give away everything and everyone?

Laban studies him for a moment, as though trying to determine if he believes him. Then he grips his shoulder again. "I'm glad you came to your senses. Where are the others?"

Shane shrugs. "I'm not sure, sir. I left as secretly as I could."

"You did good." Laban turns, and his gaze finds mine. Hatred, bubbling and dark, boils in his eyes.

He stalks toward me, like I'm his prey. The scar on his nose catches my attention.

The scar *I* gave him. And he's never forgotten it.

I doubt he ever will.

I grind my teeth, but fear spirals up and down my spine. I'm trapped and about to be attacked by a man who hates me. He will do anything he can to hurt me.

"Bria Averton," he growls my name. "I've waited far too long for this opportunity."

I straighten my shoulders and refuse to back down. I won't show him fear. No matter how afraid I am. I'll never cower before this evil man.

He pulls his arm back, preparing to strike me, and I brace myself.

Matthias steps in front of me, deflecting Laban's blow before it can land. He punches Laban across the jaw.

The air electrifies as another soldier tases Matthias.

His body convulses, shakes, then drops to the ground, limp.

"Matthias!" I move toward him, but before I can reach him, Laban grabs me by the extra fabric of my suit and delivers a blow to my stomach. The suit keeps the blow from knocking the air out of me.

Laban's eyes narrow. He yanks the helmet off my head and clutches a fistful of my hair, dragging me closer to him.

My scalp screams in pain, but I keep my face an impassive mask.

"When your boyfriend wakes up, tell him I'll make sure he regrets getting in my way. Understand?" He twists my head so that I'm forced to look at him. His cheek is red from where

Matthias struck him, but his eyes shine like he's actually *happy*.

The man is twisted.

I don't respond.

He grins.

"Get them bound. And let's get back to Talionis," he shouts to the soldiers.

He throws me to the ground, and I land on my hands and knees. He steps on Matthias's back as he walks to the transport. A wave of anger crashes on me, and I spring to my feet, ready to attack him.

Two soldiers flank me, gripping my arms. They bind my hands behind my back and drag me to the transport. The anger seeps out as quickly as it came upon me.

We failed.

I strain to look back at Matthias as the soldiers propel me along. Two men hoist his unconscious body off the ground. His head rolls to the side, but they don't seem to care.

Once we are on the transport, Nika, Kemena, and I are secured to the wall, and Matthias is dropped at our feet. He doesn't so much as flinch. He's lying there because he stood up for me.

"He'll be okay," Nika murmurs to me.

"None of this is okay," I say.

Laban gives the order, and the transport lifts off the ground. We are soaring back to Talionis.

Back to the place of my nightmares.

A thought stirs, even as I wonder if I'm going to die today. Ari still has something that Ark wants. She still has the encrypted files. And if she's right, she might have figured out how to decrypt them.

Maybe there's still a way to stop this man.

Oh God, show me what to do.

FIFTY-TWO

As soon as we arrive in Talionis, soldiers remove our suits and place us in shackles. Laban informs us that the High Council is convening to sentence us for our crimes. Matthias is conscious again, which is a relief, though he still seems a little out of it. When Laban mentions the High Council, Matthias's gaze sharpens slightly.

A group of soldiers lead us toward the building, and apprehension crawls through me. I barely listened in Elva Trill's educational classes, but I still remember the one she gave about the High Council. It's the only trial hearing where the Commander himself is present, and it convenes for treason. According to Trill, the only sentencing ever passed by the High Council is death.

A private shackles the four of us to the floor in the center of the room, and Shane is instructed to stand apart from us. Not too far away, but far enough that it's clear he is no longer associated with us, the fugitives.

I can barely look at him. He's a traitor, but a small part of me knows he mostly acted out of fear. Even now, he casts uncertain glances at us. His eyes catch mine, then he quickly looks away.

Colonel Keenan Valarius goes over to Shane and shakes his hand, smiling at him. I can't hear what he's saying, but Shane's face brightens. My stomach twists, and it's my turn to look away.

There's no way I can watch him gladly receive the praise of our enemies.

Because of his actions—because I failed to stop him—Ark has the items he wants. So what will he do to Storm and Cai now?

I push the question aside, and focus on the others arriving. I recognize many of the members of the High Council as they enter and take their seats. Mandeville. Major Tay Vasco. Elva Trill. She has a smug expression on her face as she gazes down at us from the elevated platform. I force my face to remain neutral. I will not show my fear or anger. They won't have the satisfaction of thinking they have defeated me.

Even though right now it feels like we've lost, I don't regret trying. *God, if this is it, I hope You are pleased with me.* A peace, strong and intense, clothes me like a thick blanket. I feel settled. Okay.

I'm facing death, and I'm not terrified. My mouth drops open slightly.

"I'm not scared," I whisper to Nika.

"No talking," Sergeant Andor Valarius says sharply from where he stands behind us.

Nika gives me a smile, and I know she understands.

I've messed up, made bad decisions, but, even though I don't *want* to die, I'm not scared.

Those in the High Council murmur among themselves, gesturing at us. Colonel Valarius isn't talking to anyone. He sits straight, and his eyes bore into Matthias. The calm look on his face unsettles me, and some of my peace ebbs away. I've seen that expression before. That look. It came before he shot me. It was on his face when he watched Laban beat Dex Tildon because he received the lowest marks of all the recruits.

That look means pain is coming.

And this time, it'll be directed at Matthias.

I focus on Matthias, but he stares straight ahead at nothing in particular. The shackles on my hands chafe against my wrists. I wish I could hug him, thank him for being a constant friend. More than a friend. Tell him once again how much he means to me.

A small sigh escapes. Even though I'm not afraid to die, I still have some regrets. Is that how it will be no matter what? Will I always regret what I didn't do ... and what I *did* do?

The doors behind us open with a clang. The murmurs in the room cease, and everyone on the High Council stands. I don't have to turn to know Demetrius Ark has entered the room.

My shoulders tense.

His feet clack against the tiles as he makes his way to his seat: the one in the center, directly in front of us, and higher than the rest. He passes without a glance, and I stare at his perfectly styled dark hair. He moves with grace, fluidity, poise. Like he's in control and nothing, no one, can take it away.

He turns and faces us, then settles into his seat. After a brief pause, the rest of the High Council follows suit.

Ark's dark and intense gaze finds mine. The hairs on the back of my neck stand. The man is unnerving. He takes in the room.

"Let it be recorded that on this day, the sixth of June, the High Council is brought to order to determine the punishment due those who have acted traitorously against Talionis and its laws," Ark's slightly accented voice carries through the room in an almost melodic way. But there is a weight to it that demands it be heard. "Our first matter of business, however, is to address the actions of Elite Recruit Shane Malton."

Shane snaps to attention, sweat beading on his brow.

"At ease."

Shane drops his hands and links them behind his back, looking anything but relaxed.

"Shane. Although at first you acted against Talionis and her interests, in the end, you made your allegiance known. I move to have all of Elite Recruit Malton's charges removed from his record and see him rewarded for the good he has done for Talionis. And for me, his Commander."

The words seem to surprise Shane. His composure slips a bit, and he looks up at Ark. Ark smiles at him, and Shane's chest puffs out, his lips turning up.

I want to spit out the bile rising in my throat. It's disgusting to watch Shane so honored and pleased by the words of such an evil man.

"All in favor?" Ark says.

The right hand of every member of the High Council raises.

Of course no one would go against Demetrius Ark. If they did, I doubt they would live to see tomorrow.

"Then it's settled. Shane, you will take your place once again in our city. You're a part of the Talionis family, tied by your actions to the destiny of this great city. Welcome home, son."

Out of the corner of my eye, I see Nika shaking her head in bewilderment. I follow her gaze to find Shane with a huge smile on his face. Like he fully believes every word coming out of Ark's mouth, despite the crushing amount of evidence he's seen that the man is a liar.

How is that possible?

"Bria," Ark says, yanking my focus to him.

Matthias tenses.

"You had so much potential. Yet you threw it all away."

The words settle in the room, and the stares of the council members bore into me.

This is it. Time for me to receive my death sentence. I study Ark, looking him straight in the eye. I'm not afraid, and I want him to see that.

His eyes light up, and his mouth twitches.

My forehead furrows. That was not the response I expected.

"I'm truly disappointed," he continues. "You betrayed my trust, my authority as your Commander, and that is something I'll never be able to forgive."

I bite my tongue to keep from lashing out and telling him he was *never* my Commander. *Just get it over with. Tell me you're going to have me killed.*

He leans forward in his chair, the eagerness in his eyes sickening. What kind of man so enjoys murdering people? "I'll never be able to trust you again. But, you will be useful to me."

I blink. What? Murmurs start up, and I realize I'm not the only one surprised by Ark's words. What does that mean?

Ark raises his hand in the air, not taking his eyes off me. The murmurs cease. He snaps his fingers, and the doors behind us open. Something about the way he's looking at me unnerves me, and I'm unable to stop from turning to see who is entering.

A gasp is strangled from my lungs.

Storm.

She's led into the room by two soldiers, and I want to scream, to yell at them to take their hands off her. To do *anything* to get the terrified look off her face. When she sees me, she draws in a sharp breath, but otherwise she allows the soldiers to guide her. Her warm, brown eyes are filled with fear, but also strength.

A strength a girl her age should never have to know.

God, please protect her. Please. I can't do anything, but You can.

Ark allows the silence to stretch interminably, but I stay quiet and watch the little girl I love like a sister. She stares back at me, and I offer her a small smile. She smiles back. A broken, sad smile. My heart breaks. What have they done to her?

And where's Damara? A pulse throbs in my neck. I don't know if I'm ready to discover what happened to her.

Ark clears his throat. "Bria Averton, you have committed treason against Talionis, stolen items from the Commander, and disgraced the uniform you once wore. You are hereby stripped of your rank of Elite Recruit." He pauses as though to let that sink in, but I don't care about the stupid rank. "And you will now work as a laborer in Talionis, primarily using your skills in Warfare Strategies to further the goals of Talionis."

My eyes narrow in confusion. This is ridiculous. How could they expect me to *work* with them?

As though hearing my unspoken questions, Ark continues, "If you don't comply, the girl will be punished. Follow my orders, do as I say, and she'll be fine. You have my word. Understood?"

My mouth gapes, but I nod. Yes, I understand. But I don't know what to do.

"Good. Then we will proceed with the sentencing. Next: Matthias Valarius."

A fresh bout of fear encapsulates me. I was ready to die, but I'm not ready to see the guy I care about or my friends die.

"It is clear you have a bit of your mother's rebellious spirit in you, but I have hopes that you will become more like your father."

The look of loathing on Colonel Valarius's face tightens the dread building in my chest.

"The penalty for your treasonous actions will be this: you'll be placed under the authority of your father."

Matthias's eyes drift closed.

I wish I could run to Matthias. Protect him from what's to come, but also cry in relief that he's not going to die.

"Sir," Colonel Valarius speaks up. "I beg your pardon for the interruption."

Ark lazily waves the words away with his hand. "Say what you need to say, Colonel."

Colonel Valarius clears his throat. "Treason is deserving of death, sir. The High Council does not need to forgo the needed sentencing on account of me. A traitor like Matthias is no son of mine." The words are acidic, and I flinch, even though they're not directed at me.

Matthias's head stays bowed.

"My dear Colonel," Ark intones, "have you not yet learned there are fates worse than death?" He says the words as though he's sharing a wonderful secret. "I have no doubt you will find a way to get your son in line."

"He's no longer my son," Colonel Valarius says. "But I will do as you command, sir."

I want to scream, to tell them to leave Matthias alone. But no words come. Even if they did, I know they would do no good.

What will he be forced to endure now?

Matthias looks over at me. The side of his lip tilts up in a half-smile, and there's a peace on his face. My fear remains, but his calm eases it slightly.

"Kemena Bromeliad," Ark says. "You have not yet experienced Talionis and all the good we are doing and will do here. Your association with these traitors does not bode well for you, but we'll give you the opportunity to prove yourself. You'll be assigned to work labor."

"I will not work for you," Kemena says, each word perfectly enunciated, calm, and confident.

A spark flashes in Ark's eyes. "You'll do what you're commanded to do."

Kemena stares back, and her strength gives me courage.

A small bit of hope springs up in me.

Ark isn't sentencing us to death. I don't know what is going to happen or what the future holds for us, but we'll be alive.

God must still have a purpose for us.

And we have friends not far away. Friends who will fight for us. Fight against Talionis.

"And finally, Nika Bromeliad."

I offer my friend a small smile before focusing on Ark. His eyes are on me, and for a reason I can't identify, that unnerves me. I try to shift, but the shackles binding me to the floor cut into my ankles.

"Because of your acts of treason against Talionis, you are hereby sentenced to death." Ark's eyes never leave mine.

The air rushes out of my lungs, and it feels like everything around me is falling to pieces. This can't be happening.

"No!" Kemena cries out.

"Don't do this!" I scream, finding my voice as tears rush down my face. I can't lose my best friend. Not now. Not like this. Not to this man.

Ark seems unfazed by our cries. "The sentence will be carried out immediately. Sergeant Andor Valarius, you will see it done."

Sobs wrack my body, cries I can't control as I try to reach for Nika, unsuccessful because of my restraints. Her face is drawn down in shock, and Kemena is fighting against the shackles binding her, furiously screaming as Sergeant Valarius steps forward and unshackles Nika from the floor.

Something snaps in Nika's gaze, and she struggles against Sergeant Valarius, but his grip remains firm.

Unyielding.

Kemena is crying now. "No. Please, no." Her tears make her words sound strangled, but at least she can form words. My throat is closed. "Take me instead. I can't lose her again."

"I love you, Kem," Nika calls out as Sergeant Valarius half-drags her from the room. "I love you." Her words are choked with tears.

"I love you, baby girl! Oh, my baby girl." Kemena doubles over as sobs rip through her.

Nika is ready to see Jesus. I know that. But this. This is more than I can handle. Everything inside me shreds.

Then Nika is gone. The door slams behind her.

Tears blur my eyes, and my heart thunders in my ears.

"If you *ever* consider defying me again," Ark says, "I want you to first stop. And remember this moment."

The words slam against me with bone-shattering force. He's doing this, murdering Nika, to get to *me*.

Oh God. Oh God. Please help me. I can't bear this.

FIFTY-THREE

I'm not sure what happens next. Everything passes in a blur. I once thought that perhaps Sergeant Andor Valarius was different from his brother. That maybe he didn't believe in Talionis the same way Colonel Valarius does. He wasn't as passionate, but he's always been terrifying. A soldier no one would dare cross. And he's just like everyone else in this terrible place. Willing to murder at a mere word from his *Commander*.

And now my best friend is gone.

My head is pounding, the ache almost unbearable, as Ark concludes the hearing.

Colonel Valarius descends from his seat and slaps Matthias across the face so hard his head whips to the side, but he doesn't so much as grunt. Then Colonel Valarius unshackles him and drags him from the room, the look on his face a promise that Matthias will experience pain tonight.

A hollowness fills me. How can this be happening? How could God perform such a miracle in healing Ari, only to have *this* be the result? I don't understand.

The soldiers who brought Storm in earlier lead her out of the room now. I want to cry out to her. Tell her to be brave. But as our eyes connect, I can't even manage a smile. Tears are coursing down her face, but she doesn't make a sound. Then I can't see her anymore.

Sergeant Valarius returns to the Tribunal. According to the ornate clock on the wall, only twenty minutes have passed since he left. But Nika is already dead. I retch, heaving up whatever is in my stomach and depositing it on the floor. A low moan comes from Kemena, and I wish I could go to her, talk to her. Wish we could mourn the loss of Nika together.

But she's led by Major Vasco from the room, and Sergeant Valarius comes for me. He unshackles my feet and leads me out of the room and through Talionis to the Main Headquarters building. I don't resist, even as hatred wells up within me.

He killed my best friend.

He weaves us through hallways, and I keep my head down, not wanting to see anyone. Finally, we stop before a door.

"This will be your room. It's high security. Any attempts to escape will be impossible." Sergeant Valarius's low voice scrapes against me.

I hate him.

Maybe I shouldn't feel that way, but I do.

He scans his hand on an identifying screen by the door, and it whooshes open. Then he leads me inside. I yank my arm away from him, anger building inside me.

I spin to face him, not caring about the consequences. I open my mouth, then freeze.

The look on his face brings me up short. Almost . . . weary. Upset. I close my mouth, confusion muddling my mind.

"You killed her," I say, but instead of anger sharpening the words, they come out broken. Raw.

He presses his lips together. "I follow orders. And you will learn to do the same."

Tears track down my face, and I clench my jaw. "I'll *never* be like you."

The scar on Sergeant Valarius's face bunches. Then he reaches forward and grabs my shackles, forcing me closer to him. I want to pull away, but know it's foolish to remain shackled if I don't have to.

He places the key near the lock, but not in it. "Don't react to what I'm about to say." His voice is so low, I'm unsure if I even heard it. "She's not dead."

It takes everything in me not to gasp or step back, but somehow, I remain still. This has to be a trick. A trap to lull me into trusting him so I'll do everything they want me to do.

"Why should I believe you?" I whisper.

"Believe what you want." His eyes focus on mine, and he unlocks my shackles without looking at the lock. "I didn't think it was safe for you to know, but Cai insisted."

Cai's alive. And instructing Sergeant Valarius on what to do.

Before I can form a question or get him to prove what he's saying is true, he takes the shackles and leaves the room.

I stare after him. Could it be true? Is Nika alive? Or is it just another ploy to make sure I follow orders?

I sit on the bed in the small closet of a room and realize I'm holding a piece of paper. How did he slip it to me without me even realizing it?

My gaze darts around the room, but I see no signs of cameras. Carefully, I unfold the note. I draw in a quick breath. I know this handwriting.

It's my mom's.

I scan the short note, not breathing.

Remember, Bria, the greatest mistakes and the most profound discoveries are in the details. Don't lose heart. It's not over yet.

Then the handwriting changes, and the last few words make me smile:

Girl, God is gonna work.

Nika is alive. And with my mom. A rush of emotions fills me, but one rises above all the questions I want to ask. *Thank You, God. Thank You.*

I don't know what's about to happen, but if God can use one of the scariest soldiers in Talionis to keep my friend alive, then *maybe* this fight isn't over yet.

———

WHAT'S YOUR BATTLE STRATEGY?

You and your friends have faced more enemies than you ever dreamed possible since escaping from captivity. Each of you has their own strengths and weaknesses, and together you've managed to survive. But the fight isn't over. As you continue forward, what's your battle strategy?

Answer these questions to find out!

Take this quiz to find out!

CHARACTER & WORLD GLOSSARY

Bria: Main Character, fugitive of Talionis
Matthias Valarius: Love interest, son of Colonel Keenan Valarius, fugitive of Talionis
Nika: Bria's best friend, fugitive of Talionis
Ari: Bria's close friend, fugitive of Talionis
Shane: Ari's boyfriend, fugitive of Talionis
Bryson: Ari's brother, fugitive of Talionis
Cai: Bria's uncle and mentor who was taken by Laban after they escaped Talionis, former leader in Eryndale
Storm: the little girl Bria bonded with in Talionis and who she's desperate to protect
Nalani: escaped from Talionis with Bria, but stayed behind on *The Fearless Lady* after almost drowning

BRIA'S FAMILY

Elena: Bria's aunt, the woman who betrayed her to Talionis; Cai's wife
Josiah: Bria's dad
Lily: Bria's mom
Eli and Zeke: Bria's twin eight-year-old brothers
Ezri: Bria's brother who died when she was younger

THE FEARLESS LADY CREW

Catori: captain of The Fearless Lady
Davey: part of Catori's crew who helped Bria and her friends
Nate: Davey's brother who was also part of Catori's crew, but died standing against Talionis while helping Bria and her friends
Quwani: part of Catori's crew, but she was on leave when the crew helped Bria and her friends
Hosea: the man who brought Bria and her friends to Catori when they were on the run
Micah: Catori's husband who has been missing for years
Shep: Catori's well-trained dog

TALIONIS SOLDIERS

Commander Demetrius Ark: Commander and leader of Talionis who is desperate to get back the items Bria stole from his safe
Sergeant Laban Meritas: one of Ark's most trusted soldiers who hates Bria and is leading the hunt for her and her friends
Lieutenant Colonel Keenan Valarius: Matthias's dad and a leader in Talionis
Staff Sergeant Andor Valarius: Matthias's uncle, senior Drill Instructor
Shay: Bria's neighbor from Derbe, she fully believes everything she's been told by those in Talionis and is now a soldier who is helping hunt for Bria and her friends
Major Tay Vasco: Warfare Scenarios Instructor for Talionis
Elva Trill: Educational Instructor for Talionis

ERYNDALE SCOUTS & LEADERS

Max: the leader of the scout team who found Bria and her friends
Chul-Min Lee: on Max's team, brought Bria and her friends into Eryndale

Enya: on Max's team, brought Bria and her friends into Eryndale
Zoe: on Max's team, brought Bria and her friends into Eryndale
Essie: leader and founder of Eryndale; Cai's mom
Azarias: Cai's son; well respected scout in Eryndale who oversees various scout teams
Emmi DeFort: Malachi, Moses, Micah, and Jordyn's mom, well-respected woman in Eryndale
Kassre DeFort: Emmi's husband, a well-respected retired scout who took on a mission to fight against Talionis; met Bria and her friends when he rerouted *The Fearless Lady*
Levi: Azarias's six-year-old son
Malachi DeFort: Micah's older brother, Eryndale Scout, the Wild Dogs team leader
Moses DeFort: Micah's youngest brother, Eryndale Scout, part of the Wild Dogs team, most of his friends call him Retro
Jordyn DeFort: Moses and Malachi's adopted sister; she is one of the youngest scouts in Eryndale and she's excellent at navigation; part of the Wild Dogs team
Glacier: Eryndale Scout, part of the Wild Dogs team
Karyss: Eryndale Scout, part of the Wild Dogs team
Isaac: Eryndale Scout, Wild Dogs; he's also good with tech
Kemena: Nika's older sister
Thaddeus: older scout, member of the S.O.C. and head of cartography in Eryndale
Wolf: Eryndale Scout
Lorenzo: older scout, excellent fighter, leader of the S.O.C.
Bill and Paul: Older brothers who live in Eryndale who lead a team of master craftsmen (Wade, Fred, and Joey)
Brandi: head of tech development in Eryndale
Gabe: a younger member of the C.A.E.
Reginald Finnigan: high-ranking official in the C.A.E.
Ajax: a well trained dog in Eryndale

OTHER ENEMIES

Broche: a mercenary who has been working with Talionis in the hunt for the fugitives

J: Broche's top lieutenant who abandoned him in the battle with Bria and her friends

Callypso: a believed myth and legend throughout the North American region, she's a Raider who destroys anyone who gets in her way; she calls those with her her pirates

MAIN LOCATIONS

Talionis: The hidden city built on the ruins of what was once Philadelphia; the place responsible for kidnapping teens throughout the North American region and training them to become soldiers

Sitreea: a country across the ocean that believes Talionis is being used as a hidden intel gathering base and does not realize Demetrius Ark is using it to train soldiers

Eryndale: a refuge city built in the mountains that was established after the Demise of North America; it became a place that provided a home for those who did not have one, and the scouts from Eryndale help create new towns and villages for the survivors of the Demise

Derbe: Bria's hometown

ABOUT THE AUTHOR

Award-winning author CJ Milacci writes stories for teens and young adults with heart-pounding action and hope. As the podcast host for Read Clean YA with CJ, she loves talking about books and the deeper themes woven into the pages of each novel. She's passionate about crafting stories of good overcoming evil, finding hope in the midst of seemingly hopeless circumstances, and true acceptance.

Always willing to get real about hard issues, C.J. also enjoys the cheesiest of puns. She chats about writing, her faith, bubble tea, and other fun adventures online (@cjmilacci) and at cjmilacci.com.

SPREAD THE WORD

Can you think of two people who could use this book in their lives? Maybe they are your friends, teens in your church, someone you know who loves young adult fiction. Maybe they are avid readers and always looking for a new book. Or maybe it's someone you know who needs an escape from the crazy life she is immersed in, someone desperate for hope.

If so, I would love it if you could connect them to this book so they can experience the hope found in this book.

Thanks again for reading!

ACKNOWLEDGMENTS

First and foremost, thank you to my Savior and King, Jesus Christ. You so faithfully led me each step of the way with this story. Thank You for guiding me, teaching me, and creating with me time and time again. I love you!

There are countless people who have had a part in supporting me and bringing this book to life. To thank them all by name and in detail would take as long as this book, so I'll keep it short for now.

My amazing parents. Mom, thank you for reading early drafts of this book, encouraging me every step of the way, and listening as I worked out difficult elements. I couldn't do this without you! Dad, thank you for being one of my biggest fans and for loving my books. I hope you enjoyed meeting Bill and Paul in this story.

Ani, the little sister of my heart who is such a blessing in my life. Thank you for your support and excitement, and for helping me accomplish far more than I ever could on my own.

Rachael, my cousin who helped dream up Callypso and bring her to life. I love seeing a character we created together in my stories! (Even though she is a bit creepy.)

My talented and amazing beta readers. Katie Robles, Katie Briggs, Lily, and mom. Your feedback, encouragement, and insights helped strengthen this book and make it so much better.

To my incredible family. Uncle Paul, I am so thrilled you love my books, and I had to add you into this one with *Bill*. Aunt Tommie and Uncle Fred, thank you for your support and enthusiasm every step of this journey. I loved writing Emmi and Kassre DeFort and I hope you love reading about them. "That's just how we are." Ellen, thank you for creating Lorenzo with me! He was so much fun to add into this story.

And to all my other fabulous family members. There are too many of you to list by name, but I can't imagine a more supportive crew, and I'm so thankful for all of you. I love you guys!

Becca Wierwille, my outstanding editor. You helped hone this story and make it so much stronger. Thank you!

Emilie Haney, my cover designer, who is amazing to work with. Thank you, Emilie! You outdid yourself with *another* gorgeous cover.

Chris Pearce, my proofreader, who can catch the littlest of mistakes. Thank you for cleaning this up and for loving the story.

My BLB Marketing Mastermind Group, Candace, Katie, and Karyne, you guys are the best! The marketing brainstorms we have always get me excited, and I love knowing I have friends who will pray for me when this journey gets tough.

And to my Kickstarter backers who made all this possible and helped bring this book to life in ways I never imagined, thank you. You all made this project an amazing experience, and I'm honored that you chose to be a part of this. Without further ado, here's the list of Kickstarter backers (in order of when they backed):

Mom & Dad, Heiko Koenig, Ani, Alice, Darlene N. Böcek, Peter DeHaan, Brandon Petcaugh, Kelly Jo Wilson, Josh and Tori Bair, Cayla, Jacob H Joseph, Alicia Jacques, Karah Little, Katherine Malloy, Marcy B., Amy Ullrich, Elizabeth Grace, Bella Raine, Aunt Kelly, Maria Jacques, Eddie Joo, Laurie Christine, Lance and Angie Emma, Bob, jennben17, Jeremiah Friedli, Author Candice Pedraza Yamnitz, Naomi Joy Dadson, Janet DiAntonio, J F Rogers, Abigail L. Wilkes, Madi Joy, Naomi Sowell, Joshua C. Chadd, Krystina Roupe, Lee Anne Womack, Jennifer Dyer, Rachael Jacques, Abigail B., Karyne Norton, Maria Broome, Tiffany Goldman, Joelle DiAntonio, Author Given Hoffman, Maryann Landers, Chris Pearce, Sacred Bunny, Margaret Hamlin, Jeremy Jacques, Patty R, Ronie Kendig, Kathy Brasby, Erin Dydek, David Holzborn, E. A. Hendryx, Jessica Gwyn, Charmagne Kaushal, Aunt Judy and Uncle Gene, Thomas Umstattd Jr.,

Zachary Dale, Matt & Sarah Scales, MJ Kasowski Family, Mahina, Emily Hutnyak, Remington Cloutier, Pamela Hart, Christen Krumm, Abbye Scales, Becca Wierwille, A.C. Williams, Rachel Strehlow, Kevin and Mary Spencer, Christa Stoltzfus, Rachael Ritchey, Becky Sorensen, Keith & Becky Woods, Kenneth Ost, Shelley Pegman, Deb and Drew McGuire, Pat Zaborowski, Sarah Beckman, Elliana and Josiah Seyller, Kayla Ann, Katie Robles, Uncle Fred and Aunt Tommie, Katie Briggs, Tyrean Martinson, Natalya Cerebe, Candace Kade, Liz Jacques, Jake Stoddard, Jacey Veltman, RuthAnna Miller, Kristin Flanagan, Ophelia Grace, Harold van Bolhuis, Elisha Snowdon, Leah E. Good, Connie Hendryx, Renee Miller, Andrew Milacci, Mindy Hite, Janine B, Erica Martin, Jeanna Simmons, L.E. Richmond, Benjamin J. Wright, Josiah DeGraaf, Z. R. McCormick, David Lapp, Ellen Centore, Chad Abbs, Nick McPherson, Isabella Blair, Kylin and Kale Lay, Jonas, Cathy McCrumb, Hannah Summers, Jerry Paradise, Maria Jung, Jewell & Robert Rowlands, Hannah Scales, Ethan, M. Weedin, Zoe Krouse, Zach and Bridgette Huebener, Alexandra Corrsin, Michele Collauto, Micah Madden, Susan K Macias, Brett Harris, T. A. Hernandez, Uncle Paul and Aunt Linda, Nicole O'Meara, Morgan G., Doug Erling, Kim, Lily Hall, Suzie Anne, Chelsea Rich, Beth, Kristin Cooney, So Peculiar Games, Hannah, Meagan Myhren-Bennett

ALSO BY C.J. MILACCI

Talionis Series

Recruit of Talionis

Fugitive of Talionis

Enemy of Talionis

Talionis Series Short Stories

Dying Embers

Shattered Ashes

Differing Paths

Rise from the Ashes

Talionis Series Companion Novel

Abandoned Shores